The
Liverpool
Girls B

Pam Howes

bookouture

Published by Bookouture in 2017
An imprint of StoryFire Ltd.
Carmelite House
50 Victoria Embankment
London EC4Y 0DZ
www.bookouture.com

ISBN: 978-0-34913-249-5
eBook ISBN: 978-1-78681-338-1

Printed and bound in Great Britain by Clays Ltd, Elcograf S.p.A.

Papers used are from well-managed forests
and other responsible sources.

Dedicated to the memory of Allan Williams, 1930–2016. The Beatles' first manager, and founder of the Jacaranda Coffee Bar in Liverpool, where my character Sandy Faraday works.

Chapter One

Fazakerley, Liverpool, February 1966

Jacqueline Evans pulled the pillow around her head as her mam Dora bellowed up the stairs for the third time in as many minutes.

'Jackie, come on, are you getting up today, or what? I've a lot to do. If you don't want to come shopping in town with me, just say so. You can go and take some flowers to Granny's grave for me, save me having to go over later.'

Jackie groaned and threw back the covers. She sat up slowly and dangled her feet over the bedside rug. Saturday morning, and she'd been hoping for a lie-in. She stared around the spacious bedroom that she'd once shared with her older sister Carol, who now lived in Allerton with their dad and his second wife Ivy. They'd seen little of Carol since she'd started working full-time at Lewis's department store, and begun dating a new boyfriend. Carol had told Mam it was quicker to get to work as Dad's house was closer to the city centre than here. Jackie secretly thought that was just an excuse to move out as Carol thought she'd get more freedom to do as she pleased at Dad's. Mam hadn't been too happy with her decision. They'd had a few arguments about it. But at eighteen, Carol was old enough to make her own choices and had told their mam so. Carol had lived with Dad for a time when their mam had suffered depression and then again when – due to a wrongful accusation against Mam of child neglect – the welfare department had decided Carol should be returned to Dad's care. She'd eventually come back to live with their mam and Jackie, but had never been as close to Mam as Jackie was.

Jackie knelt up on her bed and pulled back the floral curtains. They did little to keep out the cold this morning. It was freezing. She chipped at the ice on the window with her fingernail. She'd bet anything that Carol didn't have ice on *her* bedroom window; she'd told them they had central heating. For a brief moment she wished that she too had gone to live with Dad and Ivy in their new house, then immediately felt guilty. Mam did her best. Her job as an early-morning cleaner at Fazakerley hospital helped pay the rent and she also ran a small dressmaking business from the spare bedroom, having been a seamstress all her working life. They managed, just about. Mam was fiercely independent and refused to accept money for Jackie's keep from Dad, even though he constantly offered it.

In a few months it would be Jackie's turn to look for a job. She finished school in July after O levels, but didn't have much of an idea of what she wanted to do. Well she *did*, but Mam didn't have the money to support her dreams of going to drama school.

Slaving away in a factory was not an option Jackie fancied, she was adamant about that. Although Mam had mentioned Hartley's paid good money; perhaps she could save a bit for the future and study drama at night school. Jackie yearned for more from life than factory work though. She loved to sing and dance, and as a child she'd attended dancing classes and even taken part in a few shows and Christmas pantos at the Empire Theatre. But the nearest she got to a stage these days was at school. She always involved herself with the annual summer and Christmas shows and enjoyed teaching dance routines to her fellow pupils.

Carol worked in Lewis's wages office and had told Jackie she might be able to get a job in the store when she was ready, which would also be a great temporary measure. Carol got a discount on her clothes and makeup and always looked dead fab and trendy. Jackie envied her older sister, who was a Mod and had recently had her light brown hair cut short like the model Twiggy. She wore spiky lashes and pale lippy and had told Jackie that her new boyfriend had a scooter. The pair belonged to a crowd that went to all the clubs in town. Jackie hadn't met the boyfriend, Alex, yet, but she aspired to be a Mod too. Maybe he'd have a mate with a scooter who Carol could introduce her to. She wouldn't want her hair cutting short though; she preferred to keep it long.

Her friends at school often told her she had a look of Marianne Faithfull with her blonde hair and dark blue eyes. It was her clothes that left a lot to be desired, Jackie thought. Apart from her school uniform she'd hardly anything else to wear. She really needed something new before she was ready to meet a nice lad and start dating. She'd grown a few inches in the last twelve months and the clothes Mam had made her last year were far too short now, even shorter than would be acceptable as mini skirts and dresses. Mam kept saying she'd get cracking and make her some new clothes, but finding the time to do it on top of her cleaning and sewing work was almost impossible, and Jackie didn't like to mither too much.

Maybe Carol could ask if there was a Saturday job for her at Lewis's to be going on with, perhaps on one of the makeup counters. It would tide her over and give her a bit of spending money to treat herself. She'd try and see Carol soon. She could sneak a day off school and go into the city; meet her in the Kardomah for a bit of dinner. If they lived in the same house Carol would probably lend her something nice to wear. She may just take up her dad's invite to stay over at the new place occasionally at the weekend.

'Jackie!' Mam's repeated yell broke her thoughts. 'I won't tell you again. If you're coming with me you need to be ready in ten minutes tops. I'm waiting to go.'

Jackie ran down the stairs and stood shivering in the hall in her nighty. 'Mam, you get off. I need breakfast first, and then I've got some homework to do. I'll get the bus up to Knowsley this afternoon and take some flowers to Granny's grave. Shall I put some on Esther's grave as well?'

Esther was the late wife of her mam's old boss, who'd been like a second grandma to Jackie when she was little.

'That would be lovely, chuck. Tidy them both up for me as well, if you will. But go before it gets dark. You don't want to be hanging around graveyards in the dark and by the time you get back from Knowsley it *will* be. We'll be able to get some daffodils to brighten the graves up in a week or two. Esther loved her daffs. So did my mam. I do miss them both.'

Jackie nodded. 'So do I. Poor old Gran. It was a shame she went so quickly in the end.'

'I know, love, but her memory loss was bad. It must have been so frightening for her at times and she was in shocking pain with her joints. I don't think her body could take much more. Her passing was for the best. She's at peace now.'

Dora's mother had spent her final years in a nursing home, after being transferred from a residential home where she'd lived previously. A bump to the head a few years ago had set her on the road to losing her memory. Coupled with crippling arthritis in her knees and hips, it had meant she'd been wheelchair-bound for the last few months of her life. She'd been laid to rest in St Mary's churchyard in Knowsley village, alongside her late husband and baby granddaughter Joanna, Carol's twin, who'd died shortly after birth.

Dora handed Jackie a ten-shilling note. 'That should be enough for the flowers and your bus fare. I'll see you later, love.'

'Okay, don't forget I'm going over to Patsy's tonight.' Jackie kissed her mam on the cheek and closed the front door behind her.

❦

Jackie put two slices of Mother's Pride under the grill and rooted in the fridge for the margarine and marmalade. She made herself a mug of coffee and rescued the bread before it burned. Sitting at the little kitchen table, she buttered her toast and spread the orange marmalade thinly, her mind drifting to its usual dilemma. How could she get a career on stage when there was so little chance of her going to drama school after her exams? It was all she'd ever wanted to do.

Her mam had worked for a city centre drapery business owned by a Jewish couple, Sammy and Esther Jacobs, for a few years after she and Dad had split up. Amongst other things, the business used to make and repair costumes for theatre productions. Jackie had accompanied her mam and Sammy to the theatres to deliver the costumes, so she'd sat through many rehearsals and shows and been enthralled by what she'd seen. Everybody had said she was destined for a career on stage when she was older.

But after Esther passed away, Sammy decided to retire. He'd sold the business and his house, and gone away to visit his and Esther's families in Israel and America. Jackie hadn't set foot inside a theatre since as Mam had no spare money. Jackie, Mam and Carol had lived in the flat above the shop for a few years and Sammy had been very good when they were forced to leave, looking after them by paying the rent on their new Fazakerley home until Mam got on her feet. But she wouldn't accept his charity, as she called it, for *too* long, which was why she was now doing an extra job and Jackie's stage career dreams were up the Swanee. In spite of her mam's objections, her dad had really wanted to help, but Carol told them his wife Ivy had pulled her face at him handing over money now that Jackie had grown up. She'd even moaned at having Carol living with them again. But Dad had told Ivy to stop complaining; they were his daughters, and it was his duty to help out.

Jackie finished her breakfast and went back upstairs to get ready for her visit to Knowsley. Esther's grave was just up the road in the Jewish cemetery on Long Lane in Fazakerley, and they looked after it for Sammy when he was away travelling. It was the least they could do after all that Sammy and Esther had done for them.

❁

Back upstairs Jackie rooted in the wardrobe for her blue jeans. They'd seen better days, but Mam had let the hems down recently so they'd do her for a few more weeks. She took a red sweater from the chest of drawers in the opposite alcove to the wardrobe. Boxed games and school books sat on top of the drawers. A few grown-up novels and her diary, kept hidden from Mam's eyes, were in the top drawer under her knickers and socks. Not that she'd got much to hide with her diary, but Mam would go mad if she knew she was secretly reading *Lady Chatterley's Lover*, borrowed from a school friend who'd told her it was dead sexy in places.

Her single bed, covered with a pink candlewick bedspread, stood under the sash window that overlooked the small paved backyard. The bright winter sunshine was beginning to melt the ice on the windows. She ran to get a towel from the bathroom, rolled it into a sausage shape and sat it on the windowsill to catch the drips before they ran onto her bed. Carol's old bed was still upended against the wall waiting to be chucked away. Her mam had hung onto it in case Carol came back home, but as time went on it was looking unlikely that would happen, and Mam had finally said it could go so that Jackie's bed could be moved away from the windowsill.

A small bedside table with a pink-shaded lamp stood next to the bed. Jackie loved the way her room took on a warm glow when it was switched on; it made her feel instantly cosy. A copy of *Peter Pan* sat next to the lamp; it was a childish book to be seen reading now, but the story had comforted her when she was missing Carol and her dad, as he used to read it to them when they were small. She still wished they could all be together as a family, but it wasn't possible. Mam had never forgiven Dad for his affair with Ivy, who he'd worked with at the Royal Ordnance Factory in Kirkby. Some things were best left in the past, was all her mam would say when Jackie tried to bring up the subject.

She put on her navy-blue duffle coat, locked the front door, slung her bag over her shoulder and strolled down the pavement, feeling happy and proud as Punch to be living in the area known as The Avenues. She could hold her head up high in school with that snobby cow Marcia Phelan, whose mother originated from across the water on the Wirral. Marcia was forever boasting about relatives that lived on the same road as Cynthia Lennon's mother. The way she went on about it, you'd think she was bloody royalty because of her vague Beatle connection. Well that was nothing, Jackie thought, because *she'd* seen John Lennon playing his first gig with The Quarrymen at a summer fête in Woolton when she was a little girl, before he was even a Beatle, and she'd danced to his skiffle music. It was a hazy memory but as soon as Dad or Uncle Frank talked about that day, happy childhood thoughts came flooding back, banishing the sad ones of the times she'd cried herself to sleep at night because she was missing her dad.

Chapter Two

Jackie smiled as she turned the corner on her way home. Uncle Frank's car was parked outside the house. Frank was Mam's elder brother and he'd always looked out for them. He'd been married to Mam's best friend Joanie, who had sadly died in a factory fire many years ago. He'd never remarried and had made looking after his sister and her daughters his mission in life.

'Here's my girl,' he said, sweeping Jackie into his arms as soon as she walked indoors. She gave him a hug and a kiss on the cheek.

Mam came down the stairs and gave Jackie a hug. 'Frank beat me to it today; he was here before I got home. How did you get on? Did you manage to get some nice flowers with the money I gave you?'

'Yes,' Jackie said. 'There's not much about with it being so cold, but the lady did me two mixed bunches and added some green stuff. They looked lovely. I split Granny's between Joanie's grave as well. There was nothing much on it.'

Frank nodded. 'I'll nip over tomorrow and sort it out before I come here for my roast dinner.'

'Thanks, Frank, Joanie's mam hasn't been well enough to go herself recently and her brothers all live miles away now,' Mam said and smacked him on the arm. 'And anyway, who said you're invited to dinner?'

'Aw, you wouldn't see your brother starve, would you, Dora? Besides, I've just put a nice leg of lamb in your fridge.' He winked.

'That's the beauty of having a key. I can surprise you. There's fish and chips keeping warm in the oven as well.'

'Oh, Frank, you are a love, thank you. And of course you can come for your dinner, I was only teasing. We'll be eating a bit later though because there's a special service at the church in the morning and I want to go. Mr Faraday's being officially ordained as the vicar. I know he's been in Liverpool for a while at various parishes, but from tomorrow St Paul's will be his church and he'll be our own Reverend Faraday. Our Jackie's coming with me, aren't you, chuck?'

'Looks that way,' Jackie said, raising an eyebrow at Uncle Frank. The family had never been strict church-goers, but since moving to Fazakerley her mam had started to attend nearby St Paul's church every Sunday and Jackie and her best friend Patsy went to the youth club in the church hall on Wednesday evenings.

Frank nodded. 'Good to support your local rev,' he said with a grin. 'Just need to get something from the car. Back in a minute.' He dashed outside and came back in with a cardboard box and a record player.

'Frank, what's all this?' Mam asked.

'Little pressie for my favourite girl,' he said, putting them down and giving Jackie a hug. 'A Dansette, plus the top ten forty-fives in the hit parade this week.'

Jackie's jaw dropped and she ran to her uncle and hugged him. 'Thank you so much. I've never had a record player before.'

'I know, chuck. Thought it was high time you did.'

'Frank,' Mam gasped. 'Oh, what would we do without you? You do spoil us. You're so kind.'

Frank looked embarrassed and shrugged. 'A mate of mine's off to sea and had to empty his rented room, so I got the record player from him. He'd only had it a few months and he's looked after it well. The records are all new, though. I thought you can't have a record player and nowt to play – so I popped into NEMS.'

He laughed as Jackie rifled through the records, her eyes lighting up at labels bearing names like Manfred Mann, Twinkle and The Righteous Brothers, who currently had the number one song in the hit parade, 'You've Lost That Lovin' Feeling'.

'Oh thank you so much,' Jackie repeated. 'I can't believe this. Wait till I tell Patsy.'

'Come on,' Frank said, 'let's get the fish and chips down us, we can listen to the records later and I'll light us a nice fire in the sitting room.'

⊛

Jackie popped her head around the sitting room door and thought how cosy it looked with the coal fire blazing in the grate and the red velvet curtains drawn against the cold night. Mam and Uncle Frank were seated side by side on the black vinyl sofa clutching glasses of pale ale, which Frank had nipped out to the off-licence to buy.

An armchair that matched the sofa stood in the bay window area. The record player was in pride of place on top of a chest of drawers in the alcove next to the chimney breast. Uncle Frank was singing along to Del Shannon's 'Keep Searchin'', trying to reach the falsetto notes and failing miserably. For a moment Jackie almost felt like she'd rather stay in and be nice and warm, but she'd promised Patsy that she'd go over to hers tonight and she didn't want to let her friend down.

Mam had produced a dark pink silky eiderdown that she'd bought earlier on Paddy's market and put it on Jackie's bed. It made the room look quite posh and it matched the pink roses in her bedside rug. It would be toasty tonight when she got back. She wouldn't want to get up tomorrow morning. But Mam would have her up for church at the crack of dawn, no doubt.

'See you in a bit,' Jackie called, above the noise of Frank's singing and Mam's laughter.

'Okay, chuck,' Mam said. 'Don't be too late back, and be careful coming home on your own. Hey, guess what Frank just told me? He's only getting us a new telly next week to replace the broken one. They said it can't be fixed at the shop, so he ordered a new one from NEMS. Won't *we* be the bee's knees?'

Jackie smiled. 'Oh brilliant, thanks, Uncle Frank.'

She wouldn't need to lie any more when that snobby Marcia Phelan asked her what she'd thought of certain programmes, and she had to pretend she'd seen them rather than admit to having a broken telly that her mam couldn't afford to replace. Patsy usually helped out by whispering bits of information to her. She'd be able to watch *Top of the Pops* and *Ready Steady Go!* again and her mam would be able to catch up on her favourite *Coronation Street* programme, instead of relying on the women at work to keep her up to date.

Jackie wrapped her scarf tightly around her neck against the cold wind and hurried up to the top of Fourth Avenue, onto Longmoor Lane and then left into Second Avenue. It was easy enough to find your way around here without getting lost. The six avenues ran in numerical order.

A few teenage lads were making their way home, kicking a ball between them. They were noisy, but none of them looked rough like the lads that had hung around near the old house on Wright Street, where she and Mam had lived before they moved to the flat above the Jacobs' shop. She passed a middle-aged man walking a Jack Russell and he touched his cap and smiled. Jackie smiled back and stopped to stroke the little dog. She looked up as someone called her name. Patsy was hanging out of the bedroom window of the house opposite, her red hair billowing in the stiff breeze. Jackie waved and crossed over as the front door flew open and Patsy, smoothing down her ruffled locks, beckoned her inside. She took Jackie's coat and scarf and hung them on the hall stand and they ran upstairs and flopped down onto Patsy's comfortable bed. Jackie told her about Uncle Frank's surprise gifts and the promised television.

'Wow, the whole top ten in one go? You lucky thing. I got 'Keep On Running' by the Spencer Davis Group today. Me and Mam went into town this afternoon. I popped into NEMS to listen to some records while she did her shopping. Love it in there and there's always the chance of seeing a Beatle. I'd die if John Lennon walked in, mind, even though we've already seen him when we were little!' She rolled her eyes and grinned. 'Chance'd be a fine thing these days. Too famous to be walking the streets with the likes of us now they've been to America.'

'I suppose so,' Jackie said with a sigh. 'Think we've missed the boat there. Our Carol saw them play The Cavern at lunchtimes when she first started working. They'd just come back from Hamburg then. Still, other good groups are playing there now. As soon as we leave school and get some money we'll start going out properly at night. Mam said she'd make me some new clothes when she gets the time. I've hardly got anything to wear at the moment. Nothing fits me any more.'

'Haven't you?' Patsy frowned and jumped to her feet. Her huge wardrobe was twice the size of Jackie's, and she rummaged inside and pulled out a short black needle-cord skirt and a white polo-neck, skinny-rib sweater. 'Here, I don't wear these now. You have them. On Wednesday it's youth club night again so you've no excuse not to go this week. You could wear those nice black knee boots your dad bought you for Christmas as well. They'll look great with those clothes. If you come round here for seven we can do our makeup and hair together.'

'Thanks so much,' Jackie said, beaming. 'Feels like Christmas today. Loads of presents, and it's not even my birthday for a few weeks.'

'Let's go downstairs and I'll ask Mam if she can find the pattern she bought for a shift dress. Then your mam can borrow it to make one for you. I know she likes to make her own designs, but it'll save her some time if she's already got the pattern.'

Jackie followed Patsy downstairs and into the lounge (not 'the sitting room', like Mam called their front room) where Agnes was sitting on the sofa reading a magazine and smoking a cigarette. Patsy's mam had the same red hair as her daughter, but wore it fastened into a neat French pleat. She had good taste and the room was furnished in the latest style.

A brown tweed three-piece suite, with curved wooden arms, took pride of place and the shiny cream-tiled fireplace held a modern gas fire. The green carpet felt thick underfoot, and velvet curtains in a rich shade of gold hung at the windows. Patsy said her mam liked G Plan furniture. The house was full of it. Her dad had a good job in air traffic control at Speke airport and Agnes was the secretary at Fazakerley primary school. The family went on holiday every year and Patsy had told Jackie that she would ask if they could take her with them to Butlin's at Pwllheli this summer. Jackie hoped they'd say yes. She'd never had a proper holiday. Just the odd day trip with Mam and Dad to New Brighton on the ferry and then again with Dad and Ivy once they were married.

'Hiya, girls,' Agnes greeted them. 'Sit yourselves down; I'll make a cuppa in a minute.' She stubbed out her cigarette in a green, push-down ashtray. The chrome top made a whirring sound and swallowed up the dimp. 'Is your mam okay, Jackie?'

'Yes, she's fine, thanks. She was having a drink with Uncle Frank when I left her.'

'Glad to hear it. Now listen, tell her that twin-tub washer she's having of mine will be with her on Monday morning. I've arranged for it to be dropped off in-between her hospital shift and dinnertime.'

'I'll tell her. It's very kind of you.'

'Mam, we won't bother with the tea because Jackie can't stop long anyway,' Patsy said. 'Will you have a look for the shift dress pattern, and then her mam can use it to make her a new dress?'

'Of course.' Agnes got to her feet and stretched. 'It's going to be a cold one again tonight. Make sure you wrap up warm when you go back out, chuck.'

'We'll play a few records and then Jackie can pop her head around the door before she goes, Mam,' Patsy said. 'Or you can leave the pattern on the hall table, then we won't disturb you.'

'Don't have that record player turned up too loud,' Agnes called after them.

Patsy raised an eyebrow and winked at Jackie. 'I never do.'

Back in Patsy's bedroom the pair sprawled on the bed and sang along to 'Terry' by Twinkle.

'Do you fancy lads with a motorbike like Terry or would you rather have a scooter boy?' Patsy asked, twirling a length of hair around a finger.

'Oh scooter boy, definitely. I like the Mods. Our Carol's lad's a Mod. We haven't met him yet, though. But she says he's at art college and he's got a scooter. She says he collects glasses at the Jacaranda at the weekend.'

'The Jac's another good club we can go to,' Patsy said. 'I'm sure I can persuade Dad to take us into town and pick us up again if he's not on shift.'

'Don't think I'll be allowed into town until we finish school and exams.' Jackie pulled a face. 'Still, we can ask, I suppose. But youth club will have to do for now.'

'Have you had any more thoughts about what to do after school finishes?'

'Yep, but I can't see Mam agreeing. If she doesn't shove me into Hartley's factory, she'll want me to get an office job like our Carol. I wouldn't mind working in Lewis's, but I'd rather be on a counter, then I can watch the world go by. Study people, you know, ready for acting parts. We could really do with an amateur dramatics club around here. I suppose the library would be a good place to ask where the nearest one is. If my O levels are good, I wouldn't mind art college as an alternative. Now I'd love that. I could learn to design and paint scenery maybe.'

'You're determined to do something on stage, then?'

Jackie smiled. 'It's always been my dream. What about you?'

'Me? Oh well, I'm hoping Brian Epstein will spot me singing along to the groups when we go to The Cavern, like he did with Cilla.'

'But you can't sing,' Jackie said, laughing as Patsy strutted up and down the carpet holding a hairbrush in her hand like a microphone. 'You can dance, and you've certainly got Cilla's red hair, but not her voice.'

Patsy shrugged. 'Well, modelling, then. I'll never be another Twiggy, but the Shrimptons are curvier. And I can strut my stuff as well as they can.'

Jackie looked at her friend. She was slim with curves in the right places, long legs and a pretty face with an almost permanent smile. The lads at school ogled her constantly, but Patsy remained aloof and said she wanted more than a schoolboy to take her out.

'Have to see what the careers officer says when he comes to see us.'

Patsy snorted. 'He'll try and bung us into a typing pool, you'll see.'

'Not if I have my way.' Jackie jumped to her feet. 'I'd better be making tracks. Mam wants us to go to church tomorrow for the new vicar's special service. She'll no doubt have me up at the crack of dawn.'

'Oh, poor you,' Patsy sympathised. 'Still, if the new vicar's son's around, you're in for a treat. I managed to catch a glimpse of him the other day. Fit as a flea *and* he's got a nice scooter too. Has a look of Paul Jones from Manfred Mann; sexy eyes and a cheeky grin.

Somebody said he's seeing a girl from across Liverpool somewhere, but that doesn't mean anything. He's not engaged to her and in my eyes that makes him free and single.'

Jackie laughed. 'Trust you. He sounds nice though. What's his name?'

'Sandy,' Patsy replied. 'Sandy Faraday. He's got an older brother, Roger, but he's doing politics at uni in Manchester. Sandy's nearly eighteen and he goes to the art college where John Lennon went. Bet your Carol's fella would know him if it's the same place. He's got a dead posh accent as well because the family's from down south. Kent, I believe. Right, let's get that pattern and I'll see you out. Knock on for me on Monday morning for school.'

Chapter Three

Jackie sipped her coffee, half listening to what nosy Mrs Baker was saying, something about her mam helping with alternate after-service coffee mornings. She put her empty cup and saucer down on the trestle table and glanced sideways under her long fringe at Sandy Faraday, the vicar's youngest son. His likeness to Paul Jones – the wide smile, twinkling blue eyes and dark brown hair – was unmistakable. He was talking animatedly to another dark-haired teenage lad, laughing and using his hands to describe something. Both looked smart but trendy, in beige, slightly flared trousers. Sandy wore a black double-breasted pea coat and his friend a navy one. Jackie had seen The Small Faces wearing similar outfits in a pop magazine feature about London Mods.

She sighed and looked down at her own outfit, the duffle coat hiding her pleated school skirt, but at least she had on her new black knee-length boots, and a red woolly scarf tied around her neck that helped to give a healthy glow to her pale cheeks. She hoped Sandy might think she was a student, but knew she looked about twelve, despite her Marianne Faithfull hairdo, which she'd backcombed a bit higher today, using hair lacquer to hold it in place. It was rock-hard and she'd never get a comb through it later.

Mam wouldn't let her wear the outfit today that Patsy had given her, saying it wasn't suitable for church. She willed Sandy to look at her, but even if he did, he wouldn't be impressed by what he saw. Anyway, he already had a girl who was no doubt as trendy as he was. A bit of a kid like her wouldn't interest him. She was sixteen soon, so it was time to grow up a bit, like Patsy, who had an air of maturity and confidence about her that Jackie would give her right arm for.

The remaining congregation hung around in the community hall next to St Paul's church, some of the men looking decidedly bored and uncomfortable, as though smart suits were not their usual attire. Jackie guessed most of them were eager to get a move on to catch opening time at the pub, after enduring the long, and slightly boring, morning service. Then they'd no doubt go home to Sunday dinner and listen to *Two-Way Family Favourites* on the radio. Her stomach rumbled at the thought of dinner and she realised she was starving. Her mouth watered as she conjured up the smell of roast lamb. She'd only had time for a quick cuppa at breakfast.

Reverend Faraday was a nice vicar but there was only so much bible stuff she could endure in one go. She'd bet the bored-looking men felt the same. None of their wives seemed in a hurry to stop gossiping though. They were swarming around her mam like bees around a honey pot, each trying to out-talk the other. Probably wanted the lowdown on why her husband wasn't with her, Jackie thought. They asked nearly every week. But Mam had never told anyone she didn't know well enough that she was divorced. All those daft hats pinned to the women's heads, and the outlines of whale-bone corsets adorning big backsides, evident through their tailored skirts.

She stifled a grin at her ungodly thoughts and turned her attention back to Mam, whose cheeks were pink, lips pinched into a thin line. Her mam didn't wear daft hats, but she looked really smart in her best gold-coloured duster coat and her well-polished black shoes. She clutched her favourite handbag tight, knuckles white. Her blonde hair curled softly onto her cheeks, and she'd done her best with a Max Factor crème puff and her Sunday-best pink lippy. Jackie felt proud that her lovely, slim mam looked at least twenty years younger than most of the swarm.

'What's up?' Jackie whispered. That look meant someone had said something Mam didn't agree with. It was time to go before an argument started.

'Come on,' her mam whispered back, and then louder, 'Right, ladies, thanks for your hospitality. We'll see you next Sunday.'

She put her cup and saucer down on the table with a conversation-stopping clatter.

'But you will be coming to the WI meeting on Tuesday, Mrs Evans?' one of the women asked as another tutted at Mam's banging down the crockery with such force.

'Er, I'll see.' She grabbed Jackie by the arm and bundled her outside.

'What was that all about?' Jackie asked, trying to catch a last glimpse of Sandy Faraday before the door closed behind them, but he'd vanished from sight.

'That bloody Barbara Baker woman, turning her nose up when I told her that I did a bit of early-morning cleaning for a living,' Mam said, striding out of the church grounds and down Formosa Drive with purpose. 'That's why I like to keep our business private, Jackie, apart from the dressmaking, of course, which they all know about anyway. My little cleaning job pays our rent. It's all right for her, never lifts a bloody finger all week, and her daft husband runs around like a scalded cat, pampering to her every whim, while she sits on her fat arse and does sod all! And then she expects *me* to agree to helping with coffee after the service and joining the WI as well. I've got quite enough to do at the moment, thank you.'

'Ooh, she's really annoyed *you*, Mam,' Jackie said, trying not to laugh. Barbara Baker had picked the wrong one to look down her nose at. Her mam could give as good as she got. God help the insensitive woman, because next time Mam would be ready for her with both barrels blazing. 'Give her a chance. She probably doesn't mean any harm.'

'Huh, from what the others were saying when she was out of earshot, she's a right snobby cow. The rest are always friendly enough, and the new vicar's wife is *very* nice. Her youngest son was there but I didn't get to meet him, did you? Think he's a similar age to our Carol.'

'Er, oh, is he?' Jackie said airily. According to Patsy, Sandy was in fact not quite eighteen, almost a year younger than Carol. 'No, I didn't get to meet him. Do I have to go to church every week, Mam? I'm up to my eyeballs with homework now my exams are coming up. I could do with Sunday mornings to keep on top. It's not like we're Catholics. We won't get struck down or anything if *I* don't go.' She paused as an idea popped into her head. 'I could make a start on Sunday dinner, save *you* time,' she finished, hoping to sway things her way.

Mam shrugged as they turned onto Longmoor Lane. 'I don't suppose it'll matter if you give it a miss. I only go out of habit really. It's just something to do and it gets us out for a couple of hours. But I have to say, I could have slept in this morning. I was that tired.'

'Me too.' Jackie smiled. She could work on her wardrobe planning. When she felt ready she would go to church with Mam on the odd Sunday, looking like a trendy teenager instead of a bit of a kid. Now she'd clapped eyes on the vicar's son, she couldn't bear him to see her again until she'd got herself sorted out fashion-wise. She was conscious of Mam rattling on again. 'What?'

'That Baker woman, you could tell by her face that she doesn't believe I was ever married. Always asking after my husband, like she cares. She thinks I'm an unmarried mother. Blooming cheek. Wait till I see her again. At least I've *got* kids, which is more than she has. Mind you, it's no surprise when you look at her weedy husband. Bet he hasn't got it in him anyway.'

'Mam, behave!' Jackie giggled. 'And at least you've got a bay window.' It had become a family joke after they moved here – that Mam had finally got her much-coveted bay window.

'Well,' Mam said, as they turned into Fourth Avenue, then she saw the funny side and started to laugh with Jackie. 'Yes, we're a bay-windowed family, all right. I guess that makes us as good as the Bakers. Oh, look who's here already.' She waved at Frank as he got out of his car. 'That damn woman, keeping me talking. We'll all have to muck in. I left the lamb roasting on a low light and the spuds are peeled, so it shouldn't take too long to do the rest.'

⊛

After dinner, all of them stuffed with roast lamb and all the trimmings, Uncle Frank lit the fire and Jackie switched on her transistor radio, last year's birthday present from her dad. They sat side by side on the sofa and caught the end of *The Clitheroe Kid* while Mam brewed up in the kitchen. Jackie laughed as her uncle mimicked the gormless, stuttering Alfie Hall character, thanking Mam as she handed him his cuppa.

'I'll take mine upstairs,' Jackie announced. 'I need to finish my homework. Be down later for *Pick of the Pops*.'

'Okay, chuck.' Mam sat down on the seat Jackie had vacated. 'Me and Frank'll just shut our eyes for five minutes.'

Jackie smiled as she made her way upstairs. Five minutes, eh? Knowing those two they'd be flat out until teatime. It was so nice to have Uncle Frank here for Sunday dinner. They felt like a proper family when he was around. It was a good feeling.

She took her diary from the drawer and sat down on the bed, chewing the end of a pen. After giving it some thought she wrote briefly about the morning in church, and then a bit about seeing Sandy Faraday and his friend. She closed the diary, lay down with her hands under her head and allowed herself a little daydream. What would Sandy be like to kiss? She'd bet he was good at it.

Those lovely lips that curved into that wonderful smile. Lucky bloody girlfriend, whoever she was.

She wondered if they'd done it and then felt her cheeks heating at the thought. Why had that come into her mind? Reading *Lady Chatterley*, no doubt. The things Mellors and her ladyship got up to would make your hair curl. Last time Carol had been round she'd sworn Jackie to secrecy and told her that she'd done it with Alex. Jackie had told Patsy as they told each other everything, but she knew that Patsy wouldn't tell anyone. Jackie wondered if her sister felt power now in using the sex thing over Alex. From what she'd read it seemed to be that a woman could hold on to a man by keeping him wanting more rather than saying no, but that seemed to go against other advice she'd read in agony-aunt columns. This growing-up lark was very confusing at times.

❀

When Jackie left the room Frank turned to his sister. 'Dora, I've got summat to tell you,' he began, feeling nervous as she frowned.

'Oh aye, what have you been up to then? You're looking a bit sheepish, our Frank.'

'Well, you know I've been helping out at the Legion, standing in while the concert secretary's been off poorly.'

Dora nodded. 'Yes, and?'

'Maureen, you know, the nice little barmaid with the red hair, well I've taken her out a couple of times and I've kind of fallen for her. I didn't know how to tell you, well, because of Joanie.'

Dora stared and then flung her arms around him. 'Frank, it's been ages. It's time you found another nice lady to love. Oh, fancy being worried about telling me. If it's what you want then there's nobody happier for you than me. Joanie wouldn't want you to be on your own forever, love. And how does Maureen feel about *you*?'

'The same, I think. I, er, haven't told her yet, but I see it in her eyes. I wanted to talk to you first.'

'Then you must tell her how you feel. Don't waste any time. You've both suffered loss. I know her husband was killed at work and it's been hard for her bringing up their little lad on her own. Just do it, Frank. Life's too short.'

'Aye, I will.' Frank beamed and breathed a sigh of relief. He looked across at the framed photo on the bookcase: Joanie, his late wife and Dora's best friend, who'd died so young and tragically in a factory fire shortly after their wedding. 'She would want me to be happy, wouldn't she?' he whispered, almost to himself.

Chapter Four

'Keep still while I backcomb it higher,' Patsy ordered as Jackie balanced on a dressing table stool in front of the mirror. She'd already rimmed Jackie's eyes with kohl and plastered her lashes with mascara. Blue eye shadow brought out the colour of her eyes in a face pale with foundation, while light-pink lippy defined her full lips. Satisfied, Patsy squirted the neat little bouffant with lacquer and stood back to admire her handiwork. 'Bloody hell, you look fabulous! More like Marianne Faithfull than ever.'

Jackie smiled and looked closely at her reflection. 'Do you really think so?'

'Course I do. Right, shift out the way while I do *my* face.'

Jackie sat on the end of the bed while Patsy plastered on her own makeup and took her rollers out. She teased the crown of her red hair with a tail-comb and smoothed the sides, sweeping them into cheek-fanning curls. A blast of Bel Air lacquer and she announced she was ready.

'Hope the disc jockey's got some new records this week,' Patsy said, buttoning up her coat as Jackie retrieved their handbags from the floor. 'Last week he played really ancient stuff. He's a bit too old, don't you think? He's at least thirty. They could do with asking someone up from one of the clubs in town. They'd get loads more people in and we might meet some nice lads.' She led the way downstairs. 'See you, Mam,' she called.

The lounge door opened and Agnes popped her head around it. 'See you, girls. Have a good time, don't be too late home, and behave yourselves.'

'Always do,' Patsy muttered as they left the house. 'Fat chance of anything else around here, eh, Jackie?'

❁

The church hall was fairly crowded as the girls wandered in after paying their shilling admission fee. A classmate waved them over to a table near the back wall and they made their way through the ranks of teenagers, who all seemed to be talking at once.

'Thanks for saving us seats, Sally,' Jackie said as she took off her duffle coat and slung it over the back of a chair. She looked across to the small podium where the disc jockey always set up his equipment, but it was empty, and Reverend Faraday stood wringing his hands as he talked to the church warden. 'What's going on?' she asked Sally.

Sally shrugged. 'Dunno. But the fella with the records hasn't turned up yet.'

As Sally spoke, Mrs Faraday hurried into the hall and whispered in her husband's ear. A smile lit up his anxious face and he raised his hands to the heavens in a gesture of thanks. He got up onto the podium, fiddled with some wires and picked up a microphone. The church warden clapped his hands and called for attention. Silence fell as the vicar spoke.

'It seems we have a problem with our usual spinner of records,' he began. 'However, if you'll all bear with me, we'll have things under control as soon as possible.'

'Oh great,' said a dark-haired lad sitting at the next table. 'He'll have us all up singing hymns or summat.'

'Shurrup, Philip.' Sally smacked the lad's arm. 'He's doing his best.'

'Well that's a fine start,' Patsy grumbled and then stopped as a buzz went around the room, all eyes turning to the door. 'Oh, on second thoughts, maybe not,' she finished, smiling broadly at Jackie. 'Look who's just come in.'

Jackie felt the heat creeping up her neck. Patsy had asked her what she thought of the new vicar's son on Monday at school and she'd feigned disinterest. But her friend had seen right through her and teased her.

Sandy and his mate from Sunday carried in two record players and a large box between them. They lifted the stuff up onto the podium. Within minutes they had the record players up on two small tables and the strains of 'Here Comes the Night' by Them filled the room.

'We can't really dance to this,' Jackie said, pulling a face. 'I love it though,' she added as Patsy frowned. Them's singer, Van Morrison, was her friend's latest crush.

'We can ogle instead,' Patsy said, winking at Jackie. 'You're looking very flushed. Are you warm or is it the sight of the disc jockey and his pal?'

'Of course not. I don't even know them.'

'Well Sandy's looking right at you.'

'He isn't.'

'He bloody well is, and look at Marcia Phelan's face. Talk about jealous. She fancies him like mad, but he's not interested.'

Jackie squirmed in her seat as Sandy stared right at her and then his face lit up with a smile. She half-smiled back and wondered where his girlfriend was tonight. Marcia Phelan was looking daggers in her direction, but she turned her head away and looked down at her hands clasped around the handbag on her knees.

As Them finished singing, Sandy's friend immediately played 'When You Walk in the Room' by The Searchers and a group of girls dashed onto the dance floor. Patsy grabbed Jackie's hand and hauled her to her feet. They put their bags onto the floor, as did several other girls, and began to dance around them. Jackie tossed back her hair and threw herself into the dancing, thankful of the trendy outfit Patsy had given her.

Her confidence soared as she lost herself in the music, and six records later, feeling slightly out of breath, she was glad of a slow song so that she could sit down for a while. The Cascades's 'Rhythm of the Rain' played as she fanned herself with her hand. Patsy was up dancing with a boy from their class and swaying in his arms. The dark-haired lad wore a hopeful expression as his hands wandered up and down Patsy's back. He looked nice enough, but Jackie knew he didn't stand a chance of anything more than a quick snog with her friend, and *that's* if he was lucky. As soon as the music finished Patsy extricated herself from his arms and dashed back to her seat, laughing.

'Groping little sod.' She flopped down as Sandy announced that refreshments were on sale and to form an orderly queue at the hatch, where his parents were serving. Sandy's friend put an instrumental track by The Shadows on while teenagers queued.

'I'm gonna ask Sandy's mate if he'll play Wayne Fontana's "Come on Home",' Patsy said as she rooted in her bag and handed Jackie half-a-crown. 'Get us some Vimto and crisps while I put my request in.'

'I've got some money,' Jackie said. 'Let *me* pay.'

'No, it's Mam's treat. Go on.'

As Jackie got to her feet she spotted Sandy whispering something to his friend and then he was leaping off the podium and making his way across the room, looking directly at her. She saw Marcia Phelan toss her long dark hair back and try to catch his eye, a tight-lipped smile plastered on her face, but he ignored her.

'Hi there.' He stopped Jackie in her tracks. 'Where did *you* disappear to last Sunday?'

'Me?' she stuttered, feeling her jaw drop.

'Yes, you! After the service. I saw you looking a bit bored and was coming over to talk to you, popped to the lav first, and when I came back you'd gone.'

'Oh, I, er…' she mumbled. He'd actually noticed her. She couldn't believe it. She swallowed and looked up to see a teasing glint in his blue eyes. His lovely lips curved into that wonderful smile and her heart fluttered, her stomach looped and nothing more would come out of her mouth. In faded denims, a blue and white striped shirt with a double collar open at the neck, he looked so handsome that she could hardly breathe.

As though sensing her embarrassment, he broke the silence. 'Shall we join the queue? Your friend's making thirsty gestures.'

He waved at Patsy, who was making her way back to the table, wiggling her hips as Wayne Fontana's dulcet tones filled the hall and the teenagers hurried onto the dance floor again.

Jackie felt Sandy's hand on the small of her back, guiding her across to the hatch. 'We had to leave,' she whispered. 'On Sunday, I mean. Mam was about to have a big row with Mrs Baker.'

He laughed. 'Barbara Baker! I believe she's a right pain in the arse. My mum says it's time someone stood up to her. She's ruled the roost for too long.'

She stared at him, momentarily shocked that a vicar's son would say 'arse', almost in earshot of his parents, and then she smiled. 'Well, Mam will. Believe me.'

They were at the front of the queue now and Sandy's mother was serving. 'Yes, son?' She smiled at him, her dimples the same as his and her blue eyes twinkling. 'Or should I serve your lady friend first?'

'I think you'd better,' he said. 'Her friend's waiting impatiently over there.'

'Two glasses of Vimto and two bags of crisps, please.' Jackie handed over the money and wondered how she was going to carry everything without having to come back.

'Same for me please, Mum,' Sandy said. 'Back in a sec.' He picked up the glasses and led the way to the table, where Patsy smiled sweetly as he handed her the Vimto.

'Thank you, Sandy. You joining us?'

'Be with you in a minute,' he said and dashed back to the hatch.

Jackie sat down and put the crisps on the table.

'Well?' Patsy raised an amused eyebrow.

'Well what?'

'What did he say?'

Jackie felt her cheeks heating. 'He, er, he asked where I'd got to last Sunday after the service.'

Patsy smiled knowingly. 'I reckon he definitely fancies you.'

'Don't be daft.'

'He does. And here he comes again. Move up and then he can sit in the middle of us.'

Jackie moved across to a spare seat and Sandy sat down beside her. Hand shaking, she picked up her glass and took a sip.

'Cheers.' He clinked his glass against hers, then took a long swig of Vimto. 'So, are you gonna tell me your name?'

'Er, I'm Jackie,' she mumbled.

He smiled. 'Nice to meet you, Jackie. Do you live close by?'

She nodded. 'On Fourth Avenue.'

'Oh, good. Fancy a dance later? I'd better rejoin Stevie for now, or he'll play all the wrong stuff if he doesn't get a request. He's into the blues and I don't think Howlin' Wolf and John Lee Hooker would go down too well with this lot. I'll be back.' He dashed away.

Jackie stared after him, her mouth open. She had no idea who Howlin' Wolf was, and had that really just happened? Sandy Faraday wanted to dance with her? He'd spoken to her and she'd hardly said two words back. She hoped he'd realise that she was a bit shy and she'd tried, but not much would come out of her mouth. She'd bet Marcia bloody Phelan wouldn't have been so flipping dumbstruck. She realised Patsy was asking her something and turned her attention back to her friend.

'You look like you've been hit by a bus!'

'I'm in shock. Why me? There are loads of girls to choose from. Why does he want to dance with me?'

'Well why wouldn't he? You're lovely.'

'But he's already got a girl.'

'She's not here, and it might not be serious. He might have finished with her. Who knows? To be honest, I've never seen him with a girl; I just heard he was dating someone from the other side of town. It might be a rumour, or it's all fizzled out and he's free again. Enjoy yourself. I'd give my right arm to have a dance with him, and I bet Marcia would give her leg as well!'

Jackie smiled and willed herself to relax, sipping at her drink. She couldn't eat her crisps now; she felt all churned up inside. Patsy ate both packets, discarding the little blue wrappers, claiming the salt made her thirsty. Jackie watched as Sandy whispered something to Stevie and then he jumped down off the podium as Crispian St Peters began to sing 'You Were On My Mind'.

'Bet he's picked this for you, shows he's been thinking about you,' Patsy whispered as Sandy held out his hand and Jackie took it. He didn't say a word, just led her onto the dance floor and pulled her into his arms.

She melted into him like it was the most natural thing to do. His eyes looked into hers, a slight smile playing at the corners of his mouth. Her stomach looped all over the place and her legs felt like jelly. How she was managing to stay upright, she had no idea. Other couples were on the floor and Patsy was dancing with Sally but for Jackie it felt like she and Sandy were alone. The music came to an end and he led her back to her table.

'Save the last dance for me,' he whispered and ran back to Stevie.

Jackie flopped down onto her chair wondering what the heck had happened to her just now. She'd been struck dumb and could hardly breathe. It was like he'd cast a spell over her. She sat listening to the music, not quite believing his promise of another dance. But sure enough, as The Drifters sang out across the room, Sandy ran over and claimed the last dance.

When the song finished he dropped a chaste kiss on her lips and asked if he could take her to the pictures on Friday night.

'Erm, I'll have to ask my mam,' she stuttered, feeling a bit daft. He'd think she was a right kid when she just wanted him to think she was all grown up.

But he nodded with understanding. 'That's okay. I'll call for you at seven and we'll see what she says.'

Jackie smiled, told him her door number and said goodnight. She left the hall with Patsy and Sally, who wanted to know everything he'd said, which wasn't much so didn't take her long to relate.

'What can I wear?' she wailed as they all linked arms and crossed Formosa Drive. 'I've only got this skirt and jumper. And that's even if Mam says it's all right to go.'

'I'm sure she'll say yes,' Patsy said. 'And I'll lend you an outfit,' she added generously. 'I'll bring something into school tomorrow.'

'Thank you. Will it go with my boots?'

'Yes. You'll look fab when I've finished with you. I knew he fancied you. I could tell.'

'But what if he's already got a girl? Like you thought he had.'

'He probably dumped her,' Patsy said as they waved goodbye to Sally, who lived on Longmoor Lane. 'Why else would he ask you out? Enjoy yourself; you'll be safe as houses with him. He's the flipping vicar's son, when all's said and done.'

'Hmm,' Jackie said, not totally convinced and terrified of getting out of her depth. What if she made a fool of herself? 'We'll see.'

Patsy linked her arm, laughing. 'I quite fancy Stevie. After I requested that song he kept looking over at me and winking. Get Sandy to tell him I like him. Then maybe we can go out as a foursome some time.'

Chapter Five

For the umpteenth time, Jackie checked her appearance in the age-speckled full-length mirror on the inside of her mam's wardrobe door. Patsy's black and white hound's-tooth check pinafore dress looked perfect with the black polo-neck top and her precious black boots. She flicked her hair over her shoulders and dabbed a bit of her mam's Avon Topaze perfume on her wrists and behind her ears, loving the slightly woody scent.

Mam had kicked up a right fuss when she'd asked if it was okay to go to the pictures with Sandy. She said it didn't matter one bit that he was the vicar's son, he was still a lad and older than her. She was too young for boyfriends and what about her homework and what-have-you? Jackie had pleaded and begged and promised the homework would be done over the weekend. In the end Mam had reluctantly said yes. There'd been a lecture on behaving herself and strict instructions not to go off anywhere alone with him, and to come straight home as soon as the film finished.

Jackie reluctantly put on her duffle coat; it was a cold night anyway so she'd be glad of it later when they came out of the warm cinema. Students wore them, so she wouldn't look *too* childish. Her handbag was downstairs in the kitchen. As she hurried to get it the doorbell rang. Her legs wobbled as she went to open the door. Sandy was standing with his back to her, waving at the twitching net curtain opposite. He spun around, his wide smile lighting up his face.

Her heart skipped a beat and butterflies turned cartwheels in her stomach as she caught a whiff of spicy aftershave. He looked good in faded jeans and the pea coat he'd worn in church, an Anfield football scarf flung casually around his neck. She'd be proud to be seen out with him and hoped he'd feel the same about her. She stood back to let him in.

'Nosy neighbour,' he said, jerking his thumb towards the window across the street.

'You can say that again,' Mam said, coming out of the sitting room. 'Net curtain Nelly, that one. Nice to meet you, young man. Now make sure you have Jackie home no later than half-ten. It *is* the pictures you're going to and not a wild party or anything?'

'I promise, Mrs, er…' he said. 'It's the pictures, yes. And I'll look after her.'

'Evans,' Mam said, shaking his outstretched hand.

Jackie kissed her mam on the cheek as she and Sandy left the house.

'We'll catch the bus on Longmoor Lane,' he said, leading the way. Then he stopped dead and she walked right into the back of him. He turned, grabbed her hand and held it tight as he walked on.

The butterflies were doing cartwheels again as her small hand grew hot in his large one. 'Which picture house are we going to? Mam said the Rio in Fazakerley closed down a while ago and it's a bingo hall now.'

'It is. We're going to the Astoria.'

They reached the bus stop as the number twenty was pulling up and they climbed on board, making their way upstairs. The conductor followed as they found seats near the back and sat down.

'Two to Walton Road, please.' Sandy handed over the fares and the unsmiling man punched two tickets and handed them over with the change. He sniffed loudly and walked away without a backward glance.

'*He* clearly loves his job,' Sandy said, grinning. He reached into his jacket pocket and pulled out a packet of Embassy cigarettes and a box of matches. He offered the pack to Jackie, who shook her head. 'Do you mind if I do?'

'Not at all.' She was surprised that he'd even asked her. How polite. Her dad and Uncle Frank just lit up without bothering. She didn't particularly like the smoke that got into everything, including her clothes, but there wasn't much she could do about it so she just kept out of their way.

Sandy lit up and puffed a cloud of smoke into the air above his head. 'I only have one or two at night,' he said, as though reading her mind. 'Mum hates me smoking, so I never do it at home. I'll put it out if you object.'

She shook her head. 'It's fine.'

She looked out of the window but couldn't see much as it was dark and the windows were dirty. The streetlights winked and blinked through the filth and smuts on the outside of the glass. She couldn't remember the last time she'd been on a bus in the dark or even out at night, apart from to the youth club and Patsy's house. She sat back and willed herself to relax. She felt she should break the silence and maybe ask him something about himself.

'Who's your favourite group?' Music was a safe enough topic.

He shrugged. 'I like most music, except jazz. I don't have a particular favourite, but I'm quite into Bob Dylan at the moment.'

'Really?' Jackie wasn't too sure about Bob Dylan. Some of his stuff was okay, but his voice droned on a bit too much for her liking. She preferred the more melodic Donavan. 'What about The Beatles?'

'Well that goes without saying. We're Liverpudlians; well – I'm a token one, anyway. I think we all like The Beatles. Their latest LP, *Rubber Soul*, is superb.'

'It is. I've heard some of it at Patsy's. I love "Nowhere Man" and "In My Life".'

'Me too.' He dropped the butt end of his cigarette onto the floor and ground it out with his boot heel. He leant across her, giving her another whiff of spice, and rubbed at the glass. 'Can't see a damn thing through these windows, but I think we're off at the next stop.'

They got to their feet and hurried downstairs as the bus lurched to a standstill, brakes squealing in protest. He held out his hand to her as she jumped from the platform and landed beside him.

'Right, not too sure what's on tonight. Ah, here we go.' They stopped outside the Astoria and looked up at the poster on the wall. '*Doctor in Clover*,' he said. 'That'll do, won't it? Got a good cast. Leslie Phillips, Shirley Anne Field. Should be funny. The others in the series were.'

Jackie nodded. She hadn't seen any of the Doctor films, so had no idea if they were funny or not. Anyway, it didn't matter. It was such a treat to be taken out.

The queue for tickets was short and most people were already seated, but Sandy managed to get two on the back row of the stalls. He bought a box of Paynes Poppets to share and they went inside. Several people got to their feet to let them pass as the usherette shone her torch along the row. The newsreel had already started as they sat down and undid their coats. Sandy helped Jackie off with hers and put it across his knee.

'You okay?' He smiled and took her hand again, lacing their fingers together. They watched the rest of the newsreel and the adverts for future showings. 'I fancy that,' he said as a trailer for *Dateline Diamonds* came on. 'The Small Faces are in it. We'll come and see it next month.'

Next month? The butterflies were going crazy now. Did that mean he'd want to see her again? If he was thinking ahead, it was unlikely he had a girlfriend. Should she ask him? Better not. For all she knew, the girl may have dumped him. He might be upset deep down and hiding it. She was going to enjoy being with him and not worry about anything else.

Marcia Phelan would kill to be here right now, she thought as Sandy slid his arm around her shoulder and she snuggled against him. The girl had made a few nasty remarks today at school after she'd overheard Patsy telling Jackie she'd brought the clothes for tonight's date and they were in her locker. Jackie had ignored Marcia, but the comments about having to borrow clothes had hurt. Patsy had shoved Marcia and told her to shut her gob. She'd called her a jealous cow and told her the reason Sandy had asked Jackie out, and not her, was because she was a much nicer person than Marcia would ever be.

Sandy offered her a chocolate as the big film started and he popped it into her mouth and another one into his own. It felt nice, the way his fingers touched her lips, and her tummy tingled with a fizzy sort of feeling. He squeezed her hand and she squeezed his back. After a few minutes his lips brushed her cheek and he nibbled her ear. She liked that and turned her face to his. He dropped a tentative kiss on her lips. She took a deep breath and returned it.

As the film progressed she lost track of what was happening, just aware of laughter all around her. Sandy's kisses were demanding and she found herself responding with such fervour that it was hard to breathe as their tongues entwined and he gently caressed her through her clothes. Strange things were happening to her, like funny twinges in her tummy, and as he stroked her knees she felt a warm feeling and wanted him to move his hand up higher, but she didn't say anything. He might think she was cheap and she'd never ask him to do that anyway. As the lights went up for the interval her cheeks felt hot and she was sure she must look flushed.

Sandy detached himself from her and smiled. She fidgeted in her seat and smoothed her skirt down.

'Want a choc ice or a tub?'

'Oh, a choc ice, please.'

He got to his feet and followed a queue of people down to the front where the two usherettes were standing with laden trays around their necks. The melodic strings of Mantovani filled the air with 'Some Enchanted Evening' and Jackie sat back and relaxed, staring at Sandy as he moved slowly down the queue. He was so handsome. She couldn't believe her luck. Her first ever date and she was with the best-looking lad for miles. He was at the front of the queue now and then making his way back to her with a big smile, two choc ices clutched in his hands.

❀

Dora checked her watch for the umpteenth time since Jackie had gone out. She'd tried to get on with some sewing, but had cast it aside at nine thirty, unable to concentrate. She wasn't sure how she felt about her youngest daughter going out on a date, no matter how nice a lad Sandy seemed to be. Her elder daughter Carol had dated the odd boyfriend before she'd left to live with her dad, and although Dora had had similar qualms about her, she'd been okay and the relationships soon fizzled out. The new boy Carol had met since she started working at Lewis's hadn't been introduced to her and Jackie yet, but her ex-husband Joe had told her he seemed a nice enough lad on the one occasion Carol had introduced Alex to him and Ivy.

Dora went upstairs to her bedroom and sat in front of the dressing table, winding rollers into her hair. It was still a bit damp from an earlier washing, so would be nice and wavy by tomorrow morning when she took the rollers out. Jackie would be fine, she hoped. Sandy was polite, clean and tidy, and you couldn't get a better boyfriend than a vicar's son, surely?

Dora sighed. Joe had been a nice enough lad too, but he'd still had wandering hands when they'd done their courting. She looked at her reflection in the mirror, her cheeks flushing pink, as she thought about Joe and how things hadn't worked out for them. She'd known him since their schooldays and he'd been the love of her life, but due to circumstances beyond her control, their marriage had failed.

Carol had been born a twin, but sadly her sister Joanna had died within hours of their birth. Dora had suffered terrible depression afterwards and had been hospitalised and estranged from her remaining baby for several months. It had taken a while for her to bond with Carol again and when Jackie was born a couple of years later Dora had suffered the same crippling depression once more. The strain on their marriage had been more than either she or Joe could deal with and, when she discovered that he'd had a brief fling with Ivy Bennett, a woman from work, Dora couldn't forgive him and had ordered him to leave their marital home. With her mam and Frank's help she'd coped alone with both daughters until Carol was removed from her care and given to Joe's custody. She and Joe had made an attempt at reconciliation when Jackie was four years old, but things didn't work out, though Dora had eventually got Carol back.

Now Joe was married to Ivy; although both her daughters often hinted that their dad wasn't all that happy. Dora shook her head at her reflection and her eyes filled briefly. That made two of them then, but Joe had made his bed, and it was nothing to do with her any more whether he was happy or not. She hurried downstairs to make a pot of tea for when Jackie got back and peeped out of the front room window once more while she waited for the kettle to boil. She could just make out the silhouettes of a young couple in each other's arms, under the lamp at the top of the road. She let the curtain fall back into place as she heard voices coming down the avenue, and breathed a sigh of relief as she recognised one as Jackie's. Her daughter was home safe and sound, and why wouldn't she be?

'Get a grip, Dora, let her grow up a bit,' she muttered as she went into the kitchen to fill the teapot.

❊

Jackie relaxed into Sandy's arms as he kissed her slowly and passionately. He held her hand as they walked the short distance to

Fourth Avenue, stopping to kiss her every few yards. Jackie felt like she was floating and didn't want the night to end. He gave her a lingering kiss on the doorstep. She wished she could ask him in but her mam would be in her nighty and rollers and might throw a hairy fit. She was still up, because a light showed through a slight gap in the curtains, where no doubt she'd been nosying out, on the look-out for them arriving back.

'I'd better go in,' Jackie said, reluctantly pulling away from him. 'I don't want to give Mam a reason to moan or she might not let me out again.'

Sandy groaned and gave her another kiss. 'Can I see you Sunday afternoon? I've got to help out with church stuff in the morning. Mum and Dad expect it, I'm afraid. I don't really mind, gives me a bit of a laugh to see all the women vying for my old man's attention. But I'm free after dinner, say about two.'

Jackie nodded. 'That'll be nice. I won't be at church in the morning because I've got homework to catch up with.'

'Okay, I'll see you Sunday then. If it's not raining we'll go to Sefton Park on my scooter. Wear something warm.' He dropped another kiss on her lips and she watched him stride off up the avenue, stopping on the corner to give her a final wave.

Chapter Six

'So, are you seeing him again?' Patsy asked as she and Jackie strode up Longmoor Lane towards the Co-op.

Jackie's mam had forgotten spuds and carrots for tomorrow's dinner and the two girls had volunteered to get them. Mam said they could keep the change, so a slab of chocolate each was on the cards.

'Yes,' Jackie replied. 'He's taking me out tomorrow afternoon to Sefton Park on his scooter.'

'Didn't he ask you out for tonight?'

Jackie shook her head. 'He never mentioned seeing me today at all. But that's all right. I was seeing you anyway.'

'Wonder what he's up to then? Bet he's going to one of the clubs with his mates. Did you tell him that I fancy Stevie?'

'No, but I will tomorrow.' Lying in bed last night after Sandy had gone home, Jackie had wondered why he hadn't asked her out for Saturday night. But maybe she was too young to take into town. The clubs might not allow her in because she was under sixteen. The Cavern wasn't licensed though, and Carol had been going out in town for ages. Maybe Sandy liked a drink with his mates. He could hardly take her in The Grapes or The Phil. She sighed and willed the days to hurry by until her birthday, but even then she'd still be underage for drinking legally.

'Bet they've gone to the football match.' Patsy's voice broke her thoughts.

'Maybe. Sandy wore an Anfield scarf last night. Uncle Frank supports them and that's where *he* is today. It's a home game.'

'Then they'll be out for a drink afterwards and doing the clubs. No time for girlfriends.' Patsy laughed and linked arms. 'Still, you've got me.'

'Well, I'm hardly his girlfriend...' Jackie stopped and stared straight ahead. Walking towards them were Marcia Phelan and two other girls from their class. 'Oh great. That's all we need.'

'Have a good time last night?' Marcia said loudly as the other girls sniggered. All three were dolled up to the nines; mini skirts, boots and long leather jackets, with makeup that made them look at least five years older.

'Er, yes thank you.' Jackie tried to side-step past the girl but she moved to block her path. 'Excuse me, we're in a hurry.'

'Ooh, got another date with the lovely vicar's son, have we?'

'She has tomorrow,' Patsy said. 'Not that it's got anything to do with you. Now gerrout the way or I'll make you.'

Marcia smirked and moved slightly. 'I guess he'll be seeing his *real* girlfriend tonight then.'

With that she walked away with her entourage, leaving Jackie staring after her.

'Bitch. Ignore her,' Patsy said, looking daggers at Marcia's back. 'She's a jealous cow who couldn't get a fella if she tried,' she yelled after the trio.

'Leave it.' Jackie walked on, feeling like she'd been hit in the stomach with a lead weight. 'Told you he'd already got a girl.'

'He hasn't, I'm sure of it. Ask him tomorrow.'

'Maybe.' Jackie led the way into the Co-op, feeling sick inside. Sandy's actions last night, the way he'd kissed her and held her hand, had made her feel special. But maybe that was what boys did to win a girl round. How would she know? He was the first boy to ever ask her out and she hadn't a clue really what had been expected of her. She just did what came naturally in responding to his kisses and caresses, and he hadn't complained.

With their purchase of vegetables in a paper carrier bag, the girls made their way back to The Avenues, calling first at Jackie's to drop off the shopping and then on to Patsy's, where Jackie was invited to spend the afternoon and stay for tea. Her mam was going out with Uncle Frank and his friends to the Legion tonight to see a turn; a fellow who sang like Elvis, apparently. Jackie was glad that *she* was going to Patsy's and not spending the night alone. Marcia's comment had hurt her more than she was letting on.

⚜

After a tea of grilled lamb chops, chips and peas, followed by home-made apple pie and custard, sitting in Agnes's posh dining room, with a fancy embroidered cloth on the teak table, and matching napkins, Jackie and Patsy headed upstairs to listen to records. Patsy had asked her mam if Jackie could sleep over and her dad had offered to go and push a note through the letterbox on his way out for a quick pint, so that Mam wouldn't worry when she got home and found Jackie missing.

'So come on, you've hardly said a word about what you got up to last night,' Patsy said as they lay sprawled on her comfy bed with Manfred Mann 'Do-Wah-Diddying' in the background.

'We just went to the pictures,' Jackie said. 'He bought us some Poppets and a choc ice and that was it really.'

'And he didn't snog the face off you?'

Jackie grinned, her cheeks heating.

'Course he did. You're blushing like crazy. So, tell us what the film was about then.'

'Erm, it was a comedy, one of them Doctor films.'

'But you hardly saw any of it, did you?'

Jackie laughed and shook her head. 'Not really. And yes, he's a great kisser, not that I've anything to compare him with of course.

But he made me feel special and he put his arm around my shoulders the whole time and held my hand when we walked for the bus.'

She missed out the bit where his hand had caressed her body. That was her secret, although she'd written it in her diary.

'Lucky you,' Patsy said, jumping up to change the record. 'Sounds like he's dead keen. I'd ignore Marcia and her comments earlier. She's just jealous. Enjoy tomorrow with him, and don't forget to mention a foursome with Stevie.'

'I won't,' Jackie said, staring up at the ceiling as Otis Redding sang 'My Girl'. She still felt a little unsure about things, but she wouldn't let it spoil her afternoon out with Sandy tomorrow.

❀

Dora slammed the front door shut and thundered up the stairs, a feeling of fury coursing through her body.

'That bloody woman,' she muttered. 'I'll show her.'

Jackie popped her head round the door of her bedroom, where she was finishing the last of her Sunday morning homework. 'What's wrong, Mam?'

'Her. That bloody Baker woman. She ignored me this morning, apart from giving me smug looks every now and again,' Dora said, storming into her own bedroom.

Jackie followed her and sat down on the double bed. Dora pulled the wardrobe door open and reached for a cardboard box from the shelf. It was the box she kept important papers in, like birth certificates.

She sat down next to Jackie and began to rifle through the papers, tossing some down on the bed.

'What are you looking for?' Jackie picked up her parents' marriage certificate, a copy of the decree absolute and her own birth certificate.

'I'm going to wipe the smug look off that cow's face and I'll do it in front of all her cronies too. One of the ladies said that during the WI meeting last week Barbara bloody Baker told them that I'd never been married and that Evans was my maiden name. She said she knew someone who used to go to school with me years ago.'

'Well it is,' Jackie said. 'You changed our surnames to your old name after Dad married Ivy. You said you didn't want the same name as her.'

'Yes, I know, chuck. But this way I can prove I *was* married and now choose to use my maiden name, and I'll also tell them I changed yours to make it easier for us both. You can change yours back to Rodgers any time you want to now you're older, Jackie.'

'I'm quite happy to stay an Evans for now,' Jackie said.

Dora gave her daughter a hug. Her shoulders were shaking but she felt a bit calmer now.

'Come on,' Jackie said, leading the way downstairs. 'I'll make us a brew. The shoulder of lamb's in the oven and the spuds are peeled ready. You didn't tell me if Uncle Frank was coming, so I peeled extra.'

Dora rolled her eyes. 'There's no keeping him away on a Sunday and I don't mind feeding him. He tips up money towards the housekeeping and every penny helps. You're a good girl, love. I don't know what I'd do without you. That bloody woman must have nothing better to do with her time.'

'I'm sure she doesn't. But don't let her get to you, Mam. She's just a bored old biddy. Enjoy the rest of your day with Uncle Frank, knowing that you can swan in there next Sunday and prove her wrong. Think what a fool she'll feel when you show her up in front of all her friends. By the way, have you remembered I'm going out with Sandy after dinner?'

'Yes. He reminded me.' Dora laughed. 'He's a nice lad and his mother's a lovely lady. But you be careful on that scooter. Make sure you hang on tight. I'm going to write to our Carol tonight and invite her round soon; maybe we can have a little birthday party for you next month. She won't make excuses not to come then, and she might even bring that new boyfriend of hers.'

'I wouldn't hold your breath, Mam. But it'd be nice to see her again soon. And hopefully I'll get to meet Uncle Frank's new lady friend if we ask him to bring her along too.'

'I'm sure you will. She's lovely, is Maureen. Just what our Frank needs. My mam would have been that chuffed for him. It was always her wish that he'd find a new lady.'

'We need to get you sorted out next,' Jackie said with a teasing glint in her eyes.

Dora shook her head. 'I don't think I can be bothered, love. Your dad was the love of my life. I don't want to go down that road again. I'm quite content on my own for now.' Dora swallowed hard and blinked rapidly as she hung her jacket on the coat rack in the hall.

Chapter Seven

Sandy put the last of the clean glasses back on the shelf and hung the damp cloth up to dry. It had been a busy night working in the Jacaranda. They'd had a great new local group on, The Lamplighters, who'd gone down well, and now the crowd was slowly dispersing up the stairs and out onto Slater Street. The Jacaranda was a favourite haunt of Liverpool's music lovers, probably second in popularity only to The Cavern.

It had been a good day all round. Anfield had won three–two at home against Manchester United, so jubilant supporters had been out drinking in the city tonight. Although the Jac only sold soft drinks, the punters would visit the pubs first before coming in to listen to the groups and maybe pick up a fit little bird to take home. Rarely was there any trouble and it was a pleasure to work here. He'd done well for tips tonight. An extra shilling here and there bulked out his small allowance from his parents. He was skint today after taking Jackie out last night. He'd had to borrow money from his mum for the match this afternoon, but now he could pay her back with his tips and wages and still have a bit left over.

It had been well worth taking Jackie out though, he thought as he straightened chairs and tables, emptied the overflowing ashtrays into a bin and wiped a sticky mark from the mural of faces near the stage area. The mural had been painted by the late Stuart Sutcliffe and his art student pal, John Lennon, and was much cherished by the Jac's owner. He strolled up the stairs to the ground floor, his mind still on Jackie. He'd been smitten from the minute he'd set eyes on her in the church hall last weekend and had been so disappointed when she'd vanished while he'd nipped for a pee. He'd rushed to the door and looked up and down Formosa Drive, but there was no sign of her, *or* her mother. She'd been on his mind all week and he'd been delighted to see her at the youth club. She was a doll, and her fragile Marianne Faithfull looks were a turn-on in any man's books.

He'd just wanted to hug the life out of her at the pictures last night and was desperate to be alone with her, but that would take time and planning. He had no idea how old she was and hadn't got around to asking her yet, but he guessed sixteen at the most as she was studying for her O levels. She may still be underage, so he'd better find out tomorrow before he made any moves he might regret.

He checked his watch. Caz would be here soon. She'd want to come back to Stevie's and spend the night with him, no doubt. She and her mates had popped in earlier to see the group, but had gone on to The Grapes for a drink as it was one of the girls' birthdays. She'd promised to be back in time for him finishing his shift. He always stayed at Stevie's flat on a Saturday night after work and then rode his scooter, which he left parked in Stevie's yard, back to the church on Sunday mornings to help his folks out. Caz usually stayed with him at the flat if she and her friends hadn't got anything else planned.

She'd told them all he was her boyfriend and they were going steady. It wasn't strictly true. He enjoyed sex with her on a regular basis, but had no intentions of it getting serious and *definitely* not now that he'd met Jackie. He had a feeling he might well be half in love with her already. He couldn't stop thinking about her and had never felt this way before. If things worked out with Jackie he'd need to break up with Caz. He didn't want to hurt her, but he knew he'd have to finish things soon.

He looked up as the door opened and Caz strolled in, her eye makeup and neat brown hair, cut like Twiggy's, complementing her black mini-dress, and shapely legs clad in pale tights and long white boots, her bottle-green leather coat draped casually around her shoulders. She smiled and he dutifully walked towards her and received a kiss, which he returned. He knew he was in for a good time when she opened her handbag and showed him a half-bottle of vodka.

'Ready to go, Alex?'

At nearly nineteen, she was almost a year older than him and always called him by his Sunday-best name. Even his parents didn't call him Alex or even Alexander. He'd always been nicknamed Sandy and he liked it. But he'd been introduced to her as Alexander by a college friend, and that was that. He'd never taken her home to meet his family, so she had no idea of his childhood name. Alexander Faraday sounded sophisticated, and as he was hoping to make a living selling his paintings when he left art college, his real name had a more professional ring to it. But even Stevie called him Alex in Caz's earshot, although there'd been no agreement that he should do so; it just happened as a matter of course.

'I'll get my jacket. We'll have to walk, I'm afraid. No spare dosh for a taxi.' He wanted to keep what little he had for tomorrow so that he could at least offer to buy Jackie coffee and cake at the park café.

'Oh bloody hell, Alex; my feet are killing me in these boots,' Caz grumbled. 'It'll take us ages to walk down to Scottie Road. Come on, I'll treat us to a taxi.'

'It's not that far, couple of miles at the most. But if you've got enough money for a taxi, then fine.'

Caz worked at Lewis's department store as a wages clerk and earned a lot more money than he did, so he wasn't about to argue with her. Stevie's flat was above his parents' grocers shop. They'd recently moved to a new bungalow in Woolton, and allowed their son to live in the empty flat. It was a fair walk from Slater Street but normally he didn't mind. He called goodnight to his workmates and his boss Allan Williams, the Jac's owner, who used to manage The Beatles before Brian Epstein, and he and Caz set off up the street to the main road, where they quickly flagged down a taxi.

❀

Sandy sat at the kitchen table with a mug of coffee, listening to Alan Price singing 'Any Day Now' on Stevie's record player. He flicked ash into an old saucer that doubled as an ashtray, and sang along to the chorus. He could hear the seagulls kicking off down near the docks through the open window. Noisy buggers, they'd waken the dead. It was early but he needed to get back to Fazakerley, clean, tidy and ready for church.

He felt a bit hung-over from too much vodka last night. But he'd enjoyed it, and feeling slightly pissed had taken the thoughts of Jackie from his mind as he'd stripped Caz's clothes off and they'd made love on the mattress in the spare bedroom. Stevie's folks had taken the bed frames from both bedrooms with them, but had left the old mattresses behind. With a few colourful blankets and cushions chucked on them they made great alternating sofas and beds and no girl had complained yet, according to Stevie, anyway. The light and airy living room, with its double windows, was Stevie's studio, and out of bounds to drunken women.

Sandy stubbed out the last of his cigarette as his pal came stumbling into the kitchen, bleary-eyed and stubbly-chinned.

'Do you mind if I give coming to church with you a miss this week, mate?' Stevie said as he stuck two slices of bread under the grill. 'Toast?'

'Yeah, ta. No, not at all. But I might need you on Wednesday to help with the youth club again.'

'That's fine. Just let me know at college. I want to work on my abstract today. It needs to be ready for the exhibition next month. Old Wagstaffe said he wanted as many finished as we can manage.'

Mr Wagstaffe, the coordinator in charge of all college exhibitions, had been pressing students to get their work in as soon as possible.

'I've no chance of finishing mine for this one,' Sandy said with a sigh. 'There's no room at home to swing a cat, let alone put up my easel and work.'

'You can always move in here, you know, mate. Feel free. Much easier for getting to college as well. No lugging bloody big portfolios on the train or bus, or trying to keep your scooter upright with them strapped on the back.'

Sandy chewed his lip. He was tempted, but… He lowered his voice; Caz was still getting ready in the bedroom. 'Thanks, Stevie. Trouble is, if Caz knows I'm here permanently, she'll be round every spare minute. She'll want to move in with me.'

Stevie rescued the toast from under the grill and plastered the slices with Stork margarine. He reached into the one and only wall cupboard and pulled out a jar of marmalade.

'Help yourself,' he said, handing a plate and the toast to Sandy. 'And you don't want that? Sex on tap, I mean. Sounds okay to me.'

Sandy smiled. 'There is that. But no, I don't want to live with her. I'm thinking of dumping her. I'll see how it goes with that little blonde from the youth club first. I really like her.'

'How old is she?' Stevie sat down opposite him and took a bite of toast.

'Not sure. Sixteen-ish. I'm taking her out this afternoon, so I'll find out then.'

'Potentially jailbait.' Stevie smirked. 'And you, the son of a vicar. Where are your morals, man?'

Sandy grinned. 'Left 'em down south. If she is – underage, that is – I can wait. Meantime, like you said, I've got sex on tap with Caz.'

He thought back to last night's session. Caz was pretty good in bed, had taught him a lot about what women like, and that's probably why she assumed she had a claim over him.

He looked up and nodded as she sauntered into the kitchen, fully clothed, makeup immaculate, hair neat and tidy. She must carry the contents of her dressing table in that handbag of hers, he thought. 'Hi. Coffee?'

'A quick one please, Alex. Then you can run me home and I'll go back to bed for an hour or two. Do you fancy meeting up later, after your church duties, I mean?'

'Sorry, no can do today,' he said, making her a mug of coffee. 'My old fella has roped me in to help give the church hall a lick of paint.'

Where did that lie come from? He'd be struck down from above at this rate.

'Oh, that's a shame. Ah well, never mind. See you in the week then. Meet me from work one night or give me a call at home, *if* you can get through. The party line is always engaged with the neighbours using the phone, you know?'

Sandy knew all right. The number was nearly always engaged when he called her and by the time he got through it was often too late to be bothered riding over to Allerton. It wasn't the attitude of a love-struck suitor; but maybe right for a relationship that was coming to an end, almost. He couldn't quite do it yet – finish with her, that is. To have no sex life at all was unthinkable for a fella of his age. If it was a case of wanting his cake and eating it, then he'd try not to feel too guilty.

Chapter Eight

'Hold tight,' Sandy instructed as Jackie wrapped her arms around his parka-clad waist. He whipped up Longmoor Lane on his bright red Vespa SS180 with its multiple chrome mirrors attached to each side of the front carrier, and followed the signs for West Derby and Queen's Drive. Thankfully the forecast rain had held off so far today and the sky was mainly blue with a handful of fluffy white clouds. He was conscious of Jackie tightening her hold on him as he turned into Mossley Hill Drive and the entrance to Sefton Park. They'd arrived in no time as there was little traffic on the roads. Most of Liverpool was probably slumped on their sofas at this time in the afternoon, stuffed full of Sunday dinners.

He pulled into the car park and helped Jackie off.

'You okay?'

Smoothing her windswept hair from her eyes, he dropped a gentle kiss on her lips. Her face was white and she let out a breath, holding onto him for support.

'You'll get used to it. The first time riding pillion is always the worst. Come on, let's stretch our legs and explore a bit and then I'll treat us to coffee and cakes.'

He held her hand as they strolled down the path leading into the park.

'I haven't been here for ages, not since I was a little girl,' Jackie said. 'Before my dad married his second wife our parents used to bring me and my older sister for picnics. Dad would take us out on the lake on little boats while Mam sat and watched. She doesn't like water, can't even swim.'

'Neither can mine.' He laughed. 'Thought you were an only child? I didn't know you had a sister.'

'Yep, Carol lives with our dad and stepmum over the other side of Liverpool. I hardly ever see her because she works full-time and she's always out with her mates or her boyfriend. Tell you what I'd love to see again, now we're here, though.'

'What's that?'

'The Peter Pan statue.' Her face lit up as she spoke and Sandy smiled, thinking how pretty she was. So young and innocent, like a breath of fresh air. 'Can we?'

'We can.' From behind he put one arm around her head with his hand over her eyes and led her across the park, guiding her with his other arm. 'You ready?' he said and removed his hand from her eyes. 'There you go.'

She ran her hands over the base of the bronze statue, smiling up at the figure of Peter Pan outlined against the blue sky.

'It was my favourite story when I was a little girl. Dad used to read it to us at bedtime. I called one of our dolls Wendy after my favourite character. If ever I'm lucky enough to have a daughter I'll call *her* Wendy, too.'

'Wendy Moira Angela Darling,' he said with a grin. 'No kid will thank you for that mouthful. I should stick to Wendy Angela if I were you.'

'*You've* read it too?'

'I think everyone has.' He looked at her, blue eyes shining, rosy colour back in her cheeks, blonde hair framing her heart-shaped face, her luscious lips curving into a gentle smile, and thought he'd never seen such a beautiful girl. Sandy realised at that moment that he'd like to spend the rest of his life with her. She was *the one*, and he wanted to get to know her more than anything he'd ever wanted before. But he was also conscious not to frighten her off by being too over-eager at such an early stage. He bent to kiss her, holding her close. She responded eagerly, her arms reaching around his waist.

He drew his head back and smiled. 'I could stand here kissing you all day. But we might get thrown out by the park-keeper.' He took her hand. 'There are loads of statues by the Palm House, and the café is over that way too.'

They strolled around the park, Sandy pointing out areas of interest to her: follies, shelters and boathouses that he told her had been designed by someone named Lewis Hornblower. They walked around the huge man-made lake that Jackie remembered childhood boat trips on, and then made their way to the elegant Palm House conservatory with its three-tier dome. The huge building had eight corners where the statues stood, and Sandy told her the names of each one as they walked by them. He'd done a project on the park in his final year at school when they'd first moved to Liverpool, and certain things had stayed with him, including the fact that statues of Christopher Columbus, Captain Cook and Charles Darwin, the explorers, were situated there. He'd admired the stories behind each man and would put his future art career on hold in an instant to go off and explore new continents as these men had done. His dad had taken him to the docks regularly when they'd first moved up here and he'd enjoyed watching the big ships leave for far-flung places, envious of the throngs of passengers waving excitedly to friends and family as they sailed away to their wonderful new lives.

'Do you fancy travelling when you finish your education?' he asked.

'Oh, er, I've never really thought about it,' Jackie replied. 'To be honest, I've never been out of Liverpool.'

'We haven't done much either. Dad gets so little time off and there's not a lot of money in being a vicar, so we could hardly ever afford to go away on proper holidays. Mum's sister had a guest house in Herne Bay – not far from Canterbury where we used to live. Mum used to take us to stay there in school holidays when I was a kid.' He sighed. 'I fancy America myself. Maybe one day, if I ever get remotely famous and sell some paintings, it's the first place I'll visit.' *And hopefully I'll take you with me*, he thought.

In the café inside the Palm House Sandy ordered coffees and two huge slices of Victoria sponge, the layers of moist cake thickly sandwiched together with strawberry jam and fluffy buttercream.

'Ooh, this is a real treat,' Jackie said, tucking in at a table that overlooked a collection of colourful and exotic plants.

'Mum makes cakes like this,' he said. 'Maybe you could come for tea one day and sample hers.'

He couldn't believe he'd said that. Not once had he even thought of asking Caz to his home. But he'd really like Jackie to meet his parents away from the church and youth club environment.

She looked at him, eyes wide. 'I'd love to, thank you.'

'I'll arrange it then.'

'You said something about selling your paintings before. What sort of things do you paint?'

'Surreal and abstract stuff that no one can make head nor tail of,' he said with a laugh. 'At least that's what my mother says. I suppose you could say it's in the style of Salvador Dalí. Trouble is, I need to get on with doing some more painting. I was supposed to have something ready for the college exhibition next month. But it's nowhere near finished, nor is it likely to be.'

'Why not? Can't you just get on with painting at night after college?'

'I wish! But there's no room at my parents' place. I've nowhere to erect my easel. My mate Stevie said I can move in with him. He's got a flat down Scottie Road and uses the old living room as his art studio. There's room for me too, he has a second bedroom, but I can't really afford to live away from home. I hardly earn a penny and I'd probably starve to death for the sake of my art. Isn't that what most artists do though; starve while living in a garret or something?' He laughed and tucked into his cake.

Jackie finished her slice and took a sip of coffee. She wiped her lips on a paper napkin. 'I have an idea that might help.'

'You do?'

She nodded. 'How often does the church hall get used at night time?'

'Only Tuesday for WI meetings and Wednesday for youth club,' he replied. 'Actually, thinking about it, it's every other Tuesday.'

'Well there you are then. Why not use the hall? It would be brilliant and I bet the lighting would be fine because of the high ceiling in there.'

He stared at her for a long moment. 'You're a bloody genius. Why didn't *I* think of that? I'll have to ask Dad of course, but I can't see there being a problem. I've gotta do something or there's little point in me continuing my course. This is the first big art work we've been asked to produce. Eventually I'll rent a studio, but for now I'm stuck.'

Jackie smiled. 'Glad you think it might work.'

'Fantastic idea. What about you? Any plans after O levels?'

'Er, well, I'd like to go to college to study drama. I just love acting, dancing, that sort of thing, and I enjoy singing too, so I'd like to be involved in musical theatre.' She sighed and shook her head. 'But it's just a dream really. I doubt Mam will say yes to that plan. She'll want me to get a job because we really do need the money.'

He frowned. She sounded so enthusiastic; it would be a shame if her mother denied her the chance to reach for her dreams.

'Have you had any experience, lessons or anything? I mean, I saw you dancing the other night and you were totally lost in the music. Best dancer on the floor.'

'Thank you.' She blushed. 'Yes, I used to have dancing lessons and I've been in a few revue shows and pantos at the Empire when

I was little. Now I just do stuff at school. I'm always involved in whatever show we're putting on, and I usually get a good part too. But of course that will all be over this year. I could do with joining an amateur dramatics club, but there's nothing near us.'

Sandy chewed his lip. 'Mum used to run an am-dram club in Kent. She was talking about starting one up here, but of course we've only just been given a permanent parish, so she's not got around to it yet. I'll let you know if she's still thinking about it when I've spoken to her.' He was dying to ask how old she was without seeming obvious. 'There might be, er, age restrictions for joining something like that, with you still being at school, I mean. Are you sixteen yet?' There, that was easy enough.

'Next month,' she said. 'Thank the lord. I'm one of the youngest in the class and I hate it. Everybody's always going on about what they get up to now they're sixteen.' She blushed and looked away. 'You know what I mean?'

'Lads are always trying to make out they're super studs. You'll be ready in your own time, Jackie.' He reached for her hand and squeezed it. And when she was, he'd be there, waiting to make her his. 'Let's have one more stroll around and then we'll make our way back to the car park.'

As he helped her onto the scooter she clapped her hand to her mouth and started to laugh.

'What's so funny?'

'I almost forgot,' she began. 'Patsy will kill me. She said to tell you she likes Stevie and will you let him know.'

'Does she now?' He laughed. 'Yeah, I'll tell him. He'll probably be coming to help me with the music again on Wednesday. Make sure she's there.'

❀

After dropping Jackie off and arranging to see her at the youth club on Wednesday, whether he was needed to play records or not, Sandy made his way home to Haven Road. He wasn't that keen on living in the Morgan Heights tower block, but at least they were on the ground floor in the caretaker's flat for now, and it meant he could take his precious scooter inside and park it in the corridor by the front door.

The two-bedroom flat came with his father's job and was rent free. They were here on a temporary basis, and would move into a new bungalow in the grounds of the church and hall, but there had been delays with the building work and that had been going on for a while now. After the huge draughty old rectory they'd left down in Kent, living here was like camping out in a shoe box and it drove his mother mad. She was forever going on at his mild-mannered father that he should never have accepted a position in Liverpool without the promise of permanent accommodation. It was too far away from her family and friends. But his father chose to ignore her grumbles and just got quietly on with his work. Sandy loved living in Liverpool and he enjoyed his course at the art college, treading in the footsteps of John Lennon and Stuart Sutcliffe. He'd made some good friends and was quite happy to settle in the city.

He let himself into the quiet flat; his parents would be down at church for the evening service. There was a note propped on the table against the teapot. Instructions from his mother about what to have for tea. He smiled. Didn't she realise he could make his own decisions about food at his age? Besides, he wasn't really hungry after that enormous slice of cake.

There were boxes packed with belongings all over the place, his mother getting ready for the big move that showed no signs of being sooner rather than later. No wonder there wasn't anywhere to paint. Maybe asking Jackie round for tea wasn't the best idea for now either.

He went into his bedroom and lay down on the narrow bed, hands behind his head, thinking about her and how good she'd felt in his arms. He wished he could spend every waking minute with her, every sleeping minute too. If only. Roll on next month and her sixteenth birthday. Hopefully her mother would allow her a bit more freedom to go out with him.

He needed more money to take her to places and wondered if Allan Williams would give him another shift at the Jacaranda. He couldn't ask for an increase in his allowance. His parents were stretched to the limit. Mum had given him extra money last month for new jeans and his pea coat. Trouble is, if he got extra work in the Jac, then he'd have to sleep over at Stevie's, and if Caz got wind of that she'd be there wanting to stay over with him, so that wasn't an option. Not any more. He would definitely finish with her soon.

A nice thought struck him. If his father said yes to him using the hall to paint, Jackie could come and keep him company. It would give them somewhere to be alone, if she could get out, that is. Maybe her friend Patsy would cover for her. She looked game enough for anything, that one. And she'd owe him for fixing her up with Stevie, who'd said last week that she looked a fit little bird. So hopefully it shouldn't be a problem.

Chapter Nine

Something was wrong. Alex's recent indifference towards her was puzzling. It was unusual for him not to call, but there'd been nothing for a couple of days. On Saturday night he'd seemed a bit distant and not his usual friendly self. He'd been keen enough when they'd arrived at Stevie's, but they usually made love at least three times before she left to go home on Sunday, and after the first time he'd rolled over and fallen asleep. When she'd woken up and reached for him he was already up and in the kitchen.

Carol wondered if he'd met someone else: maybe a girl from college who moved in the same arty circles as he did. She knew they had little in common. She hadn't a clue about art and who he was going on about when he raved over paintings he loved. She'd heard of the fella who'd cut his ear off, Van Gogh, and that Andy Warhol bloke who painted pictures of tins of soup and Marilyn Monroe, but that was about it. Alex liked Bob Dylan and *she* loved Tamla Motown and soul music. He was a Mod and rode a scooter and she thought they'd have loads in common, with her being a Mod too. Everyone said how good they looked together, a real Mod couple, but looking good and feeling good were two different things.

She liked to go out with her friends from work and have a girly time and get pissed. And although Alex liked a drink, he never got rolling drunk. He always seemed to be in control of himself, *too* controlled at times. It seemed almost impossible for him to relax some nights. And he'd never asked her to his home. She knew he lived with his parents in Fazakerley and that his dad was a vicar and they were quite posh because they came from Kent. But she had no idea which church his father did his vicar-ing stuff in. Alex always went home early Sunday morning to help out, but she was never invited. Maybe he was ashamed of her and her short skirts and makeup. Although he never complained about the length when he was shoving his hand *up* the short skirts. She could do with getting to know some of his college pals a bit better, to try to find out more about him. They'd been going out together nearly six months now and she was tired of feeling used and only seeing him half of the week, if that.

She'd been hoping he'd want to make their relationship more permanent when his course ended. Maybe get engaged or something. But that was looking highly unlikely now. Besides, he never had any spare money. His only income, apart from the allowance from his parents, was the money he earned at the Jacaranda, which was peanuts compared to *her* wages. She couldn't see an artist making much money. Did people really pay a fortune for what looked like tins of paint chucked willy-nilly over a canvas?

Maybe it was time to move on and find another fella who would give her a future to look forward to. Someone she could understand and not feel so dim in his, and his friends', company. The lad she'd been seeing before Alex had worked down the docks and always had plenty of money to take her out. Except it wasn't just *her* he was taking out, as she'd discovered when he turned up at The Cavern one night, after she'd told him she was staying in and then changed her mind. He had another girl clinging to his arm. He'd tried to pass her off as his sister, but the girl said she was his fiancée and had threatened to scratch Carol's eyes out if she didn't leave her fella alone. After further altercations in the ladies with the girl, Carol had finished with him there and then and left the club in tears. Her mates had taken her to The Grapes and got her drunk. She'd dumped him not long after he'd robbed her of her virginity too, the bastard! But she wouldn't stand for being mucked around. She was nearly nineteen and could end up on the shelf at this rate. Some of the girls she'd been at school with were already married and starting families.

She felt sad when her thoughts turned in that direction. Alex was the best-looking lad she'd seen in a long time and she was certain she loved him. It was the only reason she'd slept with him, after promising herself she wouldn't be taken in again. She thought he loved her too, although he'd never actually told her that he did, but his actions spoke volumes at times and it had been enough for her to trust him.

'Oi, Caz. Wake up, gel, you nearly missed the stop. Youse dreamin' about that lovely fella of yours again?'

Carol got to her feet and waved at Susan Wilkes, her tubby, bottle-blonde workmate who'd just descended from the smoky upstairs of the bus they were travelling on. Carol hated fag smoke and refused to go upstairs. She pushed the thoughts of Alex to the back of her mind and linked arms with Susan as they got off the bus and made their way into Lewis's department store to begin the day's work.

❀

'We're going to the Kardomah at lunchtime, Caz, you coming with us?'

Carol jumped as Susan's voice broke her reverie. 'Yeah, that'll be nice. Thanks.'

Alex might be in there. He sometimes met up with his college mates for lunch. She'd joined them a couple of times in the past. With that thought cheering her up a bit, she chewed the end of her pen and tried to concentrate on her work but it was impossible. She could do with a holiday; maybe the Easter break in April would be a good time. She might suggest to Alex that they go away for the weekend if she offered to pay: New Brighton, or maybe

Blackpool. They could go on his scooter and she'd stand the cost of accommodation. It would be nice to know that Stevie wasn't lying in the room next to them. Not that it inhibited them, but still, she always felt a bit conscious on a Sunday morning that he might have been listening to them making love. As Susan got to her feet on the dot of twelve and grabbed her coat and bag, Carol pushed back her chair and sighed.

Outside the pair walked briskly down the road and crossed over, following a couple of other girls from the wages department. One of them, Ann, had recently got engaged and talked non-stop about her forthcoming wedding and what she'd bought for her bottom drawer. Carol found the whole thing nauseating and held back while the girls got well in front. She'd love to share talk of wedding plans with Ann, if she only had some of her own.

'What's wrong?' Susan asked. 'You're very quiet lately.'

Carol shrugged. 'Nothing, just a bit fed up with work and my love life, or lack of it.'

'Thought you liked your job. Have you had a falling-out with Alex?'

'No. But he hasn't called me for a couple of nights and I haven't seen him since Sunday morning. And yes, I *do* like my job. But I'm ready for a break, a bit of a holiday. Might see if Alex fancies a few days away at Easter.'

'Oh, well if you fancy making it a foursome, we could hire a caravan. Me and my Pete could do with a bit of a holiday. Mum's neighbour has a van over in Formby that he hires out. Be cheaper if four of us share. I'll ask him how much.'

Carol's heart sank. While she was fond of Susan, and her boyfriend Pete was okay, she would rather spend the time alone with Alex. She smiled, trying to look enthusiastic.

'We'll see. I haven't actually asked Alex yet.'

They reached the junction of Stanley Street and Whitechapel and the Kardomah Café. Inside the smell of hot toast and coffee perked Carol up and her stomach rumbled. She'd probably feel better once she'd had something to eat. The café was crowded and she glanced around but there was no sign of the students Alex hung about with. Ann and Sandra from work were already in the queue and beckoned Carol and Susan over.

'I'll order,' Ann said, 'and youse can all settle up with me at the table. Go and bag that one by the window.' She pointed to the Stanley Street side.

'Beans on toast and coffee, for us two,' Susan said, steering Carol across the crowded café. 'That okay with you?' she whispered to Carol, who nodded. 'Don't mention holidays to those two,' Susan added.

'I won't.' Carol took off her coat, hung it on the back of a chair and sat down. She rubbed at the steamed-up window and stared at the people rushing past, wondering idly where they were going and for what reason.

'Penny for them,' Susan said.

'Not worth a penny.'

'Can I ask you summat? And don't bite my head off.'

Carol looked up from her people-watching. 'What?'

'Are you preggers?'

Carol threw back her head and laughed. If only. Alex was the ultimate in being careful. 'Am I heck,' she said. 'What makes you say that?'

'Well, it's like your mind's elsewhere all the time. Like you've got a problem you're not sharing with me, as you normally do. And that's the usual one for us gels, ain't it?'

'Not for me.' If she were, then she was sure Alex would do the right thing, him being a vicar's son. At least then she'd have him and know he was hers for good. But there was little chance of it happening. He was too damn cautious to take chances for one thing. 'I'm just feeling a bit fed up, that's all. Be glad when it's summer. Only another couple of days to go and then it's March. We can start looking forward to spring.'

It was nearly her kid sister's birthday, too. Jackie would be sixteen next month. She must remember to get her a card and a bit of something from work. Perfume, maybe.

Ann and Sandra brought laden trays across and dished out the lunches. 'They took ages today,' Ann grumbled, sitting down opposite Carol. 'I'm bloody starving. Tuck in, gels.'

❀

On the way back to Lewis's, Carol looked around at the sound of a loud wolf-whistle. She stopped and pulled Susan back with her. Alex and Stevie were crossing the road and came up behind them.

'Didn't you hear me calling?' Alex said as they drew level.

She shivered as he dropped a light kiss on her lips. 'No.' Her stomach fluttered as she looked into his eyes. 'I just heard you wolf-whistle.'

'Ah, that was Stevie, not me.'

'Oh. Oh well, it did the trick. We're, er, we're just going back to work.'

'Not to worry. Catch up with you again. Busy tonight, but I'll meet you under Nobby Lewis after work tomorrow,' he said, referring to the naked statue of the Liverpool Resurgence above the front doors of the department store. 'We'll go for a drink. I did try and call you by the way, but your bloody phone was engaged all the time.'

Carol nodded. 'Okay. We'll have to dash or we'll be late. See you tomorrow then.'

'Feel better now you've seen him?' Susan asked as they hurried up Whitechapel.

'A bit. But what's he doing tonight, that he couldn't meet me? And to be honest, our neighbour with the party line has been out two nights on the run. So the phone couldn't have been engaged all night. He's lying.'

Susan frowned. 'He doesn't seem the type to lie. Didn't you say his dad's a vicar?'

Carol half-smiled. 'He is. But that doesn't make Alex any different to other lads his age.'

Chapter Ten

Her stepmother was ironing when Carol arrived home from work. She got on well enough with Ivy, her dad's second wife, to a point, although at times she really missed her mam and younger sister and wished her dad Joe had not got involved with Ivy in the first place. Dora, her mam, was blonde, slim and still looked young for her age, while Ivy was dark and chubby and not half as pretty. What *had* he been thinking? She was a bossy woman too, but looked after them both okay. Her dad seemed happy enough, most of the time, although sometimes he seemed miles away when spoken to and occasionally had a sad look on his face.

'Hiya, Carol,' Ivy greeted her. 'Your tea's in the oven. Just watch your fingers when you lift the plate out. Use a cloth.'

'Thank you.' Carol hung her coat on the hall stand.

She sat alone in the small dining room, with its mish-mash of furniture and colours. Ivy had never been good at putting things together and Carol was certain she must be colour blind. Who in their right mind put purple and blue floral curtains with a dark orange carpet? Thank God the walls were plain white. She wondered why her dad was late home. He usually ate his tea with her, but his plate was still in the oven. She looked up from her sausage and mash as Ivy bustled in with a teapot. 'Where's Dad?'

'Doing overtime. We're saving up to go to Spain. So he's taking extra hours while they're on offer.' Ivy poured two mugs of tea and handed one to Carol. 'You okay, you look a bit peaky.'

'Fine thanks. Just tired.'

'Oh, while I think on.' Ivy dug into the large pocket of the green nylon overall she did her cleaning in, and pulled out a creased envelope. She laid it on the table and ran a hand across it, trying to smooth it flat. 'This came today. Looks like your mam's writing. She's posted it first class as well. Hope it's not bad news, her wanting it to get here quick, like.'

Carol frowned and looked at the postmark. 'She would have phoned me if there was bad news. But this was posted a few days ago. It should have arrived sooner than today.' She looked closely at Ivy, whose cheeks flushed pink. 'Odd that it's taken a while to come. Still, not to worry, it's here now. I'll take it upstairs with me to read.'

She picked up her mug of tea and the letter and strolled out of the room, conscious of Ivy's beady eyes staring at her back.

On closer inspection, she could see that the envelope had a dried substance oozing slightly from the flap. Bet Ivy had panicked when the glue wouldn't dry. She sat down on her bed. Nosy bugger. She was so jealous of anything to do with Mam and it would only cause ructions for her dad if Carol said anything.

If only he and Mam could have sorted themselves out, life would be much nicer. But they'd had a lot of problems early on in their married life. Carol's twin sister had died the day they were born and Mam had suffered really bad depression for a long time and the same following Jackie's birth a few years later. They hadn't even lived in the same house then; Jackie and Mam had stayed at Granny and Frank's while Mam recovered and *she'd* stayed with Dad in their prefab bungalow until Mam was well enough to come home. But Dad had had a brief affair with Ivy and, when Mam found out, it had been the beginning of the end and they'd split up. Then when they decided to give it another try, Ivy had told Dad that she was expecting his baby and ruined it for them for ever. Ivy eventually claimed she'd lost the baby. But Carol had overheard her mam talking to Agnes on more than one occasion, and had sussed out that Ivy had lied and there'd been no baby at all. But Mam wouldn't have Dad back and he'd felt obliged to marry Ivy. The lost baby was never discussed in front of Carol and Jackie and Carol had no idea if her dad even knew he'd been lied to.

She lay back on her narrow single bed and ripped open the envelope Ivy had given her. She wasn't one for letter writing, her mam, but it was nice to catch up with her news. Uncle Frank had got a new lady friend. Her name was Maureen and her mam said she was a lovely person. Carol smiled. It was time he moved on. His late wife Joanie had been dead for many years now. There was an invite to tea on the Sunday just after Jackie's sixteenth birthday. Mam hoped she would be able to come, and to write and let her know, as Jackie hadn't had a birthday party for years so it would be a nice surprise for her if Carol would come.

Carol nodded. It would be lovely to see the other half of her family again. She'd felt a bit lonely at times since she'd moved in here, even though it was much more convenient to get to work, and better for going out at night. That's why she enjoyed being out with Alex or her friends so much; it got her out from under Ivy's feet. She wished she could persuade one of her mates to flat-share, but they were all saving up for holidays with their boyfriends or to get married. She sat up and reached into her bedside cupboard for pen and paper. She wrote a lengthy letter to her mam, and added that she'd love to come and see them both and celebrate Jackie's birthday.

Footsteps thundered up the stairs and broke her reverie. Dad was home. She jumped up and opened her bedroom door. 'Hiya, Dad.'

'Hiya, chuck.' He gave her a hug and dashed into the bathroom, calling, 'Give us a minute.'

She went back into her room and sat down on the bed again, plucking at the blue candlewick bedspread. Another mismatched

room, with yellow curtains and a red patterned carpet square. If
only Ivy would allow her to redecorate the room it would look
lovely. Lewis's had some nice bedding and curtains and she'd get
a staff discount too. But Ivy said there was nothing wrong with
the way it was now and Carol had to wait until she got her own
place. Ah well, maybe it wouldn't be too long. She heard the lava-
tory flush and water running and then her dad popped his head
around the door.

'All right, queen?'

His wide grin brought a smile to her face. Carol was like her
dad, similar light-brown hair and smile, same hazel colour eyes
too. Mam and Jackie were blonde-haired and blue-eyed and looked
alike. Two matching pairs. Tonight her dad's eyes looked tired. And
deep lines were etched each side of his mouth where stubble grew.

'I'm fine, Dad. You?'

'Knackered, chuck. But Ivy wants this bloody holiday in Spain
and seeing as she can't work because of her bad back it's all down
to me to save up for it.'

Carol raised her eyebrows. There wasn't much wrong with Ivy's
back when she was shopping and waltzing off to the hairdresser's or
meeting her friend Flo. When the Royal Ordnance Factory, where
both Ivy and Dad had worked, had closed down and her dad had
started work at the Ford Motor Company in Halewood, Ivy hadn't
even bothered looking for another job. It was Carol's opinion that
she was lazy and just wanted to be kept.

'Got a nice letter from Mam today,' she announced. 'She's
invited me to tea for our Jackie's birthday.'

She smiled as her dad's face lit up at the mention of his ex-wife
and youngest daughter. Carol knew he missed them as much as
she did and would rather be with Mam than married to Ivy, but
Mam had made it clear that she wouldn't have him back.

'Are they okay, chuck?' He came into the room and pushed
the door closed. 'I want to send Dora something for our Jackie. I

feel bad that I haven't supported them as much as I should; your mam makes it so hard for me to help. But Jackie's getting ready to leave school soon, so I'm sure a bit of extra money would come in handy. Write me down the full address, love. Ivy mustn't know I'm sending anything. I'll never hear the bloody end of it.'

'They're fine, Dad. And Uncle Frank's got a new girlfriend at last. Ivy won't hear anything from me, I can assure you,' Carol said, writing down her mam's address.

'Ta, love. That's smashing news about Frank. He's a great bloke and it's time he found happiness again. Right, chuck, I'll go down and get my tea now. See you later.' He shoved the piece of paper in his trouser pocket and left the room.

❦

Carol ran a bath and lay back in the lavender-scented bubbles. After her dad had finished reading tonight's *Echo* she was planning on looking at the adverts section to see if any Easter breaks were available. If she just went ahead and booked it, Alex would surely feel obliged to go with her. After all, who'd be daft enough to turn down a free holiday? She would tell him tomorrow night when he met her after work. There was no way she wanted to share a caravan with Susan and her boyfriend. She wanted some privacy with Alex. That was the whole idea of a break. To get him to loosen up a bit and enjoy being just the two of them, and hopefully then he'd see they were meant to be together. She knew she could make him happy if he'd give her the chance.

She wondered if her mam's house was anywhere near Alex's dad's church. Mam was a regular church-goer so she may well know the family. She'd make a point of asking when she went to the birthday tea-party. Meantime, she'd think about what pressie to get for Jackie and maybe a nice little something for her mam too.

Chapter Eleven

March 1966

After a cuppa and a slice of birthday cake, Jackie sat back on the sofa surrounded by the contents of her birthday parcels from Mam and Uncle Frank. She'd never had so many pressies in one go and her wardrobe had certainly benefitted today. Mam had made her a shift-style mini dress from Agnes's pattern in a blue paisley-design fabric, which she planned to wear later with her new black kitten-heeled shoes, and she'd also got a matching black handbag. Uncle Frank had given her a pair of Levi jeans and a fabulous long black leather coat like the Mods wore.

Dad had sent money recently. It wasn't her birthday money as he always got her a present, guided by Carol, so she'd told Mam to keep it as it was nice for her to have a bit of spare cash in her purse. Now Mam had been more than generous towards her and she felt moved to tears.

'Thank you so much, Mam and Uncle Frank. I'll feel like the bee's knees at youth club tomorrow night. I can't wait to show everything to Patsy.'

'It's time you had some new clothes, especially now you're doing a bit of courting.'

Jackie smiled and felt her cheeks warming. Trust Mam. 'Courting' sounded so old-fashioned. The last couple of weeks she'd seen lots of Sandy in that she'd been sneaking to the church hall for an hour or two while he'd been painting. His dad had given permission for him to use the premises and his abstract was nearly ready for the college exhibition. It was lovely, all bright colours and what looked like faces and slices of fruit and feathery things.

Not the sort of picture you'd hang in a house like theirs, she thought, but something that would grace the walls of an art gallery, Sandy had told her. He'd also taken on the disc-jockey job at the youth club permanently now as the older man had moved away. Stevie helped him on those nights, and he had taken Patsy out to the pictures and they'd all four of them been for a walk down to the docks and to a coffee bar one Sunday afternoon.

Patsy had hinted at her and Jackie going to the Jacaranda one night, but Stevie said it wasn't a good idea to go wandering around on their own in town, and then he and Sandy had exchanged glances and raised eyebrows and promised to take them one day when they had time. Jackie wondered why the raised eyebrows, but didn't ask as she wasn't one for prying. Sandy always stayed over at Stevie's on Saturday; he said it was too late to come home when they'd been on a lads' night out to the pubs. He was always around to take her out on Sunday afternoons though, so she wasn't too bothered.

She was looking forward to catching up with her sister on Sunday, and hopefully Dad would drop Carol off and pop in for tea and cake. She was dying to see him again and even if he only stood in the hall for a few minutes, it would be better than nothing. Tonight she was invited for tea at Sandy's place. She felt nervous and excited all at the same time. Patsy was coming over soon to help her do her makeup and hair.

'Any chance of another cuppa, Dora?' Uncle Frank asked.

'Aye, why not? Fancy a bit more cake as well?'

'Go on then. I think my waistline can stand it.'

Jackie laughed. Her uncle was tall and skinny and didn't carry any extra fat around his waist. She gave him a hug.

'I'm looking forward to meeting your Maureen tomorrow. Mam says she's really nice and she must be something special if *you've* fallen for her,' she teased as he blushed slightly.

There was a knock at the door and Patsy and Agnes came in, carrying parcels and cards. After Jackie had unwrapped new tights, a pretty floral sponge bag and a manicure set, she and Patsy made their escape upstairs for the makeup session. More tea had been brewed and cake sliced and they left the adults to it, carrying all Jackie's new things between them.

'Are you nervous about going to Sandy's place?' Patsy asked as she gave Jackie's hair a lift with extra backcombing on the crown.

'Sort of, but his parents seem to be really nice and easygoing, so I'm sure it will be all right.'

'And now you're sixteen, are you and he going to, er, take the plunge?'

Jackie chewed her lip. 'Maybe. He said we might be able to get away for a day or two in the summer holidays. But you and Stevie will have to come with us or Mam will definitely say no. And me and you might be working by then anyway, so we'll have to see.'

She didn't tell Patsy how close she and Sandy had come to going all the way during their evenings together in the church hall. She knew it was only a matter of time, but like Sandy, she'd prefer it to be somewhere special and not on a pile of sweaty old gym mats used by the Monday afternoon keep-fit class.

'Love this new coat,' Patsy said, stroking the soft leather. 'Wait till Mardy Marcia sees you in it. You should wear it tomorrow at the youth club. Swank it off a bit.'

'I will.' Jackie twisted around on the stool in front of the dressing table and sighed. 'I'm not looking forward to the careers officer coming in to school tomorrow. Bet he won't even listen to me when I tell him what I've got in mind.'

'Nor me. But I'm standing for no nonsense and won't be fobbed off. I'm telling him straight – I want to be a model, and it's his job to point me in the right direction.'

'Don't you fancy hairdressing?' Jackie asked as Patsy twiddled the tail-comb between her fingers. 'You're really good at it.'

Patsy shrugged. 'It's on my list, but I don't fancy being stood on my feet all day. Might get veins in my legs. That would put paid to a modelling career before I even got started.'

'Well, there are only office jobs and factory assembly lines where you get to sit down for most of the day.' Jackie pulled a face. 'Boring! I've made a list too, and office work is right at the bottom.'

Patsy smoothed Jackie's fringe down and blasted it with lacquer. 'Wouldn't be too bad if we got jobs in the same office to be going on with, like Littlewoods Pools or something. We could ask.'

'We could.' Jackie cocked her head to one side. 'Is that the door?'

'Jackie, your young man's here,' Mam yelled up the stairs.

'Coming,' she yelled back. 'Do I look okay?' She'd changed into her new blue paisley dress and black shoes and a pair of fashionably pale tights.

'You look amazing. He won't be able to keep his hands off you,' Patsy teased.

Jackie raised an eyebrow. 'He'd better, in front of his parents.'

❀

'Sandy tells me you have an interest in amateur dramatics.' Mrs Faraday offered Jackie a slice of home-made birthday cake. Sandy's mum had surprised her with the cake, a beautiful sponge sandwiched together with raspberry jam and buttercream, iced in white with little pink flowers around the edge, and sixteen candles in a circle. She'd felt quite emotional as the family sang 'Happy

82 PAM HOWES

Birthday' to her and cheered when she blew out the candles. Sandy said he hoped she'd made a wish and as she looked into his eyes she knew that *he* knew exactly what she'd been wishing for.

'Er, yes I do.' She put down her tea cup carefully. They had white china cups and saucers with a gold rim, not sturdy mismatched mugs like at home, and dainty sandwiches on a tiered plate, with matching side plates. The table was set with white linen and real napkins, like Agnes used. Everything was home-made, including the sausage rolls with their delicious flaky pastry. It was all so elegant and she was terrified of breaking anything.

'Well in that case, I've a proposition you might care to consider.' Sandy's mum pushed her wavy brown hair back behind her ears and smiled.

'Really?' Jackie wiped her mouth on the pristine napkin and folded it neatly on her plate.

'I've been toying with the idea for a while, but now we're settled in the parish it might be a good time to put my plan into action. How would you like to help me set up our own am-dram group in the church hall?'

Jackie gasped. 'Oh, I'd love to. I really would.' She looked at Sandy, whose wide grin was splitting his face.

'Told you she'd be keen, Mum. And I can help out with any scenery painting that needs doing.'

Sandy's dad smiled. 'And no doubt I'll be expected to pull my weight too.'

'Well of course you will, Arthur. I help *you* with all that goes on in that church of yours. Well, it's settled then. I'm delighted, my dear. We shall call ourselves St Paul's Players.' She patted Jackie on the shoulder. 'Perhaps we can retire to the sitting room and Sandy can pour us a drink so we can toast your birthday. Nothing alcoholic for Jackie, mind,' she said, looking at Sandy.

Jackie followed Sandy's mum into the sitting room, where the walls seemed to be lined with boxes and packing cases.

'Please excuse the mess. We were supposed to be moving into our new home soon, but it's still not quite ready.'

'Yes, Sandy told me you were due to move,' Jackie said. 'Bet you can't wait. My mam would be able to help with costumes for any shows we put on at the hall. She used to make outfits for the shows and pantos at most of the theatres in Liverpool before the owner of the business she worked for retired.'

'Oh, did she really? That would be wonderful. I admire your mother very much. I was a bit concerned after her run-in with that Baker woman recently, but she stood her ground and waved her marriage certificate in Mrs Baker's face and forced her to apologise. I know I shouldn't laugh, being the vicar's wife, but I howled and so did everyone else.'

Jackie grinned. 'Mam's got spirit all right.' She took the glass of Coca-Cola Sandy handed her and smiled at him. 'Thanks.'

Sandy gave his mum a glass of sherry and his dad a whisky and poured a small one for himself.

'To Jackie, happy birthday,' he toasted and his parents joined in, raising their glasses.

Jackie smiled her thanks. She didn't think she'd ever felt so happy. Sandy had given her a silver bracelet with a heart charm attached and he told her he'd buy her more charms for Christmas. Well that was nine months away so he seemed to be thinking long-term with their relationship, which made her feel warm inside. His parents were so nice and had made her feel really welcome. They'd given her a black leather purse and inside it were a pound note and a brass charm, like a little pixie. His mum said it was for luck and would ensure her purse would never be empty. And now she wanted her to help run an am-dram group. Life was pretty good and she was so glad the Faradays had moved to Fazakerley. She couldn't wait to tell her mam, who she was certain would love to be involved with making the costumes.

Walking back to Fourth Avenue, with Sandy's arm around her shoulders and him stopping every few yards to pull her into his arms for kisses, took them ages.

'Wish I'd thought to bring the hall keys out with me,' he whispered. 'I need to spend some time alone with you.'

'Not sure that's a good idea,' she said, looking into his eyes. 'You know what might happen.'

'Yep.' He nodded. 'You're right. But then you wished for it earlier.'

'How do you know?' she teased. 'Was it that obvious?'

'Totally.' He grinned and squeezed her so tight she squealed. 'Come on, better get you home or your mother will be after me.'

They ran the rest of the way and arrived breathless on the doorstep.

'I'll see you tomorrow at the youth club,' Sandy said. 'I need to stay over in town on Friday night this week. We've got to start putting things together for the exhibition. But I'll see you on Sunday, after your family birthday party.'

'You can come to the party, you know. Mam said it was okay to ask you.'

'I'll be staying in town and going into college to help on Sunday. Stevie will be doing the same. But I'll be back about teatime and I'll come straight to you. Save me a bit of grub. I'll be starving by then.' He pulled her to him for a last kiss and whispered into her hair, 'See you tomorrow.'

He dropped a kiss on her lips and hurried away, leaving her standing on the doorstep staring after him with longing. She went inside, her head filled with thoughts of seeing him again soon and the chance to start up the proposed am-dram group with his mum.

Chapter Twelve

Sandy hurried home, thinking about Jackie and how much he wanted to spend a night with her. It would take some planning, but hopefully she might be able to meet him from the Jac one Saturday soon and stay with him at Stevie's place. He really *did* think he'd fallen in love with her. He'd never felt so strongly for any girl before and certainly not Caz.

He hated lying to Jackie about Friday night but he really needed to see Caz and end it with her as soon as possible. He *was* staying late at college, but planning to call her tomorrow night after youth club and arrange to meet her outside work. Trouble with Caz, she would try and talk him round, so he would have to be strong. He'd stay over at Stevie's and hope she wouldn't want to stay with him. He knew she was still annoyed with him for letting her down a couple of Wednesdays ago, when he'd arranged to meet her under Nobby Lewis's statue. He'd forgotten it was youth club night and that he'd promised to help his dad again, until Stevie had reminded him on the way back to college. Still, he'd pretty much smoothed her ruffled feathers on the Saturday night, so hopefully she wouldn't go on about it again, although the Easter weekend break she'd booked in Blackpool was another matter. That's why he needed to finish it as soon as possible. He had no intentions of going away with her.

Carol ignored Susan calling her name as she hurried from the store on Friday night and stood under Nobby Lewis. She would kill Alex if he let her down again. Sending one of the students with a note last time was unacceptable, especially when the girl had asked if she was Caz, looked her up and down and remarked that she was just as Alex described her. Except it was said with a sneer. The girl had a posh accent that, like Alex's, sounded more southern than Liverpudlian. She was dressed in the typical student fashion of duffle coat, jeans, boots and an art college scarf flung casually around her neck, a portfolio tucked under her arm. She'd thrust the note at Caz and walked away.

She'd ended up going for coffee with Susan instead, as she hadn't felt like going straight home. Susan told her to dump him if she was fed up and find another boyfriend. But she wasn't fed up; despite having a good moan about him, she loved Alex and desperately wanted him to love her back. She'd booked the Easter break in Blackpool and he still hadn't committed himself. He told her she should have asked him first but she'd replied it was supposed to be a surprise and if she'd said anything it would have spoiled it.

Since Susan had asked her if she was pregnant, it had been on her mind. Would he stay with her and marry her if she were? Or would he just walk away like other lads had done to girls she'd known in the past? Dare she take a chance and try to trap him, or was that just a really bad idea? What if he wouldn't marry her? Then she'd be stuck at Dad and Ivy's with a baby no one wanted, least of all her. And she only had to look at her dad to see how unhappy *he* was at being wrongly snared. But if it was the only way of getting Alex to stay with her, should she take that chance? Trouble was, he wouldn't make love without a rubber johnny. He wouldn't even do it when she told him it was a safe time, without using something. Maybe she could wriggle about a lot and it would slip off or tear. She'd need to think of a way before they spent another night together.

Susan came up behind her and made her jump.

'Let's hope the bugger turns up tonight, eh, Caz?' she said, giving her arm a squeeze.

'He'd better,' Carol muttered. 'Ah. Here he is.'

She smiled as Alex appeared around the corner of Ranelagh Street. He looked so good in his khaki fish-tail parka, faded Levis and college scarf. Her stomach fluttered as he pecked her on the cheek and nodded at Susan, who said goodbye and hurried away.

'Where are we going?' she asked as Alex took her hand and pulled her along the street.

'The Phil. I need to speak to a mate and he's probably in there.'

Carol fumed inwardly. The Philharmonic pub was usually packed at this time of night with students and men, grabbing a pint on their way home from work. She'd hoped they might go somewhere quiet so she could try to persuade him that the holiday at Easter was a good idea. 'Do we have to?'

He stopped and looked at her in surprise. 'I'll see you to your bus stop then if you don't want to come.'

'I didn't mean that,' she stuttered. 'I just wanted to be alone with you, that's all.'

He shrugged. 'Can't be helped, I'm afraid, Caz. I've a lot on at the moment with the exhibition and I need to check that my pal Tony's bringing his stuff in tomorrow. The coordinator's coming in especially. Tony left college tonight before I got a chance to speak to him. Someone said he was going to the Phil.'

'Okay.' She hurried along beside him. 'Where's your scooter?'

'At home. Dad gave me a lift into college today. I had to bring my exhibition piece down with me and it's too big to balance on the scooter, or bring on the train. I'm staying over at Stevie's tonight.'

'You managed to get it finished then, your painting?' He sounded so enthusiastic that she knew she should take an interest.

'I did. The coordinator thinks there's a good chance I might sell it as well. He's really pleased with the result.'

'Did you give it a title? Is that what you do, name them?'

He looked surprised that she was questioning him, but he answered with enthusiasm, so she assumed she was doing the right thing.

'It's called *Forbidden Fruit*,' he said.

'Oh, so what is it, a bowl of fruit, like?'

'No, Caz, you wouldn't understand.'

He almost snapped his answer and she frowned. They turned the corner of Hope Street and hurried inside the crowded pub.

'Grab that table.' He pointed to the back of the room. 'Just need a pee.'

He dashed away as she pushed through the smoky bar area and sat down. She took off her coat and hung it on the back of the chair, glancing around the rich, wood-panelled room to see if there was anyone she recognised. Mostly students, the drinkers were in the main clad in jeans and she felt a bit overdressed in her work suit, even though the skirt was fashionably short and her jacket neat and boxy. Alex seemed to be taking ages and when he reappeared he was talking animatedly to a lad similarly clad to him. The lad waved his goodbyes and dashed away and Alex came over to the table. He took off his parka, flung it down on a chair and asked her what she'd like to drink.

'Bacardi and Coke, please.'

He rooted for his wallet and looked inside, his face flushing. 'Er, not enough money for that, Caz. Have a cider or something.'

She tutted, took her purse out of her bag and gave him a ten-shilling note. 'Get whatever you want and a bag of crisps for me.'

'I'm sorry,' he mumbled. 'I'm just so skint at the moment; had to buy a family friend a birthday pressie.'

She shrugged. Him being skint was nothing new. 'Doesn't matter.'

He put his wallet down on the table and walked away. She picked it up to shove back in his parka pocket. But something stopped her and, making sure no one was observing, she took a quick look inside. It was empty, except for half-a-crown and two one-shilling pieces in the coin bit. But tucked inside the notes section were two Durex contraceptives. Her hand shaking, she stuffed the wallet into her bag and got to her feet. Alex would realise she'd gone to the loo when he came back, but the bar area was heaving so he'd be a while getting served.

Heart beating so hard it boomed in her ears, Carol locked herself in a cubicle and rooted in her bag. She took the two foil packs from Alex's wallet and put them on the lid of the toilet seat. She rummaged down her top for her bra strap that had come adrift this morning. With no time to find a needle and thread, she'd fixed it with a tiny gold safety pin. Hands trembling, she removed the pin and quickly stuck it into both contraceptive packets, twice. She examined them to make sure the tiny pin-prick holes were invisible to the naked eye, rubbing her thumb over the area. Satisfied that she couldn't see the holes without actually squinting, and thinking that it was usually dark in the bedroom anyway, she put both packets back into Alex's wallet, fastened her bra strap up again, pulled the toilet chain and walked out.

Alex was just being served and she slipped his wallet back onto the table. She had enough money on her for a couple more drinks and hopefully she'd persuade him to let her come back to Stevie's place for the night. Once he'd had a few pints he was usually quite amenable.

❀

Sandy sat at the kitchen table, head in his hands. Caz was in the bathroom getting ready to go home. He couldn't believe he'd agreed that she could stay over again after he'd been determined to finish with her last night. The plan had been to tell her no to the Blackpool trip and that they should split up as the relationship wasn't working for him any more. He felt sick at betraying Jackie.

Not that she'd find out, but *he'd* know and that was bad enough. As soon as she was ready he'd walk Caz to the bus stop and tell her it was over. He knew she'd be upset, but at least it was Saturday and she wouldn't be going into work in a state. He looked up as she came into the kitchen.

'Coffee?' he offered. She sat down and reached for his hand. He jerked away and she frowned as he got to his feet and picked up the kettle.

'Alex, what's wrong?'

'Look, Caz,' he said, spinning around to face her before he lost his nerve. 'Last night was a mistake. I want us to finish. Now. Today. It's not working for me. I'm sorry,' he added as her eyes filled with tears.

'But, Alex, I love you.' Tears were running down her cheeks now and she wiped them away with the back of her hand. 'You can't just end it like that. Surely I mean more to you, after everything we've been to each other?' She took a deep gulping breath. 'I thought we'd get engaged, that you'd want to marry me one day. Why did you make love to me then if you knew this was going to happen?'

'Caz, I tried to tell you last night that I would sleep in Stevie's studio.'

'You were eager enough when you *did* come to bed with me though,' she hissed. 'You bastard. I can't believe you'd use me like that and then dump me right after. That's so unlike you.'

'Yeah, I know. I shouldn't have. And I'm sorry. But that's it, we're over.'

She got to her feet, her face a mask of fury. 'You reckon? You've got somebody else, haven't you?' She grabbed her bag and coat and stomped towards the door. 'Don't think this is the last you've heard from me,' she flung at him.

Sandy breathed a sigh of relief as he heard the door slam shut downstairs. He *was* a bastard, dead right, but he *had* insisted on sleeping in Stevie's studio, until Caz stripped off right in front of him. He'd been slightly pissed and feeling horny, thanks to her generosity with the drinks, and he couldn't resist. It had only been the once and then he'd feigned sleep and ignored her.

Stevie appeared in the kitchen. 'Is it safe to come out now? What was that all about?'

'She's angry because I've finished with her.'

'Ah right, a woman scorned, eh? So, you had a final shag before you dumped her? That was a bit mean, mate. No wonder she's mad. But still, it's done with now and you can concentrate on your career and the love of your life.'

'Last night wasn't supposed to happen,' Sandy muttered, feeling embarrassed. 'But yeah, it's just me and Jackie now and a whole new future to look forward to. I think I love her, you know. In fact, I'm pretty sure I do.'

※

Jackie said goodbye to Sandy's mum and hurried back to Fourth Avenue. Mrs Faraday had sent a message home with Mam after bumping into her yesterday afternoon. The message had been to say that if Jackie wasn't busy on Saturday, could she pop into the church hall after lunch for a meeting about the am-dram group.

The meeting had been productive in that Sandy's mum had managed to spread the word and had rounded up ten people, a mixture of men and women, who were all eager to involve themselves with St Paul's Players. A poster, inviting new members, had been roughly designed and one man, who ran a small printing company, had offered to print flyers to hand out at morning service next week, as well as designing the poster. It had been decided that Mrs Faraday and Jackie would be in charge of deciding which plays and productions to put on, and when. The aim at the moment was to produce a musical play, possibly *Oliver!*, in the autumn, and a pantomime, as yet undecided, at Christmas, and to encourage some of the primary school children to take part.

The next meeting had been arranged for the following Saturday afternoon and Jackie had said goodbye and come away buzzing with excitement. She dashed into the house and flung her duffle coat over the back of the sofa. She sniffed the air and her stomach rumbled. She was starving. In the kitchen she lifted the saucepan lid and savoured the wonderful aroma that rose from the lamb scouse, simmering on the stove. Her mam had been busy; there was a tray of sausage rolls on the worktop, alongside two plates of buns as well as a batch of scones. She dropped the lid back onto the pan as Mam came bustling into the kitchen.

'Hiya, chuck. I was just putting the ironing away upstairs.' She filled the kettle and put it on the stove. 'How did the meeting go?'

'It was good. Quite a lot turned up. All dead keen. We're thinking of putting on a production of *Oliver!* in the autumn. Mrs Faraday said that would be the best time as it gives us ages to get it all together, and people will be back from their summer holidays by then. *You've* been busy.'

'That scouse is for tea tonight and what's left will do for a quick dinner tomorrow. Saves me cooking after church. I'll ice them buns later. All I'll have to do then is make the sandwiches for your birthday tea. Is your young man coming? Because if he is there'll be eight of us to feed: Agnes, Patsy, Frank and Maureen and our Carol and then me, you and Sandy.'

'He's coming later, Mam, but we can save him some food. They're finishing setting up for the exhibition tomorrow at college so he said he'd come straight here when he's finished. Did you invite our Carol's lad? Be nice to meet him.'

'No, I completely forgot to be honest. She might just turn up with him anyway. We'll have a quiet night in tonight. I think Frank will be round later after he's finished helping out at the Legion, so we can watch a bit of telly, and maybe he'll pick us up a treat from the off-licence.'

Jackie's face lit up. 'Dandelion and burdock and crisps. Yum.'

Chapter Thirteen

Carol ran up Scotland Road towards the bus stop, tears blinding her. Thank God it was Saturday and her day off. At least she could go straight home and stay in her room out of the way. She felt sick and upset and her head was all over the place. She'd been so certain that Alex would be keen to go away with her, that his recent indifference was just due to worrying about the exhibition, and that he'd be fine once it was all over. In her head last night she'd had visions of him selling the painting and using the money to surprise her with an engagement ring, which he would present to her in Blackpool. Being dumped was the last thing she'd been expecting. She took a great gulping breath and a large woman standing at the bus stop, headscarf covering her rollers, turned to look at her.

'Youse okay, queen?'

'Yeah, thanks. Just something in my eye.' Carol turned her back on the woman and pulled a tissue from her handbag. Her face would look a right mess now; mascara running in trails down her cheeks. She blew her nose and decided to walk into the centre and get the Allerton bus home later, when she'd calmed down a bit. She could do with a coffee, and some toast to settle her stomach as well.

She set off walking, her mind working overtime, hoping she wouldn't bump into any of her own or Alex's friends. The one thing in her favour now was that last night he'd used one of the Durex she'd pricked holes in and she knew for certain it had definitely leaked, but Alex hadn't noticed. She was bang in the middle of her monthly cycle too. But it really didn't seem such a great idea now. In fact, it was the worst one she'd ever had in her life. What the hell was she going to do? She had two weeks of agonising in front of her now. Why had she been so bloody thoughtless and stupid? Alex was a penniless student with no chance of supporting a wife and baby. A kid would be the last thing he'd want to be lumbered with. He'd often talked about travelling when they'd been out with their gang of mates, but he'd never included *her* in his plans. It was usually lads' talk about what they'd all do when they finished art college.

She hurried along, head down, mind in a whirl, and rounded the corner of Stanley Street, where The Kardomah Café was opening its doors for business. She thankfully dashed inside and ordered a toasted teacake and a mug of coffee. She chose the same table she often shared with her friends at lunchtime and carried her order across on a tray. It was early and the café was fairly quiet. She was glad as she didn't want to see anyone she knew. She couldn't face any questions and had just about got her tears under control. She set about buttering the teacake, and took a sip of coffee.

She would hang around in town for the morning, window shop, pop into NEMS and listen to a few records. She needed to get a card for Jackie for tomorrow's birthday party, and some wrapping paper. Dad had asked her to get *him* some, too, as he'd bought a watch for Jackie. He'd also told Carol that he'd give her a lift over to Fazakerley, but not to tell Ivy, who always visited her old friend Flo on a Sunday afternoon. Uncle Frank would be at Mam's, so he would probably bring her home as Dad wouldn't be able to stay and her mam might not even let him in, depending on her mood.

She finished her breakfast and paid a visit to the ladies to tidy up her face, which wasn't as bad as she'd imagined it to be. Just a bit blotchy and her nose red, but she looked like she had a cold rather than she'd been crying. She took a deep breath and ran a comb through her hair.

She'd make up a tale that Alex was busy with his exhibition and church stuff this weekend and staying in town tonight, if anyone asked why she wasn't going to meet him after her usual night out with her girlfriends. There'd been talk of going to The Cavern later and meeting in The Grapes first. A group called Mark Roman and The Javelins were playing and rumour had it they were really good. It was something to do and better than staying in with Dad and Ivy. Maybe Alex would have a change of heart and come looking for her. Whatever, it would take her mind off the stupid thing she'd done, the possible consequences and the fact that he just might have a new girlfriend.

❀

As Ivy left the house on Sunday afternoon, Carol's dad dashed upstairs and put on his best pair of grey slacks and a clean shirt and tie. He tapped on Carol's bedroom door.

'Come in, Dad.' She was putting the finishing touches to her makeup and trying to conceal the dark circles beneath her eyes. She'd hardly slept a wink, in spite of drinking heavily in The Grapes last night. She'd almost fallen downstairs in The Cavern, but some lad behind her had grabbed her arm and pulled her upright as she'd stumbled. Her shoulder was aching now where he'd yanked her, but better that than a broken leg, she supposed.

'I wrapped the watch for you.' She indicated a narrow parcel on top of the chest of drawers. She'd bought a bottle of Je Reviens Worth perfume for Jackie and a black ceramic cat ornament with big eyes for Mam. It reminded her of their childhood pet, Topsy, who'd sadly died a couple of years ago. All were neatly wrapped alongside the watch. 'Did you sign your card?'

'Ivy did. It's on the dining table. She thinks *you're* taking it. Let's get going then, in case she comes home early.' He dashed back to his bedroom for his tweed sports jacket and car keys. 'I'll go and turn the engine over,' he called. 'Be quick as you can, gel.'

Carol tweaked her hair into place, applied her lipstick and grabbed her leather coat and handbag. She put the presents in a Lewis's carrier bag and made her way downstairs. She still felt a bit grim and hung-over, but was looking forward to seeing her mam and Jackie again. She picked up Dad and Ivy's card from the table and joined him in his Ford Popular car.

'We won't be too early, will we?' Dad said as they drove towards Fazakerley at a leisurely pace.

'Mam said any time after two and it's nearly five to now. We'll be fine. Are you nervous, Dad?'

He puffed out his cheeks and nodded. 'A bit. I just wish your mam would talk to me properly. It would make life so much easier for all of us. Well – except for Ivy. Too late now though.'

'It's never too late,' Carol said, staring out of the window at the gloomy afternoon. At least it wasn't raining, but the weather matched her mood. 'I remember the day you and Mam brought our Jackie home from the hospital. I wasn't quite three but I can recall it. I stayed with Granny and then she brought me back to the prefab after tea.'

'Fancy that. You've a good memory, gel. I also remember the day well. I was happy as Larry with two lovely daughters and a beautiful wife. Where did it all go wrong?' He shook his head. 'My fault. I've only me to blame. I should have taken better care of your mam when she needed it. But with all that went on after with her depression and stuff I just felt neglected. Childish of me, I know. Ivy was just there. It meant nothing to me really. But I couldn't get rid of her afterwards and she trapped me.' He shuddered at the recollection. 'One day, just one day,' he muttered, 'things will come out when she's pushed me too far. I shouldn't have married her.'

'No, Dad, you shouldn't.' Carol touched his arm. 'I know there are things you didn't tell us, but me and Jackie are not daft. We overheard Mam and Agnes talking ages ago. Mam said she was sure Ivy was faking her pregnancy,' she went on. 'You should have it out with her. Let her know that *you* know she's been lying all this time. Bet Ivy was rubbing her hands with glee when she heard Mam didn't want to know. Poor Dad, if only you'd talked more instead of rowing.'

'I wanted to. It was your mam that wouldn't listen.' He sighed. 'Anyway, it's water under the bridge now. Ivy's looked after me well enough, I suppose.'

'But you're not in love with her. Not like you were with Mam.'

'No, I'm not. But what's love at the end of the day? It doesn't put your dinner on the table.'

'Oh, Dad, you old romantic.' Carol laughed. 'We're nearly there,' she added. 'It's just off Longmoor Lane and we're on that road now.'

She felt a bit perkier than she had done earlier. Talking to her dad had helped to take her mind off the thoughts of the last couple of days.

As they pulled up outside the terraced house her dad smiled. 'When we were married, it was always Dora's dream to live up here near Agnes, and have a bay window,' he said quietly. 'Funny what you remember, isn't it?'

'It is,' Carol said as the front door flew open and Jackie danced up and down on the step, excitement written all over her face. Her sister had grown a fair bit taller since she'd last seen her and her long blonde hair suited her. She looked trendy in a blue paisley mini dress, pale tights and neat black shoes. Carol got out of the car and Jackie flung her arms around her. Carol hugged her back.

'Dad!' Jackie squealed and hurled herself at their father. Carol stood by while he hugged his youngest daughter, his eyes moist.

'How you doing, chuck?' He squeezed her tight and set her back down on the pavement.

'Mam said it's okay for you to come in,' Jackie said, grabbing his hand and pulling him towards the door.

'Oh, er, I, er, don't want to intrude,' he stammered.

'Honestly, Dad, it's fine.'

Jackie led the way and showed Carol into the sitting room while their dad hovered in the hall.

'Mam, they're here,' Jackie yelled up the stairs, pulling her dad into the sitting room. 'Sit down, she won't be a minute.'

Carol took her mam's present out of the bag and handed the rest to Jackie, who laughed with excitement as she opened the cards and unwrapped her gifts.

'Oh thank you, Dad,' she gasped as she gazed at the Timex watch with its silver bracelet strap. She pulled it from the narrow box and slipped it onto her slender wrist. It fitted perfectly. 'It's gorgeous,' she said, kissing him. 'Thank you.'

Her eyes widened as she opened the perfume from Carol. 'Oh, this is posh,' she said as she took the bottle from the box. 'Much nicer than Mam's Avon stuff.' She dabbed herself behind the ears and on her pulse points. 'Smells gorgeous. Bet Sandy will love it.' She gave Carol a kiss.

'Sandy?' Carol asked, raising an amused eyebrow. 'That your pal from school?'

Jackie laughed. 'No, silly, that's Patsy. Sandy's my new boyfriend. You'll meet him later. He's busy this afternoon, but he'll be here before you go home.'

Carol smiled. Even her little sister was doing a bit of courting. How sweet was that? She was distracted by the sitting room door opening and her mam walked in, looking lovely in a slim-fitting plain black skirt that emphasised her trim figure, and a pale blue V-necked sweater, a choker of imitation pearls around her throat. Her blonde hair fell onto her shoulders in soft waves. Carol jumped to her feet and flung her arms around her mam, feeling tears welling. She blinked rapidly and kissed her cheek. Mam kissed her back and hugged her tight, whispering that it was really good to see her.

Both girls watched and held their breath as Mam's eyes turned to Dad, who was sitting quietly on the chair in the bay window, his eyes on their mother. 'Joe, how are you?'

'I'm fine thanks, Dora. And yourself?'

'Doing nicely, thank you.'

'Good. You've got this place very nice.'

'Thanks. Jackie, would you like to put the kettle on please, love. You'll stay for a cuppa, Joe?'

'Well, if that's okay with you. I don't want to impose.'

Jackie left the room and Carol moved up on the sofa to make room for Mam. The atmosphere felt a bit tense, so she handed Mam her present.

'Oh, it's lovely,' Mam said, unwrapping and holding up the black ceramic cat. 'It reminds me of Topsy.'

'That's what I thought,' Carol said as she received a kiss on the cheek. There was an awkward silence as Mam found a place for the cat on the mantelpiece and sat down again, and Dad shuffled his feet. The silence in the room was broken only by the ticking of the mantel clock and pots clattering as Jackie moved around in the adjacent kitchen.

A knock at the front door had Mam jumping to her feet to answer it and she let in Agnes and Patsy. Mam told them to take a seat and went to help Jackie. Carol smiled at Patsy, who sat on the floor while Agnes perched on the sofa. Dad got up and offered his chair to Patsy, who shook her head and said she was fine where she was. He sat back down again and twiddled his thumbs. Carol smiled at him, willing him to relax for a few minutes. She knew he'd need to go soon before Ivy got home or he'd be in bother, and a Dad-and-Ivy row was the last thing she felt like dealing with at the moment. That woman could sulk for days when it suited her, and give them both the silent treatment.

'Only us,' shouted a voice from the hallway as someone let themselves in at the front door.

'In here, Frank,' Mam called from the kitchen.

Frank popped his head around the sitting room door. 'How do, all,' he said with a big grin. 'Nice to see you, Carol, and you too,

Joe. I'd, er, I'd like to introduce Maureen.' He smiled as a petite redhead peeped out from behind him, a friendly smile lighting up her blue eyes.

Carol jumped up and gave her uncle and Maureen a hug. She could see relief in Dad's eyes at having another man to talk to.

'Very nice to meet you, Maureen; have a seat.' She gestured for Maureen and Frank to sit on the sofa and went to sit by her dad's feet on the floor.

Mam and Jackie carried in plates and a tea tray with steaming mugs. The coffee table was quickly cleared of the Sunday newspapers and Frank's pools coupon from last night, and set for tea.

'Lovely to see you, Maureen. Glad you could make it. Now help yourselves,' Mam said, handing out small plates. 'The sandwiches are ham or potted beef. Jackie, can you bring the sausage rolls through, chuck.'

As everyone tucked in, Jackie put a few sandwiches and two sausage rolls to one side. 'I'll take Sandy's tea into the kitchen,' she announced. 'Otherwise there'll be nothing left for him.'

Carol smiled to herself as Jackie left the room. She couldn't wait to meet this boyfriend. Probably someone from her class at school; all spots and gangly limbs. Although, looking at her sister as she tossed her long blonde hair back over her shoulders and laughed at something Uncle Frank was saying, she could see what a beauty she'd become. Wide blue eyes, full lips and a fabulous figure; whoever he was, Sandy was a lucky young man.

Chapter Fourteen

Jackie looked up from her seat on the rug next to Patsy. Her dad had got to his feet, an apologetic expression on his face and a look of regret in his eyes as he announced he needed to leave. She jumped up and put her arms around his waist, burying her head in his chest.

'Thank you for coming, Dad. And thank you so much for the watch. I love it.'

'You're welcome, sweetheart. And thank *you*, Dora,' he said to Mam, who was looking at him from under her full fringe, 'for your hospitality. I, er, have you got a minute?' he added, nodding towards the door leading into the hall. 'Are you coming home with me, Carol?'

'No thanks, Dad, I'll stay a bit longer.'

'We'll run our Carol back later, Joe,' Frank said. 'Maureen won't mind, will you, chuck?'

Maureen shook her head and patted Frank on the hand. 'Not at all, love. Give me and Carol time to get to know one another.'

'Thanks, Frank. See you later then, Carol,' her dad said and followed Jackie and Mam into the hall. 'I, er, just wanted to give you this.' He took an envelope from his inside jacket pocket and handed it to Mam. 'It's a bit of extra money I've put by that might come in handy now Jackie's getting ready to leave school.'

Mam looked at the envelope and then at Dad. 'I think this should go to our Jackie to look after then. She's not sure yet whether she'll get a job or go on to college, are you, chuck?'

Jackie bit her lip. 'I'd like to study drama and dance,' she said quietly. 'But I don't think we can afford for me not to work. It's time Mam took life a bit easier.'

Dad tapped the envelope with a finger. 'That's why I've given you the envelope. If you want to go to college, we'll find a way, your mam and me. You're a smart girl.'

Mam handed the envelope to Jackie. 'Put it away upstairs for now. We'll talk about this again. Perhaps you can come over another time, Joe, and then we can discuss her future once she's seen her O level results. I'll be in touch through our Carol. I won't ring the house though, in case it's not either of you answering the phone.'

Dad nodded, kissed Jackie on the cheek again and said his goodbyes. Mam closed the door and leant against it with a sigh.

'Thanks, Mam, for letting Dad stay a while, I mean. I know it can't be easy. He doesn't look too happy, does he?'

Mam shook her head. 'No, love, he doesn't. But he's made his bed…'

She went back into the sitting room and Jackie ran up the stairs and put the unopened envelope into her underwear drawer. She'd look at the contents later. It felt bulky. Dad must have been secretly saving up for ages. She looked at her watch. Almost four o'clock. Sandy would be here soon. She felt a thrill run through her and couldn't wait to see him, and then be alone with him later when her mam went to the Legion with Uncle Frank and Maureen for an hour or two.

As she ran down the stairs she heard the spluttering sound of a scooter coming up the avenue. She flung open the door as Sandy pulled up outside and stopped the engine. He jumped off as she dashed outside. He swept her into his arms, kissed her and held her tightly, like he didn't want to let her go.

'Ah, I've been looking forward to the first kiss all day,' he whispered into her hair. 'I love you, Jackie, I really do.'

She looked into his eyes and smiled. 'I love you too, Sandy, very much.'

She took his hand and led him inside. 'You've just missed my dad, but my sister is still here.'

She waited while he slipped his parka off and hung it on the hall coat pegs. He kissed her again. She opened the sitting room door and pulled him in with her.

Carol was talking animatedly to Patsy, who looked up and smiled as Jackie came into the room. Carol turned as she heard her name being called.

Jackie felt Sandy stiffen behind her and she gripped his hand tight, smiling at his nervousness. 'Carol, I'd like you to meet my boyfriend, Sandy,' she announced, a big grin splitting her face.

Carol got to her feet, her face draining of colour. She stared at Sandy, whose cheeks had flushed bright red, and he hung his head, not meeting anyone's eye.

'Sandy?' Jackie said, looking at him. 'What is it?'

Carol looked like she was about to cry, but she also looked angry and two red spots had appeared on her cheeks. 'Shall *I* tell her, or will you – *Alex*?'

Jackie stared from one to the other, her face a mixture of bewilderment and horror.

'Alex?' she said. 'But his name's Sandy.'

'His name is Alex,' Carol said quietly. 'And he's *my* boyfriend.'

'*Ex*-boyfriend,' Sandy muttered. 'We broke up, Caz, remember?'

'You were my *sister's* boyfriend?' Jackie felt confused. Was she dreaming? 'And all the time you were seeing me, was it behind Carol's back? Sandy, how could you?'

'Is this some sort of sick joke?' Carol demanded. 'Dating my little sister; cheating on me.'

'I didn't know Jackie was your sister,' Sandy said. 'I had no idea. I didn't even know you *had* a sister. And things were coming to an end with us two when I met her. You know we had problems, Caz. That's why I finished it.'

Uncle Frank got to his feet and held up his hands. 'I think you three need to sit down and sort this out. Can we decamp to your place, Agnes?' He helped Maureen and Mam, who was shaking her head, to their feet. 'Come on, Dora. They need to talk,' he said as Mam protested that she should stay. He pushed her towards the door.

'Of course.' Agnes got to her feet, gathering up her handbag and jacket. 'Come on, Patsy, and you too, Dora,' she insisted. 'This is something they need to sort out on their own. You've got some explaining to do, young man,' she directed at Sandy, who was looking shell-shocked.

'Will you be okay?' Patsy asked as Jackie chewed her lip, still feeling bewildered, tears trickling down her cheeks. 'Must be that girl from the other side of Liverpool,' she whispered to Jackie. 'Fancy it being your Carol. But don't worry, it's you that Sandy's crazy about, remember.'

Jackie took a deep breath and gave a watery half-smile to Patsy, who squeezed her arm and followed the adults out of the house. Jackie's legs would no longer hold her up and she collapsed onto the sofa, pulling Sandy down with her.

❀

'I can manage,' Dora said to Frank as he bundled her down the road towards Agnes's home. She shook his arm off and marched on ahead, leaving him walking with Maureen. She should be with her daughters, helping them sort out the mess they were in. She couldn't believe that Jackie's boyfriend Sandy was Carol's boyfriend Alex. All three of them had looked horrified when the truth came out. She really hoped that Jackie wasn't going to be hurt like *she* had been when Joe cheated on her with Ivy. It was a pain that never quite went away. Jackie had always been more sensitive than

Carol. She wore her heart on her sleeve, whereas Carol was a bit brasher and hopefully would soon pick herself up and get another boyfriend. She'd looked more angry than hurt back there. A woman scorned and all that. But she also hoped that Sandy wasn't one for running after any girl that took his fancy; he'd have Dora to answer to if he messed about with her youngest daughter's feelings.

❀

Carol stared disbelievingly at the pair as Jackie sobbed in Alex's arms.

Her kid sister. How could he? The absolute bastard. But he said he didn't know she had a sister and actually he'd never asked her about her family, or she his. Had he slept with Jackie? For a fleeting moment she thought about the remaining Durex with the pinprick holes and a sick feeling enveloped her. Jackie might get pregnant. But there was no chance of getting into Alex's wallet to retrieve it now. She couldn't say anything without landing herself in the shit. He'd be furious. He was already looking at her as though he hated her.

'How long have you been together?' she snapped.

'A few weeks,' Sandy said, smoothing Jackie's hair from her face. 'We love one another.'

Carol took a deep breath. She felt overwhelmed with jealousy. Never once had he told *her* he loved her. Not even when they were making love. Her sister and Alex looked a couple, and right with each other. Jackie didn't deserve all this upset. It wasn't her fault. She'd looked so happy as she pulled him into the sitting room. So full of hopes and dreams, just like Carol had felt when Alex first started dating *her*. But Alex had *never* looked at her like he was looking at her sister. All she'd ever seen in his eyes had been lust. It had never been anything but sex, she'd known it deep down.

She got to her feet. As much as she was fuming inside with *him*, she didn't want to break her sister's heart. 'Jackie, we *had* split up.' She kept quiet that it had only been yesterday morning. 'I hadn't got around to telling anyone just yet. I'm going now. You two need to talk.'

Jackie stared at her, lips quivering. 'I'm sorry, Carol. I had no idea he was Alex. I only know him as Sandy.'

Carol held up her hands. 'Seems it's not us girls that are at fault here. I'm sorry I spoiled your birthday party.' She put on her coat and picked up her bag. 'I'll go and find Uncle Frank and Maureen at Agnes's and get a lift home. I hope the two of you will be happy together,' she finished, almost choking on her words.

She left, shutting the front door behind her, thoughts tumbling around in her head. What the hell could she do now, and what if Friday night *had* left her pregnant? It was something only time would tell. With a ton of luck it hadn't happened, but luck seemed thin on the ground at the moment.

Chapter Fifteen

August 1966

Dora took out the official-looking buff envelope that had arrived yesterday, from where she had hidden it at the back of the kitchen cupboard. She pulled out the enclosed letter and, carrying her cuppa and the letter through to the sitting room, she sat down on the sofa to read it again. Her stomach turned over and she shivered as her eyes filled with tears.

Samuel Jacobs, her former employer, guardian angel and father substitute. The dear man who had given her a job that allowed her to bring her daughter into work, hours to suit her family situation, a roof over her head following a burglary at her home on a street with empty and boarded-up houses, had passed away two weeks ago at his sister-in-law's home in the United States. The letter had come from local solicitors Hardin and Mercer, who had acted for Esther and Sammy Jacobs all their lives. An appointment had been made for Dora to visit the office that afternoon at two thirty, and she was to call them if it wasn't convenient. She took a deep breath as she digested the news again. She knew Sammy's funeral would already have taken place, as Jewish people were usually buried very soon after death. She couldn't believe she'd never see her wonderful friend and father-figure again. He had been due a visit this year and his last letter had said he would probably come in the autumn. Dora felt numb as she finished drinking her tea.

Jackie was upstairs packing her case in readiness for a little trip away with Patsy. Dora had decided not to tell her daughter about Sammy's passing as it would spoil her holiday, or she might not want to go, and that would be the last thing Sammy would have wanted. The news would do when she got back. She wondered if his death had been sudden. She hoped he hadn't suffered. In his last letter Sammy hadn't complained of ill health or anything, but no doubt she'd find out more that afternoon. She pulled a tissue from up her cardigan sleeve, wiped her eyes and pushed the letter into her apron pocket.

❀

Jackie packed the last of her things into the small suitcase: She and Patsy were going away for the bank holiday weekend, their first time without parents. Agnes had kindly booked them a chalet for three nights at Pontins Middleton Towers holiday camp near Morecambe, along with return train tickets. Patsy's dad was taking them to the station in an hour.

What their parents *didn't* know was that Sandy and Stevie had also booked the weekend at the same place, but they were going up on their scooters. The plan was to chalet swap, one couple per chalet. It had taken a lot of arranging and lying through her teeth to Mam, but so far it looked as though she'd got away with it. She couldn't wait to get on that train and relax.

Following the revelation that Sandy had been dating her sister, Jackie had sent him away and cried herself to sleep. It wasn't that she hadn't expected him to have been out with other girls, but the thought that he'd been sleeping with her sister, when she'd have loved them to be the first for each other, made her feel sad. When he was waiting outside school for her on the Monday afternoon, looking like he hadn't slept a wink, knowing he'd skipped a really important day at college to meet her, she'd agreed to talk to him and taken him back to her home. Fortunately Mam was at Agnes's, and they just clung to each other and cried. He told her he'd never meant to hurt her and that as soon as he met her he wanted to finish with Carol. He also admitted that he and Carol *had* only just split up and that if she didn't want to see him again he'd understand. He said he'd rather she learnt the truth from him than from her sister in a fit of jealousy later.

It had taken her a while to trust him again, but she loved him and her love was unconditional, as was his for her. Mam had been a bit tight-lipped and told her that a cheating man never changed his ways and she should be careful not to trust him too much or she'd get hurt. Jackie didn't believe that for a minute. She was sure her dad had always regretted his affair with Ivy. He'd been back to the house a couple of times to visit since her party and to discuss her future with regards to college now her O level results were through. He always looked sad when he was leaving and he and Mam seemed to have reached an understanding that he was always welcome if he wanted to talk about family matters.

This was a big leap forward. Jackie secretly hoped that one day Ivy would find out he'd been coming over regularly to see them and she'd throw him out, just like Mam had done. Then he could come back to them for good. She'd noticed that Mam always washed and set her hair and dressed in her best when she knew Dad was coming. Mam had given him Agnes's phone number and Patsy would bring a message about any impending visits, which were nearly always on a Sunday afternoon when Ivy was out visiting her friend.

Carol had kept her distance, sending one letter two weeks after the birthday party fall-out, apologising, and wishing Sandy and Jackie all the best for a happy future. Mam had written back, but they'd heard nothing since and Dad just said Carol seemed okay and was out with her mates most nights, staying over with one or other of them. He'd seemed a bit concerned that she was drinking a lot and said that Ivy had found empty gin bottles in her wardrobe. They'd warned her not to bring any more drink home, and so far she'd done as she was told.

Jackie took a quick look around to check she'd left nothing behind and carried her case down to the hall.

'You got everything, chuck?' Mam said, coming out of the kitchen where she'd been making a pack-up for Jackie to take with her. 'Cheese-and-Branston-pickle sarnies, and I've put crisps and a carton of Kia-Ora in the bag too.' She handed Jackie a carrier bag and wiped her hands down the front of her flowery apron. 'Now just be careful on that train. Make sure you get off at the right station, and watch what you're doing when you go out at night. I'm sure you'll be fine. Them Pontins places seem safe enough or they wouldn't advertise them as suitable for families.'

Jackie smiled and put on her leather coat. It was a bit warm for the weather they were expecting, but would have to do as she didn't have anything else suitable. She'd got a couple of five-pound notes in her purse, taken from the money her dad had given her on her birthday. There'd been a hundred pounds in the envelope and it was safely stashed away to help with books and fares when she started college. Hopefully she wouldn't need to spend much this weekend as all meals were included. Sandy had been saving his Jacaranda money, so they should be fine.

'So where is it your young man's going?' Mam said as a knock sounded at the door. It was Patsy's dad and he carried the suitcase out to the car while Jackie said her goodbyes.

'Er, New Brighton with a few pals from college,' Jackie fibbed, praying her cheeks weren't going pink and Mam couldn't read her mind. 'One of their mothers has a caravan that they're staying in,' she added, not meeting her mam's eyes.

'Hmm, well no doubt it'll be all boozing and noisy music. I know what young lads are like when they get together. Although being the son of a vicar, you'd think he'd be a bit less wild.'

Jackie laughed. 'Sandy's not wild, Mam. He's dead quiet. Totally into his art and music, and not loud stuff either.' She gave her mam a hug and hurried out to the car.

Patsy moved over on the back seat to make room. She squeezed Jackie's arm and the pair burst into a fit of nervous giggling.

'Soon be there,' Patsy whispered as Jackie let out a relieved breath.

Patsy's dad wound his window down and shouted, 'By the way, Dora, Joe rang earlier. Agnes said to tell you to pop over in a bit and she'll give you the message proper, like.'

'Rightio, I will. Thanks,' Mam called, waving from the doorstep.

'Wonder what my dad wants,' Jackie mused as the car pulled away.

'Don't know, but whatever it is, it'll have to wait until Monday night when we get home,' Patsy said, grinning.

❀

Sandy pulled up at the entrance to Middleton Towers and stretched his legs while waiting patiently for Stevie to catch up. It had been quite a ride, further than anticipated, but it would be worth the long trek to spend time with their girls. He couldn't wait to hold Jackie in his arms all night. Since the birthday party fiasco and Carol's walk-out, he'd been expecting repercussions, but it seemed that she'd put their relationship behind her and moved on. He'd not seen sight nor sound of her since that Sunday, and now he and Jackie were back on track he couldn't be any happier. He loved her totally and tonight he was planning to make her his. They'd mutually agreed to wait until they could be somewhere perfect together and that opportunity hadn't arisen until now. From the looks Jackie's mam had given him this week, he had a feeling she knew he and Stevie would be making their way up here. Still, if she'd been at all worried she would have said something and, vicar's son or not, he would have lied to make this trip happen. He'd not be following in his father's footsteps anyway. He definitely wasn't vicar material, he thought now, as Stevie rode up next to him.

'Okay, mate, let's go and book ourselves in and then look for the girls,' Sandy said, and got back on his scooter.

Checked in, chalet located and bags dumped on the floor, they found the girls, who were in a chalet in the next row to theirs.

Jackie let them in, her face aglow, and he pulled her into his arms and kissed her long and hard. 'Thought we'd never get here,' he said. 'Are you coming to our chalet with me, and then Stevie can move in here?' He picked up her case.

'Patsy's already unpacked so he can bring his stuff across,' Jackie said. 'We'll get sorted out and then meet for something to eat. There's a group on tonight in the ballroom. It's The Fourmost and they're great. Patsy fancies a dance and so do I.'

'Fine by me. Seen them at The Cavern, they're really good.' He took her hand and they sauntered across to the chalet, Stevie following them.

'See you about six thirty then,' Stevie said as he left them to it. 'We'll knock on for you.'

Sandy shut the door behind his mate and turned to look at Jackie, who was perched on the edge of one of the metal-framed single beds. 'Well, here we are. Our own little love nest. Sorry we haven't got a double bed, but I can't tell you how much I've looked forward to this.'

'Me too,' she said and gestured for him to sit beside her. 'I'm feeling really nervous though.'

'We'll be fine. A couple of drinks to relax us first, and trust me; we'll be desperate for each other. You're never nervous when we're in the church hall.' He raised an eyebrow and smiled. 'How we stopped at times, I don't know!'

He grinned as she blushed, and he kissed her. 'Are we getting changed?'

'Oh yes, I want to put something special on so I look nice for you. Mam made me a new dress for the holiday. I'll wear it tonight.'

'You always look nice, but go on, get ready and I promise not to peep.' He took a packet of cigarettes and matches outside with him and sat on the doorstep. He couldn't believe they were here. The early-evening air felt warm and he relaxed as he lit up, took a long drag and watched the holiday-makers walking by. Fashionably dressed couples in their early twenties with little kids running excitedly ahead, making their way to the Bon Appetit cafeteria, alongside older couples who looked like they'd been married for years, some holding hands and others with a few yards space in-between them, as though being on holiday together was not where they wanted to be. He smiled and hoped he and Jackie would never reach the stage of simply tolerating each other.

'I'm ready,' she called and he stubbed his cigarette out and went inside.

She did a twirl and smiled. 'Will I do?' She smoothed her hands over her short black and white striped dress, with its neat white Peter Pan collar, and walked towards him, flicking her hair over her shoulders.

Would she do? He felt the heat in his groin. 'You'll more than do.' He pulled her into his arms and kissed her. 'I'll have a quick freshen-up and change into a clean shirt and trousers. I got oil on these jeans before I left home. Everybody's dressed up out there so we need to look the part.'

Jackie sat down on the bed again and put on her strappy white sandals while he filled the sink and had a quick wash. He stripped off his jeans and she averted her eyes from his skimpy black briefs. He pulled on his black Sta-Prest trousers and a black and white striped shirt.

'Matching pair,' he laughed, pointing to her dress. 'Or do we just look like two humbugs?'

'Silly,' she said, smacking him on the arm. 'But *I've* got black undies on too.'

Before he could answer there was a knock at the door and he let in Stevie and Patsy, both dressed up in their best. Patsy's emerald green mini dress set off her red hair and Stevie's beige flared trousers and brown shirt suited his dark colouring.

'I'm starving,' Stevie said, 'and I can smell fish and chips, so that's what I'm having.' He grabbed Patsy by the hand and pulled her outside. The pair walked on ahead while Sandy locked the chalet door and took Jackie's hand.

'So, are they lacy?' he whispered as they followed their friends.

'What?'

'The black undies?'

She grinned and squeezed his hand. 'That's for me to know and you to find out.'

'Oh I will.' He felt so happy, like he was walking on clouds. This was going to be a wonderful weekend. One they'd look back on for the rest of their lives with fond memories.

❀

Jackie rolled onto her back and stared at the ceiling. Daylight crept in through a gap in the thin blue curtains and she guessed it was mid-morning, judging by the noise and chatter of people walking by the window. Probably nearer dinnertime. Beside her Sandy was still sleeping, snoring softly, which was no surprise as they'd been awake most of the night and he'd woken her about six this morning to make love again.

She stretched slightly so as not to disturb him and slid out of the narrow bed to creep into the toilet. There was no shower or bath and she could do with one. The communal showers were at the end of the chalet block and with so many people around she'd feel embarrassed at being so late up. Still, there was no choice if she wanted to freshen up. She fastened her hair on top of her head, pulled on jeans and a T-shirt, picked up a towel and her sponge bag and hurried barefoot outside.

The shower block was empty and she was in and out in less than ten minutes. She rushed back to the chalet, feeling refreshed. Sandy opened his eyes as she crept back in.

She knelt beside the bed and stroked his hair from his face. 'Good morning.' She dropped a kiss on his lips. 'There's no one in the showers if you want to dash in quickly.'

He sat up and rubbed his eyes. 'No surprise. Bet we're last up. Have we missed breakfast?'

'Yep. It's almost dinnertime. I swear I could smell roast beef while I was out there.'

'Right.' He flung back the bedclothes and got to his feet, stretching his arms above his head.

Jackie's breath caught in her throat. He was so good-looking and he'd made love to her with such passion, but also taken care not to be rough with her. He'd been right about them being desperate for one another by the time they got back to the chalet. They'd all danced and sang and drank until well after midnight. Although the boys had bought Coca-Cola for her and Patsy, they'd also shared their alcohol. The group had been brilliant, but all she'd been able to think about while Sandy had danced her around the huge ballroom was that she hoped he wouldn't be disappointed.

She was determined to show him that she could love him better than her sister had. She wasn't shy with him, as they'd spent a lot of time getting to know one another on the old gym mats in the church hall; she knew what pleased him and him her, but that first time, when he'd pushed inside her and she'd wrapped her legs around him, had been the most wonderful feeling she'd ever experienced. The whole sense of belonging, of being one at last, took her over the edge maybe sooner than she'd liked, but the next time, and the one after, had both been amazing. Now she felt complete, grown-up and truly loved, and she knew he did too.

'Back in a sec,' he said after pulling on his oil-stained jeans and grabbing a towel.

Jackie changed into a new white sleeveless top that Mam had got her from TJ Hughes last week and a pair of below-the-knee navy pedal-pushers. Her white sandals completed the outfit. She tied up her hair into a neat ponytail. If the day was as warm as yesterday it would be cooler fastened up out of the way. Last night someone had told them about a special evening show for the bank holiday at the SS Berengaria entertainment centre.

She'd spotted the centre as they came into the campsite on the small bus that picked up holiday-makers from the station. It was a huge building with the spectacular appearance of an ocean liner complete with funnel. Sandy said he would take her to watch the show tonight if the tickets weren't sold out. She was looking forward to it. It was right up her street. Musical acts, dancers, a comedian. She might be able to glean a few ideas for the St Paul's Players, who were in the middle of rehearsals for *Oliver!*

Sandy dashed back inside bare-chested, and pulled on a clean T-shirt and his spare jeans. 'Just seen Patsy and Stevie. They'll meet us in the Rendezvous Coffee Bar in ten.' He rubbed his hair dry with the towel and ran a comb through it. 'First sitting for lunch is twelve, so we'll go for the later one as families with kids will probably be at the first. Be a bit noisy, don't you think?'

'Yes. Let the families get out of the way. Shall we swim this afternoon? The pool looks quite nice and it's warm enough. I brought a swimsuit with me.'

'Bikini?' His eyes lit up.

'Sorry, it's a one-piece. I didn't think.'

'Silly.' He pulled her to him. 'I'm only teasing. I don't want men ogling you anyway. I'll whiz over to the Berengaria and get the tickets for later. I'll check our scooters are okay in the car park too. Back in a minute.'

Jackie went outside and took a deep breath. She could smell the sea but not actually see it from where she was standing. Seagulls swooped and dived all over the camp, making a racket and waiting for titbits. The campsite looked lovely, lots of grassy areas and colourful flower beds, with the majestic bulk of the SS Berengaria just across the way. The ballroom last night had been spectacular too with its massive dance floor and twinkling lights, and was surrounded by indoor gift and clothes shops. There was a chemist as well as a smaller coffee bar and tea shop. Mam had told her to buy some calamine lotion in case she got a bit of sunburn. She'd pop in the chemist's after they'd had coffee. She looked up as Sandy came running towards her.

'Got them,' he puffed as Jackie clapped her hands with excitement. 'You ready?'

They strolled across the gardens to the coffee bar and joined Stevie and Patsy, who were already seated at an outside table, gazing into one another's eyes.

'You two want a refill?' Sandy asked, reaching in his jeans for his wallet.

'We're fine, you get yours,' Patsy said. 'Isn't it warm? We thought we might have a swim later.'

Jackie smiled. 'Us too. Sandy got tickets for tonight's show. I know you said you didn't fancy it, but if you do, there might be some left.'

Patsy blushed slightly and said, 'Stevie wants an early night.'

'Ah, okay. Well, enjoy.'

'We will.'

Sandy went to the counter, carried back two frothy coffees to the table and sat down. 'I'm starving. We missed breakfast. Did you two?'

'Yep,' Stevie said. 'But Patsy had some biscuits in her bag so we had those to be going on with.' He checked his watch. 'Only half an hour and then we can go and eat.'

The cafeteria crowd was thinning as they queued for food. Sitting down, plate piled high with roast beef and vegetables, Jackie said, 'Think that dark-haired woman server had her eye on you two, flirting with her just to get extra roasties.'

'We're growing lads,' Stevie said, adding, 'and I need the energy for our early night.'

'Behave.' Patsy tapped him on the hand and laughed. 'Honestly, what's he like?'

Jackie smiled; it was good to see her best friend and Stevie as smitten with each other as she and Sandy were. She couldn't help thinking how lucky the four of them were.

Back at the chalet after lunch and getting their swimming things together, Sandy pulled her close and kissed her. 'I love this, us being together, and I know we're only young and we've got years ahead of us to plan a future, but I want to tell you something.'

'Oh, what?' Jackie looked at his serious face.

'Well, I *was* saving this as a surprise for nearer Christmas, but I'm bursting to say something now. I sold *Forbidden Fruit* last week; well, the gallery that took it from the exhibition did, anyway. After they take their commission they'll pay me fifty pounds. Also they're willing to showcase anything else I paint. But what I'm trying to say here is that I want to use the money to buy you a ring. So I guess what I really mean is – will you marry me, Jackie?'

Jackie stared at him, eyes wide and mouth open.

'Have I said the wrong thing? Shit, I'm sorry.'

'No, no of course not. You've shocked me into silence for once. Wow. I wasn't expecting that. But yes, yes, I'll marry you, when we're older, of course.'

'Of course,' he echoed. 'You've got college soon and *I* need to establish a career, so it won't be for ages yet, but at least we'll know we belong together.' He clapped his hand to his mouth. 'Hell, does that sound too soppy and possessive? I'm not making a very good job of this, am I?'

She stroked his cheek and smiled. 'Consider us engaged.'

He let out a relieved sigh and pulled her closer. 'We'll tell our parents soon.'

She laughed. 'We'll have to bide our time, because we're not supposed to be together this weekend. We can hardly rush home and tell them. Leave it a week or two and then you can do it properly and ask my dad and all that stuff. We've got years to plan our future, like you say.'

❈

The Berengaria Seaside Special that night gave Jackie ideas for her chosen career. She loved the song and dance routines and wondered if she could get a holiday job, taking part in a chorus line, a bit like the Tiller Girls on the Palladium show, but with singing too. It would be great experience for the future. Maybe her forthcoming college course in Drama and Performing Arts would help her in securing that sort of work. The theatre was huge inside with over two thousand seats, every one occupied. The cheers and shouts of 'MORE!' echoed around the auditorium, the thunderous applause sending a thrill through her. It was hardly the sort of career she could do for long if she married Sandy, though. Then it occurred to her that an artist could work anywhere he chose, so they could travel the country together. He'd told her that afternoon in Sefton Park that he wanted to travel. They could do anything they wanted – until babies came along.

❈

It was Sunday morning, and the last day of the holiday. Jackie lay in Sandy's arms, and they snuggled together as close as they could. She couldn't believe how quickly the days had flown. Monday would be spent travelling back. How she would miss him tomorrow night. He opened his eyes and smiled. She kissed him and reached below the bedcovers to touch him, but he held her hand aloft and shook his head.

'What's wrong?'

'We're out of supplies.' He gestured to the empty Durex box on the bedside table. 'Have to wait until the little chemist near the ballroom opens, if it even does on a Sunday.'

'But I thought we had plenty.'

'Yeah, we did, and we've had plenty of sex!' He laughed. 'I'm not taking chances, babe. Much as I love you, I'm not prepared to balls-up our future. If we start, you know we won't be able to stop.'

'But there's one in your wallet,' she reminded him. 'The loose one you pulled out along with that fiver at the bar in the ballroom last night, when Stevie teased you about tipping the waitress with it and you got all embarrassed.'

'Oh yeah.' He grinned. 'I'd forgotten all about that.' He reached for his jeans on the floor and took out his wallet. The foil packet had been in there for months and was a bit battered, but still intact. He slid it under the pillow and took Jackie in his arms. They made love with all the energy of a good night's sleep behind them.

Lying together afterwards, Sandy whispered, 'I would never have believed that I could love someone as deeply and totally as I love you. I'll love you forever. Never forget it.'

She sighed and traced a finger around lips that had kissed her from top to toe. She felt she'd really grown up in the last couple of days; she wasn't just a sixteen-year-old girl, but a woman ready to face anything life threw at her. With Sandy by her side it was all possible.

'It's the same for me,' she whispered. 'I love you to the moon and back, and I always will.'

Chapter Sixteen

Her bloody skirt wouldn't fasten at all now. The zipper was strained and the button on the waistband simply wouldn't meet the buttonhole. Carol took it off and threw it on the bed in despair. She sat down and took a deep breath. Everything was too tight. She begrudged buying anything new for the length of time she would need it, but it looked like there wasn't a choice.

She pulled the tight girdle she'd been forced to invest in up over her tights and tried the skirt again. It just about zipped up now and her loose top helped disguise her swollen belly. Fortunately, being tall, she wasn't showing too much at the front yet, her height seemed to help balance out her weight gain, but everything else was expanding. Her breasts, the tops of her thighs, even her face looked rounder. She really couldn't keep this baby a secret for much longer. It was coming up to the August bank holiday weekend and then it'd be September. And seeing as she knew the date of conception was on the last day she'd had sex with Alex, it would be born early December.

She hadn't worried too much at first. She'd been so upset at losing Alex to her sister, and emotional upsets could be a cause of late periods. She'd read about it in *Honey* magazine, on the agony-aunt page. But the following month she'd had to acknowledge the possibility of being pregnant. One half of her was pleased, because she might get Alex back, but the other half was terrified. A pregnancy test at Boots proved positive and reading the results on the slip of paper had felt unreal. Deep down she knew she couldn't have the baby and had tried to get rid of it at first by buying gin and sitting in hot baths at night. But the old wives' tale hadn't worked and now she felt she had to give it a chance and go ahead with her pregnancy. Ivy had had a right go at her for using all the hot water, and then the nosy bugger had rooted in her wardrobe and taken the empty bottles down to the kitchen to show Dad, who expressed his concern that she was becoming an alcoholic. All the gin had done was make her feel hung-over and sickly, on top of coping with the morning sickness that she'd hidden by running water and flushing the loo several times.

She hadn't even confided in Susan at work. In fact, not a soul knew she was pregnant, but that would have to change soon. She needed to tell her mam; she'd know what to do. She really couldn't confide in Ivy, and Dad would go mental. She knew she should tell Alex, but after all this time he would probably say it wasn't his, and there was no way of proving it was without confessing what she'd done. And even then, he might not believe her. Every time Dad came back from his secret Sunday visits to her mam's she dreaded him announcing that her sister was pregnant. Maybe Alex had chucked away the remaining damaged Durex, or more likely Jackie had just been lucky, or quite simply they weren't yet lovers.

She picked up her jacket and handbag and made her way downstairs. 'See you later, Ivy,' she called from the hall.

Ivy popped her head around the kitchen door where she was busy wrestling sheets into the twin-tub. 'Will you get me some Rennies from Boots on your dinner break? I don't know what I've done with that packet I bought last week. I'll settle up tonight.'

'Yep, okay.' Carol closed the front door behind her and rolled her eyes. The Rennies were in her handbag. That was another thing, the heartburn. It was something she'd never experienced before. It kept her awake at night, and as if that wasn't bad enough, the baby had started to move around a bit, when she wasn't restricting it with the tight girdle. As soon as she got into bed it began wriggling. At first it had felt like butterflies, but the movements were more pronounced now. She plodded along the pavement to the bus stop, feeling like an elephant, although she knew she didn't look like one – yet.

As the bus drew up she pushed her way inside and sat down. A few stops further along Susan got on, but instead of going upstairs for her usual cigarette she joined Carol.

'You okay, Caz? You look a bit pale.'

'Just tired. Didn't get much sleep.'

Susan nodded. 'Bet we'll be busy at the store this week. Bank holiday weekend and all that. Mind you, doesn't really affect us in the office. Can't wait for a long weekend off though. Doing anything special?'

Carol's eyes filled and she shook her head. Susan squeezed her arm. 'You still missing Alex? You're better off without him, you know. Dating your kid sister behind your back like that. What a bastard. You need to find another fella to give you a good time.'

'It's not that easy. And Alex didn't know Jackie was my sister.'

Susan shrugged. 'No matter who she was, he was seeing her while he was still with you.'

'He tried to tell me it was over,' Carol said. Although somewhat sympathetic, Susan only saw things in black and white. There were no grey areas for her. 'I misread the signs. Thought we were together forever.'

'But he was sleeping with you and seeing *her*. Cheeky bastard. You're still best rid of him as far as I'm concerned.'

'Maybe. Come on, we're here.'

As the girls alighted from the bus, the woman behind them, carrying a toddler and a trolley, caught her heel on the platform and fell forwards, the trolley hitting Carol firmly in the back. She dropped heavily to her knees, winded by the blow.

'God, chuck, I'm so sorry. Youse okay?' the woman said, putting down the little boy and crouching beside Carol on the pavement.

'That bloody conductor should have helped me. Lazy sod,' she shouted after the departing bus, shaking a fist.

Susan unfolded the trolley and sat the little boy in it before he got the chance to run away. She helped Carol to her feet. 'Come on, let's get you into work and have you checked over. You've gone white as a sheet. We're only over there in Lewis's,' Susan told the shocked woman, who looked like she was about to cry. 'We've a first-aid nurse on site.'

'I'm so sorry,' the woman said again, fastening her little boy's reins on the trolley. 'I really am.'

'I'll be fine,' Carol said, looking down at her bleeding knees. 'Nothing that a new pair of tights won't put right.'

'Let me at least give you the money for another pair.' The woman reached into a shopping bag that was attached to the trolley.

'It's okay, don't worry, we get staff discount,' Susan said. 'We better go, we're already late. Goodbye.'

She took Carol's arm and led her across the road, into the store and straight to the first-aid room, shouting to someone in their office as they passed to let the supervisor know that Carol had had an accident.

The nurse took one look at Carol and helped her up onto a small bed at the back of the room. Susan explained what happened.

'Are you in any pain? What about your back? It took the full brunt of the trolley by the sounds of it. And we need to get those stockings off and your knees cleaned up.'

'They're tights,' Carol said. 'I'll pull them off.' Christ, she'd got that bloody girdle on and once she removed it she'd spill out like an exploded cushion. She chewed her lip, feeling embarrassed and not sure what to do.

The nurse took it as a sign that she'd like privacy and pulled a curtain across. 'I'll be back in a moment. Hot tea with sugar? Good for shock. Make yourself comfortable.' She left the room.

Susan frowned as Carol sat unmoving on the edge of the bed. 'Shall I help you? Is your back painful? Can you move all right?'

Carol hitched her skirt up and wriggled the girdle down as quickly as she could, then removed her damaged tights. She couldn't meet Susan's eyes but knew from the sharp intake of breath that the cat was out of the bag. She held her breath and pulled the girdle back on again.

'Caz?'

'Don't say anything. Please. Nobody knows.'

'How far?'

'Five months.'

'Shit! You're joking? So it's Alex's?'

Carol nodded as the door opened and the nurse came back into the room carrying a tray with two cups of tea.

'Sit down,' she said, handing a cup to Susan. 'I'll clean Carol up and then we'll see how she feels.' She put a packet down on the end of the bed. Carol looked. New tights. They were the wrong colour, American tan, but better than a torn pair. 'The young lady on hosiery said you could pay her later.'

'Thank you.' Carol took the proffered cup and saucer, her hands shaking. Susan was looking at her with a shocked expression in her eyes. She knew she could trust her not to say anything just yet, but even so, she felt vulnerable now that someone else knew and it wasn't just *her* secret any more. She groaned. 'My back is really hurting.'

'I think I'll send you for an X-ray,' the nurse said. 'You were bent almost double when Susan brought you in here.' She lifted Carol's top up and ran her fingers down her spine, prodding as she went. Carol winced as she got to waist level. 'You're in for some colourful bruises, my dear. Finish your tea and then I'll sort out your knees and see how you are at walking for me. You both work in wages, is that right?'

They nodded and she continued. 'I'll let them know that I'm advising you to take the rest of the day off work and sending you to hospital for a back X-ray. I think you should accompany her, Susan. I'm not prepared to let her go alone. There's a bit of colour in your cheeks again, Carol, but you still look washed out to me, so I'm taking no chances.'

'Christ, you could lose the baby,' Susan whispered as they were left alone again. 'A fall like that at this stage could trigger a miscarriage. Especially being banged so hard in the back. Could have done you all sorts of damage.'

'Might be for the best,' Carol muttered, tears sliding down her cheeks. 'Nobody wants it. And I can't bring it up on my own.'

'Well Alex should take some responsibility. He can't get away scot-free. He should have been more bloody careful. You'll have to tell them at the hospital.'

Carol sighed and wiped a hand across her face. She felt consumed with guilt. None of this was Alex's fault, but she couldn't tell Susan that.

'I will. Thanks, Sue. For being here for me, I mean.'

Susan shook her head. 'Someone needs to be.'

❁

Within the hour, Carol, accompanied by Susan, was in a taxi heading towards Fazakerley hospital.

'This is close to where Mam lives,' Carol whispered as they drove up Longmoor Lane. 'I'm going to ask the driver to take me home instead. Alex lives nearby. I don't want to see him.'

'Are you mad? You *need* to see him. And that back needs checking. Anyway, he'll be at college at this time of day, won't he?'

'No, it's summer holidays. He could be anywhere around here on his scooter and *she'll* probably be with him. I can't bear to see them together.' She took a deep shuddering breath and groaned as she fidgeted in her seat.

'Right, well, let's get you examined properly and then we'll decide what to do.'

The taxi dropped them off by the entrance to the Accident and Emergency department and they followed the signs for X-ray.

A young nurse took the letter the first-aid nurse had given to Carol and led them to a private cubicle, where Carol was told to strip to her waist and given a cotton gown to slip on.

The nurse wrote down some details and then looked up over the top of her glasses. 'Is there any chance you could be pregnant?' she asked, blushing slightly as she looked at Carol's ring-less left hand.

Before Carol could deny it Susan said, 'Yes, she is, about five months.'

'Ah, well we won't be able to do an X-ray today, Miss, er, Rodgers. It could damage your baby.'

Carol chewed her lip.

Susan took charge. 'She had a nasty fall this morning. Can someone take a look at her to make sure everything's all right and with the baby as well?'

'Of course. If you'll just wait here, I'll get a doctor.'

'Someone had to tell her,' Susan said. '*You* wouldn't. And you can stop wearing that ridiculous girdle and get some clothes that fit you properly. Poor little bugger's gonna come out all squashed. It's not going to go away, Caz. You've got to face up to it. Whatever you decide to do when it's born is up to you. And when we leave here I'm taking you back to your home and you can tell Ivy and ask her to help you tell your dad. Then he can let your mother know. You can't do this on your own any more.'

Carol sat quietly while Susan spoke. She knew her friend was right. She'd still be able to work for another couple of months at least and she was hidden away in the offices and not standing on a counter all day in view of prying eyes and gossips. Facing up to the future was starting now. She squeezed Susan's hand as a young, white-coated doctor followed the nurse back into the cubicle.

Ivy looked up from mopping the kitchen floor and stared in grumpy suspicion as Carol let herself in mid-afternoon, followed by Susan.

'What are *you* doing home this early?' She put down her mop and followed the pair into the mismatched front room that no one was allowed to sit in during the day, but Carol was past caring and didn't even take off her shoes before walking on the green speckled carpet. She sat on the blue tweed sofa and gestured for Susan to sit down too. She ached all over, her back was killing her and she just wanted to crawl into bed and sleep until the pain went away. The doctor had reassured her everything was fine with the baby and estimated it was due the first week of December from the dates she'd given him, just like she'd worked out for herself. He'd advised her to see her own doctor as soon as possible.

Ivy plonked herself down on an armchair, arms folded expectantly. 'Well?' She sucked on her dentures. 'I hope you haven't got the sack. *We* can't afford to keep you.'

It was always about money with Ivy. Carol was grateful once more when Susan took charge.

'Er, Mrs Rodgers, no, Carol *hasn't* got the sack. She had an accident this morning on her way to work. We've just got back from Fazakerley hospital.'

Susan went on to explain what had happened, that there was no damage to Carol's spine but she had severe bruising to her back and knees and she needed to rest. She paused and then looked at Carol, who took up the tale.

Staring at a length of wallpaper in a hideous pattern of orange flowers in brown vases above her stepmother's head, Carol blurted out, 'I'm sorry, Ivy, but I'm expecting a baby.'

Ivy's eyes bulged and her face flushed a darker shade of pink than the full-blown roses on the curtains. Her chins quivered and her pale blue eyes flashed angrily. Her words, when they came out, sounded strangulated.

'You're *what*? Well, I hope he's going to marry you. And don't think you can live under this roof either. I'm having no baby here. Wait till your father hears about this. He'll go bloody mad. You're old enough to know better. Not as if you're sixteen like your sister. You can go and pack your bags, and as soon as Joe gets home he can take you round to your mother's. Let *her* take responsibility again. I've done my bit.'

She took a breath and continued with her onslaught. 'And you needn't think you can tap him up for money either. *I've* to do without my holiday now because he's helping out so your sister can go to bloody college. Waste of money if you ask me. Fanciful ideas she has. She'll only end up like you, dropping her drawers for the first lad who takes a shine to her.'

Carol burst into tears and Susan gasped, staring open-mouthed at Ivy. She moved up the sofa and put an arm around Carol's shoulders. 'Has anybody ever told you that you're a right unfeeling cow, Ivy? How Carol's dad's put up with you all this time I do not know. Biggest mistake he's ever made was getting you to drop *your* drawers!'

'How dare you speak to me like that in my own house?' Spittle flew from Ivy's lips as she turned on Susan, her face crimson. 'You can just get out, right now.'

'Oh, don't you worry, I'm going, and I'm taking Carol with me. My mam will look after her until her dad gets home. Then they can talk and decide what to do for the best. Go and pack a few things, Caz, and I'll phone us a taxi.'

'Well you needn't think *I'm* paying for it,' Ivy snapped.

'You're not, but I'm using *your* phone,' Susan said, her angry glare defying Ivy to refuse permission as Carol wobbled to her feet and left the room.

Upstairs Carol threw a few things and some toiletries into a small case. She found a pair of jeans and a dress that had been too big earlier this year, but would fit her fine now, and a couple of loose tops. Maybe her mam would make her some maternity clothes once she knew about the baby. Now she was facing up to it being a reality, she felt an overwhelming need to tell Alex. If it meant splitting up his relationship with her sister, she didn't really care. She felt numb inside at the moment, but she owed her baby a chance. If Alex didn't want to know, and she doubted he would, then she'd have to face up to a future alone when it happened.

⊛

Ivy was sitting on the sofa in the front room, nursing a mug of tea, when Joe arrived home from work. As he took off his boots in the hall she called out that she needed to speak to him.

'Won't be a minute. Just need a pee.' He popped his head around the door, then retracted it just as quickly when he saw the sour look on her face. What the bloody hell was up with her now? Never happy unless she was moaning, that one. He dashed upstairs and was back within moments. 'Right, what's up? You've a right miserable look about you.'

She slammed her mug down on the coffee table and glared at him. 'And so would you if you'd had the afternoon I've had.'

Joe shrugged. 'Get on with it then.' He was in no mood for shilly-shallying around the houses with her. He was tired and hungry and couldn't smell his dinner cooking either, which was unusual.

'That daughter of yours,' Ivy began, 'she's brought trouble to our door.'

'Eh? Trouble? Which one? Our Carol?' he asked, as she nodded. 'Why, what's she done now?'

'She's only gone and got herself in the family way,' Ivy snapped. 'It's disgraceful.'

Joe frowned. 'Now hang on a minute. No woman I know of has ever got herself pregnant. There's usually a bloke involved as well.'

'Yes, well, you know what I mean,' Ivy blustered. 'No need to be so sarky with me.'

'Where is she then? Is she okay? Did you find out who the lad is? Must have got herself a new boyfriend after that vicar's son fiasco.'

Ivy shook her head. She told Joe the events of the afternoon. 'So I told her she had to go. I don't want her under this roof, showing us up,' she finished and folded her arms under her ample bosom.

'You did what?' Joe exploded. 'You had no rights to do that. She's my daughter. She needs our help, not chucking out on the streets.'

'She's not on the streets. She's with that awful Susan that she works with. She gave me such cheek, that one; she was downright rude to me. *She's* no better than she should be either.' Ivy sniffed and got to her feet. 'I've been too busy to cook your tea. You'll have to make do with a tin of soup.' She shuffled out of the room.

Joe stared after her retreating back. He jumped to his feet and ran upstairs to Carol's bedroom, found her address book in her bedside drawers. With no idea of her friend's surname, he leafed through until he found a couple of Susans. One was only a short distance from here. That would be her. The other lived in Birkenhead, which was too far for being a workmate.

'Right,' he announced, walking into the kitchen as Ivy put a bowl of tomato soup on the worktop and sliced some bread. 'You can stick your bloody soup. I'm going for my girl and bringing her home.'

'You'll do no such thing,' Ivy yelled. 'She's not coming back here. I'd be too embarrassed.'

'Oh you would, would you? Well, no more so than I was when *you* announced you were up the duff. I was bloody mortified.' Joe put on his jacket and picked up his car keys.

'Don't you dare speak to me like that; and I'm warning you, Joe. Don't bring her back here, or you can both get out.'

'Don't give orders to me in my own home.'

'It's my home too and I don't want the neighbours talking about us.' Ivy folded her arms, a mutinous expression on her face. 'This is a decent area. People will point fingers.'

Furiously, Joe grabbed her by the upper arm and frog-marched her into the front room.

'Sit down,' he ordered. 'It's time for some home truths, and then I'm bringing our Carol back here whether you like it or not. This house was paid for with the money my mother left me when she passed on. Well, the deposit was, anyway. The rest of the money she left *you* spent like it was going out of fashion, buying all this mismatched crap.' He waved his arms around. 'Ever since you got your claws into me you've never lifted a finger financially, apart from a bit of part-time work before the ROF closed down. You knew I had Dora and two kiddies to support. But you never offered to help me in any way. Always saw them as a burden. Dora once told me that you really saw me coming, and by God she was right. I've been a bloody fool, I know I have. I should never have got involved with you. Poison Ivy, they called you at work and they weren't far wrong. You were determined to trap me. You knew I wanted my family back and to be with my wife again. But you ruined that for us.'

'I was pregnant, Joe. You ruined it yourself. What was I supposed to do?' A single tear forced its way down her cheek and dangled from her double chin. She swiped at it with her hand.

'Stay there,' he demanded and left the room. He was back within seconds and thrust a sheet of paper at her.

Ivy looked at it and her face blanched. It was a copy of her medical notes. 'How did you get this?' she gasped.

'Never mind how. That isn't important right now. I've had it a good few years, but I've been waiting for the right time to show it to you. I think that's now, don't you? There never was a baby, Ivy. You lied to trap me and then had a very convenient non-existent miscarriage. I hate you for what you did to me and Dora. You wrecked everything we were rebuilding with our daughters. I can't live with you any more. I want a divorce. This marriage is a sham, all built on lies and your greed. I was an easy meal ticket for you.

I got you out of your shabby old flat, gave you a roof over your head and you pay me back with lies. You hardly ever welcomed my kids over. Always made out they were an inconvenience. You begrudged every penny I gave to Dora for their keep. And now you want to see my poor young girl out on the streets when she's expecting a baby and needs support. I want you out of here when I bring Carol back.'

'You can't do that,' Ivy cried. 'I have as much right to be here as you do. I'll see a solicitor tomorrow. I must be entitled to something. You have no grounds for divorce.'

'Oh yes I do. This house can go up for sale as soon as possible. Do what you want until that time, but I'll be sleeping in the spare room from now on.'

'You're having an affair with Dora, aren't you?' Ivy accused. 'I knew it. Well I'm divorcing you and I'll take you for every penny.'

'Whatever. But you're barking up the wrong tree there.'

❀

Ivy stared after Joe as he slammed the door on his way out. She'd done it now, accusing him of having an affair with Dora. But nothing would surprise her. She felt sick at the thought of giving up her lovely home. She needed to know what rights she had and what she was entitled to, if anything. The idea of going back to work filled her with horror after having had a cushy lifestyle here. Coming and going as she pleased and always having a bit of spare money to spend. She couldn't bear to think of giving it all up and starting again. Once word got out as to why Joe was divorcing her, she'd never get another man to take her on.

Chapter Seventeen

'Only me,' Jackie called as she let herself into the house. There was no reply and she stood her case up against the hall wall. She popped her head around the sitting room door. The room was immaculate: cushions plumped, hearth rug straight, no old newspapers lying on the coffee table, but no sign of life. She walked through to the kitchen, where the back door stood open. She could see her mam in the garden, taking washing off the line and dropping it into a laundry basket.

'Hiya,' she said as her mam picked up the basket, a wooden clothes peg between her teeth.

'Hiya, chuck,' Mam said, spitting out the peg and walking into the kitchen. She popped the basket onto the table and gave Jackie a hug. 'Have you had a good time?'

'Yes, thanks. It was fabulous. The weather was great and there's so much to do on the site. The shows are brilliant and the food was lovely.' Jackie knew she was gabbling and trying not to blush at the same time because all she could see in her head was Sandy's limbs entwined with hers at night. It was all she'd thought about on the train home, that and his marriage proposal. She was bursting to say something – she'd told Patsy of course, but she knew her friend would keep the secret until it was officially announced. Patsy asked if she could be the first to tell Marcia Phelan and they'd fallen about laughing on the train.

'Was the chalet all right? Clean and comfortable?'

'Er, yeah, it was really nice. We had to have a shower in a block nearby, but we had a toilet and sink in a little room just off the bedroom.'

'I'll make us a brew and you can fold that dry washing for me. Your dad's coming with Carol at half-three. He wants to discuss something, but he wouldn't say what it was about. I spoke to him on Saturday after he'd left a message with Agnes for me to call him. He didn't sound too happy.'

Jackie frowned. She hadn't seen or spoken to her sister since the day of her birthday party five months ago and there'd been no communication with their mam apart from the one letter.

'Do you think Dad and Ivy have had a falling-out and he wants to come back to you?' Jackie asked, folding tea towels and slipping them into a kitchen drawer.

Mam raised her eyebrows. 'Oh dear, I hope not. It's one thing him visiting occasionally, but I don't think I could go down that road again, love.'

'He still loves you, Mam. I can tell by the way he looks at you.' Jackie felt she knew enough about love now to know what she was talking about. 'You could sort things out if you really wanted to.'

'Don't talk daft.' Mam busied herself spooning tea leaves into the brown pot, but Jackie could see her cheeks pinking, *and* she'd washed her hair. It was soft and curling on her shoulders and she was wearing her Sunday-best pink lippy as well as her good black skirt and a new white blouse.

'Why are you all dressed up then?' she teased as Mam poured boiling water on the tea leaves. '*And* you're blushing.'

'Behave yourself!' Mam burst out laughing. 'Be nice to see our Carol again after the last fiasco. Maybe she thinks it's time to make amends. She's no doubt got another boyfriend by now. Just try and get on with her, let's have a peaceful teatime. I'll make some sandwiches and there's a bit of cake left over from the weekend.'

'Is Uncle Frank coming for tea?' Jackie asked and helped herself to a custard cream from the packet her mam pushed across the table. She nibbled a corner and took a sip of tea.

'No, he's taken Maureen over to visit her pal in Formby. He's back on the docks tomorrow, first thing. I expect they'll go straight home.'

'I got him a little pressie and one for you and Dad as well.' Jackie went out to the hall, rooted in her case and brought in a carrier bag. 'It's just an ornament thing for on the bookcase. And I got boxes of fancy sweets for Uncle Frank and my dad.' She handed the tissue-wrapped gift to her mam and sat down at the table to finish her brew.

Mam unwrapped the glass snow dome with a model of the SS Berengaria inside.

'If you shake it, snow settles on the building,' Jackie said. 'That's the place where we saw the show. It's built like a huge ship, even got a funnel. It was amazing. The song and dance routines were fantastic. I'd love to be in a show like that one day.'

'I'm sure you will be. That college course will be good training for you. By the way, I'm currently helping Sandy's mother with the costumes for *Oliver!* She's really excited about the show and said what a lovely girl you are to work with. I felt proper proud of you, love. Bloody Barbara Baker wanted to get involved but Mrs Faraday told her we had enough help, thank you. Soon put her in her place, she did. Did Patsy enjoy the show as well?'

'Er, oh yeah, she, er, loved it.' Damn, she'd better make sure Patsy remembered to say they'd seen the show together, just in case Mam asked *her* mam if she'd enjoyed it too. 'Shall I take this washing upstairs out of the way while you make a start on the sandwiches? I'll have a quick freshen-up before they arrive.'

She ran upstairs with the laundry and came back down for her suitcase. She wondered if Sandy and Stevie had arrived home yet. They'd left before the train did to get a head start. Sandy told her he'd pop over later to see her. He was expecting to be home mid-afternoon. She couldn't wait to see him again; even after just a few hours she was missing him like crazy.

❀

While Jackie was upstairs Dora started to make sandwiches for their visitors. She could really have done without Joe and Carol coming today. She wanted to tell Jackie about Sammy passing away and what had happened on her visit to the solicitor on Friday. She hadn't told a soul yet, not even Frank or Agnes. Her head was still in a whirl. As she buttered the bread her mind went back to the conversation with the solicitor Mr Mercer as he explained the contents of Sammy's will. She'd sat facing the man, feeling stunned as he'd told her she was to receive an interim payment of three thousand guineas from the estate. He'd handed her a cheque and she'd stared at it, unable to take in the news. As the room swam in front of her eyes, Mr Mercer had called his secretary in to give her a glass of water.

'But I can't accept this,' Dora began, her voice wavering. 'It's way too much. I'm not a relative or anything.'

'It's Mr Jacobs' wish that you have enough money to buy a little house to secure your future. It states it quite clearly here in his will. He's also written you a letter.' He handed her an envelope with her name written on the front. It gave her a warm, but sad, feeling when she saw Sammy's sprawling handwriting. She opened the envelope with shaking hands. As she read his affectionate scrawl her eyes filled with tears. The words broke her heart and she wished she could fling her arms around her wonderful surrogate father and give him the biggest hug ever.

❀

My dearest Dora,

I fear I won't be well enough to make a further trip to England this year. My health is failing and I'm told by the physicians that

I don't have too much time left. I have written a new will and have made you sole beneficiary. You are the daughter my darling Esther and I never had, but you and your children meant so much to us both. I don't want you to ever have to scrimp and scrape again. A sum will be paid out to you as soon as I pass and the rest once the solicitors have dealt with my estate. As you know, I have no property in the UK now, but I have a small house here in Brooklyn that will be sold after my passing and you will, in time, receive the proceeds from that sale.

I'll tell you now that nothing has been left to my estranged son, Sonny. I have had no contact with him since he wrote to tell me he was going to Australia to make a new life for himself, and that was over five years ago. As far as I am concerned, I no longer have a son, and I know that Esther would have agreed wholeheartedly with my decision.

I have just one final request of you, Dora. Under Jewish burial rules I will be interred in the USA on my death. There will be no time to return me to the UK nor is cremation permitted to allow my ashes home. Will you please ensure that my dear Esther's grave is looked after for as long as you are able?

I hope that you and my surrogate granddaughters enjoy a long, healthy and happy life and that my bequest helps you all to achieve just that. Thank you for making my life without Esther a happy one. Just receiving your letters has been such a joy and my visits to the UK were always pleasurable times, thanks to your hospitality.

Goodbye, my darling girl.

Much love to you and yours.

Sammy. Xxx

❀

Jackie helped her mam make the sandwiches and they were just finishing slicing the left-over cake when the door-knocker went.

She ran to answer it and invited her dad and Carol in and showed them into the sitting room. Dad gave her a hug and a peck on the cheek but Carol hung back silently, not meeting her eye.

'Sit down, we won't be a minute. Mam's just brewing the tea and then we'll bring everything through.' Jackie slipped out of the room and back into the kitchen, pulling the door to behind her.

'What's up?' Mam said. 'Why are you closing the door?'

'They're a bit odd,' Jackie whispered. 'All sort of quiet. Our Carol didn't even speak to me and she looks dead pale. I wonder if Ivy's chucked them both out.'

'I hope not. We haven't really got the space to put them up here. And I doubt you'll want to share a room again with Carol – or her with you, for that matter.' Mam picked up the tea tray and chewed her lip. 'Come on; let's find out what's wrong with them.' Jackie followed her with the plates of sandwiches and cake.

After Mam had handed around mugs of steaming tea and told them to help themselves to food, she turned to Dad. 'So, what's up, Joe? You look a bit miserable. And you too, Carol. Are you not taking your coat off, love? It's roasting in here.'

Carol shook her head and pulled her coat tightly around her body.

Jackie frowned. It *was* warm, very. She was boiling in just one of her little cotton shift dresses and sandals. Carol had on jeans as well as her full-length coat and she looked very pale. Her short Twiggy hairstyle had grown out and she wore no makeup at all. That wasn't like her sister, who normally wouldn't dream of going out unless she was dolled up to the nines. A little shiver ran down Jackie's spine and she shivered. Something was wrong and she had a bad feeling about it. She chewed her lip as Mam asked a few more questions and then Dad put down his mug on the coffee table.

'Right,' he began and cleared his throat. 'Well, there's no easy way to say this so I'll just come straight out with it. Our Carol's expecting a baby.' He laced his hands together round his knees and looked at Mam, who nearly dropped her mug.

'No! You're not? Oh, love.' Mam put down her mug and reached for Carol's hands.

Carol burst into tears and Mam pulled her close. 'It's okay, chuck. Don't worry. These things happen. We'll cope. How far gone are you? What about the father? Is he around? Are you still seeing him?'

Carol shook her head, choking on her sobs.

Jackie watched the scene unfold, her insides turning to liquid. Her heart hammered in her chest and her head felt like it was going to explode.

'So he dumped you when you told him? Is that it? Well – the little swine!' Mam looked across at Dad. 'He can't get away with this. You need to get out there and sort this lad out, Joe, whoever he is.'

'Well that's the problem. We *know* who he is, but…' Dad looked at Jackie, who got to her feet, her colour draining.

She shook her head slowly. 'No!' She wagged a finger at them. 'Not Sandy. You're a liar, Carol. He hasn't been near you since March. There's no way you can blame him. You're just out to make trouble for us because you're jealous.'

Carol stood up and took off her coat. The jeans she wore with her loose top were partly unzipped and fastened with a thick elastic band looped around the button.

'I'm five months, Jackie. It is Alex's baby, I'm afraid. There hasn't been anyone else since we split up.'

Jackie launched herself at her sister and their dad caught hold of her and held her close as her heartbroken sobs and screams filled the room. She yelled at the top of her voice: 'You're lying. There's no way that's his baby. He would never take chances. He loves *me*. We're getting engaged.'

She ranted on and on, and then, because there was nothing to lose now, and everything to fight for: 'We've been away together this weekend. Yeah, that's right, Mam, Dad,' she said as they both stared at her, mouths open with shock. 'We spent it in the same chalet. That's when he proposed. We've made plans for our future. He'll be famous one day with his paintings; and *me*, well I'm going for a career on stage, and we'll travel the world with our work. And *you*, you think you can come along and ruin everything we've planned by lying that you're expecting his baby. I hate you.' She pulled away from her dad and made for the door.

'Whoa, young lady, get back here,' Mam ordered, her face white. 'You've lied to me about the weekend. Jackie, I trusted you, and Agnes trusted Patsy. I suppose Sandy's mate was there too, was he? So the pair of you spent the weekend with the lads when you were supposed to be together. Well I don't know what Agnes is going to say when I tell her about this, I really don't.'

'No, Mam, you can't tell Agnes. That's not fair. I only said it because I'm so angry at *her* trying to cause trouble for me and Sandy.' She couldn't even say her sister's name; it would stick in her throat.

'So you didn't spend the weekend with them?' Mam looked confused.

'We did,' Jackie confirmed. 'But I wouldn't have said anything if I hadn't been trying to make *her* tell the truth. That she's *not* expecting Sandy's baby.'

'I *am*.' Carol stood her ground, defiance written all over her face. 'And because of your precious boyfriend I have nowhere to live, and Ivy and Dad have fallen out too.' She made for the door, muttering that she needed the toilet.

Jackie turned to her parents, tears still running down her cheeks. 'She's lying. I know she is. Mam, I'm sorry for what I did this weekend in not being honest with you, but I know for a fact that Sandy wouldn't have taken any chances with her. He just wouldn't, trust me.'

'Trust you?' Mam snorted. 'It'll be a long time before I trust you again, madam. And lads are lads. I know what they're like.

He's obviously slipped up. That belly of hers is easily five months gone and she was with him for a long time before he started seeing you. Think how she's felt on her own, trying to cope with this and keeping it from your dad and Ivy. Stop thinking about yourself.'

Dad nodded his agreement. 'We've only just found out ourselves. She had an accident on her way to work this week. Ended up at Fazakerley hospital. Her friend brought her home and between them they told Ivy. She hit the bloody roof, threw Carol out and she's been sleeping on her mate's mam's sofa for the last few nights. She won't come back home while Ivy's there. Me and Ivy have had a great big row. I told her a few home truths and that I want a divorce and in retaliation she's accused me of having an affair with you, Dora. It's all a right bloody mess.' He sat back and sighed heavily.

Jackie sat down on the hearth rug, sobs still racking her body. She needed to see Sandy, to warn him what was going on. He would be back home by now, surely.

'Where does this lad live?' Dad asked. 'I think we need to get him and his parents round here for a bit of a discussion, like.'

'Why?' Jackie looked up from under her fringe as Carol came back into the room and sat down next to Mam, who put an arm around her shoulders. She didn't look as pale as she'd done earlier; there was a steely glint in her eyes and Jackie didn't like the look of it. 'What's the point? There's nothing to discuss. Sandy's *my* boyfriend and he's going to marry me in a year or two.'

They all ignored her and started talking to each other like she didn't exist. Jackie got to her feet.

'Back in a minute,' she muttered and slipped out of the house. She took a deep breath and started running down the avenue and onto Longmoor Lane, fury at her sister carrying her along. Just as her lungs felt like they were about to burst the familiar sound of a scooter engine came towards her. She stopped as Sandy pulled up, killed the engine and leapt off. She collapsed into his arms.

'What's wrong? Jackie, babe, what is it?' he asked as she sobbed and clung to him. 'Is it your mam? Does she know about the weekend? Is she mad? Shit!'

'Yeeees,' she cried and clung to him. 'She knows.'

'Don't worry. We'll choose a ring as soon as I get paid for the painting and that will show her we're serious about each other. I love you so much.'

'Love you too,' she sobbed. 'But it's not just that. Something else has happened. Something awful. Take me home and sort it out, please. I can't bear it.'

'Okay. Jump on. Nothing can be that bad, surely? Hold tight.'

❁

Carol listened to her parents talking and just let them get on with it. If anything good was coming out of this mess it was that they seemed united in their efforts to help her and that was no bad thing. Dad still loved her mam and they should be together. He had an arm around Mam's shoulders and she wasn't pushing him away. Jackie had been ages upstairs but she was probably in her bedroom, crying. Well, she wasn't the only one who'd cried into her pillow. *She'd* done it for weeks after Alex dumped her. Her dad got to his feet and picked up his car keys.

'Back in a bit,' he said and went into the hall. 'Dora, front door's wide open.'

Mam got to her feet and hurried out of the room. 'Jackie,' she yelled up the stairs. No reply. 'Bloody hell, she must have gone out. Probably gone to find Sandy.'

She stood on the doorstep and looked up and down the avenue but the only sign of life was the twitching net curtain across the road.

'What shall I do then? Look for our Jackie or go and see Sandy's parents?'

'I don't know,' Mam said as the sound of an engine turned into the avenue and Sandy's red scooter, with Jackie on the pillion seat, clinging to him, came into view. 'Here they are. Better get this over with. Maybe he can ask his parents to come here after we've spoken to him.'

'Aye, go back inside and prepare our Carol.'

Carol looked up as her mam came back in the room.

'Our Jackie had gone out. She's back now and she's got Sandy with her. Are you okay about this, love? Now, you are sure it's his baby? While there are just us two here, tell me the truth.'

'Mam, of course it's his. I don't sleep around.'

'No, of course you don't, chuck. But I had to ask, you do understand? This is going to break our Jackie's heart.'

Carol sighed. Jackie and Alex came in holding hands, followed by Dad, shaking his head as though not having a clue what to say or do. Alex did a double take when he saw her and she guessed that Jackie hadn't had a chance to say anything to him yet.

'Sit down, Sandy,' Mam ordered, pointing to the chair in the bay.

He did as he was told, Jackie sitting on the floor beside him, her arm lying possessively across his knees. His hand reached out to touch her hair, a puzzled look on his face. She leant against him and smiled. That one action of his made Carol harden herself to what she must say and do. A loving action, done without thought, just naturally. Her stomach tightened with jealousy and she clenched her hands into fists. Her baby did a little wriggle, reminding her that *it* was there, too. She took a deep breath as Dad took up position in front of the fireplace and cleared his throat. Mam, seated next to her on the sofa, patted her hand reassuringly.

'Right, young man, we have a few things to discuss,' Dad began. 'First things first, I believe you and our Jacqueline have spent the weekend together?'

Carol saw Jackie squeeze Alex's knee as he answered. His cheeks bright red, he stumbled over his words.

'Er, yes, we did, er, sir.'

'No need for the sir, Joe will do,' Dad continued, putting on his best stern voice. 'So, getting girls to lie to their mothers about whom they're away with doesn't bother you?'

Sandy chewed his lip before replying. 'I'm really sorry for the deception. I love Jackie and she loves me. We just wanted to be together. It was a special time for us and I, er, I've asked her to marry me. I've sold a painting. The money I made is for an engagement ring.'

Carol frowned. Did he mean he'd sold that fruit painting? And then it dawned on her. *A special time*. The forbidden fruit had been her underage sister and now she wasn't, and looking at the pair, they'd obviously made the most of their few nights away together.

'Well, son, I'm sorry to be the one to burst your bubble, but it'll not be our Jackie you'll be marrying.' He looked at Carol. 'Stand up a minute, chuck. I think you should be the one to tell him.'

Carol rose to her feet and stood in front of him. As he stared up at her and it dawned on him, she would never forget the way his jaw dropped or the look of horror on his face.

'I think that speaks for itself, don't you?' Dad said.

'What? You think that's *mine*?' He pointed to her belly. 'Is this some sort of sick joke, Caz? We split up months ago. *How* can it be mine?'

'No joke, Alex,' Carol replied, sitting down again. 'It's due early December. I think even *you* can work out that it's yours.'

'You know that's impossible. I was always careful. You know my feelings on that score.' He sat back on the chair, his face mutinous. 'You must have slept with someone else. There's no way you're blaming this on me.'

'I said it wouldn't be yours,' Jackie said, grabbing his hand. 'She's doing this to split us up. She's a jealous bitch.'

'Jackie,' Mam said, 'watch your language.'

Carol shook her head. '*Why* am I jealous? He's not worth it. He cheated on me with you. He got me pregnant and doesn't want to know, and he's made *you* lie to Mam about going away. Quite a catch, Jackie, isn't he? I bet his vicar dad will have something to say when our dad goes round to theirs and tells them.'

Alex stared at her, hatred gleaming in his eyes. As if he could see his shiny happy future sailing off up the Swanee. *Serves him right for being so cocky*, she thought.

'There's no need to go to my parents' place. I'll go home and ask them to come back here with me. I've nothing to hide. That baby isn't mine and I'm not taking the blame for it.'

He got to his feet and Jackie saw him out. Carol watched her kiss him goodbye through the window and then glared at her sister as Jackie curled up on the armchair while Mam rushed around collecting pots and taking them into the kitchen.

'Well,' Dad said, lighting a cigarette. 'This is a pretty kettle of fish. He's determined not to take responsibility. Are you sure it's his, Carol?'

'Dad, of course I'm sure. What do you take me for?'

'Now there's a question,' Jackie said, scowling. 'I'll never forgive you for this, Carol. Never. You saw how upset and shocked he was. Not in the least bit guilty. He knows you're lying. I hate you and I hope that baby's got two heads.'

'Jackie,' Mam said, coming back into the room, wiping her hands on a tea towel. 'Don't say things like that. If it *is* Sandy's then he'll have to do the decent thing by our Carol.'

Jackie jumped to her feet. 'What? Marry her, you mean? Not a chance. He hates her. You can see it in his face. Anyway, why should he when we all know she's lying?'

Carol could feel herself building up to telling them she could prove the baby was Alex's and why. But not unless she had to use that ace would she deal it. *Keep calm*, she told herself inwardly.

'I'll make some fresh tea,' Mam said. 'It always helps in a crisis. Jackie, dash round to Agnes's and ask if she's got a bit of cake to spare. A Swiss roll or something. Be quick as you can. And don't stop to gossip about this.'

❀

Dora stood with her back against the sink unit waiting for the kettle to boil. She couldn't believe the events of the last half hour. But then the whole week had been unreal. Not only was she probably the richest woman in The Avenues – although she didn't feel able to tell anyone about it just yet – she was also not far off becoming a grandmother. How could her life get tipped so upside down in just a few days?

Thank God Joe was here. She didn't have the energy to deal with all this upset on her own. She felt moved that he'd stood up for Carol and told Ivy he wanted a divorce. But would he really go through with it? Half of her hoped he would, while the other half wondered what it would mean for them if he were free. Could they make things work again? Could she trust him? They'd got much closer since Jackie's birthday party; he'd been calling round every Sunday for an hour or two to discuss their daughter's future. But was it enough to go forward? She shook her head. She was jumping the gun a bit here. He'd probably decide to take the easiest option – to go home and make things up with Ivy. And then there was poor Jackie. Although she was angry with her youngest for lying to her about the holiday, her daughter must be feeling heartbroken; much like she had felt herself when she'd learned of Joe's betrayal and Ivy's so-called pregnancy.

'It never rains,' she muttered as she poured boiling water into the brown teapot, gave the leaves a stir and popped the knitted cosy on to keep the tea hot. And where could she put Carol? She'd need looking after but there was no room here really for her and a baby. The small spare room was full to the brim with her sewing paraphernalia and Jackie certainly wouldn't want to be sharing *her* room with her sister. No doubt Ivy wouldn't want Carol back under her roof now that Joe had given her what for either, not unless he returned cap-in-hand to apologise, and Dora hoped he wouldn't do that. And what if Sandy denied it was his child and refused to marry Carol? Then what would they do? Her hands shook as she got the best cups and saucers out of the cupboard and placed them on a tray. She could afford to buy a bigger house with Sammy's inheritance, but Jackie still wouldn't want to live under the same roof as Carol, she was sure of that. What a bloody mess.

She sighed and went back into the sitting room to join Joe and Carol, who was still crying. She sat down beside her and took her in her arms, wearily shaking her head at Joe above their daughter's head.

❀

Jackie shot out of the house and ran round to Second Avenue. Patsy's dad was in the front garden and he told her to go straight in. Patsy was standing in the hall, combing her hair in front of the mirror.

'Can we go to your room, quick?' Jackie gasped.

Patsy nodded and led the way. 'What's happened?' she asked as Jackie collapsed onto the bed and burst into tears. Between sobs and gulps of air she explained the situation, including that Mam knew about the boys and the holiday.

'She's too mithered about Carol to be bothered coming telling your mam at the moment. But at least you know now.'

'Don't worry. Sounds like you've all got enough on your plates. I'll soft-soap Mam if I have to. But oh my God, Carol gets herself up the duff and tries to blame Sandy? What a cow she is. You must be feeling so gutted as well as angry. What will his parents say? Shit, and he's the vicar's son too. The gossips will have a field day.'

'I know. I need to get back. Mam sent me to borrow a cake. Is *your* mam in?'

'No, she's visiting her sister, you know, the one whose daughter lives in London now, my cousin Janet. But come on down to the kitchen and I'll see what I can find.'

Patsy rooted in the kitchen cupboards and produced a chocolate Swiss roll. 'Here, that'll do. Bet nobody will feel like eating cake but I know what mams are like for having stuff in. Net curtain Nelly will have a field day when the vicar and his wife turn up in their big car.'

Jackie nodded. 'I feel sick. After the fabulous time we've had, to be hit by this as soon as I get home. It was so special for me and Sandy too.'

'I know.' Patsy hugged her. 'Sandy loves you. And like you say, how can it be his baby if he's taken no chances with her? She's lying, you'll see. Go on, get back and stand your ground. Fight for him. I'll see you tomorrow. Come over as soon as you can.'

Jackie hurried back to Fourth Avenue and arrived at the same time as Sandy and his parents pulled up in their shiny black Humber saloon. They got out and greeted her, Mrs Faraday, neatly attired in a tweed skirt and jacket, and the vicar with his dog collar, looking more suitably dressed for church business than an informal meeting with his parishioners.

Sandy wrapped his arms around Jackie and kissed her. His dad coughed with embarrassment and turned to listen to something Sandy's mum was saying.

'Have you told them?' Jackie whispered.

'No,' he whispered back. 'They haven't a clue. They just wonder what's going on and what the urgency is.'

'Your mum looks really worried.'

He nodded. 'So does my old fella.'

'We'd best go in then. I love you.'

'I love you too. I can't believe this is happening.' He squeezed her hand and she led them inside, into the hall.

'Mam, Sandy's parents are here,' Jackie called, taking the chocolate Swiss roll through to the kitchen.

Mam came out of the sitting room, looking anxious. 'Oh, please come through to the lounge, Mrs Faraday, Vicar.' She stood back so they could squeeze past her.

Jackie frowned. Lounge? Mam was going posh all of a sudden. Sandy's parents weren't royalty. They were dead friendly and normal. Not that it mattered when you considered what a bombshell Carol was going to chuck at them.

She pulled Sandy in with her and they sat down on the floor, their backs against the large chest of drawers. He held her hand tightly as Carol, who was sitting at the end of the sofa, glared at them. Mam invited the vicar to take the chair under the window and Mrs Faraday sat down at the other end of the sofa while Mam perched awkwardly in the middle. Dad, as before, stood in front of the fireplace, looking decidedly uncomfortable.

'So, is someone kindly going to tell us what's going on?' Mrs Faraday began. 'Sandy hurried us over here, saying it was urgent. Has there been a death in the family, Dora?'

'Oh, no, no, nothing like that,' Mam said, her face flushing. 'Joe, would you like to explain?'

Carol got to her feet, her face pale, but her expression determined. 'No need. It's my problem, I'll tell them.'

Mrs Faraday's eyes narrowly raked Carol up and down and her lips formed a thin line. 'And you are, young lady?'

'Me, oh I'm Carol, Dora's eldest daughter, and Jackie's sister. I'm also your son's ex- girlfriend.'

'I see.' Mrs Faraday frowned.

'Yes,' Carol continued. 'And *this*,' she placed her hands protectively over her swollen belly. 'This is your son's baby, but he's denying responsibility, because he thinks he's in love with my sister.'

Carol stopped, all bravado gone, and burst into tears. She sat down again and Mam put her arms around her and held her.

'Sandy, is this true?' the vicar roared, turning to look at his son.

'She *is* my ex, yes, that much is true, but it's not my kid,' Sandy said, his expression stony.

'Why is the young lady accusing *you* if you're so certain you're not responsible?' his father asked.

'She's lying,' Jackie piped up, her lips trembling. 'She's jealous and wants to split us up.'

'Jackie be quiet, love,' Dad said. 'You're not helping. There's no reason why Carol should lie about this. She could have kept quiet and let us believe she doesn't know who the father is.'

Carol looked up. 'Alex *is* the father. I can tell you the exact day and date this baby was conceived. It was the Friday before your party here, Jackie; the day before he and I split up. If you work it out there's no way it can be anyone else's. And Alex knows that.'

'Is this true, Sandy? You had, er, intimate relations with this young lady on the date she says?'

Sandy hung his head and nodded.

His father took a deep breath. 'So this baby *could* be yours?'

'I took precautions, Dad. I was careful, I always am.'

Jackie nodded. 'He is. I can vouch for that.'

His mum whimpered and her colour drained. 'Oh, Sandy!' She shook her head wearily.

'Not careful enough, it would seem,' the vicar said. 'Well, this *is* a mess.' He mopped his brow with a large white hanky and shook his head. 'What are we going to do about it?'

'I'll bring the tea through.' Mam got to her feet and nodded at Dad, who took his cigarettes from his pocket. She left the room as he gestured with the packet to Sandy, who shook his head, and the vicar, who took one.

'I've given up,' the vicar said. 'But this situation calls for something.'

'I'd offer you a drink but there's no alcohol in the house,' Dad said.

'Tea will be fine.'

The silence was deafening as they waited for Mam to return with the tray of mugs and sliced cake.

'So, what are we going to do about this situation?' the vicar asked again. 'I mean, are there any plans in place for the future of the child?' He looked at Carol. 'There are many couples waiting to adopt. We may be able to arrange something privately through the church. Then we can keep this amongst ourselves. I'm sure you'll all agree that would be for the best all round.'

Carol looked horrified at the suggestion. 'No. This is *my* baby. I'm not giving it away to strangers.'

'It might be for the best, chuck,' Dad said. 'You're too young to be saddled with a kiddy.'

'Well Sandy *certainly* is,' Mrs Faraday said, finding her voice. 'He's a student. He's not even working yet. He's only eighteen. You *knew* that,' she snapped at Carol. 'You shouldn't have let this happen. You stupid, irresponsible girl.'

Carol flushed redder than the velvet curtains in the bay window. 'I *didn't* let it happen. I trusted him to be careful.'

'And I *was*,' Sandy protested. 'So *how* can it be mine?'

'We're just going around in circles here.' Joe took charge. 'The point is, no matter *who's* to blame, my daughter is pregnant and in four months that baby will be here. She's managed alone for the last five, trying not to upset anyone, and now she can't manage any longer. She doesn't want to have her baby adopted. I'm putting my house up for sale due to my marriage problems and Carol won't come home until it's all sorted out. Dora doesn't have the room here for Carol *and* a baby in the long term, and she can't sleep on the sofa at her friend's for much longer. No matter what your son says, that baby could well be your grandchild,' he directed at the vicar and his wife. 'It's certainly ours and we need to pull together here.

'Dora will accompany Carol to the doctor's for her appointment next week and she'll get it in writing when the baby is due, or thereabouts. Your lad was seeing Carol for a good few months before they split up. He broke it off with her because he started seeing our Jackie here. And I hope to God he's been careful with her, because I'll kill him if he's not.'

'Dad,' Jackie gasped. 'How could you embarrass us like that?'

'Oh, I think you do a good enough job of that on your own,' her dad replied. He turned to Sandy's mum. 'Are you aware he's just spent the weekend with Jackie at a holiday camp behind her mother's back? Your lad's not as white as you seem to think he is, madam. And for the wife of a vicar it's time you took him in hand.'

Sandy's mother pursed her lips and rounded on her husband. 'I told you not to take a position in Liverpool, didn't I? All that stuff I read in the papers about those scruffy groups and their wild ways and how it would influence our boys. *Now* look what's happened. This is all *your* fault, Arthur.'

The vicar shook his head. 'I think we should go home. We need to talk with our son privately. This is getting us nowhere. I can only apologise for your daughter's plight. But surely you can see there's little Sandy can do to help. He's just a student. I feel the best option is to have the child adopted and then we can all put this unfortunate episode behind us.' He got to his feet and helped his distraught wife up.

Sandy also got to his feet. 'There's nothing to talk about.' He turned to Carol. 'I don't know what you expect of me. Until you can prove that's my baby, Caz, I want nothing to do with it.' He looked at his parents. 'I'll have a lift back with you and then I'm going to stay with Stevie.'

Jackie jumped up and grabbed his hand. 'What about me?'

Sandy pulled her to the door and outside. 'I'm so sorry about this. I don't see how I can prove one way or the other that it isn't mine. I guess blood tests are the answer once it's born. I just don't know.' He ran his hands through his hair, his eyes moist. 'Oh God, Jackie, what a fucking mess.'

Sandy hardly ever used the f-word, which Jackie put down to him being a vicar's son. He must be feeling really in despair right now and she didn't know what to say or do that would help him. 'Are you definitely going to stay at Stevie's?'

He nodded. 'I'll go home with them first and get my clothes and scooter, and then I'm off. You know where he lives. If you still want to see me, come down to Scottie Road.'

'Of course I want to see you. I'm just so scared they'll make you marry our Carol or something.'

He raised his hands in a gesture of hopelessness. 'How? I have no job; the only money I've got is my allowance and Jacaranda wages and the money from the painting when I get it. I can't keep myself at the moment, never mind a wife and kid.' He pulled her close. 'And I love *you*. I don't want to marry Caz, baby or no baby.'

'But what if it *is* yours?'

He shrugged. 'God knows what I'll do. Like my dad suggested, it would be better to get it adopted.' He turned as his parents came out onto the street.

His mother, tight-lipped, her face an angry shade of red, marched to the car and waited while his father opened the door and helped her in.

'Sandy, in the car, now,' he demanded.

Sandy raised his eyebrows, pecked Jackie on the cheek and walked to the car. He turned and half-smiled, mouthed 'I love you' and climbed onto the back seat. As the car pulled away he blew her a kiss and waved; his expression was one of sorrow. Jackie felt her stomach lurch and an overwhelming feeling of sadness enveloped her; things would never be the same again.

Back indoors Carol was sobbing in Mam's arms and Dad sat slumped in the armchair, staring at the ceiling. He looked up as Jackie walked in the room.

'I don't want you to see that lad again,' he began and lit a cigarette, blowing a cloud of smoke into the air.

Jackie looked at him, her mouth open. 'Dad, that's not fair. He's my boyfriend, he's done nothing wrong.'

'Nothing wrong!' He stared at her, his expression weary. 'He's got your sister into trouble. I mean it, Jackie. You're not to see him again. He's a bad lot. If he had an ounce of decency in him he'd offer to marry Carol, or at least support her and admit to what he's done.'

'Yeah, according to *her*,' Jackie spat. 'I'd rather believe Sandy than Carol. I knew she'd do something to split us up. She's been planning this all along.'

'Don't be stupid,' Mam said. 'If she'd been planning anything, she'd have told us before now. She's had months of carrying this baby and kept her mouth shut. Anyway, that's it now. Like your dad says, you're not to see Sandy again until all this mess is sorted out. And don't think you can go sneaking off behind my back again, because I'll be watching you, lady,' she called as Jackie ran out of the room.

⚜

Joe stared after Jackie as she stomped away. He shook his head as he heard her thumping up the stairs. Dora raised her eyebrows in his direction.

'We need to sort out some accommodation for Carol,' he began. 'I can go to my old mate Don's for a few nights and then I'll look for a flat to rent until I get the house sold.'

Dora nodded. 'Ivy should move out and let you and Carol move back in. You own the house, Joe, it's not right.'

'Aye, I know that. But it'll take time, Dora. I'll go back later and see what's what.'

'Okay, well Carol can stop here tonight. You'll have to sleep on the sofa until we get sorted out, chuck.'

Carol smiled through her tears. 'Thanks, Mam. I don't think Jackie will be too happy about that though.'

Chapter Eighteen

Sandy hadn't got around to unpacking his holdall, so he just shoved a few clean items in and zipped it back up. He slung it in the hall near the front door and walked into the sitting room, where his mum, her face drained of colour, was sitting on the sofa, nursing a schooner of sherry. His old fella, slumped low in an armchair by the window, red spots high on his cheeks, clutched a glass of whisky, looking furious. His pale-faced mum had tearstains on her cheeks and her lips trembled as she attempted to sip her drink. His dad knocked his whisky back and banged the glass down on the coffee table. Sandy felt angry that they assumed he'd let them down. All right, sleeping with sisters maybe wasn't the best conduct for a vicar's son, especially when they were the daughters of a parishioner, but that aside, he genuinely hadn't linked the pair.

'Sit down,' his dad ordered, pointing to the other armchair.

Sandy knew he couldn't get away before his dad had read him the riot act, so he plonked himself down on the chair nearest the door. His scooter keys were on the side table and he reached for them and pushed them into his parka pocket; just in case his old fella had any ideas about trying to keep him here by removing his only form of transport.

'Well, I really don't know what to say to you, Alexander, other than that your mother and I are very disappointed.'

'Sorry, Dad, Mum.' His old fella never used his full name. 'I don't know what to say either. But I'm standing my ground here. Unless Caz can prove otherwise, that baby is *not* mine.'

'Then I think all we can do is wait until the birth of the child, ask for blood tests and take it from there. But I don't think you should have any more to do with either sister until we know for sure.'

Sandy nodded his agreement, although there was no way he wasn't seeing Jackie – as long as she still wanted *him* after this fiasco. She'd be starting college next week and he'd hopefully see her around town.

'I also think you should stay away from church and the hall while this mess is sorted one way or the other. You know how those women love to gossip. Your poor mother will have to make excuses about Jackie leaving St Paul's Players. It's a shame, because I know she really enjoys working with them, but as I'm sure you can imagine, it won't be possible for her to continue to be part of the group once the rumours about the father of her sister's child begin to manifest. I can't for one minute see that young lady, Carol, keeping anything to herself now that her family is aware of her predicament. It's going to be a very embarrassing time for your mother and she doesn't deserve it. After everything she's done for you too. It was her idea to allow you to go to art college when I would have preferred you to do something more academic, like your brother. Roger is a credit to this family.'

Sandy gritted his teeth. Dad was playing the prodigal son card again. He felt bad for his mum, but he wasn't backing down at this stage. He got to his feet.

'I'm off. I'll be in touch soon. Hope things don't get too bad, Mum. Just ignore the old biddies, you're better than them.'

'Yes, she is,' his dad agreed. 'But *they're* not the ones with the wayward son. Now go, take care and have a good think about what I've said. If you have any thoughts about doing the right thing by that girl, call us. I don't mean marrying her, as that would be a recipe for disaster at this stage, but at least owning up to fathering the child.'

'Yeah, okay,' Sandy said as he picked up his holdall and left the flat.

❀

Stevie shook his head in disbelief as Sandy poured out his story over coffee at the little table in the kitchen of the flat on Scotland Road.

'Shit, mate. Don't know what to say. And after we've all had such a fabulous weekend too.' He handed over the remains of the ciggie he'd been smoking as Sandy arrived. 'Finish it. You look like you need it more than me.'

'Thanks.' Sandy took a drag and inhaled deeply.

'How the fuck are you gonna get out of this mess?' Stevie said. 'And what about Jackie? She must be so upset.'

'She is. Heartbroken.' Sandy took a final drag and stubbed the end of the ciggie out on the old saucer ashtray. 'But what can I do? Caz is adamant it's my kid. I'm damn sure it's not. I never have sex without using a rubber. Must have been a faulty one or something. Just my fucking luck.'

Sandy sighed and ran his hands through his hair, leaving it standing on end. 'Is it okay if I stay here for a while? My dad wants me out of the way. I'll get a few more hours at the Jac and do some paintings. The gallery said they'd take what I can come up with, so at least I'll be on my way to earning a living.'

'Of course, mate. Keep a low profile though. Caz will still be working, I suppose, and you might bump into her.'

'Yep she is. For a few more weeks anyway.'

'And your dad reckons blood tests will prove if it's yours or not?'

'Apparently, when it's born. But she's getting a letter from the doc's this week with the due date and she says we'll be able to work its conception back to the night before I dumped her, or near enough. And I've got to admit, she doesn't sleep around and even if she did, she'd have to have been bloody quick off the mark, like right the next day or that week at the latest.'

'And what if it is yours? Can she get it adopted?'

'Dad suggested that, but she wants to keep it. So if it *is* mine, I'm lumbered for life. And being the good vicar's son that I am, I'll probably have to marry her in time, much as I really don't want to. But if it means my parents can hold their heads up again in the parish, I guess I don't have much choice. I do have *some* morals, for what they're worth.'

❀

Jackie got off the train at Lime Street station and hurried down Roe Street. Sandy was meeting her in Mathew Street outside The Grapes pub. He'd got a message to her via Stevie, who'd called Patsy. They were going back to Stevie's flat for the afternoon. She'd told Mam she had an induction day at college. The induction was on Friday, but she'd worry about an excuse for that when Friday arrived.

As she turned into Mathew Street her heart leapt as she spotted Sandy looking up at a poster on the wall outside The Cavern. She ran towards him, calling his name. He turned, caught her in his arms and swung her round and round, covering her face with kisses. He squeezed her so tight that she squealed.

'Do you want a drink in The Grapes first? Or shall we go back to Stevie's place?'

As she looked into his eyes she saw her own hunger mirrored there and caught her breath.

'Oh sod it,' he said, 'we're going straight back to Stevie's. C'mon.' He grabbed her hand and pulled her along.

She was desperate to be alone with him. It seemed ages since a week last Monday when they'd had their final hours together before leaving the holiday camp, and the nightmare that followed. She'd been dying to get away from the house and Mam and Carol going on about the bloody baby all the time. Turned out the dates the doctor had written down more or less coincided with Carol's last night with Sandy, but it made no difference to how Jackie felt about him and it still didn't really prove anything. He didn't know yet, and she wasn't going to be the one to tell him and ruin their afternoon. Mam had collared his mother at the church hall on Sunday and showed her the letter. But there had been too many people around for them to discuss it properly, and so far the vicar and Mrs Faraday had not taken up Mam's invite of calling round to take the matter further.

Mam and Dad had gone on about him marrying Carol and taking some responsibility. But Carol had said it was up to him. She was determined not to hide the fact that she was carrying his baby, she'd said so in a fit of anger the other night, but she wasn't prepared to chase him. Mam told her to say nothing to anyone yet as it would make her look cheap and people would talk, and it was best to keep her mouth shut until another meeting of both sets of parents could be arranged.

Arms around one another, they rounded the corner onto Scotland Road, windswept and out of breath, and ran up the stairs to the flat. Stevie was out for the afternoon and Sandy switched on the gas fire in the kitchen and offered coffee. Jackie shook her head and peeled off her leather coat and scarf. She dropped them over the back of a chair and looked at him. His eyes met hers and he led her into his bedroom, lowering her onto the mattress. They were in each other's arms, kissing and eagerly tearing off clothes, naked within seconds, caressing and rolling together in desperation. Sandy paused to reach for a rubber; even with senses as heightened as theirs, Jackie trusted him to take care of her. She quickly pushed the thoughts of Caz, and how it could have happened, from her mind and enjoyed their frantic lovemaking. They lay in each other's arms for ages afterwards, loving that feeling of sleepy tenderness and complete fulfilment that engulfed them both.

'Coffee?' he offered again as she stirred.

'Please.' She sat up, flicked her tangled hair over her shoulders and stroked his arm. 'I love you so much, you know.'

He knelt up in front of her and took both her hands in his, his eyes moist.

'You have no idea how much I love *you*, Jackie, and I'm so sorry for the mess I'm in. I'm surprised you haven't told me to get lost. No matter what happens, it's you I love, I always will. Please remember that.'

❀

With Bob Dylan's *Blonde on Blonde* playing in the background, Sandy flung a handful of red paint at the canvas and ran his fingers through it, creating swirling waves down the centre. He had no idea what he was painting, but getting the anger out of his system on canvas helped him calm down.

He could see his life mapped out in front of him and it wasn't the life he'd planned. He wished he'd never met Caz. She'd chased him, pursued him, until he'd finally asked her out. A one-night stand had developed into something that he'd begun to regret almost as soon as it started. She was always there, needy; wherever he went with his mates she'd turn up, and even if he was talking to another girl she'd make sure they got the message that she was his girlfriend. It was his own fault for not dumping her sooner, or at least making it clear to her that they were not in a serious relationship. They had so little in common and the thought of spending the rest of his life saddled with her and a kid he didn't even want filled him with horror.

His parents had been strict to a point and he'd been brought up to always do the right thing, no matter what. If marrying Caz and giving his child a name was the right thing, then he didn't think he had a choice. He felt sure his parents would eventually insist, even if just to save face for themselves. But for now his life was on hold until the blood tests had been carried out.

On their way to Lime Street earlier, Jackie had told him that she wanted to continue seeing him for as long as possible, until they knew the truth. They both realised they were grasping at straws and the chances of them being together forever were slim, but it was all they had for now and neither wanted to let go.

❀

Jackie dragged her feet on the walk back from Fazakerley station. She decided to call at Patsy's house as she couldn't face going home just yet. Her friend led the way upstairs and Jackie collapsed onto the bed and burst into tears.

Patsy put an arm around her shoulders. 'You saw him then?'

'Yes,' Jackie sobbed. 'And I have a horrible feeling it was the last time we'll be together. I don't know what to do. I love him so much. I can't bear to be around Carol any more. Now she's got the letter from the doctor she's so bloody smug. The blood tests could still prove he didn't father the baby, but it's looking very likely that he did.'

'Did you tell him about the letter and the dates they'd confirmed?'

'No. I didn't want to spoil our afternoon.'

'Oh, Jackie. I feel so helpless that there's nothing I can do for you.'

'You can.'

'What?' Patsy frowned.

Jackie fished a tissue from up her sleeve and wiped her eyes, smudging her mascara in the process.

'If Sandy marries Carol I can't stay around here. I'm going to London. I've got the money Dad gave me for college and when I'm there I'll get a job and join another theatre group or something. And I'm not coming back to Liverpool.'

'But you can't do that. You're too young and your mam would never allow it.'

'She won't have a choice because I won't tell her. I'll run away.' Jackie stuck out her chin in a determined manner. 'What

I need from you is a contact. Your cousin Janet lives and works in London, doesn't she? You said she did the other week when I came to borrow cake.'

'Yes.' Patsy nodded. 'She works on a cosmetics counter in Selfridges. I'm not sure which one, but I can ask Mam. I won't say why I want to know; I'll ask casually, like. Janet flat-shares with a girl she works with. She might be able to help you or show you where to get help. I'll miss you like crazy and I don't think you should go. But if it's what you want then I'll do what I can and I'll keep it to myself. But for God's sake be careful. It's a scary world out there on your own.'

'I don't really want to go. But I can't stay here. I just can't. And you must promise that you won't tell Stevie. Sandy mustn't know where I've gone. He'll have enough on his plate, marrying my bitch of a sister.'

❀

Joe took Dora's arm as they walked up the avenue towards Longmoor Lane. Dora had told him she needed to talk to him, but with Carol upstairs and Jackie dozing fitfully on the sofa, there was no privacy in the house. Agnes said they could have her dining room for the evening as she was busy upstairs and Patsy was out with her boyfriend. Alan was at work at Speke airport, so it was the nearest to a private place they could hope for. Ivy was still in residence at Joe's house and she'd told him she would remain there until she could find somewhere else to live.

Agnes welcomed them inside, made them a mug of coffee each, showed them into the dining room and closed the door, leaving them to it. As Joe looked expectantly at her, Dora took two envelopes from her handbag and laid them on the table. She pushed them towards Joe and told him to look at the larger one with the letter enclosed first.

She sat silently while he took in the contents of Sammy's letter. He looked at her, shock, sadness and surprise on his face. He shook his head.

'I'm so sorry, chuck. I know how much you all loved him. But what he's done here – well – I don't know what to say. Blimey, Dora, fancy him making you sole beneficiary.'

Dora nodded. 'That's how I felt when I was sat in front of the solicitor. I wanted to tell you, but what with all the upset with the girls we've had, it didn't seem the right time.' She nodded at the other envelope. Although he knew now that she had an inheritance, he wasn't aware of just how much yet. 'Look at it.' In the envelope was a bank book with the details of the amount of money now sitting in her account.

She smiled as his face blanched. 'Bloody hell, gel! Three thousand guineas!'

'And there's more to come,' she told him. 'That's what the solicitor said was an interim payment.'

'But Christ, three thousand, one hundred and fifty pounds. Bloody Nora! It's a fortune. What are your plans? Are you going to give up your cleaning job?'

'Eventually. But if I do that right now people might get wind of why and I want to keep this between ourselves, Joe, until I feel ready to share it. What I'd really like to do is help our Carol a bit and make sure Jackie has all the help she needs with her drama course and future.' She stopped and chewed her lip as Joe looked at her. 'And then, well, maybe buy a family house of our own. Somewhere nice with a garden for our grandchild to play in.'

Joe smiled and took her hand. 'With a bay window?'

She smacked his arm. 'Oi you, stop teasing! But yes, you know how much I love my bay windows. What do you think?'

Joe stared at her with longing in his eyes. 'I think it sounds wonderful. I'm sure you'll all be very happy.'

'And you too, Joe. I'm including you in my family plans. If it hadn't been for Ivy and her lies, we'd have been together again all this time. I've enjoyed you being with us and coming over and helping to support me with the girls. Unless of course you have other plans for when you sell your own house?'

Joe took a deep breath. 'Are you saying what I think you're saying, Dora? You want to give us another chance? I can't believe it,' he finished as she nodded her head, a big smile lighting up her face.

'Yes,' she replied. 'I think we need a stable family life for the girls. Seeing how Jackie has forgiven Sandy has made me realise that I can forgive you too. Carol is going to need us more than ever now as well. And, well, I love you, Joe.'

Joe's eyes filled. 'I'd resigned myself to us just being pals for the future. But I've never stopped loving you, you know that. I'll pool my money from the sale of my house with yours, after I've paid *her* off. I begrudge giving her even a penny, but she's entitled to something, apparently.' He took Dora in his arms and she melted into him. It felt good to hold her close. 'We'll enjoy the time we've got left and make the most of each day from now on. It can only get better.'

❀

Ivy pushed the last of her clothes into her holdall and zipped it up. She sat down on the bed she'd shared with Joe. He was out and wouldn't come back until later. No doubt over at Dora's with that wastrel of a pregnant daughter and the one with ideas above her station. Well he needn't think he'd get away lightly. She'd done her best, fetching and carrying for him and Carol and looking after both the girls at the weekend when he'd had them to stay over. They'd been hard work and all Joe's attention had been on them and not her. She deserved a medal for all that she'd put up with during their marriage. She'd always known deep down he'd go back to Dora. He'd never been happy since the day they married. She was surprised really that he'd stuck it out with her for as long as he had. He'd harboured that secret about her never being pregnant all this time and just needed the right time to chuck it in her face.

She was going to stay with her old pal Flo for a few weeks until Joe gave her any monies that were due to her. She'd already put her name on the council waiting list for a flat, telling them she was being made homeless through no fault of her own and that her husband had left her for another woman. They didn't need to know who or why, it was her business only. She'd need to look for a little job again once she got herself sorted out. Perhaps a nice bakery shop where she could get involved with making bread and cakes. At least it would get her out and about and she would meet new people. She took a last look around the bedroom, placed her keys on the bedside table and slowly made her way down the stairs, dragging her holdall behind her.

Chapter Nineteen

October 1966

On Wednesday morning, the house empty, her mam, dad and Carol already having left for work half an hour earlier, Jackie sat on her bed and looked around to make sure she'd left nothing unpacked. Her small case, with a few changes of clothes and toiletries, was hidden in the garden shed. The envelope of money her dad had given her was safely stashed away in her handbag, along with a book for the train journey and Patsy's cousin's contact details. With Carol's marriage plans to Sandy now well under way, Jackie's need to get away was overwhelming.

She hurried downstairs and went out to the shed to collect her case. To avoid being spotted by net curtain Nellie across the street, she dashed down the passage at the back of Fourth Avenue and out onto Longmoor Lane, just in time to catch a bus into Liverpool centre. At Lime Street station she purchased a one-way ticket to London and made her way to the platform to wait for the train.

❀

Standing outside Euston station, Jackie stared at the piece of paper with Janet's details from Patsy. Janet, who had been sworn to secrecy by her cousin, knew Jackie was coming, and had issued instructions to meet her in the Selfridges store at six pm, closing time. She was far too early; it was only just after three. First of all she'd need to locate the store and then find a coffee shop to while away the time. She had the *Lady Chatterley* book in her bag that she hadn't had time to finish, so she could have a read and rest for a bit. Patsy had told her to get a taxi to the store as it wasn't far so wouldn't cost too much, and it was better than getting herself lost. People surged by, pushing their way into the station. It was busier than Lime Street and it wasn't even closing time. She needed to get out of the way and find a taxi. She watched as several people stuck their hands out at approaching taxis that stopped to pick up the fares.

Within minutes she was sitting in the back of a black cab, her small suitcase down by her feet. She told the Cockney driver her destination and he chatted to her in a friendly manner. She responded with polite replies and asked him if there was a place to get a snack near the store.

They pulled up outside the front of Selfridges on Oxford Street in no time. 'There's a restaurant in-store, luv, but if you're after something a bit cheaper you can get a decent coffee and bite to eat in there.'

He pointed to a coffee shop a few doors down as she paid the fare and gave him a tip. She thanked him and clambered out of the vehicle, dragging her case with her.

Inside the little café she ordered a pot of tea and meat pie, chips and gravy from a tall, well-built man who styled his hair like Elvis, and chose a table in the window. The café was quiet; just a few older men reading papers and smoking, mugs of tea on the tables in front of them. It wasn't a fancy place, nothing like she'd thought all coffee shops in London would be, all trendy and what-have-you, but it was clean and homely with red and white gingham tablecloths, the food was good value and the radio played pop music in the background. She felt inconspicuous and that suited her just fine. No one had given her a second glance so far. The owner brought her meal across. He produced a knife and fork, wrapped in a white paper napkin, from his apron pocket and reached across to the table behind her for a plastic caddy containing salt and pepper pots and vinegar and brown sauce bottles.

'Enjoy your meal,' he said as a slim young girl, her dark hair fastened up into a ponytail, brought a tray with tea things and a slice of bread and butter to the table.

'Oh, I didn't order bread.'

'It's complimentary with your pie and chips,' the girl said and smiled as she walked away.

Jackie tucked in. She hadn't realised how starving she was. All she'd had for breakfast was a quick bowl of cornflakes; and then a bag of crisps and chocolate bar on the train to keep her going. She'd been relegated to sleeping on the sofa for the last couple of weeks as Mam had insisted she give up her bed for Carol, who was too uncomfortable on the sofa now she was getting bigger with the baby. Everything they said and did felt like they were rubbing her nose in it, almost like her feelings counted for nothing. Sandy had been round with the vicar and Mrs Faraday and it had been agreed by both sets of parents that he would do the right thing and marry Carol at the end of the month. His father had brought up the adoption subject again but her sister remained adamant that she wouldn't even consider it.

Sandy had managed to get away briefly by going to the bathroom in the hopes he could talk to her. She was supposed to be upstairs, keeping out of the way, but was sitting on the bottom stair straining to hear what was being said behind the closed sitting room door. They'd exchanged a furtive hug and kiss on the landing, where he'd told her he felt devastated by what had happened, that he still loved her, and this wasn't his choice. She told him she knew that, and she still loved him too, but he had to do what he felt was right. And at that point she knew her only option was to run away to London, to get completely out of his life.

Patsy had helped her make arrangements, and with Dad's envelope of money stashed away in her handbag she felt she'd done the right thing. She'd only had a month in college and she'd loved the course work, but hopefully it was something she might be able to continue with down here; maybe at night school, or something. The theatres may have job vacancies, selling tickets or programmes or even ice-creams during the intervals. She could start at the bottom doing anything and work her way up. There were plenty of theatres in London so hopefully she'd find some sort of work soon.

She'd miss her mam. She felt her eyes fill as she thought of her. Mam would miss her too. They'd been a team, the two of them, for such a long time now. She felt jealous that Carol was taking her place. Mam and Dad did nothing but fuss around her, rubbing her feet when she came in from work, putting an extra cushion behind her back, giving her larger portions of food to fill her up now that she was eating for two. Mam had made Carol a whole new wardrobe of maternity dresses after the pair had visited Paddy's market and come home with parcels of fabric. Mam was knitting every night for the baby too, producing pram sets and blankets. She seemed to be in her element. Uncle Frank had brought an almost-new cot round and Mam had scrubbed it and made soft fluffy sheets and a quilt.

Dad said he'd buy the pram when the baby arrived. Mam and he were closer than ever now. Although they couldn't do anything about remarrying yet, Mam said she'd change her name back to Rodgers as soon as his divorce came through, but not before as she still didn't want to share the name with Ivy. They were all busily planning Carol's wedding. Jackie felt like a cuckoo in the nest and the last straw had been when Mam designed a pattern for an empire-line wedding dress and then asked her opinion whether she thought ivory or pale pink would best suit Carol, as it wouldn't be appropriate for her to get married in white. Jackie couldn't give a flying fig what colour Carol got married in and they should all know that, surely. They acted like she and Sandy had meant nothing to each other, as if she'd got over it already.

Getting to London before the wedding next week had been her priority and now here she was. She felt sick when she thought of how upset her parents would feel when they knew she was missing, but there was no going back now. She couldn't bear to see Sandy with her sister. Not that he came round very often, as he was working extra shifts at the Jacaranda and painting like crazy at Stevie's place to get more work hung in the gallery that had sold *Forbidden Fruit*. It made Jackie feel sick to think of him spending that hard-earned money on a wedding ring for Carol, when it should have been for *her* engagement ring.

Sandy was determined to finish his course and one of the conditions laid down by his parents in giving him permission to marry was that Carol should be willing to go back to work after her maternity leave and that Mrs Faraday and Mam, who would give up her early-morning cleaning job, would share baby-minding duties. Carol had pulled a face at the suggestion but the vicar said that without the condition being fulfilled the wedding would not take place as his son was unable to support a wife and child unaided. With no choice, Carol had been forced to agree. Jackie didn't think for one minute she'd stick to her part of the deal, but it wasn't her problem to worry about now. It was Sandy she felt sorry for, not her sister.

Another condition was that Carol should continue to live with Mam and Dad, and Sandy with his parents, until after the baby's birth, when suitable accommodation for the three of them would be sought. As Patsy had told her, following a conversation with Stevie, Sandy was reluctantly doing his bit for appearances' sake, but if the baby proved not to be his following the blood tests and the marriage remained unconsummated, he could quickly get an annulment. Jackie hung onto that one thin thread of hope, but pushed it to the back of her mind for now as dwelling on it would drive her mad.

She finished her meal and paid the bill, leaving a small tip on the table, and set off to walk back towards Selfridges.

⊛

As Jackie approached the Mary Quant counter it was easy enough to spot Janet. She had the same red hair as Patsy, but styled in a neat geometric bob. It was years since Jackie had last seen her, at Patsy's ninth birthday party. Janet had been twelve years old then and worn her hair in two fat plaits that hung down her back. She caught Janet's eye and her face broke into a welcoming smile. Jackie guessed she'd recognised her from the description issued by Patsy.

'Be with you in a minute,' Janet mouthed, fiddling with something behind the counter.

Jackie nodded and turned her attention to the stand opposite, trying a couple of perfume samples. She wrinkled her nose as the cloying scent of Rive Gauche hit her nostrils. She turned as Janet called her name.

'Just popping to the staffroom for my stuff. Won't be long.'

Within moments Janet was back and leading the way out of the store. 'Right, shall we grab a coffee and you can fill me in with what's going on. We'll go to Bar Italia; it's not too far to walk. Are you okay carrying that case?'

'Yes, it's not that heavy.'

Outside the store the pavements were heaving with people rushing towards bus stops and the station, and flagging down taxis. Jackie hurried along trying to keep up with Janet's long strides; she walked almost as fast as Patsy did. She was struck by how like her friend the now grown-up Janet was. Same greeny-blue eyes and similar build and height, as well as the hair colour. But their mams were sisters, so no surprise with the resemblance. It was nice though, to see some familiarity. She swallowed the lump that rose in her throat as she thought about her best friend and how much she would miss her. Her eyes filled as they turned into Frith Street and she blinked rapidly.

In Bar Italia Janet bagged a table and ordered two frothy coffees. A slim, dark-haired waiter brought them over and smiled as Janet greeted him.

Janet spooned sugar into her cup and stirred. 'So, Patsy filled me in a bit with your story, but Aunty Agnes was hovering nearby in the hall so it was quite cryptic, although I think I got the gist of it. Your boyfriend's marrying your sister who's pregnant with his baby. Is that right, or have I got the wrong end of the stick?'

Jackie blew out her cheeks. 'That's about right, I'm afraid.'

'God, you poor kid. I'd want to kill him!'

'Well, it's not quite as cut and dried as that.' Jackie went on to tell her the tale and when she'd finished Janet patted her hand and offered her a Sobranie cigarette. Jackie refused, but was fascinated to see the pastel shades that looked more like crayons than cigarettes. Janet lit a pink one and blew a neat smoke ring into the air above her head.

'Do you think running away from home is the right thing, Jackie?' she said gently. 'I mean, I can see how upset you are, and quite rightly so. And I can see it's your sister you'd like to kill and not Sandy, poor lad. London living isn't easy though. Finding a place to stay is hard and quite expensive, although finding work might not be too difficult and with your O level results you should get something. There are plenty of shops and offices looking for junior staff. But it can be lonely until you find your feet and make friends. You're very young to be doing this. I didn't leave home until I turned eighteen and it was such a wrench. I can put you up on our sofa for a few nights, but we don't have a spare bedroom, I'm afraid. Our flat's really tiny. I live with my boyfriend, Don. My mother thinks I share with a girl from work, so for God's sake don't blow me out on that one.'

'Thank you.' Jackie's heart sank. She'd been hoping that Janet would say she'd got a place where she could stay permanently. The thought of living on her own in a strange place filled her with dread. 'Tomorrow I'll look for work and find a room or something.'

Janet finished her ciggie and coffee and got to her feet. 'Come on then, let's head for home and we'll find you something to eat and get you settled. Don and I have booked to see a film tonight so I hope you'll be okay on your own for a few hours. It'll give you the chance to get a bath in peace and speak to our Patsy to let her know you're okay.'

⚘

Jackie stirred in her sleeping bag at the sound of whispering voices. Janet and her boyfriend had crept into the flat in the dark and were doing their best not to wake her, so she pretended to be sleeping while they used the bathroom, swearing as they bumped into things, before finally closing the bedroom door the other side of the narrow hallway.

She sighed and wriggled to get more comfortable. The sofa was even harder than the one at home and shorter too, so she couldn't stretch out her legs fully. Now she had cramp in her left calf and the pain was agony. She thought back to her earlier conversation with Patsy and how Patsy had told her that Mam had been round at teatime asking if they'd seen her as she'd not arrived home from college at the usual time. Patsy had told Mam that she might have gone for a bite to eat with some of her new college pals and it had seemed to pacify her. But Jackie knew that by now Mam would be worried sick about her. She felt bad thinking about it, but it was too late now. She closed her eyes but sleep wouldn't come. She must have dozed off again, though, as the next thing she knew, Janet was shaking her gently by the shoulder.

'I'm off to work now. Don's already gone. There's a spare key on the coffee table, a street map and a bus timetable with the bus numbers from the main road that'll take you into the city centre. I'd leave trying to find your way around on the tube for now. It can be confusing. I'll show you how it works at the weekend. Help yourself to breakfast, there's cereal and eggs and bread. I'm having an early dinner out tonight with my friends, it's a regular thing, but we'll talk some more when I get home. Good luck with your job hunt. Be careful.' And with that she was gone.

Jackie sat up and rubbed her eyes. She needed a plan of action. Job hunt first and then look for a bedsit or something. No one would give her lodgings unless she could prove she was working. Landlords usually wanted employment references.

Standing in the narrow hallway after breakfast, she checked her appearance in the long mirror on the back of the front door. Dressed in a black and white hound's-tooth check skirt and black sweater along with her boots and leather coat, carefully applied makeup and hair hanging neatly on her shoulders, Jackie thought she looked smart enough to be employable. After she'd eaten toast and scrambled eggs she had made a list of theatres she'd heard of, and looked up the addresses in the phone directory. And if she had no luck she could go to the labour exchange and ask about office or shop work.

❀

Janet's flat was situated in the downstairs part of a small converted house on Southolm Street in Battersea. Jackie locked the front door, trying the handle twice to make sure it was properly locked, and hurried to the main road. She found the bus stop easily enough. Four of the theatres on her list were close to Covent Garden. She waited until a bus bearing 'Covent Garden' on the front appeared and boarded, taking a window seat downstairs.

As she paid her fare she asked the conductor if he would let her know when they arrived at her destination. He nodded and handed her a ticket and change. 'You're from Liverpool,' he said with a grin.

'I am, yes. How do you know that?'

'Your accent. You sound like Cilla Black.' He winked and made his way down the bus, shouting, 'Any more fares, please?'

Jackie stifled a giggle. She didn't think she sounded anything like Cilla. But she stored it away ready to tell Patsy next time she spoke to her. As she got off the bus, waving goodbye to the friendly conductor, she consulted her list and asked a passerby for directions to the Novello Theatre.

By the time she'd tried there and the Lyceum, and the Royal Opera House, with no luck, she decided to find a coffee shop. The lady she'd spoken to at the Novello told her to come back on Saturday morning at ten sharp as they were auditioning for extras, but it was the same story at them all: she'd need an Equity card to prove her worth and to get work on the stage. It seemed a bit pointless to trek round to any of the others without one. There were no unskilled jobs going, not even a vacancy for an usherette. Might be an idea to phone around the others tomorrow, and if there was a chance of anything, she could make her way directly to them. She really needed drama school qualifications and she'd blown that now.

Sitting in a little coffee shop, toying with a flapjack, she crossed things off her to-do list. Theatrical agencies might be a good place to try, except she hadn't a clue where to look for one, and again, it would be the same tale – no Equity card, no work.

By four o'clock she was weary of tramping round, had a blister on her heel and felt totally despondent. She'd been in several shops with cards in the window offering employment, but without work experience under her belt, no one was interested in taking her on. She hadn't a clue how to get to Camberwell Green, where the labour exchange was, so she'd have to wait until later and ask Janet to help her. The couple of estate agents she'd popped into to enquire about room rentals had practically laughed her out of the door. At sixteen she was too young to sign a lease and would need a parent or guardian to act as guarantor. One of them had suggested she try a youth hostel. She'd been given the address of one on Carter Lane near St Paul's Cathedral but she hadn't tried to find it yet. That would be tomorrow's job.

❧

Janet's boyfriend arrived home as Jackie was easing off her boots and examining her blistered heel. The left foot of her tights was bloody, so she limped into the bathroom to strip them off, conscious of Don staring after her. He hadn't said a word other than grunt 'Hi' in her direction as he came in. He didn't seem to be very sociable and she felt a bit intimidated by him. Last night, before he and Janet went out, he'd hardly spoken two words to Jackie. He was a couple of years older than Janet and worked in a bank, but that was the only information she'd been told. There was something about him, the way he stared, like he could see through her clothes. She didn't feel comfortable near him. When she'd finished cleaning up her heel and applied a plaster that she found in the bathroom cupboard, he was seated on the sofa sipping a mug of coffee, but he hadn't offered to make one for her.

She went into the kitchen and made herself a mug of tea. Back in the tiny lounge she sat down on the armchair opposite Don, pulling her short skirt down towards her bare knees. She should have put her jeans on right away. He looked at her and nodded, his half-smile not quite reaching his eyes.

'Any luck today?'

She shook her head, surprised that he'd asked. 'It was hopeless.' She told him of her efforts and failures.

'You don't stand a chance,' he said harshly. 'You're too young to be in London on your own and you're not qualified for anything. You should get yourself off home and back to college. Bet your parents are worried sick about you. You can't stay here beyond this week. We haven't the space and we're not keeping you for nothing.'

Her eyes filled at his harsh words. 'I'll be gone soon. I've got a bed in a hostel near St Paul's for next week,' she lied. 'I'll find a job. And I *will* go back to college eventually.'

'Good luck.' He got to his feet. 'I'm off out. See you later.'

As he slammed the door shut she burst into tears. This was the worst idea she'd had in her life. She'd have been better off going to Manchester; at least it was close enough to home if she decided she wanted to return. But she couldn't go home until after the wedding, she couldn't face it. Nor did she fancy living in a hostel with strangers.

'Damn you, Carol,' she cried. 'I hate you for stealing my life.'

Chapter Twenty

Sitting on the sofa, Carol chewed her lip as her mam wiped her eyes and pushed the tissue up her cardigan sleeve. She stroked Mam's arm and watched as the young constable, seated on the chair in the bay, slipped a photograph of Jackie inside his notebook. It wasn't a totally up-to-date one, being last year's school photo, but it was the only recent one they had and, as Mam had told him, she hadn't changed that much except for her hair being a bit longer.

'Try not to worry, Mrs Evans, I'm sure we'll find Jacqueline safe and well and have her back home with you soon. From what you say, it would appear she's left of her own free will, taking her belongings with her. Now are you certain she hasn't confided in, or been in touch with, a close friend?'

Mam shook her head. 'Her best friend Patsy would be the first person she'd make contact with, they have a phone you see, and Patsy would let us know right away. It's been five days now and no one has seen or heard from her. It's not like our Jackie to do something like this. The college principal has questioned a couple of people she's recently palled up with but they're as shocked as we are.'

'And does Jacqueline have a boyfriend?'

Carol shifted uncomfortably and looked at the constable. 'Not any more. They've recently split up.'

'Hmm. So it's possible she's run away because she's upset? Teenagers take these things to heart. Do you have an address for the ex-boyfriend? I'll need to ask him a few questions, to establish when he last saw Jacqueline. Is there a possibility they've made up and run away together? Do you have any idea what the falling-out was about? Could it be that your daughter is, er, in trouble, Mrs Evans, and that's why she's gone on the run?'

Mam shook her head and started to cry again. Carol swallowed hard, feeling guilty as hell, and told the constable the sorry tale of *why* her sister and Alex had split up, and that she knew with absolute certainty he didn't know of Jackie's whereabouts.

Carol knew for a fact that Alex had no idea of where Jackie was, because he'd done nothing but blame himself since she'd gone missing, and he'd blamed Carol too. She was worried sick that he would call off next week's wedding. He didn't want it, and the least excuse to pull out would do.

Cheeks flushed with embarrassment, the constable kept his head down as he scribbled in his notebook. 'We may need to interview Mr Faraday, even so.'

Carol nodded and told the constable he could get in touch with Alex via the church. Ridiculous as it seemed, she still hadn't been invited to his home and had no clue of his address, apart from the Scottie Road flat where he stayed with Stevie, which seemed to be most of the time now. Alex wouldn't thank her for sending a policeman round to Stevie's place. Her mam said she didn't know the address as most of her dealings with Sandy's parents were done at the hall or church.

The constable folded his notebook, slipped it into his jacket pocket and got to his feet, saying that he would be in touch as soon as there was anything to report. Carol showed him out. Back in the sitting room, she looked at her mam, who was sobbing again.

'I'm so sorry, Mam. I wish I could make things right.'

'It's not your fault, love. It's that bloody Faraday lad who's to blame for this mess.'

Carol took a deep breath. She should confess. It was so unfair to blame Alex. But if she told the truth she knew he would refuse to marry her and she couldn't take that risk. There was no way she was giving him the chance to get back with Jackie. She was convinced that she could make him happy once they were settled in their own place. After all, the blood tests would show for sure that he *had* fathered her baby and that was all she needed. They'd be fine once the dust settled; he'd get over Jackie and they'd soon make a nice home together.

❀

Jackie sat on the edge of her metal bed in the shared dorm and took a look around. It was clean but sparse, the walls painted a pale shade of green, worn beige linoleum on the floor and each bed covered with a dark green bedspread. It reminded her of the hospital ward she'd stayed in when she was ten years old and had her tonsils removed; but without the antiseptic smell. This place had a fresh-air aroma due to the windows being wide open, even though it was a cold day. She hadn't met any of her room-mates yet, but it was early afternoon and she'd been told the six-bed dorm would be shared with casual backpackers and a couple of short-term lodgers who worked in the city.

Although grateful to Janet for giving her a temporary roof over her head, she was glad to get away from Don and his increasingly lecherous ways. God, what a creep he was. She hadn't a clue what Janet saw in him. The last straw had been him walking into the bathroom last night while Janet was at the launderette. There was no lock on the door but he'd known Jackie was in there as she'd announced she was taking a bath. When she'd yelled at him to go away, and hurriedly wrapped a towel around herself, she realised he'd probably been listening at the door for her getting out of the bath, and he knew she'd be naked.

His reply had terrified her. That if she'd not been such a frigid little cow they could have had a bit of fun while they were alone. He tried to pull the towel away, but she'd hung onto it for dear life and told him that she'd scream if he didn't leave. She knew the neighbours above were in as she'd heard them walking about. She threatened to tell Janet and he laughed and said she wouldn't believe her, and anyway, he'd say *she'd* come on to *him*.

When he and Janet had gone to bed she'd packed her case, and had left the flat shortly after Janet went to work, pushing the key through the letterbox. She'd left a little note to thank Janet and told her she'd got a place to stay and not to worry about her.

The hostel on Carter Lane, near St Paul's Cathedral, fortunately had a vacancy and she booked in for the week, telling them she was on a study break to visit theatres in the city. There'd been no problem with them believing her tale and she had enough money to stay longer, but they were booked up after this Saturday. At least it would give her some time to try to find a job and lodgings and, more importantly, if she had to go home, Carol's wedding would be over and done with.

She tucked the envelope with the rest of her dad's money into her handbag and stored her case in a locker by the side of her bed. She'd been told not to leave anything of value while she was out as the management couldn't be held responsible for any losses. She was starving, so something to eat was next on the agenda and she left the building, calling goodbye to the friendly concierge who'd booked her in.

Sandy had told her that one day he hoped his paintings would grace the walls of the Tate and National Galleries in London. She planned to find the galleries and look at the paintings on show. It would make her feel closer to him, admiring something he loved. And some day, hopefully, his dreams would come true, but not if it had anything to do with her sister. She'd be quite happy for him to be labouring down the docks like Uncle Frank did, ruining his lovely soft hands and getting the calluses most dockers were prone to. Jackie shook her head. Sandy was too posh for that sort of work. She pushed angry thoughts to the back of her mind and hurried on her way.

❊

'Are you sure you don't know where she is?' Sandy asked as he, Stevie and Patsy sat around the little table in the Scottie Road flat, sharing two portions of fish and chips between them. Patsy had said she wasn't hungry but as soon as Stevie walked in with the newspaper-wrapped parcels, and the appetising aroma reached her nostrils, she'd changed her mind.

Patsy looked away before shaking her head. 'She's safe and that's all you need to know.' She rammed a chip in her mouth and got up to put the kettle on.

'Well, don't you think her family should be told she's safe?' Stevie directed at Patsy's ramrod-straight back. 'Her parents are worried to death.'

'No. And don't *you* dare say anything to them,' she said to Sandy. 'You've done enough damage as it is with that bloody sister of hers. She can't handle it. She needed some space, time to herself to get her head around things.'

Sandy sighed and ran his hands through his hair. 'Shit, this is all my fault. If anything happens to her I'll never forgive myself.'

'Well Jackie's not your problem now. Carol is.'

'She *is* my problem, Patsy. I love her. I don't wanna marry Caz.'

'Too late for that now, Sandy. You made your bed, as my mam's always saying.'

'Please just tell me where she is. I promise not to let on to anyone. And if she calls you, tell her I'm so, so sorry.'

Patsy brewed three mugs of tea and plonked them on the table. She sat down and took a sip, looking over the rim of her mug at Sandy's tear-filled eyes. 'She's in London.'

'London? Jesus, I thought you'd say Manchester or somewhere closer. Oh God, to think of her all alone in London. Anything could happen to her.'

'She's not all alone. She's staying at my cousin's flat. She's perfectly safe. So you can stop worrying and get on with your new life. After the wedding I'll tell my mam and she can tell Dora. But I'm saying nothing until after the weekend, because they'll try and bring her home and she doesn't want that. I'll phone my cousin on Sunday and check everything's all right.'

Sandy nodded, knowing that was the best he was going to get. Patsy was stubborn and it was pointless asking for her cousin's phone number. Life was shit and in three days he was getting married to Caz and the thought of that filled him with more than dread. He wished with all his heart that he'd run away with Jackie.

❀

'What do you mean, she's not there any more?' Patsy's voice rose an octave. 'Well where the heck *is* she then? A hostel? But why? Well, if she gets in touch again, tell her to call me here.'

Patsy slammed down the phone. Janet's boyfriend had answered and seemed unconcerned that Jackie had upped sticks and gone off on her own. Janet was out shopping, so she didn't get to speak to her. Shit, she'd been hoping to persuade Jackie to come home now that sham of a wedding was over and done with.

She didn't think she'd ever seen a more miserable-looking bridegroom than Sandy. Carol had smiled bravely throughout, looking reasonably pretty in her pink tent of a dress made by her mam, with matching pink rosebuds in her hair. There had been hardly a soul at the ceremony, just a friend of Carol's from work and her boyfriend, Uncle Frank and Maureen, and Carol's mam and dad as well as herself, Stevie and her mam. Mrs Faraday wasn't there and it seemed like the vicar had rushed through the service as quickly as he could.

A quick sandwich and cup of tea back at Carol's mam's place, and then Sandy, giving Carol a hasty peck on the cheek, had left with Patsy and Stevie to spend his wedding night at Scottie Road with them instead of with his new wife. What a waste of time. But like he told them again last night, after they'd all got drunk, he'd done his bit, and by not consummating the marriage he could get out of it more quickly once the blood tests were done. Patsy felt really sorry for him, because she was as certain as everyone else that he was lumbered for life now, but if it gave him a few more weeks of hope, then so be it. She could think of nothing worse than being tied to someone you didn't even fancy, never mind love.

'You all right, chuck?' Her mam's voice broke her thoughts as she passed her on the stairs, her arms full of bedding for the washer.

'No, Mam, I'm not all right.' Patsy's eyes filled. 'I need to talk to you. Put the washing in and I'll make us a coffee.'

Sitting at the kitchen table, Patsy poured out her tale. When she got to the part about Jackie leaving Janet's flat, Agnes's hand flew to her mouth.

'So she's wandering around London on her own? Oh my God, anything could happen to her. She's only sixteen. I need to go and see Dora right away. And *you* can come with me. You should never have encouraged her to go. She'd have got over that lad eventually.'

'I don't think she would, Mam, but that doesn't matter right now. We need to get her home.'

❀

Carol handed round mugs of tea while they waited for her dad to get back with Uncle Frank. They were doing a round of the pubs in town with a photo of Jackie in the hopes that someone would say they'd seen her recently. Her mam was in a right state, crying her eyes out. Agnes had a comforting arm around her shoulders and Patsy sat stony-faced on the floor by the big chest of drawers.

'If anything's happened to my girl I'll kill that bloody husband of yours with my bare hands,' her mam cried, looking at Carol, who plonked herself down on the chair in the bay.

Carol burst into tears. She too was worried about Jackie. What if something did happen to her? She'd never forgive herself and knew she had to come clean.

'It's not Alex's fault,' she cried. 'This mess, I mean. It's all down to me.'

'Why is it down to you?' Mam asked, frowning.

Carol wiped her eyes and took a deep breath. Her voice breaking, she told them what she'd done with the contraceptives Alex had carried in his wallet.

Mam stared at her open-mouthed. 'You stupid, stupid girl,' she began. 'What on earth possessed you to be so bloody irresponsible? You've ruined three lives with your selfish actions, not to mention that poor little bugger's in there.'

She pointed an angry finger at Carol's baby bulge. 'I don't think your young man will be too happy when he hears what you've done, trapping him like that. What a pity you didn't think to mention it before the wedding. You've condemned that kiddy to a life without a father now.'

'Mam, you can't tell Alex, you just can't,' Carol cried. 'I need him. Our baby needs him. It's bad enough that he doesn't want to be anywhere near me at the moment. And *you*,' she pointed at Patsy, 'don't you dare tell anyone. I've got to think about what's best for my baby now.'

Patsy jumped to her feet, her green eyes flashing angrily. 'Well, having a jealous cow for a mother isn't going to be best for it, is it? You evil bitch. Jackie and Sandy love one another so much. You've no idea what damage you've done to them. He'll never love you like he loves her, and your stupid marriage won't last five minutes once he knows.'

Agnes also got to her feet. 'Patsy, come on, love. We need to go home and try and get hold of our Janet again. Our priority is getting Jackie home safely. Though to be honest,' she turned to Dora, 'I don't think for one minute you'll persuade her to come back here with Carol still under your roof. She can stay with us for a while until *she* moves out.'

Carol looked up with a pleading expression on her face. 'Please don't say anything to anyone. I had to let you know that Alex isn't the one at fault here, it's me; it's all my fault. But I need him and so does our baby.'

'Well no one will hear anything from me,' Agnes snorted, 'I can assure you, nor from my Patsy either. But you owe it to that young man to come clean and tell him what you've done. Then it's up to him whether to stay or walk away, and I know what I'd do if I was him! I'll come over later, Dora, if I've any news.'

Mam saw them to the door and Agnes gave her a hug. 'I'd keep this from Joe and Frank for now if I was you,' Agnes advised. 'Least said, soonest mended. But what a devious little madam your Carol is.'

Carol blew her nose as her mam came back into the sitting room and sank down on the sofa again. 'I'm so sorry, Mam. Please don't say anything to Alex, I beg you. The baby really is his and as soon as he knows that for sure we can move into a place of our own and be out from under your feet.'

'It's not my place to tell him, but *you* must. It was a wicked thing to do and you can't keep a secret like that. They have a habit of blowing up in your face.'

Carol nodded, but knew she wouldn't tell him. Not yet anyway. If Patsy let the cat out of the bag she'd have to come clean, but for now she'd buy herself some time until the baby's birth.

⸙

Dora let her head fall back on her shoulders. She felt weary as she closed her eyes and stretched out her stockinged feet. Carol was upstairs in the bath. Joe and Frank would be back any minute from their round of the town's pubs in the search for Jackie. She couldn't believe what Carol had done. Trapping the lad like that was on a level with Ivy's trapping Joe. Why would any woman be so desperate? Had Ivy's deception been behind the reasons for Carol's thinking when she'd damaged the contraceptives? Maybe being brought up by Ivy for some of her young life had had more of an effect on Carol than Dora had realised. That woman had gone out of her way to get what she wanted, not caring who she hurt in the process, and it seemed her daughter was now following in Ivy's footsteps. Much as she loved Carol and she would ensure that she was looked after both during her pregnancy and afterwards when the baby arrived, the whole thing was a recipe for disaster.

❀

Patsy sat on the bottom stair as her mam hung up the phone and turned to face her.

'Janet said she just walked out, she doesn't know why. She left a note thanking Janet for putting her up and that was all she'd written. But she also said her boyfriend Don had told her that Jackie had mentioned she'd booked a bed in a hostel near St Paul's Cathedral. She's just looked it up in the phone book, it's on Carter Lane. She's given me the number. I'll try them now, see if I can talk to her or leave a message for her to call us here.'

Patsy got up from the stairs and paced up and down the hall, looking at her mam, who looked agitated as she slammed down the phone. 'What's up?'

'She's not there. She was only booked in until yesterday morning. They don't know where she was going after she left the hostel. So what do we do now?'

'Wait until she calls us, I suppose,' Patsy said, biting her lip. 'Maybe she's got a room in a lodging house, or something. Be like looking for a needle in a haystack without an address though.'

'I'd better nip round and tell Dora. You stay here in case Frank and Joe are back; I don't want you shooting your mouth off about Carol in front of them. It's up to that young madam to come clean herself. Peel me the spuds for dinner, chuck, I won't be long.'

Patsy called Stevie while her mam was out. He told her Sandy wasn't there, that he'd popped home to see his mother, who wasn't very well, apparently. Probably all the worry of the stupid wedding and all the old gossips getting to her, Patsy thought. She told him where Jackie had been and how she'd now moved on without any forwarding address.

'Shit! Well I'm not telling Sandy that, he's in a bad enough state as it is without upsetting him further.'

'I agree,' Patsy said, so tempted to tell him about the damaged contraceptives and Carol's deceit. But she knew she daren't. 'I'll let you know as soon as we hear anything.'

❀

'Right,' Frank said. 'I know my way around London quite well, and I'm off work for a week's holiday now. I was going to go fishing with a pal, but I'll take myself down to the metropolis and search for our Jackie instead.'

'Oh, Frank, thank you,' Dora said, grasping his hand. 'Agnes is calling the police with an update on her whereabouts so *they'll* be on the look-out too.'

'Shall I come with you, Frank?' Joe asked. 'I'll see if I can get a few days off, but you know what that place is like when it's short notice.'

'It's okay; I'll go on my own. Ford's is not the most compassionate employer, I know that. Me and our Jackie are close and if there's anything bothering her she'll confide in me, I'm sure. You've not really been in her life that much for the past few years, Joe, so I think I know her best. I'm not criticising here, I can see what this is doing to you, but let *me* do it. You stop here and look after our Dora and Carol. They need you.'

❀

Joe lit a cigarette and paced up and down the path in the back garden, deep in thought. He was grateful to Frank for offering to go and get Jackie but it hurt like hell that she was closer to Frank than to him. He had a lot of making up to do. His poor little girl would be feeling heartbroken right now. He felt so sorry for her – and for Sandy too. The pair were besotted. God help the lad. Nobody knew better than Joe what it was like to be trapped in a loveless marriage. Carol's determination to keep the baby and marry Sandy had overwhelmed everything else lately. Only time would tell if it was the right thing, and maybe by then, Jackie would have picked up the pieces and thrown herself into her stage career and found another lad to fall in love with.

Chapter Twenty-One

Jackie fidgeted, trying to get comfortable on the pile of cardboard boxes she'd found in a shop doorway at the rear of Oxford Street. It was Sunday, her second night of sleeping rough, and she hated it. She shivered, tears running down her cheeks. The October night was cold and she felt chilled to the bone. Tomorrow morning, the boxes and all the other rubbish piled in the small back lane would be collected by the dustbin men and she'd have to go looking for somewhere else to sleep. She'd bought a knitted blanket from a second-hand stall on Covent Garden market and tucked it around her body and under her chin. She had on several layers of clothing and she'd managed to have a bit of a wash and brush her teeth in the toilets at Euston station that morning.

She wanted to go home now; she'd made her point and was lonely, frightened and missing her mam badly. But while freshening up she'd put down her handbag and turned her back for seconds, and when she'd picked it up the flap was open and the envelope with all her money had gone. She'd hurried outside and looked up and down the street but the pavement was crowded, as always, and the thief could have been any one of the hundreds of people pushing past her.

She'd cried as she sat down on a bench to take stock. A thick-set man with a round face and camel-hair overcoat sat down beside her and asked if he could help. He offered her a cigarette but she declined and moved away. He inched closer and asked if he could treat her to breakfast, but warning bells rang in her head. He was so close she could smell his hair-cream, like her dad's Brylcreem, and her stomach did a little flip at the familiar scent. She told him she was fine and waiting for a friend. He'd shrugged and walked away, but she'd seen him later talking to another young girl who looked as aimless as she did, and as the girl nodded he'd taken her arm and led her away down the street.

Jackie shuddered, wondering what the man's intentions were, and if the girl would be safe. She didn't feel brave enough to follow them though. She'd spent the day wandering around, sightseeing, as there was nothing else to do. She'd been to Carnaby Street and window-shopped and thought she'd spotted a couple of The Kinks in one of the outfitters, but couldn't be sure, although a group of mini-skirted girls were hovering around the door, grinning and pointing. It should have been an exciting experience, but her frame of mind was all wrong and she couldn't summon up enthusiasm. Fashionably dressed young people thronged the pavements both sides of the street. Mods on fancy mirror-and-fur-bedecked scooters rode past, reminding her of Sandy and Stevie and their friends. She wished Patsy was with her. They'd often joked about coming to London and finding rich and famous boyfriends.

She hunkered down as far as she could into her blanket when she heard footsteps thudding by and tuneless whistling, followed by a loud rumbling burp and a gagging noise. She hoped that whoever it was wouldn't choose to throw up his stomach contents over her boxes. Then a rustling and squeaking noise nearby terrified the life out of her. What if it was rats? Uncle Frank had told her that rats near the docks at home were sometimes the size of small dogs and could go for your throat if they felt threatened. She heard a loud meow and further squeaking and then silence apart from the hum of traffic on Oxford Street. Must be a mother cat and her kittens living in another box in a nearby doorway. Fingers crossed they wouldn't get thrown into the dustcart tomorrow. She planned to go into Selfridges in the morning and ask Janet for help. If it hadn't been for Janet's horrible boyfriend she wouldn't be in this mess. Luckily her purse had been in her coat pocket when the thief struck, but all she had left was a couple of shilling pieces, a half-crown and a ten-bob note. Not enough money to buy a train ticket home.

Food was expensive and she'd had two snack-meals today of tea and toast, and had lingered in the café for as long as she could to keep warm, and to save wandering aimlessly around. She was so hungry now she could cry. She didn't feel well either. She'd been sick this morning almost as soon as she woke up and now felt like she was starting with the flu. Must be a bug she'd picked up at the hostel. She closed her eyes, her hand clasped around the little silver heart on the bracelet that Sandy had given her for her birthday. She never took it off and it comforted her to know it was with her always.

She thought about how he'd probably be curled up in bed right now with her sister on their first weekend of marriage. Or maybe not, and he had stayed with his parents while Carol stayed with Mam and Dad, as had been part of the conditions. She hoped he had. The image of him in her head, making love to Carol, broke her heart. With that thought she closed her eyes and tried to sleep, willing the morning to come soon.

❀

'Sorry, she's not in today,' the girl on the Mary Quant counter said. 'Taken a few days' holiday and gone to Brighton with her boyfriend.' She switched her glossy smile to the customer standing behind Jackie and asked if she could help.

Jackie's shoulders slumped and she walked away, head bowed, and made for the ladies' toilets. Janet had been her last hope of getting home. Locked in a cubicle, away from the prying eyes of the purse-lipped attendant, who'd eyed her dishevelled state with suspicion, she sank to the floor and retched over the bowl. There was nothing to come up. The one slice of toast and cup of tea she'd allowed herself an hour earlier had already gone down the café loo. She closed her eyes, head resting against the cool green wall tiles. She felt so ill and just wanted her own bed and her mam to look after her.

'Are you okay in there, young lady?' a stern voice called as someone banged on the door.

'Yes.' She wiped her clammy face on a tissue, got to her feet and flushed the toilet. She took a packet of Polo mints from her bag and popped one into her mouth as the knocking on the door grew louder. 'Coming,' she called and walked out to face the miserable woman attendant whose eagle-eyes raked her up and down.

'Hope you haven't made a mess in there.' She barged past Jackie, brandishing rubber gloves and a bottle of bleach.

Jackie ignored her, dragged her case out into the store and headed towards the lift. Outside the store entrance a distant clock chimed ten. If she called Patsy's house now she might just catch Agnes before she left for her job at the school. Patsy wouldn't be in, as she'd begun her new job at Littlewoods Pools at the same time as Jackie had started college, and she left the house at eight. She hurried to the corner and joined a queue of people waiting to use the phone box. The two men in front walked away when the older woman who'd been using the phone came out and beckoned them to follow her. Jackie dashed in and laid her coins on the shelf. Agnes answered after a couple of rings.

'It's Jackie,' she burst out and started to cry. 'I want to come home. Will you tell my mam and dad that I'm sorry?' She listened as Agnes told her not to worry and that Uncle Frank was on his way to London to look for her.

'Where will he be able to find you? He's phoning here later when I get back in from work to see if you've been in touch and I can tell him where to go. He should be there late afternoon, traffic permitting.'

Jackie's legs almost gave way with relief as she told Agnes she'd stay around the Oxford Street area and would wait near the entrance to Selfridges from four o'clock. She hung up as the pips went and walked slowly down the street and back into the little café for another cup of tea and a slice of toast, feeling much more cheerful. She'd be able to use her left-over money to buy a bowl of soup for her lunch now and even a bread roll. Hopefully she'd hang onto it – she was feeling really sickly.

❀

Agnes dashed round to Fourth Avenue with the good news. Dora sobbed on Agnes's shoulder when she heard that Jackie was safe and would be home later. Agnes patted her back until the sobs subsided.

Carol stood in the doorway between the hall and sitting room looking pale and red-eyed, as though she'd not slept a wink. 'Thank goodness for that,' she muttered.

'When Frank phones later I'll ask him to bring her straight to our place,' Agnes said, ignoring Carol. 'You can come back with me, Dora, and we'll get the spare room ready. I'm sure Carol can look after herself.'

'She'll be fine. She's got an ante-natal appointment today. That's why she's not in work.' She gave Carol a peck on the cheek. 'Good luck.'

Agnes nodded and she and Dora left the house, linking arms. Agnes knew that Dora had suffered bouts of severe depression when her girls were younger and she'd been worried sick that the upset of the last few weeks would tip her back over the edge again. Hopefully she'd be okay, but she'd be keeping a close eye on her for a while.

❀

'Is everything okay?' Carol asked anxiously as the midwife listened to her baby's heartbeat through a funnel pressed against her abdomen.

'A strong and healthy beat,' the midwife assured her as she stretched a tape measure from the top to the bottom of her bump. 'The fundal height's correct for your weeks, too.'

Her blood pressure was fine. The midwife asked her to confirm the date she expected to start her maternity leave, and she made a note of it.

'The accident recorded in your notes seems to have had no effect on baby. Try and rest as much as you can as your ankles are slightly swollen today. Nothing to worry about at this stage, though. I expect your husband will be looking after you well, Mrs Faraday. I'm sure he's as excited as you are.'

'Yes, oh yes, he is,' Carol fibbed, feeling her cheeks heating. 'We're both looking forward to becoming parents.'

On leaving the clinic Carol got on a bus into town and made her way to the Kardomah Café, where she was meeting Susan for lunch.

She bought a coffee while she waited and took her usual window seat. Susan arrived minutes later with her arms full of cards and brightly wrapped gifts.

'From the girls in the office,' she announced as she laid the parcels on the table. 'So, how's it going, Caz? I know you've only had a couple of nights of wedded bliss, but is everything okay?'

Carol's eyes filled and she shook her head. 'It's a disaster. I haven't even seen him since the wedding. He knew I had the clinic appointment today but didn't seem interested when I told him on Saturday. He hates me and it's going to get even worse.' She told Susan that Jackie had been in touch with Agnes and was being brought home later. 'So as soon as he claps eyes on *her* that's my marriage over and done with.'

'Not necessarily. Did he spend the wedding night with you?'

'No.' Carol lowered her voice. 'He doesn't want the marriage consummating. He spent the night at Stevie's. He's married me to save face for his parents with the gossips, and to give the baby a name, but he'll be off at the first excuse, I just know it.'

'I don't know what to say.' Susan sat back, arms folded and a look of astonishment on her face. She stared silently at Carol, who opened her mouth to speak and then closed it again, as though changing her mind. 'It might be okay if you give him a bit of space.'

'Space is all I *do* give him. Apart from Saturday and the day he came round with the ring to make sure it fitted, I haven't seen him. All the wedding arrangements were done by Mam and the vicar. Mrs Faraday kept her distance, and as you know, she didn't even come to the wedding.'

'You need your own place,' Susan said, getting to her feet. 'Let me order lunch and then we'll talk some more. Do you want another coffee?'

'No thanks, but I'll have a slice of Welsh rarebit please.' Their own place would be a dream come true. But she'd have to wait until after December for that to happen, if it ever did. Finding somewhere they could afford would be difficult on her wages alone. Alex was going to have to sort himself out and look for a job that paid more than the Jacaranda did, never mind finishing his bloody college course first. He'd had things all his own way, and she'd agreed – to keep the peace and to hold on to him. Well, now the worm was about to turn because she was fed up of her needs being ignored.

Susan arrived back with a laden tray. 'Got us a cherry Bakewell each for afters. Tuck in.'

Carol picked at her Welsh rarebit, pushing it around her plate. 'Jackie will be staying at Agnes's,' she said, for want of something to say. 'She'll be better off there for now because I've got her bedroom and all the baby stuff is lying around the house.'

Susan nodded, forking up a mouthful of baked beans. 'Well, it would be cruel to rub her nose in it. There's a place to rent not far from where *we* live. It's in a house that's been divided into four small flats. You should go and have a look and see what it's like. I wrote the address down for you.' Susan rooted in her handbag and handed Carol a piece of paper. 'Make an appointment and I'll come with you.'

Carol chewed her lip as she looked at the address. Luxmore Road in Walton Vale wasn't a bad area and close to shops and facilities. Bit of a trek when she went back to work, to drop the baby off at Mam's and then get into town for nine, but she would face that problem in the future. If the rent was reasonable she could take it on with the savings she had put by, and hope that Alex would join her eventually. It was worth a thought anyway.

'Thanks, Sue. I'll call them later.'

※

Carol signed the lease with a flourish and handed over forty pounds, most of her savings, to cover the damage deposit and the first two months' rent. She had almost nothing left now, but at least the flat was furnished and would do them for a year or two until they qualified for a council house. The walls were freshly painted in cream emulsion and the doors in white gloss. Slightly faded fawn carpet squares covered the floors. The bedroom, separate from the sitting room and kitchen area, was small, and as there was no hallway, the door leading into it was off the sitting room. It was furnished with a double bed, small wardrobe and dressing table and a chest of drawers. The furniture was old-fashioned but cared for, and she could make the room look nice with rugs, and lamps on bedside tables. Bedding and curtains from Lewis's new autumn range would look nice in here when she could afford it. Alex could cough up a few quid to help. There was just enough room to squeeze the cot into the corner near the window.

The sitting room furniture was also old-fashioned but clean and looked after. A brown tweed sofa and armchair, a polished drop-leaf dining table with two wooden chairs and a matching bookcase graced the room. A wall-mounted gas fire on the chimney breast was the only form of heating, but it would be fine as she could leave the bedroom door open to take the chill off when the baby went to bed. Her excitement mounted as she pictured cosy nights in with Alex, eating food she'd cooked on the tiny gas stove and opening a bottle of wine when they could afford it. She was certain that once he saw the flat he'd be okay and would feel happy that they could start their married life properly.

It felt good that she was taking control now instead of letting his father dictate to them about *when* they should live together. She was a married woman; she needed her husband by her side. She hadn't even waited for Susan to view the flat with her. As soon as they left the café at lunchtime she'd called the landlord from a nearby phone box and got on the bus to meet him, armed with her envelope of savings that was always in her handbag. She knew that if she'd thought about it for too long she wouldn't have done it.

On the bus back to Mam's she felt quite proud of herself. Jackie could come home now and have her bedroom back. Alex would have no need to turn up at her mam's place and there was less likelihood of him bumping into Jackie.

❀

By the time Mam dashed back from Agnes's to ask how the ante-natal appointment had gone, Carol had packed all her clothes, the baby's new stuff and everything else that belonged to her. She'd also dismantled the cot and carried the pieces downstairs to the hall. Mam looked at the stacked boxes, which Carol had got from the Co-op on Longmoor Lane.

'What's going on here?' Mam demanded. 'You shouldn't be lifting boxes and stuff in your condition.'

Carol explained that she'd taken a lease on a flat and was hoping her dad and Uncle Frank would help her get everything across to Walton Vale when they had a minute. 'It will be best if I'm gone so that Jackie can come back home.'

'But you don't need to move out, chuck,' Mam said. 'Jackie will stay with Agnes for a few days. It's all arranged. Frank will be too tired to start lugging stuff around when he gets back from London.'

'I *do* need to move out, Mam. We can do it tomorrow then, if tonight's not convenient. I want me and Alex to start a proper married life and I want it now.'

Mam pursed her lips. 'And does this *proper married life* involve you telling Sandy what you did?'

'Of course,' Carol said, feeling her face heating. She turned away and began to fiddle with one of the boxes.

'Hmm,' Mam muttered. 'Well in that case, you might be moving in on your own. I hope you've thought about that, young lady. And how you'll manage I don't know. I've struggled all my life after me and your dad divorced. I don't envy you. And if you'd just waited a bit longer we may be buying a new house in time. Somewhere with a garden for the baby to play.'

'We'll be fine. It won't be like that for me and Alex. I won't ever divorce him. And the flat is lovely. Wait until you see it. You'll love it, and so will Alex.'

Chapter Twenty-Two

November 1966

Sandy stared at the letter Stevie had thrust into his hand. His pal had called at Patsy's place tonight to collect her for their pre-arranged date, but she'd cancelled when he got there because Jackie had been brought home from London by her Uncle Frank. Caz was still at her parents' house, so Jackie was staying with Patsy's family for a while. Patsy wanted to stay at home with her and keep her company. Stevie had joined them for a brew and then come back to Scotland Road.

'From Caz,' Stevie announced, shrugging out of his parka. 'Jackie's mam brought it round while I was there.'

Sandy threw the letter onto the table and carried on eating his tea.

'Aren't you going to read it? Might be urgent. She *is* your wife, mate. You gotta face up to that now.'

Sandy sighed and tore open the envelope. He skim-read the contents, eyebrows rising slightly, and then continued to eat his tomato soup.

'So, what does she say?'

'Read it.'

Stevie read the letter and sighed. 'What you gonna do? Move in with her?'

Sandy shrugged. 'Who knows? Anyway, how's Jackie? Is she okay? No worse for wear for her adventures? I'm just so relieved that she's safe. I can't even begin to get my head around *that* yet, never mind moving in with Caz.'

'She's fine. A bit off-colour but they think she's got a bug she picked up from somewhere. She was sleeping rough the last few nights in a shop doorway. Poor kid.'

'Jesus! I should be there for her.'

'No, mate, you shouldn't. You've got Caz and your kid to think 'bout now. You have to put Jackie out of your mind. Just be grateful for what you had, and that she's safely home.'

'Easier said than done.' Sandy wiped a piece of bread around the dregs in his bowl and shoved it in his mouth.

⁕

Carol finished putting away her clothes and the rest of her belongings. Uncle Frank had fixed the cot back together and it sat in pride of place in the bedroom, all made up with the new blankets her mam had knitted. In spite of the old-fashioned furniture, the flat was already starting to look like home. She hoped Alex would pay her a visit soon. He would have got the letter inviting him round by now, as her mam had given it to Stevie last night. She was sure that once he'd seen their new place he'd be as pleased as she was. She tweaked the cushions on the sofa and sat down to admire her handiwork.

The few ornaments dotted around the room, wedding gifts from her workmates, looked nice, and Mam had given her the hearth rug from Fourth Avenue. It still had a lot of wear left in it and the red pattern added colour to the otherwise brown and cream room. She'd brought the red velvet curtains with her that Mam had recently replaced; Uncle Frank had put up a track and hung them. Drawn against the dark night, they made the room feel warm. With the gas fire lit, and a couple of lamps with nice cream shades that she'd got cheap in a sale at work, the room felt and looked quite cosy. She could do with a mirror for the chimney breast wall and a painting or framed print above the sofa. Maybe Alex could paint her something, a nice vase of red flowers or a landscape, mountains or the ocean or something. She'd suggest it when he came to see her.

⊛

Jackie stretched out on the bed in the spare room at Agnes's and let her mind wander. Everyone had gone to bed and she'd been drifting in and out of sleep for hours. She felt glad to be back in Liverpool and was so grateful to Uncle Frank for coming to her rescue, but something was bothering her and it scared the life out of her. Until she got home and found her diary she was trying not to get too concerned. It hadn't even crossed her mind until Patsy had mentioned it earlier – that the sick feeling she seemed to have each morning might be more than a bug. But it couldn't be, surely, because Sandy had been so careful. It was obviously the worry of running away that was taking its toll on her, and not having enough to eat. She was just being paranoid now. There was no way she could possibly be pregnant. Lightning didn't strike twice in the same place and he couldn't be that unlucky, could he?

Still, she knew she hadn't seen a period since before they went away at the end of August. Not that she'd ever been very regular, and she needed to check the date to be sure, but it was now the beginning of November. Mam and Dad would kill her. More to the point, they'd probably kill Sandy too. She turned onto her side and willed sleep to come.

⊛

Patsy ran upstairs as soon as she got home from work, and burst into the bedroom.

Jackie looked up from the magazine she was reading. 'God, you made me jump. What's up?'

'Got you a job,' she gasped. 'You can start on Monday if you want it. I know you said you couldn't face going back to college in case you bumped into Sandy in town. My supervisor said she'd be happy to give you an informal interview tomorrow afternoon and if it suits you, then it's yours.'

'Oh that's fantastic!' Jackie's face lit up. 'I can't go back to college anyway because the money my dad gave me has gone, so I've no choice but to get a job. I'll try and get on a night school drama course in time.'

'Bet some of the theatres in town do courses. You need to ask around when you get on your feet.'

'I will. Be better off working because my head's playing tricks with me lying around here all day. I'm imagining all sorts and I can't deal with it. Did you see Stevie after work tonight?'

'Yeah, he met me and we went for a quick coffee but he's had to dash off to get a painting sorted. They've got another exhibition coming up.'

'Did he say how Sandy is? Does he know I'm home now?'

'Yes, he does. He blamed himself, you know. He's very down; I *do* feel worried about him. Stevie said he hasn't been to the new flat to see Carol yet.'

'Can't believe she's done that, moved out of Mam's, I mean. After Sandy's dad laying down the law about not living together until after the baby's born. What's she going to do if it's not his, I mean just on the off-chance? She'll be all on her own.'

Patsy raised an eyebrow. 'I don't think there's much chance of it not being his, do you?'

Jackie sighed. 'I suppose not. I'm going back home tomorrow. Mam came round this afternoon and said she's got my room ready. Dad's given it a fresh coat of paint, so it's all nice and clean, and there'll hopefully be no trace of Carol left in there.'

'And don't forget to check your diary,' Patsy said. 'Are you sure it was before we went away?'

Jackie chewed her lip and stared up at the ceiling. 'Definitely. But don't forget, I've had all this upset from the minute I got home, and I was never regular anyway, I've gone two months before. So I can't be; it's impossible.'

'Well I hope it is, for your sake, not to mention Sandy's. It's nearly three months, never mind two, *and* you've been sick God knows how many times.'

Jackie blew out her cheeks and groaned. 'That's a bug, I'm sure. I'm putting it out of my mind for now anyway. Please don't say anything to Stevie. I don't want Sandy worrying; he's got enough on his plate.'

❀

Jackie was up early, ready and out of the house for eight o'clock on Monday morning. She'd been sick again, but recovered quickly. At least her mam had left for her early shift at the hospital and Dad for work, so they were unaware of anything untoward, but tomorrow was Mam's morning off so she'd have to try to drown out the retching sounds somehow.

The diary had confirmed her last period date as August the 19th and today was November the 7th. The holiday had been the last week of August, so there was a possibility of her being ten weeks pregnant. The thought filled her with horror. But she had to push it to the back of her mind and start the new job. The informal interview had gone well and she was to be placed in the same office as Patsy. It was coupon checking, nothing too complicated, so she was certain she could do the job easily enough, and it would get her through the long days of being without Sandy. As she left the house and hurried around to Patsy's place her spirits lifted a little. Her friend ran out to meet her and the pair scurried along Longmoor Lane to the bus stop.

'Did you check that date?' Patsy whispered as they took seats downstairs on the bus; Jackie said she couldn't face the smoky smell of sitting upstairs as it made her feel even more sickly.

'Yes, and I was right.'

'Shit!' Patsy exclaimed.

'I know. But if I can get through to Christmas and Caz has her baby and it's not Sandy's, then we can be together and it will all be okay. I don't even want to think about it until then. I've lost weight in the last few weeks anyway; I'm skinny as a rake, so no one will guess.'

Patsy stared out of the window as though miles away.

'What's up, why have you gone all quiet?'

'I'm just worried about you, that's all.'

'Well don't be. Let's just enjoy working together for now.'

❀

Carol shifted uncomfortably in her seat. Her back was killing her and she couldn't wait to start her maternity leave. She'd decided to work an extra few weeks as she knew she'd be bored at home alone, but was now looking forward to her time off. The money would be a lot less than her normal wages, but she'd just have to manage.

She really didn't want to come back to work as the problems of getting to her mam's or Mrs Faraday's with the baby, and then into town, would be a nightmare, and there was no way she could rely on Alex for help. He'd finally popped in to see her on Sunday afternoon and left an envelope with some money in it towards the next lot of rent. She told him she'd use it to pay the rates and water rates and would need some more for rent in a few weeks.

He'd also brought a bag of hand-knitted baby clothes, all in white, which his mother had made. That had surprised Carol. So all in all things were looking up, but he'd refused her offer of making him something to eat, and said he had to dash home to Stevie's place as he was busy with work for the Christmas exhibition. When she mentioned the possibility of him doing a nice picture for the wall above the sofa he'd shaken his head at the suggestion. He told her he didn't paint that sort of thing, but he'd see what he could find amongst the other students' work that might be suitable.

He'd kept his distance, sitting on the armchair while she sat on the sofa. He'd hurried his mug of coffee down, and then given her a quick peck on the cheek and dashed away having made no commitment as to when he'd come round again. He'd just told her he'd see her soon. He was determined to stick to the original plans: that once he knew for sure he was the father, he'd take responsibility. It wasn't too long to wait now, so she'd just keep herself busy making baby clothes. Uncle Frank had got her a telly, so her nights weren't too lonely. She had to wait for visits from Mam and Dad as she'd been told not to go round to their house and upset Jackie.

Her new neighbour Kevin was very friendly. He'd moved into the flat above her at the weekend. She'd offered him a mug of tea as he seemed a bit disorganised, and on her way back from the shops he was still rooting in the car boot for his kettle, so took her up on the offer.

He'd made himself at home on the sofa while she brewed up. By the end of the afternoon she knew his life story and he hers, but he didn't pass judgement as to why Alex wasn't living with her yet, which made a nice change from people thinking it was an odd arrangement and telling her she shouldn't have married him. Kevin was ten years older than her and told her he'd just got divorced. He had a five-year-old daughter who lived with his ex in their marital home and he saw her on Saturdays; he did a bit of this and a bit of that to earn a living. But she had no idea what sort of this and that he was referring to. He didn't elaborate and she didn't like to pry. He seemed very nice and had a decent car, was casually but smartly dressed, and she felt herself relaxing in his company.

As he'd left he called out that if she needed help with anything, to give him a shout. And as she'd sat with her feet up last night it was comforting to hear the sound of another human being upstairs.

'You ready, Caz?' Susan interrupted her thoughts. 'Fancy a bite to eat? Pete's playing darts tonight so I'm at a loose end. Don't suppose you're seeing Alex?'

'No, I'm not. Why don't you come back to my place and I'll make us something. You haven't seen it since I've moved in properly.'

'Sounds like a good idea to me. I'll treat us to a bottle of wine from the off-licence.'

❀

As Carol and Susan made their way along Luxmore Road after buying a bottle of Blue Nun, Carol's neighbour pulled up alongside them. He tooted and waved. They stood on the pavement while he got out of his car and Carol introduced him to Susan.

'Enjoy your wine, ladies,' he said as he ran up the stairs to his own flat while Carol unlocked her front door. She invited Susan in and switched on the gas fire and pulled the curtains across the bay window.

'He's a bit of all right,' Susan said as she took off her coat and hung it up on the back of the door. 'Wouldn't kick him out of bed. Kevin, did you say his name was?'

'Yes.' Carol handed Susan a couple of wine glasses and a corkscrew. 'He's very friendly, divorced and got a little daughter.'

'And he fancies you, in spite of your bloody great bump,' Susan teased. 'He couldn't take his eyes off you.'

'Don't be daft, he doesn't. Anyway, I'm a married woman.'

'Not that you'd notice,' Susan said quietly. 'It looks really nice in here. Alex wants his bloody arse kicking, letting you live alone like this. It'll serve him right if you *do* find someone else.'

'I've blown my chances of finding anyone else. Nobody wants a girlfriend with a baby. It's Alex or nothing.'

'I still think you're mad. Get it adopted and move on. Your life is in limbo and so is Alex's.'

'I can't do that, Sue.'

'Can't or won't? Is that you just being stubborn so that no matter what happens, you'll always have a hold over him? His baby or not, Caz, he'll go back to your sister eventually, and I think you know that.' She handed a glass of wine to Carol.

Carol sighed and took a sip. 'I have to give it a chance. And at least this way my baby has a name and a father, whether he wants to be involved or not.'

Chapter Twenty-Three

December 1966

Sandy unloaded the panniers on his scooter; more bags of bloody baby clothes from his mother. She was doing her bit in the practical department, even though she still refused to have Carol under her roof, which was now the long-awaited bungalow in the church hall grounds.

He hitched the bulging bags up into his arms and knocked on the door of Carol's flat. He still couldn't think of it as *his* home too, not just yet. The door was opened by a dark-haired man, slightly taller than himself, and definitely older.

'You must be Alex, Caz's husband? I'm Kev from upstairs. Just dropping her some bits and bobs in. Bit slippery underfoot for a lady in *her* condition. Last thing she needs is a fall at this late stage.'

Sandy felt his cheeks heating as the guy looked him up and down with an unfathomable expression.

'She needs looking after, mate. Right, I'm off. See youse later, Caz.' Kevin pushed past Sandy and ran up the stairs.

Sandy walked into the sitting room and dumped the packages on the table. 'More baby stuff from Mum.' He jerked his thumb at the ceiling. 'Does he do a lot of running about for you, er, that Kevin fella?'

'He has been doing for the last week or two,' she replied, moving up on the sofa so that Sandy could sit next to her, but as usual he sat on the chair across the room. 'I'm scared of falling with the pavements being so icy. I'm just praying it doesn't snow for the next few days.'

Sandy nodded, glancing around the cosy little room with the gas fire throwing out heat and the curtains closed against the cold night air. In the corner near the table stood a Christmas tree in a red bucket, decorated with red and gold ornaments and lights. On the coffee table, two empty mugs and dirty plates told the tale of a shared meal. Sandy could smell fish and chips.

'So, he brought you some tea in? I was going to ask if you fancied something from the chippy, but looks like I'm too late.'

'We were hungry. And I didn't know *you* were coming,' Carol almost snapped. 'I *never* know when you're coming, and it drives me mad. This baby could arrive any day now. What if I go into labour and I'm on my own? You should be here; we're *your* responsibility, now, Alex.'

She began to cry and he stared up at a faint crack in the ceiling, wishing that she was Jackie and this was *their* cosy little home and *their* expected baby. He couldn't even go to Carol and comfort her. What sort of an unfeeling bastard was he?

He knew it was time to move in, but accepting it was almost like admitting defeat. Still, if anything bad happened, and he wasn't here, he'd get it in the neck either way; *her* mother would go mad and so would his. He'd lied to his mum today; told her he was looking after Carol and would let them know as soon as the baby arrived.

'I'll bring my things over on Sunday,' he announced. 'But I don't wanna see that Kevin bloke in here again. I suppose he got you the tree too, did he?' He nodded towards the little decorated tree. 'You can't have managed that on your own *and* the bucket of sand to stand it in.'

'He was getting his own tree; his daughter's coming to stay on Christmas Eve. He treated me, along with the bucket. Otherwise I wouldn't have one. The decorations are from Lewis's. Sue brought me them. Why are you so nasty about Kevin? At least he cares. You couldn't give a shit about me. We should never have got married.'

'At least that's something we agree on,' he muttered. 'Like I said, I'll move in on Sunday. But I don't wanna see *him* in here again. I mean it, Caz. You're a married woman. People talk. If it gets back to the church gossips that you've had men in while I'm not here my mum will go mad.'

'*Men?*' Carol rolled her eyes. 'You really are an arse, and stuff your bloody mother. As if I care about the gossips. Why the hell did I ever think I loved you? You're just a selfish kid who hasn't got a clue.'

'So why bother marrying me then? Like Dad suggested, the baby should be adopted and we can go our separate ways. It was your stupid idea to move in here on your own, anyway. You were supposed to stay at your mam's place until it arrives.'

'Oh, and that would have suited *you* down to the ground. Living at Stevie's, having the life of Riley and playing at being single.'

'Hardly.' Sandy couldn't be bothered arguing with her. He was tired. He'd worked every night after college at the Jac to help her pay the rent and bills and at weekends painted until his mind and fingers were numb, trying to get his own exhibition together for the gallery.

'Anyway, I'm not allowed at Mam's now because Jackie's living back there, and let's face it, we mustn't upset our precious Princess Jackie, must we?' She struggled up off the sofa, placed her hands either side of her back and grimaced slightly.

Sandy stared at her. Where had the trendy Mod he'd taken to bed gone? She no longer wore a neat Twiggy hairstyle; her hair was scraped back off her face with an elastic band into an untidy ponytail. Her pale face was rounder, and devoid of makeup and the false eyelashes she used to wear that made her eyes look enormous, the one feature he'd really liked above anything else. She had a huge baby-bump, breasts that looked as though they were about to explode through the dress she wore, and her ankles were swollen and nothing like the slender ankles he remembered when he used to remove her white knee boots before running his hands up her long legs. He shuddered inwardly and knew he wasn't going to be sharing the bed with her any time soon.

'I'll sleep on the sofa,' he said. 'I'll cadge a sleeping bag off one of the lads.'

She opened her mouth to protest and closed it again. 'Whatever you want, Alex.'

He pecked her on the cheek and went outside to his scooter. The upstairs curtains were still open and he could see Kevin looking at him. He stuck two fingers up and Kevin returned the gesture as he rode away. He'd bet anything the bastard would be down later, keeping Caz company. He wondered if he'd ever tried it on with her. Nothing would surprise him. Caz wasn't an easy lay, but he knew he hadn't been her first, even though she swore blind he was. She wasn't *his* first either, but he was choosy and after Jackie there was no going back. If he never had sex again as long as he lived, he couldn't sleep with Caz. But at least his kid, if it *was* his, would have a name.

❀

Carol filled the sink with hot soapy water and put the plates and mugs in to soak. She squeezed herself into the tiny bathroom, turned on the taps and added some rose-scented bath salts, a leaving present from one of her workmates, to the running water. She topped the bath up with cold, stirred the bubbles with both hands and stripped off.

Lying in the bath, she wished with all her heart she could go back nine months and have her life return to normal. She no doubt would have met someone else by now. Alex would be happy with her sister, and she'd have learned to get over him in time. Now life was just a shitty mess, she'd never felt more miserable and she knew Alex did too. The only good thing to come out of it was that Jackie was home safe and the remaining damaged contraceptive must have been chucked away. She would never forgive herself if her sister got pregnant too.

Without Kevin's help these last few weeks she'd have struggled. He'd done her shopping, cleaned her windows and tidied the bit of front garden that her sitting room window overlooked, and then his kindness in bringing her the Christmas tree had brought tears to her eyes. He made her feel wanted, for once in her life. Her mam had suffered with depression after her birth and the death of her twin sister. It had taken a few years for Mam to pull herself together and accept Carol, and then Jackie had arrived and Mam had been obsessed with cleaning and fussing over the new baby, even though she'd been told by doctors at the hospital that her baby's death had been nothing to do with anything she had or hadn't done. It was just one of those things.

Carol often felt that Mam wished it was her that had died and not her other daughter. Mam had been diagnosed with depression again following Jackie's birth and she and Jackie had gone to live with Granny and Uncle Frank to be looked after while Mam recovered, and Carol had been left with Dad at the prefab. She'd felt rejected, and although she knew now it was just Mam's way of coping, she'd never shaken that feeling; especially as later Carol had been removed from Mam's care once more to live with her dad again, and it had taken ages for her to be returned. It was always at the back of her mind that she was second best.

She'd enjoyed the short time at Fourth Avenue recently, to feel important and fussed over for once. Trust bloody Jackie to be the drama queen and do her disappearing act, robbing her of all that attention. So for Kevin to show an interest, it felt nice.

Alex could go and get stuffed. Who did he think he was, laying down the law like that? If he cared at all he'd be here now, washing her back. If Kevin knocked on later with a bottle of wine and some chocolates, like he sometimes did, she would let him in and they could watch telly together or listen to music. He'd been a perfect gent so far and hadn't even made a pass at her. Well, just wait until this baby arrived and she was back to her old self again. Slim, hair nicely styled once more, and into her trendy clothes, instead of her mam's smock dresses, which were very well made as Mam was a brilliant seamstress, but still, they did nothing for her other than accommodate her bump. And if Alex was still being distant, she might just see what Kevin could offer instead.

❀

Sandy sat down at the kitchen table as Stevie grabbed his parka and scooter keys.

'Where you off to?' He'd just got back from his visit to Caz's and was hoping to bend his mate's ear.

'Meeting Patsy off the bus. She's coming back here for a couple of hours.'

'How come you're not going to her house to pick her up?'

'Because she's coming into town with Jackie. Can't fit two on the back, can I?'

Sandy frowned. 'So, where's Jackie going?' He felt sick. Did she have a date with someone?

'Unity Theatre for an audition. She was a bit worried about coming into town on her own at night so Patsy said she'd come down with her.'

Sandy got to his feet. 'I'll come with you. Gives me a chance to see her.'

'No, mate, you won't. You can stay here. No point in upsetting her when she's going for an audition. That wouldn't be fair. She'll be a bag of nerves as it is. You can ask Patsy how she is.'

Stevie left and Sandy lit a cigarette and made a mug of coffee. He sat and blew smoke rings into the air, feeling totally pissed off with life. His spirits lifted slightly when he heard Stevie and Patsy come indoors and pound up the stairs, out of breath and holding onto each other, laughing. It was ages since he'd enjoyed a laugh and he felt envious of the pair.

'You okay, Sandy?' Patsy asked, throwing her coat over a chair and plonking herself down while Stevie made her a brew.

'No, he's not okay,' Stevie answered for him. 'He's brassed off, aren't you, mate?'

'Just a bit,' Sandy agreed, a sarcastic edge to his voice. 'How's Jackie doing? Does she like the job at Littlewoods?'

Patsy's cheeks flushed slightly, which didn't go unnoticed by Sandy and he frowned. 'She's fine. Settling in okay. The job's a bit boring after her time at college, but once she's got some money behind her she's hoping to get back on the course. She's auditioning for a dance troupe tonight. She'll be in the chorus line-up for a show next year if she gets it. It's a start. And it's what she wants to do.'

'I hope they take her on. She deserves to do well,' Sandy said. 'Tell her I was asking about her. Give her my love.'

'I will. How come you're still here at Stevie's? Thought you'd have moved in with Caz by now.'

Sandy sighed and stubbed out his butt end in the chipped saucer. 'I move in on Sunday. Right, I'll leave you two in peace and go and do some more painting.'

Stevie stared after him. 'Christ I feel for him, but what can I do? Be glad when that kid's born and he can get his head around it one way or the other.'

❀

Patsy sipped her coffee and stared thoughtfully over the rim of her mug. She had two massive secrets and she couldn't even share them with Stevie, much as she wanted to. Carol's damaged contraceptives confession, along with the certainty that Sandy *was* the father, and now the fact there was little doubt that Jackie was pregnant too. But she still wouldn't take a sample into Boots to get confirmation in case someone saw her and told her mam. She'd be four months by Christmas, in two weeks' time, but was pinning all her hopes on the blood tests that she was so sure would set Sandy free to be with her. God help her, she would be heartbroken all over again, only things would be a hundred times worse now with a baby on the way.

Doing the audition tonight was Jackie in denial and carrying on as though things were fine. Her baby-bump was starting to show and the game would soon be up. By the time the show hit the stage in January, Jackie's secret would be out and it wouldn't matter if she passed the audition or not tonight, there's no way they'd let her leap around in *her* condition. What a bloody mess. God help them all.

'You okay?' Stevie stood behind her and rubbed her shoulders. He kissed the top of her head.

She looked up at him and smiled. 'We shouldn't have all these problems at our age. Life's supposed to be fun in your teens, isn't it?'

'Well *we* haven't got any problems. It's him in there and his women who've got the problems.' He jerked his thumb towards the closed door of the living room, where Sandy was painting and listening to Bob Dylan. 'Come on; let's go to my room while we've got the chance. We won't see him again tonight, he'll be in there until the early hours.'

He took Patsy's hand and led her to his bedroom, kicking the door shut. He pulled her down onto the mattress and kissed her, his hand up her sweater, squeezing her breasts, but Patsy wasn't responding in her usual passionate way.

'What's wrong, babe?' He leant up on one elbow and traced his fingers around her lips. 'You going off me? Come on, Pats, tell me. Shit, you're not… are you?'

'No, of course not.' She half-smiled and then burst into tears.

He held her tight while she sobbed on his shoulder. 'Tell me what's wrong, please.'

She wiped her eyes on the hanky he pulled from his jeans pocket. 'You absolutely promise not to say a word to anybody? You have to swear on, oh I don't know, your mam's life. You can't tell anyone. Promise?'

He nodded, looking worried. 'I promise. Just tell me.'

And because she couldn't hold on to the secret any more, and it served Carol right for being such a bitch, she told Stevie about the damaged contraceptives. His jaw tightened and she saw the shock cross his face.

He stared at her, silently shaking his head.

'Not a word,' she repeated.

'Fucking hell! The devious cow.' His voice rose a few octaves, but Bob Dylan was still singing so Sandy wouldn't hear his expletives. 'And she told you this *after* the wedding?'

'Yes. She told *me*, Mam and *her* mam while Jackie was still missing. She promised to tell Sandy what she'd done, but I don't think she's kept that promise, do you?'

'I doubt it. He'd be off like a shot. Oh, Christ, now what do we do? He needs to know.'

Patsy shook her head. 'It's not up to us. We promised we'd say nothing, on the condition she told him. I guess she's waiting until after the birth now so she doesn't have to go through it on her own. But that baby is Sandy's, there's no doubt about it.'

Stevie lay on his back, hands behind his head, and stared up at the ceiling.

'Stevie, there's more. The shit's really going to hit the fan for Sandy soon.'

'More?'

'Jackie's pregnant too. From the holiday. She's nearly four months. Nobody knows and I just don't know what to do now, because she's pinning all her hopes on him being free after the results of the blood tests and then he can be with *her*.'

'Oh, for God's sake!' Stevie ran his hands through his hair and stared at her. 'No wonder you don't fancy a bit of the other with all that on your mind. Shit! What can we do to help them?'

Patsy shrugged. 'No idea. Jackie's mam and dad are gonna go mental and I dread to think what Sandy's parents will say to this one.'

The phone rang out in the kitchen but they ignored it, as did Sandy.

'It'll only be my mam mithering about nothing as usual,' he said. 'After *that* bombshell I can't be arsed making small-talk. I'll see them in the shop tomorrow anyway.' He lit a cigarette and coughed a cloud of smoke into the air. 'Shit, I need something stronger than fags, but I've got to take you back to the theatre and it's icy out there so it'll have to do. Thanks for trusting me, Pats. I'll say nothing, but something's got to give, and soon.'

'I know.' Patsy's eyes filled up again. 'But God help Jackie. I really don't know what's going to happen there. I feel a bit easier for confiding in you. I know I've betrayed trusts, but my head's felt like it's about to explode lately.'

❀

Carol took a deep breath and sat on the garden wall two doors down from where she lived. The pains were coming frequently now and she needed to get back inside. She'd called for an ambulance and also called Alex at Stevie's flat but there'd been no reply. No doubt he was out having a good time, she thought, angrily, doubling over as another wave of pain hit her.

She'd called up to Kevin but there'd been no reply. He hadn't come downstairs tonight, and after her bath she'd gone to bed with a magazine and fallen asleep, only to be woken an hour or so later with pains and an urgent need for the loo. Her waters had gone as soon as she stepped into the bathroom.

She'd pulled a coat on over her nightdress, discovered Kevin's car wasn't outside and made her way to the phone box on the corner. She'd kept her purse full of loose change for the past week, just in case, and what a good job she had. Agnes's phone was engaged and she'd tried three times before giving up. Uncle Frank wasn't answering either, so he must be out. Feeling very scared and alone, she'd made her way back as far as the wall she was now sitting on, terrified of slipping in her long white boots on the icy pavements. As she sat there taking another deep breath, headlights came slowly towards her and she cried out with relief to see Kevin's car. He pulled up outside their flats and ran towards her.

'I'm in labour,' she gasped. 'Ambulance is on its way.'

He lifted her up, carried her back into the flat, wrapped a blanket around her and got her a glass of water. 'That fucking husband of yours wants lynching,' he said, pacing the sitting room floor. 'Where the hell is he? Right, here's the ambulance. Where's your bag and stuff. Have you packed it?'

'In the bedroom,' she cried as another contraction took her breath away.

He let in the two attendants and dashed to the bedroom to get her case and followed them out as they helped Carol into the waiting ambulance.

'You getting in with her, Dad?' the taller of the men asked.

'Oh, he's not—' Carol began but didn't finish as a mask was placed over her face with instructions to take deep breaths. She closed her eyes and left them all to it, floating skywards with blessed relief on the gas and air.

Kevin perched beside her as the ambulance pulled away, bells ringing. He took her hand and she gripped it tight, glad of his presence, even though she felt embarrassed by her half-dressed state and the fact that one of the ambulance men had whipped off her wet knickers and stuck a huge pad between her legs in front of Kevin. A pink nighty and long white boots weren't exactly a flattering combination. She'd never be able to look him in the eye again when this was over.

'I've done this before, remember?' he said, as though reading her mind. 'You need someone with you. They don't need to know the details,' he said, nodding towards the front of the ambulance. 'Do you want me to try and call Alex when we get to the hospital?'

She pulled the mask to one side. 'I've tried. He wasn't there. Don't bother. He'd be nothing short of useless anyway.' She took another breath of gas and air and closed her eyes as another pain hit her. 'Jesus, this is the last kid I'm ever having. Aggghhhh!'

She dug her nails into Kevin's hand as he smoothed the hair from her face with his free hand. Why oh why couldn't she have met someone like him before getting mixed up with Alex? Fleetingly, she wondered why his ex had thrown him out. But that wasn't her problem. Getting this bloody thing out of her body was her main priority right now.

❀

Stevie opened one eye slowly and checked his watch. Who on earth was calling at six in the morning? He ignored the ringing phone but it was relentless. There was no sign of life from Sandy's room except gentle snoring, so he crept into the kitchen wearing nothing but skimpy black pants and a T-shirt. His head thumped and he breathed in the heady scent of cannabis. After Patsy's double whammy last night he'd come back home from dropping her off and he and Sandy had got stoned. How he'd managed not to say anything to him he didn't know, but Sandy had crawled happily off to bed and was still there.

He snatched at the phone and mumbled, 'Hello.'

It was Caz's mam wanting to speak to Sandy. God, what now? he thought as he banged on Sandy's door. Sandy appeared, pale-faced, bleary-eyed and his hair standing on end.

'What?'

'Yer ma-in-law's on the phone.'

'Who?'

'Caz's mam, on the phone. I'm going back to bed. Tell me what's up when you finish.'

Sandy rubbed his face and stumbled into the kitchen. He tried to remain focused as Caz's mam ranted on at him for not putting in an appearance at the hospital last night and that his seven-pound-four-ounce son had arrived at just after two thirty this morning and wasn't it a bloody good job the neighbour had been around to help or that poor baby would have been born in the street.

Sandy sat down heavily on a chair and asked if the baby and Caz were okay.

'They are. No thanks to you. You can visit this afternoon. Fazakerley hospital. Two until four. Don't forget to let your parents know. Tell our Carol me and her dad will see her tonight.'

Sandy hung up and sat with his head in his hands. He'd got a son. Maybe. The blood tests would be done and by the end of the week he'd know for sure. Caz'd be in hospital for a few days. So he could stay here for now and not move in on Sunday as planned. If the boy was his, then he'd move in next week and get things ready for them coming home. Time to face up to his responsibilities.

Chapter Twenty-Four

January 1967

The christening of Paul John George Faraday took place on the third Sunday in January. Sandy had put his foot down when Caz expressed her wish to add Ringo to the list. The child's grandfather, Reverend Faraday, performed the service and briefly attended the small buffet afterwards at Fazakerley British Legion. Mrs Faraday, conspicuous by her absence, had feigned yet another migraine rather than face the gleeful gossips in the congregation. Her youngest son had shamed his family and it would take a long time before she could even begin to forgive him.

The blood tests had shown the likelihood of Sandy being the baby's father was higher than the likelihood he was not. He knew that was as good as it was going to get, and he'd accepted this and moved in with Caz and took his turn in caring for baby Paul to the best of his abilities. Money was always tight and it was looking increasingly likely that he'd have to give up his art course and find some labouring work, or something. Caz's Uncle Frank had told him he could get him a job any time down at the docks. His first thought was that he'd rather die than do that, but it seemed there wasn't much choice. Her mam and dad had given them a hundred pounds when Paul was born. Caz would soon make short work of that, no doubt. She was due back at work soon, but was constantly harping on how she was going to manage to get from their flat to her mam's and then on to work without having to get up at stupid o'clock and that Paul couldn't be dropped off early if Jackie was still in. Kevin had offered to help with lifts but Sandy had told Caz they'd manage without his help. He didn't trust the neighbour, who looked at his wife with lust in his eyes. Not that he was jealous; he didn't love Caz and was married as a matter of duty only, still choosing to sleep on the sofa rather than get into bed with her.

He had no intentions of consummating their marriage and if Caz wanted to use that reason to get a divorce, he wouldn't contest it, as then it would be *her* choice. But she seemed happy enough with the situation as it stood, and spent all her time devoting her attention to Paul, and speaking to Sandy only when she had to. In front of their few and infrequent visitors she portrayed the part of a happily married woman, but as soon as they were alone the shutters came down again and she ignored him, shutting him out completely.

He was still spending time and nights at Stevie's flat as it was the only place with room to paint. He wondered if, on those nights, Kevin kept Caz company. If he ever found out that he was shagging her he'd have grounds for divorce, but the pair acted innocently enough in front of him. It was simply a case of biding his time until an opportunity presented itself with a genuine reason to leave her that wouldn't embarrass his mother further.

Standing at the bar now, downing a pint with Stevie, Paul's godfather, he wished he were anywhere but here. Jackie had refused to attend the christening. In fact, she hadn't even acknowledged her nephew and he couldn't blame her, in spite of the fact he felt quite proud of his son, who, everyone told him, was his spitting image. He couldn't see it himself; didn't all babies look the same, a bit like Winston Churchill?

Patsy sidled over to the bar and took Stevie by the arm. She whispered in his ear and he nodded.

'I'll come for you in an hour or so,' he said.

'Okay.' She turned to Sandy. 'Thanks for asking us to be Paul's godparents.'

Sandy smiled. 'Thanks for accepting. I know it wasn't easy, with Jackie and stuff, but I didn't want *her* pals to be any part of it.' He looked pointedly at Carol and her friend Sue, who was throwing back her head, shrieking drunkenly at something her boyfriend was saying. 'My mother would have had a fit. *Salt of the earth*, she'd say, *but quite unsuitable for the job, Alexander.*' He mimicked his mother's prim tone perfectly. 'Choosing you two and Caz's Uncle Frank has gained me a few brownie points.'

Patsy smiled and stroked his arm. 'I'm sorry things didn't work out the way you hoped they would, but Paul *is* a cute baby, and I guess you can only do your best and see what happens.'

'I know what I *want* to happen,' he said quietly.

'I know you do.'

'Give her my love.'

'How do you know that's where I'm going?'

'Intuition.'

She raised a neat eyebrow. 'I will. See you later, Stevie,' she said, giving him a peck on the cheek.

'Wish I could slope off with her,' Sandy muttered and turned to the barmaid. 'Two pints when you're ready, please.'

⌘

Patsy dashed into the ladies before leaving the Legion and was in a cubicle, hitching up her tights, when she heard two women talking as they came in. She recognised Carol's drunken friend's loud voice and then Carol's voice, slightly lower.

'Well you did it, gel, didn't youse? Snared him I mean. Bet you were glad them tests turned out in your favour as well. Imagine if they hadn't, you'd be in a right mess now.'

'But I knew they would. Paul couldn't be anybody else's. I don't sleep around.'

'Well no, I know that. But you've said yourself in the past that Alex never took chances, so *you* getting up the duff was a bloody miracle in itself.'

'Yes, well.' Carol laughed. 'I found a way around it.'

Patsy straightened her skirt and picked up her handbag, anger rising as she flushed the toilet. Both girls fell silent when they realised they weren't alone.

Carol's eyes opened wide and her cheeks reddened as Patsy left the cubicle and pushed past the pair of them to wash her hands. She dried them on a paper towel as Carol stared at her, mouth opening and closing.

'Don't mind me,' Patsy said, taking her lipstick out of her bag and slicking her lips. 'Aren't you going to finish telling your friend what a devious bitch you've been? How you trapped poor Sandy because you were jealous of his relationship with your sister? Oh, and don't forget to tell her how you made a promise to me and your mam and *my* mam, that you'd tell him what you'd done, and that you still haven't kept that promise.'

Carol burst into tears and Susan put an arm around her shoulders. 'Hey, you vicious little mare, don't you speak to Caz like that.'

'I'll speak to her how I like,' Patsy yelled. 'Tell her,' she shouted at Carol. 'Because if you don't I'm going out there now and *I'll* tell Sandy. He hates you. He still loves Jackie and you know it. He tells me all the time to pass on his love to her.'

Patsy stopped, realising the Babychams she'd drunk were loosening her tongue more than they should. She chewed her lip and stared at Carol, who was wiping her eyes on a tissue that Susan had given her.

'Please don't say anything to Alex, I beg you. I need him, *Paul* needs him. He won't leave us because it will upset his mother and there's no way I'll *ever* divorce him. I'll tell Susan what I did when you go.'

'Never mind Susan,' Patsy said, pushing her face close to Carol's in a threatening manner. 'Tell Sandy.' Those crocodile tears weren't fooling her one bit. 'Because if *you* don't, *I* will. You have no idea of the damage you've done to your sister and Sandy, no idea at all.'

She stormed out of the ladies before she said anything she shouldn't, and anger kept her marching furiously up Longmoor Lane to Fourth Avenue.

❀

Carol chewed her lip as Patsy stormed out and Susan stared questioningly at her. She needed her friend on her side; not many people were, and she didn't think telling her the truth would go down too well. What she'd done wasn't something she was proud of.

'So come on then, what did you do that she thinks is so bad?'

Carol swallowed hard.

She took a deep breath. 'It was just one night, we got really drunk and Alex had no rubbers left but couldn't keep his hands off me. So although it wasn't, I told him it was my safe time and we did it without using anything. And bingo, Paul happened.'

Another lie. She was getting good at it. Like the lies she told Alex when he stayed over at Stevie's after working late, or to paint, and she allowed Kevin to keep her company at night and ply her with drinks. Kevin was getting a bit friskier and she knew it was only a matter of time before something happened between them. She was almost back to normal following Paul's birth and couldn't wait to be loved again. She missed the way Kevin made her feel when Alex was around, and it was a long time since *he'd* had that effect on her. She also missed the alcohol, as they couldn't afford even a bottle of the cheapest wine. Alcohol made her feel free and sexy again. No wonder she responded eagerly to Kevin's wandering hands and insistent kisses.

Susan shook her head. 'Is that all? Bloody hell, the way she went on I thought you'd shagged him at knife point or something. Slip-ups happen all the time. So, why does she say you have to tell Alex? Surely he realises when it happened and how?'

'Well of course he does. She's just being a drama queen like my bloody sister. I'm that wound up today that she caught me unawares, hence the tears,' Carol finished.

Susan smiled and gave her a hug. 'Right, let's have a quick pee and get back to the celebrations.'

Carol breathed a sigh of relief and hurried into a cubicle. Another drink was just what she needed, in spite of Alex telling her to go easy earlier. Uncle Frank was buying the drinks anyway, so it wasn't like Alex was dipping into his own pocket. Miserable bugger, begrudging her celebrating their son's special day. Kevin would happily have got her drunk, she'd bet her life on it.

❀

Jackie got up off the bed when she heard the loud knocking at the door. No doubt it would be Patsy, who'd told her she'd get away as soon as she could after the service and come and keep her company while the rest of the family were at the Legion. She hurried downstairs and let her in. Patsy gave her a hug and asked for a coffee as she was feeling a bit drunk and her head had started to bang. They sat in the kitchen while the kettle boiled.

'How did it go?' Jackie asked, spooning Nescafé powder into two mugs.

'Okay. Paul was good, he didn't even cry. He's a sweet little thing really. Pity I can't say the same about his mother.'

'Don't even mention her name,' Jackie said, pouring water into the mugs. 'Let's go into the sitting room. I need to talk to you.'

They sat side by side on the sofa, Jackie pale and her eyes red-rimmed. Tears were never far away.

'I've made a decision,' she began. 'If Dad goes on to the pub with Uncle Frank after the christening, Mam will come home, because she's got to get up early for work, so – while we're on our own – I'll tell her I'm pregnant. I can't keep it to myself for much longer, all my clothes are tight and she's going to guess soon anyway.

I've seen her looking at me with a frown on her face so it's only a matter of time.'

'Oh my God, you're brave. I'd rather slit my wrists than tell my mam. She'd kill me.'

'She wouldn't, she'd be angry at first but she loves you and would want to look after you, like Mam did with my bitch of a sister. Anyway, I can't keep this baby, can I? And Sandy must never find out. He'd be beside himself and he's already in a bad way, from what you and Stevie tell me. I don't want to send him over the edge.'

Patsy blew out her cheeks. 'What will you do? You're too far on for an abortion, even if they said you could get one. You can't stay hidden away here until it's born, and then what about afterwards?'

'I'll go away to a mother and baby home, and then I'll have to get it adopted.'

Patsy clapped a hand to her mouth. 'Oh, Jackie, you can't do that, you just can't. There must be another way.' She burst into tears and Jackie patted her arm, blinking back her own tears.

'There isn't. I've done nothing but think about it since that girl at work told us about her younger sister who's in Prospect House in Hoylake. She's just had a little boy and she's looking after him for six weeks, then he'll be taken away and she'll come home and that's it. Mam can tell people I'm away with the dancing show. I got the part, but I can't accept it in my condition, can I? Even Dad doesn't need to know where I am. And at least he'll be here to look after Mam now he's moved in properly. They've talked about remarrying when his divorce comes through.'

'You seem very calm about all this,' Patsy said, wiping her eyes.

'Patsy, I have no choice. If I can't have Sandy, how can I possibly keep our baby? It wouldn't be right. His mother and father would just disown him completely, and he needs them at the moment. At least I'll be giving her a start in life that *I* can't.'

Patsy gasped. 'You said *her*.'

'I know. That's because I'm certain it's a girl. Wendy Angela. Sandy chose the name, although he has no idea that he did.'

Tears rolled down Jackie's cheeks as she thought back to the afternoon in Sefton Park, near the Peter Pan statue, when he'd told her that Wendy Moira Angela Darling was a mouthful and she'd be better to just use Wendy and Angela as names for any daughter she may have one day.

'The thing is, I don't understand how it's happened. On holiday we never made love without him using something, he was so insistent on being careful and not ruining our future.'

Jackie thought back to the Sunday morning when he wouldn't let her touch him because they were out of supplies, and she'd reminded him of the one in his wallet. She told Patsy, whose face drained, and she wondered why.

'You mean the one he accidentally pulled out with his money when he was paying for the drinks?' Patsy said. 'We teased him about tipping the waitress with it.'

'Yes. He bought two new packs before we went away, but we used them all. Maybe they go off after a while or something and that one didn't work. There's no other explanation. God, if only we hadn't bothered and just got up for breakfast instead that day.' She looked at Patsy, who had tears rolling down her cheeks. 'Don't cry. It will all be okay. Whatever happens, Sandy must never find out. There's nothing he can do now and he has to get on with being married to Carol, whether he likes it or not.'

'Poor you, poor Sandy,' Patsy sobbed. 'This is awful. You two should be happy and together.'

Jackie nodded and sipped her coffee. Voicing her plans had helped her feel calmer, but numb at the same time. Giving her baby up for adoption would be horrendous, knowing how lovingly it had been conceived. But she had to be brave. Hopefully, Mam would stand by her as she had with Carol and not be too angry.

'Do you want me to stay with you while you tell your mam?' Patsy's voice broke her thoughts.

'Would you? Thanks, Patsy, I'd really appreciate it.'

'Stevie was picking me up later, but I'll tell him I'm staying home tonight. He won't mind.'

'Thank you.' Jackie smiled tearfully as Patsy squeezed her hand.

❀

Mam arrived back as Jackie and Patsy were sharing a cheese sandwich for tea. Stevie had been and Patsy explained that she needed to stay with Jackie tonight and that she'd see him tomorrow.

'I'll pour you a cuppa, Dora,' Patsy said as Mam took off her coat and kicked off her shoes.

'Thanks, chuck.' She flopped down on the armchair in the bay and sighed. 'Well that wasn't too bad, although our Carol and that Susan were making a right show of themselves towards the end. The more they drank the louder they got. I think Sandy felt a bit embarrassed. He took Paul to his parents' house and then came back and ordered Carol into a taxi. I worry about that girl and her drinking, I really do. It's not as if they've got money to throw away.'

'Mam, if you don't mind, I don't want to know.'

'Oh, I'm sorry, love. I've had a drink or two and my tongue got carried away.' She took the mug Patsy held out to her and took a sip. 'Oh that's a nice brew. Are you two okay? You look a bit teary-eyed. Have you been listening to those daft sad songs about lads on motorbikes again?'

Patsy chewed her lip and nodded at Jackie, who took a deep breath and began her tale.

Patsy leapt up and took the mug from Dora as she almost dropped it. Her hand flew to her mouth as she stared in horror at her youngest daughter, her colour draining completely.

'Oh my God, Jackie! Not you, too? Where the hell have I gone wrong?'

'Mam, you haven't. It's not *your* fault. Please don't blame yourself. No one needs to know. I want to go away and give the baby up for adoption.'

Tears running silently down her cheeks, Dora said, 'Dare I ask? Is Sandy the father?'

Jackie nodded. 'I'm so sorry, Mam.' She jumped up and ran out of the room.

Dora looked helplessly at Patsy, who shrugged. 'Is this our Carol's fault?' she whispered.

Patsy nodded. 'Yes, it definitely is. I haven't told Jackie what Carol did. She'd be even more upset. She should be with Sandy and I know they would be so happy together.'

'Bloody hell. How can I be angry with her after everything she's been through? Or with Sandy, poor lad. But what the heck am I going to say to Joe?'

'She doesn't want her dad to know.' Patsy filled Dora in on Jackie's plans as Dora let out a long breath. 'Please don't say anything to her dad,' she finished.

'By rights he should know, but if she's absolutely sure it's what she wants, well then I'll see what can be arranged. I'll take her to the doctor's tomorrow and ask if they can help.' She choked on a sob. 'Oh, my poor little girl; my heart's breaking for her.'

'Mine too,' Patsy said tearfully. 'But I don't think it would help her to know what Carol did, at this moment.'

Dora nodded. 'I don't know how I'm going to keep this to myself, I really don't.'

Chapter Twenty-Five

March 1967

Jackie stood by the narrow bed in the large dorm room she was to share with three other girls. Two were already mothers, and the third girl's baby was due the same date as hers, in three months' time at the beginning of June. At least she'd have someone with whom to share the day-to-day worries of becoming an unmarried mother, no matter how temporary it would be. She felt numb as she clutched her diary to her chest. This all felt so unreal. It was only just over a year since her first date with Sandy, but it seemed a lifetime ago.

The other girls were out, walking on the promenade with the babies, so she was alone for the time being. Matron had given her a list of rules and told her tea would be served at six in the dining room. Prospect House, on Trinity Road, was a large building comprising two Victorian semi-detached houses knocked into one. There was still a grand air about the place, with highly polished mahogany panelling in the entrance hall, thick carpets and a sweeping staircase. All the rooms running off the hall were large and airy and painted in light colours, and the home was close enough to the seafront for bracing walks, time and weather permitting. Time certainly would be, although the girls were expected to help with light housework and various domestic chores until the babies arrived. Then there was the hardest part of all, looking after the baby until it was adopted at six weeks old. Someone was coming to see her tomorrow from the Manchester and District Child Adoption Society, to discuss her case.

She slipped her shoes off and lay down on the bed, resting her head on the pillow. She shivered and pulled her cardigan around her; it was a bit chilly with the large bay window open to let in air. Matron had told her where to hang her clothes, and all the bits Mam had got her for the baby were stored away in a small chest of drawers in an alcove. In the few weeks since she'd told her mam, it had been increasingly difficult to keep it from her dad. For starters she'd put enough weight on that her bump had become noticeable, requiring a firm girdle that she'd hated wearing. Now she could discard it and be comfortable. One of the hardest things had been when Dad proudly presented her with a shoe box containing gold strappy dance shoes for the tour he'd been told she was going on with the troupe of dancers from the Unity. Patsy had sneaked them out of the house for her and hidden them in the wardrobe at home.

Giving notice at work had been another trauma, as everyone had wished her well for her new career and she'd been presented with a red leather vanity case for her makeup, and a good luck card. Mam had confided in Agnes. She said she had to, she couldn't do this without some support, and as Patsy knew anyway, Agnes would help *her* shoulder the worry too. Agnes had recently passed her driving test and borrowed the family car this afternoon to bring Jackie over to Hoylake. Mam and Patsy had accompanied them. Matron told them they could visit each weekend, so Sundays had been decided on if the car was free. Agnes said she'd make sure it was and they'd tell Patsy's dad they were looking at stately homes or something, which would put him off wanting to come with them.

She stared up at the ornate ceiling and blinked away a sudden rush of tears. All her hopes and dreams of ever being with Sandy were just that now, dreams, broken dreams. As soon as she'd heard that the blood tests on Paul were confirmation that Sandy was his father, her world had crumbled. There was no way she could tell him about their baby now. His parents would be so angry with him and he needed all the support they could give him. She would deal with this on her own. Christmas had been an ordeal to get through. Patsy had been the most supportive, best friend she could ever wish to have, keeping her company when she'd stayed indoors after work every night, doing nothing but lie on her bed, listening to sad songs and crying until she was all cried out. Patsy had cried with her. Jackie had contemplated taking an overdose of the sleeping pills that her mam had been prescribed, but they were still in her bedside cupboard.

Even though there was nothing to live for, or wake up for, any more, she'd thought about her baby and how she couldn't hurt it. Although she knew she couldn't keep it, she could at least give it life and hopefully a nice new family who would love it as much as she would have liked to love it herself.

Carol still hadn't come to the house while she was at home, but she knew Mam had helped with Paul for a couple of hours a day when her sister went back to work, although Mam said last week that Carol had got the sack for being late and taking days off without permission. So she and Sandy would have even less money coming in and, unless she got something else soon, they'd lose the flat as Mam said the rent hadn't been paid for a month. Her mam and dad said they'd help, but Carol needed to pull her weight and get a job.

Poor Sandy would end up doing some menial job that he'd loathe and shouldn't have to do. His art career would be over before it even began and that made her so sad. If she'd hated her sister before, she hated her even more now. Patsy had told her that Sandy suspected Carol was sleeping with the man from the flat above when he stayed over at Stevie's after his shift at the Jac, or to paint in peace. But Patsy said he didn't seem to be too bothered about it and he hoped it would help him to get a divorce eventually. If only he could get one before their baby arrived, but that would be too good to be true and wishful thinking on her part. Matron had told her to have a rest before the others came back from their walk, so she closed her eyes and drifted off into a fitful sleep.

❀

Two weeks after Jackie went away, Dora was tidying up the sitting room following a visit from Carol and Paul. Carol had left in a hurry, saying she had to get home for four, but hadn't said why. She never stayed too long and had only started visiting again since she'd been told that Jackie was working away in a show.

Although it was nice to see her little grandson, it hurt like hell that Jackie was in Hoylake and would be giving her and Joe's next grandchild up for adoption. Much as she loved her daughter, Dora felt like getting hold of Carol and giving her a damn good shaking for the damage she'd caused. But she had to bite her tongue and keep her temper in check, as Jackie was still adamant that Sandy and her dad must never find out the truth of her whereabouts.

The fact that Carol had lost her job because she was too lazy to get up and go to work rankled as well. There was little money going into the household and Carol was showing no signs of looking for anything else. She'd given her daughter a fiver before she left and told her to get some decent food in. She looked thinner and Dora was concerned that she wasn't eating properly. She also seemed a bit on edge and there was an air of secrecy about her; she was behaving shiftily almost, not meeting Dora's eyes when they talked. She'd mentioned her kind neighbour Kevin who helped her out when she needed it. Dora had seen her cheeks flush at this and felt a second sense about Carol that didn't sit comfortably on her shoulders.

She plumped up the cushions on the sofa and went to make a start on cooking Joe's tea. It was a lovely feeling, knowing he was coming home to her again tonight. She'd talk with him about her concerns when he'd finished his meal. As she peeled and chopped onions and carrots for the pan of scouse she was making, Dora suppressed a smile as her thoughts turned to last Saturday. Joe had taken her into the city for a bit of dinner and they'd stopped at the market on their way home. At the fruit and veg stall they'd found themselves standing in the queue behind Ivy and her mate Flo. As Ivy turned, she'd caught their eye and her cheeks had flushed crimson as Joe pulled Dora into his arms and dropped a kiss on her lips. Ivy grabbed Flo, who was about to greet them, by the arm and dragged her away. Joe had grinned at their hasty departure, and Dora had tried not to be cross at him for making a show of her in front of all and sundry. Served the woman right. She smiled now as she threw the veg into the pan of stock and gave it a stir with a wooden spoon.

Frank and Maureen were popping in later for a drink. No doubt the talk would turn to Jackie and how well she was doing in her chosen career. Dora sighed as she put a lid on the pan and turned the flame up higher. It was hard going, living a lie. But a promise was a promise and she'd never let her little girl down.

❀

Carol slipped into a shift dress, with a design of white pop-art flowers on a black background. Suitably short, it was one of Mam's creations. Her black sling-back shoes with a kitten-heel finished the look. Alex was working at the Jacaranda and Kevin had offered to take her out. Alex wouldn't be back until tomorrow night, so it was an ideal opportunity to get out and have some fun. She was sick and tired of being tied to the flat with Paul now she'd lost her job, and also sick and tired of being skint. Her mam had given her a fiver this afternoon and she intended to buy some food and a bottle of vodka tomorrow. A drink helped her to cope better. She had more patience with Paul when he cried after a glass or two.

Next door's teenage daughter, Karen, was babysitting tonight and Kevin had offered to pay the half-crown fee the girl was charging. What Alex didn't know wouldn't hurt him and anyway, most of the neighbours thought he was her student brother who stayed over occasionally, and not her husband, which suited her very well. In the main she kept herself to herself and never asked anyone in for a brew, even though the neighbours often invited her in when they saw her passing. She usually made an excuse that Paul was ready for feeding, and another time maybe.

She peeped at Paul, who was fast asleep in his cot. He'd be fine and wouldn't even wake up; he was so good, but she couldn't chance leaving him alone, just in case Alex came back unexpectedly. He'd go bloody mad with her. He hated her, but he loved his son.

Back in the sitting room she pulled the curtains across and picked up the one and only photo that had been taken at their wedding. She shoved it into a drawer out of sight. No point in rousing the babysitter's curiosity. She'd be telling tales to her mam Doreen, a big, blousy woman with peroxide-blonde hair and a loud voice.

She answered a quiet knock at the door and let in Karen, gave her a few instructions on where to find things for the baby and told her to help herself to biscuits and a cuppa.

'See you later. We won't be too late because you've got school in the morning.'

She met Kevin in the small shared porch area and he dropped a kiss on her lips and told her she looked lovely, groping her backside as he said it. She smiled. It was worth the effort: she never got admiration from Alex, so it made her feel good about herself.

'Where are we going?' she asked as he pulled onto Luxmore Road and put his foot down.

'Thought we'd go for a drink, somewhere outside of Walton Vale. I've got something to drop off at a mate's in Toxteth first. Won't take long.'

'Okay.' Carol sat back and stared out of the window as he sped down the main road. Kevin's spicy aftershave reminded her of the one she'd bought Alex for his birthday last year. She remembered how Alex's body scent, mingled with spice, had turned her on and how much he'd meant to her before it all went pear-shaped. No one could blame her for wanting a good time. She was only nineteen, too young to be ignored and feel unloved for the rest of her life.

Kevin intrigued her. He always had plenty of money to spend but didn't seem to go out to work at normal times, like other people on the street. He wasn't a pools winner, because surely he'd live somewhere better than a tiny rented flat, although he'd told her he owned a nice detached house in Woolton, where his ex-wife and his daughter lived for now. She didn't like to pry, as it wasn't her business, but it made her feel a bit uneasy at times and she didn't know why.

'Nearly there now,' Kevin said, squeezing her knee.

She smiled as he turned left onto Southport Road and pulled up outside a semi-detached house with a large car on the drive.

'Stay here. Won't be a minute.' He took a small package from the back seat and hurried up the drive.

Carol looked at the house, which was smart but had all the curtains closed, though it wasn't even dark yet. She'd thought all places in Toxteth were rough, but this part seemed fairly decent. She wondered briefly how her sister was doing with the dance troupe. She had all the bloody luck. Carol would give anything to be free to do that, and she'd bet Jackie would swap places willingly to be with Alex and have his kid. Funny how things worked out. But she'd soon get over him and meet someone else.

Kevin dashed back to the car and smiled.

'Ready? Let's get that drink then.' He drove towards Sefton Park and pulled up in the car park of a pub called Ye Olde House At Home, on Mossley Hill. 'It's nice in here,' he told her. 'Get some voddy down you then we'll park up and have a bit of fun, eh?'

Carol felt a little shiver of apprehension run down her spine, but as he trailed his hand up her bare leg she felt a familiar warm sensation in her tummy and nodded. She followed him into the smoky, busy pub, where he was greeted from the bar area by several men of his own age, who seemed glad to see him. He slung his arm around her shoulders and introduced her to them as his new girl. She felt a bit uncomfortable when a couple of them knowingly looked her up and down and winked.

Kevin ordered their drinks and led the way to a table near the back of the room. She sat down and he sat close beside her on the bench seat, handing her a glass of vodka and Coke.

'Cheers.' He clinked his glass against hers and took a long swig of beer.

Carol sipped at her drink and felt herself relaxing as the liquid calmed her churning stomach. She glanced around to make sure there was no one in the pub who might know her or, worse still, know Alex or his parents. She couldn't see anyone she recognised, but it was noisy and crowded and everyone seemed to be talking at once above the noise of the jukebox. It was one thing having a secret assignation indoors where they were out of sight, but to be in a public place was a bit risky, although it added a buzz to how she was feeling.

She finished her drink as Kevin finished his. He went back to the bar and ordered refills. She could see he had his head close to the head of one of the men he'd spoken to when they came in. She wondered what they were talking about. He was soon back, smiling. He put the drinks down, went to the jukebox, which had just fallen silent, and made a selection.

She knew he liked Rock 'n' Roll music, Elvis in particular, and he'd chosen 'Blue Suede Shoes'. He'd told her that he'd been a Teddy boy in the fifties, with his leather jacket and drainpipe jeans; and his Harley-Davidson motorbike that was still in the garage in Woolton. He was a far cry from her Mod friends and she'd die if any of them saw her now with what they'd deem to be a Rocker. Even though he was a looker, it just wasn't done to mix, but she felt she'd almost had to forgo her Mod lifestyle since becoming a mother. Kevin didn't seem to object to her Mod style of dress though. In fact, he said he liked her minis, the shorter the better as far as he was concerned.

He finished his second pint and got to his feet. 'Just got to pop to the car for a minute. I'll get you a refill on my way back in.'

She nodded. The man he'd been talking to followed him outside and she wondered what they were up to. They were back within minutes and Kevin was at the bar once more while his friend went into the gents.

Two more drinks later and Carol knew it was time to go as Kevin was looking impatiently at his watch. 'You ready?'

'Yes.' She got to her feet, swaying slightly. 'I'm just popping to the ladies.'

She hurried inside and leant against the sink. Her face was flushed and her eyes bright with expectancy. She didn't want Kevin to think she was easy, although he probably already had that impression of her anyway after all the heavy petting they'd done. She splashed cold water onto her cheeks and patted them dry with a tissue. With her lipstick renewed, she looked less drunk than she felt. She dashed into a cubicle. Had those vodkas been doubles? She really did feel pissed.

Kevin was waiting by the door and he led her to the car. She flopped onto the passenger seat and he set off for Sefton Park car park. It was dark now and his headlights picked out a couple of other cars parked up. He drove to the far corner away from them and killed the engine.

'At last,' he said, pulling her into his arms and kissing her long and hard, his tongue entwining with hers.

He tasted of beer and cigarettes, although he'd not smoked any inside the pub. She responded, eagerly kissing him back. She caught her breath as his hand crept up her bare legs and stroked her through the lace of her knickers and she moaned with pleasure.

'In the back,' he ordered after a few moments and helped her climb over the seats. He fumbled with his zip and wriggled his jeans down, slid a rubber onto his erection and yanked off her knickers. Giving her no time to touch him, or even think, he pushed inside her and clamped his hand across her mouth as she yelled out; he'd taken her by surprise, but also sent a thrill of excitement through her.

'Shut it,' he growled. 'You'll wake the fucking dead!'

He was rougher than he'd been before with her and as he banged away, Carol wasn't sure she liked it, but was too scared to stop him, so she moved in rhythm until his explosive shuddering sent him crashing over the edge. He collapsed on top, breathing heavily in her ear.

'Fucking hell,' he muttered as he slid off her and fastened himself up. 'I've been waiting a long time to do that. I want a replay when we get back, babe.'

Carol chewed her lip and pulled her underwear back on while he threw the rubber out of the window. He'd never been rough like that with her; until tonight he'd always been gentle and loving and had taken his time exploring her body without penetration. He helped her back into the front seat, lit a cigarette and drove home in silence.

He paid Karen, who told them the baby had been fine and was still fast asleep, and then he ordered Carol to strip off in front of him. He lit a cigarette and swigged from a bottle he'd brought in with him from the car, his eyes narrowing as she slipped out of her dress and unhooked her bra.

'Now take them off – slowly,' he ordered as she slid her knickers down.

She took a deep breath as he told her to sit on his knee and handed her the bottle to drink from. It was neat vodka and she usually only had it with Coke, but it stopped her trembling. He took the bottle from her and proceeded to make love to her in his usual sensual manner, taking her to heights she'd grown to enjoy with him. This time he didn't clamp his hand over her mouth and she was glad as he'd frightened her earlier. She lay with her head on his chest, while her breathing returned to normal.

He stirred beneath her and lifted her back onto the sofa from the floor where they'd ended up. 'I'd better go. I've some work to do early tomorrow.'

She nodded. 'I wish I had a job to go to. We're desperate for money and Alex doesn't get paid until Friday. We've not much food in.'

She didn't mention that her mam had given her money and that she needed a few drinks to get through the day now and was ready to climb the walls if she couldn't have any. That's why tonight had been a godsend.

He pulled his clothes back on and looked at her for a long moment. 'I can give you work. But I need to trust that you can be discreet and not tell that bloody husband of yours.'

He went on to explain that he required small packets of goods delivering to various pubs and houses around Liverpool, no questions asked. She was to collect payment on delivery.

'No payment, no goods. It's as simple as that,' he said.

'But I haven't got a car.'

'You don't need one. You can use the pram. Just shove the stuff I'll give you under the covers with the baby. I'll make sure your deliveries are within a two-mile radius so that all you'll be doing is taking the kid for a long daily walk, come rain or shine, and I'll pay you well. Your customers will be expecting you. Easy money, babe. You can treat yourself to clothes, decent scran and some booze.'

He pulled his wallet from his pocket and threw two five-pound notes down on the sofa.

'Get your rent up to date with that. I don't want you getting chucked out. I need you. And I think tonight's performance was well worth a tenner, don't you? See you tomorrow for an encore.'

And with that he was gone, leaving Carol sitting on the sofa, feeling numb and wondering what the hell she was letting herself in for, but also looking forward to the possibility of a more prosperous future that she had no intention of turning down.

Chapter Twenty-Six

May 1967

Jackie waddled along bedside her friend Veronica, who was as heavily pregnant as she, both due next Thursday, the 1st of June. They were taking in the sea air on the promenade. It was a beautiful, sunny Saturday with a bright blue sky, dotted with a handful of cotton-wool clouds. They'd eaten their sandwiches and apples on the beach, watching several colourful little boats bobbing on the gentle waves, and in the distance, the black bulk of the *Manx Maid* ferry, making its way to the Isle of Man, its large red funnel belching steam skywards. They'd giggled helplessly as they tried, without success, to help each other up off the knitted blanket they'd spread out on the sand. Jackie felt like a beached whale and was glad when she'd hit on the idea of rolling onto all fours first and *then* getting slowly to her feet, before pulling Veronica upright. Tossing their left-overs to the waiting seagulls, they carried the picnic basket and blanket between them up to the prom.

Since moving into Prospect House, Jackie and eighteen-year-old Veronica had grown close, sharing some – but not all – of their personal secrets. Veronica's 21-year-old soldier boyfriend, stationed in Germany, had dumped her as soon as she'd told him she was expecting, and her parents had shipped her off to the mother and baby home shortly after. It was good to have a confidante as Jackie was missing Patsy badly, and although she saw her on Sundays, Mam and Agnes were always there too, so it was impossible to ask how Sandy was doing.

It seemed the residents of Hoylake were used to seeing the girls from the home around town, and they encountered very few scornful looks and comments. Except for last week when a large woman at the local church had marched up to Jackie following the Sunday morning service they were expected to attend, and hissed in her ear that she should be ashamed of herself for disgracing her family, and that God would never forgive her, or accept the child she was carrying into his flock.

Jackie had seen red and turned on the woman. '*You* should just mind your own flaming business, you nosy cow! You have no idea of the circumstances that brought *any* of us to Prospect House. And for your information, my baby will be on *very* friendly terms with God, seeing as how its grandfather's my local vicar!'

She'd stormed out of the church, thinking how just like Barbara Bloody Baker the poker-faced woman was. Holier than flipping thou. Wait until she told her mam, who was coming to visit later with Agnes and Patsy. She just hoped to God that the woman didn't make enquiries as to where she'd come from, or which vicar she was referring to, or all hell would break loose and her closely guarded secret would be no more. Sandy, Carol and everyone else had been told she was working away with the dance troupe.

She'd stomped back to Prospect House to be met in the hallway by Matron, who'd demanded to know why she was back early. On explanation, Matron's mouth twitched at the corners as she'd told Jackie not to worry, but to hold her tongue in future as there were certain types of women who looked on unmarried mothers as sinful, when in fact the majority were anything but.

Jackie was invited into the kitchen for a cup of tea and, by the time the rest of the girls arrived back, had calmed down and was helping Mrs Haslem, the cook, to peel the vegetables for lunch.

Just before visiting time she'd gone upstairs to the room she shared with Veronica, to brush her hair and get ready for her visitors. She'd made a drastic decision last week and had her long blonde hair restyled. It was now chin-length and in the same style as Patsy's, like Dusty Springfield's. It was backcombed on top with sweeping curls on her cheeks and a full fringe, and Jackie thought it made her look a bit more mature. She could always grow it again when she resumed her normal life, whatever that was these days. But for now it was easier to look after and much cooler in the early summer heat.

As she'd opened the bedroom window to let in some air, she'd almost passed out with shock to see Marcia Phelan and her mother going into the house opposite. Then she remembered the girl's grandmother lived on the Wirral. That must be her house. She'd better keep herself out of sight for now. She hadn't seen Marcia for ages and the last time she did she'd had to endure the girl's smug comments about Sandy marrying her sister. Patsy had dragged her away and onto the bus to work before she'd lamped the girl one. The last thing she needed now was for Marcia to go blabbing to all and sundry that Jackie was in the unmarried mothers' home and not on a dance tour after all.

Veronica sat down on a bench overlooking the sea and took a deep breath, breaking Jackie's thoughts.

'You okay, Ronnie?' Jackie flopped down beside her.

'Not sure. I've got a low backache and a few tummy twinges, but it might be from sitting on the beach and then struggling to get up.' She fidgeted uncomfortably and looped her long dark hair behind her ears. 'I think maybe we should head back, just in case.'

Jackie nodded and helped Veronica to her feet. 'Matron will get Mrs Winters to check you over. This could be it, though. You might be early.'

The midwife, Mrs Winters, lived next door to Prospect House and kept a close watch over each girl's well-being, but as soon as labour was established, they were sent immediately to Clatterbridge Hospital and stayed there for a few days before coming back to the home for the rest of their stay. It was during the remaining five weeks that firm decisions were made with regards to the child's future. Some girls, like Jackie, had already decided that adoption was the only way forward, but occasionally a change of plan occurred, parents relented and allowed their daughter to keep her baby and arrangements were made for them both to return home. And sometimes, an errant boyfriend changed *his* mind too, and decided to do the right thing by his girl and their child.

'I'm terrified,' Veronica admitted, her dark brown eyes widening in her pale face as a pain shot through her. 'Oh shit. I think you might be right.'

Back at Prospect House Matron took one look at Jackie's worried face as she explained that Veronica, who'd sat down on the front doorstep outside, was having pains.

'Knock on next door for me, Jackie, and ask Mrs Winters to come in while I get Ronnie up to her room. Go round the back way, I think I heard voices outside.'

Mrs Winters was in her back garden and Jackie called over the fence and then let the midwife in at the back door.

'It's Ronnie,' Jackie gasped. 'She started having pains while we were out. Matron's taken her to her room.'

Mrs Winters told Jackie to stay put and dashed upstairs, so she hung around in the hall and waited. Minutes later Matron hurried down and picked up the phone from the hall table. Jackie heard her ask for an ambulance.

'Are *you* okay?' Matron turned to Jackie as she put down the phone.

'I'm fine. Will she be all right?'

'She will. She shouldn't be too long. Her waters broke as I got her into the bathroom. The contractions are coming thick and fast. Good job you came back when you did.'

'Can I see her before she goes?'

'Be quick, and then you can get yourself a cuppa in the kitchen and put your feet up.'

Jackie waddled upstairs to the room she shared with Veronica. They'd been transferred to the two-bed room after the other girls they'd previously shared with had gone home following the adoption of their babies, and now four other girls in varying stages of pregnancy were the occupants of the other room. It was like a production line, Jackie thought now. All of them with their precious teens on hold to provide childless couples with the chance of a family they'd never have otherwise. But it wasn't how the majority of the girls she'd spoken to wanted it. It was just that for most there was no other choice. It broke her heart to hear how many of them hated their ex-boyfriends, and some were the unlucky victims of drunken one-night stands with no idea who the father was. No one had said how much in love with their boy they'd been.

They weren't like her, who'd loved Sandy totally, and no one had lost their boy to their sister either. Her case was unique, it would seem, but she'd told them she'd been dumped. It was easier than explaining the whole sorry story, even to Veronica. They said they'd keep in touch, so maybe one day she'd tell her all. The one thing they'd agreed on was that they were lucky to be at Prospect House, and not one of the Catholic homes they'd heard such horror stories about, where the girls were made to work like skivvies for their sins. At least here they were looked after and treated like human beings and no one minded helping with chores, which they happily split between them. There was a lot to be thankful for, Jackie thought.

❀

Veronica's son Damien arrived safely just after midnight and mother and baby were doing well, Matron told Jackie the following morning.

'I think you should stay away from church today,' she added. 'You look tired and pale and the last thing we need is for you to start in the middle of the service. Rest is the order of the day for you, young lady, and you've got your visitors coming later, so that'll be enough excitement for one day.'

Jackie was relieved. She wondered if Marcia and her mother were visiting again and had stayed across the road overnight. They might want to take her grandma to church this morning. And also she didn't want to see that horrible bitchy woman again either.

⊛

As Veronica and Damien arrived back at Prospect House on the Thursday, Jackie went into labour. Mrs Winter had examined her and said she would be back within the hour to check her again. It was a bit too soon to send for an ambulance, so Jackie took a warm bath as instructed and lay on her bed, waiting for things to develop. Veronica popped her head around the door.

'Can I come in?'

'Yes, of course. Where's the baby?' Jackie wriggled to a sitting position, gasping as another twinge grasped her around the middle and squeezed the tops of her thighs.

'He's in the nursery on the top floor. I'll be sleeping up there tonight, in case you're still here. Although looking at you, I think you'll be in Clatterbridge soon. Well, at least yours is coming on time.'

'It hurts,' Jackie groaned. 'Like really bad period pains.'

Veronica took her hand. 'I'll warn you now, it gets worse. Make sure they give you gas and air. I was given an injection in my backside of something called pethidine. You feel like you've had loads of alcohol and it makes the pain bearable. When they tell you to push, breathe plenty of that gas and air down you.'

'Does it hurt when it comes out?'

'It does, like crazy, but as soon as it's out you forget. When you hold that baby in your arms there's no better feeling in the world and it's all worthwhile.' Veronica's eyes filled and she blinked them away. 'I really don't think I can give him up, Jackie.'

'Oh, Ronnie.' Jackie held on to her hand. 'What are you going to do?'

'I'm going to send his bastard father a photo and a letter, giving him the chance to get in touch. He's the bloody spit of him, ginger hair, blue eyes, the lot. And I'm going to beg my mam and dad to let me keep him. I owe it to Damien to try.'

Jackie chewed her lip. If only she had those options. Her mam would persuade her dad that they should let her keep the baby if she asked; she knew that would probably be okay. But then there was the whole shitty mess of Sandy and Carol and his parents and all the crap that would bring. It just wasn't doable. She screwed her eyes shut and let out a yell of pain and anguish as Mrs Winters came into the room and shooed Veronica out.

❀

Wendy Angela arrived just prior to midnight on her due date, weighing in at seven pounds and three ounces. As Jackie gazed in awe at her tiny new-born daughter, who stared unblinkingly back at her, she could see herself in the wisps of blonde hair and the large blue eyes, but her mouth was just like Sandy's and would curve into that wonderful wide smile eventually. The tears that she'd fought to keep at bay during labour as she'd tried not to think of him, and their lovely weekend away, flowed down her cheeks, and she sobbed until a nurse took the baby and laid her in a small plastic cot beside the bed.

'I'll get you some tea, and how about some toast?' she asked, her tone kind and understanding as she handed a box of tissues over. 'You've had nothing to eat for hours.'

'Thank you.' Jackie sniffed, wiping her eyes and nose. She didn't think she could bear it. She wanted to tell Sandy. He had a right to know he'd got a daughter. But how could she do it? Should she ask Patsy to get a message to him via Stevie? He'd be distraught and want to come and see her, and then what? They couldn't be together because of Carol and Paul. Carol would never agree to a divorce and let him go, and she didn't think his parents would be too happy about things either. Getting one girl into trouble had caused enough upset and trauma for his mother, two would just about tip her over the edge and his father would probably disown him once and for all. What was the point? This was something she had to deal with on her own. Once her head cleared of the gas and air she'd be thinking a bit straighter. At the moment she was just going around in circles.

❀

By the time Mam, Agnes and Patsy arrived on Sunday afternoon, Jackie's head and heart had accepted that what she'd agreed to do was the best for her daughter. They'd all brought gifts for Wendy that were to go with her to her new home: a teddy bear with a pink bow around its neck from Patsy, a white knitted shawl from Agnes, and Mam had made a pretty pink and white gingham dress with a hand-smocked yoke, and she'd knitted matching booties, jacket and a bonnet, all in white, with pink ribbon trims.

'I thought you might like to dress her in those when you, erm…' Mam's voice broke and tears ran down her cheeks as she gazed at her granddaughter. 'She's the most beautiful little girl I've ever seen,' she whispered heartbrokenly. 'She's perfect. Are you quite sure, love?'

'Mam, I've got no choice. Please don't ask me again. I can't keep her, it's impossible. Sandy's married to Carol.'

'Huh!' Patsy snorted. 'And what a waste of time that is.'

Jackie frowned. 'Are things no better?'

'They're fine,' Mam said, glaring at Patsy. 'It's a struggle but they're doing okay and Paul is coming on a treat.'

'Yeah, right,' Patsy snapped and folded her arms. 'If that's marriage you can stick it.' She got up and flounced out of the ward.

Agnes got to her feet. 'Ignore her, love; she's upset because of what's happening with Wendy. I'll go after her and see she's all right.'

'Tell her to come back before you go,' Jackie called. She turned to her mam, who was cuddling Wendy. 'If Carol isn't making Sandy happy, why are they still together?'

'They have their differences, love, but most couples do. It takes a bit of adjusting at first. They'll be fine. They seem to be managing better for money. Sandy's still at art college, and he does extra shifts at the club.'

'Is Carol back at work then?' Jackie frowned. Why wasn't Mam meeting her eye? And there was no way Sandy earned enough to keep them going, she knew that.

'No, she's looking after Paul. She says she'll find another job eventually.'

Jackie wondered how they were managing to stay afloat on peanuts, but it wasn't her business to worry. Maybe Sandy had sold another painting. That must be it. Patsy had told her a while ago that he was putting stuff together for a new exhibition. What a shame he had to waste his hard-earned money on keeping her lazy sister. She didn't begrudge him taking care of his son, but to think Carol would spend his money on herself made her feel even more angry that she couldn't tell him about Wendy.

Agnes and a red-eyed Patsy came back into the ward just before the bell that signalled the end of visiting. Mam hurriedly took a few photos on the camera she'd borrowed from Uncle Frank. Jackie blinked at the bright flash but did her best to smile. These precious photos, and the official ones the home would arrange, would be all she'd have of Wendy in a few weeks apart from her memories.

As her visitors said their goodbyes, promising to visit at Prospect House next Sunday, Jackie held back her tears and wished she and Wendy were going with them.

In the peaceful back garden, the photographer positioned Veronica and Damien under a large tree near the bottom fence and clicked several times. Jackie sat on a nearby bench with Wendy on her lap, waiting her turn for the official photo. There would be one for the adoptive parents to keep and one for Jackie. This beautiful July day would stay etched in her mind forever. The photographer beckoned her towards him and she got to her feet, smoothing down the skirt of her blue and white paisley-patterned mini dress with her free hand. By the time Friday came the photographs would be ready for them to take home.

Both Wendy and Damien were being collected by their new families this week. Veronica's boyfriend hadn't responded to her letters and her parents had said a firm no to her request to keep her son. All that was left for the girls to do now was to write a letter to their babies that would be given to them when the new parents decided it was time to tell them of their adoption. Jackie would make certain her daughter knew that she wasn't being given away lightly, and that in time she hoped Wendy would look for her, if she wished to. It would probably be the hardest thing she ever had to write in her life, apart from when she'd signed the agreement not to contact her daughter.

⚘

Jackie spent Thursday night alone with Wendy Angela in the nursery. Damien had gone with his new parents last night and Veronica's father had collected her this morning. They'd sobbed heartbroken tears as they clung together in their grief one last time. Addresses had been exchanged and they'd promised to keep in touch. The pain in her friend's eyes as she whispered that she'd never forgive her parents for this had torn at Jackie's heart. They hadn't been to visit their daughter since she'd been sent to Prospect House, and had never even set eyes on their beautiful grandson. It was their loss, when it needn't be.

Jackie couldn't sleep and sat with her back to the headboard, her daughter snuggled in her arms. She took in every inch of her, from the sprinkle of fine blonde hair on her head to her fair eyelashes and eyebrows, and traced a finger around the lips that were so like Sandy's. She kissed each tiny finger and toe and her flat little ears and button nose. Tears ran freely down her cheeks and dripped onto Wendy's face. The baby screwed up her nose and let out a loud sigh. Jackie told her how much she loved her and promised that one day they'd be together again and maybe even with her daddy, who she knew would love her so much if only he could.

Half of her wanted to sneak away in the dead of night and make her way home, or even to Stevie's Scottie Road flat, where she was sure she'd get a warm welcome. But she didn't have any money for the train fare, and even if she did, the trains had stopped running as it was now well past midnight. She was trapped and there was no way out.

Wendy woke for her feed at two thirty and greedily sucked at the teat of the ready-prepared bottle, her blue eyes staring unblinkingly up at Jackie. The girls were advised not to breastfeed because then the bond was harder to break. The first two weeks had been difficult as each time her baby cried, Jackie's breasts had flooded with milk, which leaked everywhere. It had dried up now thanks to several doses of highly effective, but equally unpleasant, Epsom salts.

Settling Wendy back down after her feed, Jackie thought about the day ahead. Agnes was coming to pick her up late morning along with Mam and Patsy. The plan was to take their time returning home and to stop for lunch before getting to Liverpool later in the afternoon in time for the arrival of the London train that Mam had told everyone Jackie would be on. The family had been informed that her current dance contract had come to an end but that she would be returning to touring with the company for a new show after a break of a few weeks. Hopefully she would be able to get another contract. She had had to lie, and tell them that there had been the death of a close relative, and so she was unable to take up her place the first time. As soon as she was able she intended to see what could be done. She'd need to get right away from Liverpool before she set eyes on Sandy and her evil sister again. Hopefully Mam would keep Carol away from the house for a while.

When Wendy awoke for her morning feed and nappy change Jackie still hadn't closed her eyes. She felt like she'd never sleep again. As she looked at her baby lying on the bed, kicking her spindly little legs up and down, she felt her heart would break and never be repaired. Tears fell as she dressed her in the pretty new dress that Mam had lovingly made and her new knitted booties, jacket and bonnet. She spread Agnes's knitted shawl on the bed and laid Wendy in the middle with her teddy bear from Patsy, and wrapped the shawl loosely around her. A knock came at the door and Matron popped her head inside, a sympathetic look in her kind blue eyes.

'You okay, Jackie? Oh doesn't she look a little picture,' she said as the doorbell rang.

'Matron,' a voice called from the hall. 'The visitors are here.'

'Thank you. Show them into my office,' Matron called back. Adoptive families were always referred to as 'the visitors' as the policy was never to reveal a surname. Matron took Jackie in her arms and gave her a good hug. 'I'm sure she'll be loved, sweetheart. They are a very nice family and will give her everything you would want her to have.'

Jackie nodded and picked Wendy up. She gave her one last kiss and handed her over. As Matron left the room and closed the door quietly behind her, she flung herself onto the bed and screamed Sandy's name into the pillow. The pain of handing Wendy over was something she would never forget. She doubted she'd ever feel happy again. She sobbed until she could cry no more and must have fallen into a deep sleep. Matron woke her a couple of hours later with tea and biscuits.

'There's been a phone call from the lady who's coming to collect you. They'll be here about twelve so it gives you an hour to gather yourself together and pack your case.' She handed an envelope to Jackie and told her not to open it until she was home. 'It's just a little card and your official photograph, but you'll get upset if you look at it now. Save it for later.'

'Thank you.' Jackie sniffed and rubbed her eyes with the palm of her hand. 'And thank you for looking after me.'

'That's what we're here for. Good luck for the future, Jackie. You'll soon pick your life up again, and one day, I'm sure you'll meet a nice boy who won't let you down.'

'I hope so.' One day, she hoped with all her heart, the boy would be Sandy and together they'd find their Wendy Angela, somehow.

Chapter Twenty-Seven

September 1967

Carol trudged wearily down the road as Paul started to cry again. He was teething and there was nothing she could do that would comfort him. She was only a mile or so from home and she needed him to be asleep when she got back, otherwise Kevin wouldn't be very happy to have his routine mucked up.

Each afternoon, following her deliveries, she'd park Paul in the sitting room and go upstairs to Kevin's flat, where she would hand over the money she'd collected from his customers. He'd ply her with drink and then force her to have sex, whether she wanted to or not. He wouldn't pay her any wages unless she'd pleased him. When she'd objected he'd threatened to tell Alex what she did for a living. Now she was trapped in a spiral of needing the money, needing the alcohol and also needing to keep Kevin sweet. And to think she'd truly thought he was falling in love with her.

She couldn't believe that he was the same nice man who'd befriended her when he first moved in, the one who'd been so kind and looked after her when she'd gone into labour. She realised now that he'd been priming her, setting her up so that she had no choice but to rely on him. Once she'd started working for him it had quickly become apparent to her that Kevin was a drug dealer and the packages she stored in the pram next to her precious son contained quantities of heroin, dope and cocaine. She collected a small fortune each day from his eager customers. He paid her well and her rent account was up to date, she had food in the fridge, a vodka supply hidden in the wardrobe, and she and Paul had new clothes on their backs.

In all his naivety Alex just thought she was a better money manager than she'd been at first and he'd handed over fifty pounds last month from another painting sale. The money was still stashed away in a drawer along with a roll of notes she'd been saving from her wages. There was enough money now to get away from here and find a bigger flat. But she knew that Kevin wouldn't let her go. She was terrified of him. She had bruises everywhere, but Alex hadn't seen them, because he never saw her naked. It wasn't that Kevin hit her; he just handled her roughly in bed. The bruises on her arms and thighs and breasts, as well as bite-marks, made her look like a battered wife. She now had an idea as to why Kevin's wife had thrown him out. But what puzzled her was that he was a great father to his little girl, who he doted on. It was like he was two people, and she couldn't understand why his ex allowed him near the child if he'd been abusive at home. Maybe he hadn't and it was just *her* that brought out the bully in him.

Either way, she knew she had to get away soon before he destroyed her completely. She couldn't wear a summer dress or a top with short sleeves without putting a jacket or something with long sleeves over the top. He went out most nights around ten and didn't get home until mid-morning, so she'd have time to make a getaway, but she had nowhere to go at the moment.

By the time she turned into Luxmore Road, Paul had dropped off and she manoeuvred the pram into the sitting room, retrieved the wad of notes from under the blanket and quietly closed the door. She crept upstairs. Kevin's door was ajar and she tapped lightly and went inside.

He was sitting on the sofa, feet up on a footstool, glass in hand. He gestured to the coffee table where a large glass of vodka and Coke waited for her. She sat down beside him, put his money down on the table and took a long and welcome swig. She was thirsty as well as desperate. She never normally had a drink before she did her rounds as she was worried about getting anything wrong.

'Oh, that's nice,' she sighed, knocking back more and relaxing slightly.

Kevin finished his drink and put his glass down. He counted the money and put a tenner on the table. That was for her, but she didn't dare reach for it. It was a good rate for two hours of walking, almost as much as she'd got for a week at Lewis's, and she was nice and slim with all the exercise, with a healthy glow from the sun, but she still felt uneasy about the whole thing.

Kevin took the glass off her and planted a kiss on her lips. He grabbed her breasts through the fine cotton of her top, pinching her nipples, and pushed his hand up her short skirt. She stiffened, knowing that once he started she was powerless to stop him. He drew his head back and looked at her.

'What was that for?'

'What?'

'You, flinching just then, as though you don't want me to touch you.'

'No, I do, I'm just a bit sore. You hurt me yesterday.' He hurt her every day, but yesterday he'd been particularly vicious in yanking her legs apart and thrusting into her before she was ready.

'But you like it rough,' he said, pulling her to her feet. 'You told me you did.' He dragged her into the bedroom and threw her onto the bed.

She couldn't recall ever telling him she liked it rough and cried out as he yanked off her knickers.

'That's it, baby,' he said, grinning and stripping off his jeans and pants. 'Tell me not to do it, I like that.'

She gritted her teeth as he pushed into her. 'Please, don't,' she mumbled.

'I can't hear you, tell me again.'

'Please, Kevin, stop it.'

'Beg me, oh yes, baby, beg me to stop,' he yelled, banging away. He had her arms pinned above her head, his full weight pressing down on her. He liked to pretend to rape her, he said, it turned him on.

She carried on begging him until he exploded and lay still, panting down her ear.

'Why didn't you come?' he demanded, shaking her roughly. 'You usually do.'

'I-I couldn't. I told you, I'm a bit sore at the moment.' Tears slid sideways down her face, soaking into her hair.

'Why are you crying?' He sat up and lit a cigarette.

'I'm tired and weary,' she said with a sob. 'Paul's teething and he kept me awake all night, I've trudged around for you today and it's so hot out there. And then...'

'And then what? You know the score. No sex, no money.'

'That wasn't the original deal though, was it? It was for me to deliver your goods and you pay me for that.'

'You couldn't get enough of me at first,' he said scornfully. 'You get nowt from the vicar's son, let's face it. God knows how he got you up the duff in the first place. All his arty-farty ways and that poncy bloody scooter he rides around on. Wouldn't surprise me if he's not a queer, and that kid of yours was pure fluke. What sort of man doesn't want to sleep with his wife when she's as fit and willing a bird as you? No normal bloke, I'm sure.'

Carol slid out of bed and retrieved her underwear, feeling dirty and sticky. And that was another thing, Kevin had stopped using rubbers. So far luck had been on her side. But the way he was with her it was only a matter of time, and it couldn't happen again, it just couldn't. She'd been prescribed the contraceptive pill a month ago, but had been instructed to take extra precautions for the first three months. Kevin had laughed at her when she'd told him and said no chance. She'd hidden her pills from Alex as there was no reason to be taking them with him. It was all such a mess and she hated her life.

'Don't forget to pick up your money on the way out,' Kevin said. 'Oh, by the way, you're gonna have to do the city centre round tomorrow. Barry, my usual lad, had his appendix out so he's laid up in hospital.'

She turned to look at him with a horrified expression. 'I can't do that. It's too far to walk, and what if I bump into Alex or Stevie or someone I used to work with? I'm sorry, Kevin, I just can't do it.'

As she turned her back on him he leapt out of bed and pinned her against the door.

'You can, and you will,' he said, his face so close to hers she could feel his hot boozy breath on her cheek. 'I'll give you the list in the morning when you come up to collect the packages. Now get out of here before I'm tempted to fuck you again.'

She ran to the coffee table and picked up her money, terrified that he'd come after her and carry out his threat. She felt like a prostitute, pocketing money for sex. What had she got herself into – and how the hell could she get out of it before Alex found out?

❀

Carol had almost completed her round of city centre establishments. She'd kept her head down, dashing in and out as quickly as she could. There'd been grumbles and suspicious stares as she'd taken the money and then handed over the packets. A few 'Where's Barry?' questions, but she'd managed to get through without too many complaints.

She hated leaving Paul outside for long and some of the drop-offs took a while as people dodged in and out at a set time, but thankfully he'd come to no harm. And she hadn't bumped into a soul she knew either, which was a blessing. It was hard to be discreet when most of the customers drew attention to themselves with their drunken expletives. And she looked like a fish out of water, whereas no doubt the errant Barry fitted into the scene well enough not to look obvious. The final drop-off was at Ye Olde Crack on Rice Street.

❀

Stevie looked up from his pint as the pub door swung open. He was waiting for Barry to drop off his dope supply, but he was late. He needed to get back to college, so two more minutes and then that was it.

He finished his drink, stood up to take the glass to the bar to save the barmaid's legs and ducked back behind the post as he realised the anxious-looking girl who'd just come in was Sandy's wife, Caz. Was she looking for Sandy, or Alex as she still insisted on calling him? Maybe the baby was ill or something. He was about to call out when he saw her take money from a fella known as Big Harry and then discreetly slip him a package. She did the same with Terry, who left the pub as quickly as he'd appeared.

Stevie slid out the door before Caz could spot him and saw a baby in a pram outside. He peeped under the sun canopy and was shocked when his godson Paul gazed back at him and gave him a small smile. He tickled Paul under the chin and received a dribbly grin.

'Right, little fella, me and you are gonna give that mother of yours the shock of her life,' he muttered.

What the hell did Caz think she was playing at? Flogging drugs and leaving her baby outside the pub was hardly the lifestyle a vicar's daughter-in-law should be leading. Barry's boss, drug dealer O'Leary, was a nasty piece of work who was well-known for getting young girls to do his dealing for him. How the heck had Caz got involved with him? And he was damn sure that Sandy had no clue what she was up to either.

He released the brake and pushed the pram around the corner, where he watched for Caz leaving the pub. He saw her come outside and glance to where the pram had been standing. Her hand flew to her mouth and she looked frantically around, her face a mask of fear. He whistled to attract her attention and she spun around.

'Lost something, Caz?' He wheeled the pram towards her and she almost collapsed as he reached her side.

'Why did you do that?' she screamed, hitting him with both fists on his chest, tears running down her cheeks. 'You scared the life out of me.'

He shook his head. 'Are you insane? I saw you in there.' He nodded towards the pub. 'And I saw what you were doing. Don't deny it, Caz,' he continued as she opened her mouth to protest. 'I was waiting in there for Barry and realised you were his replacement.'

'We need the money,' she cried. 'You have no idea how hard it is to make ends meet. If I didn't do this we'd be out on the streets. Alex doesn't care what happens to us. If he did, he'd get a proper job and look after us both. He turned his nose up at Uncle Frank's offer of something down at the docks.'

Stevie saw red then and gripped her by the shoulders. 'You selfish little cow. Sandy does his best. He works five nights a week at the bar and all day Saturday, he's in college all week and he paints after his shifts until about three in the morning. He hardly eats or sleeps, he gives you every single penny he earns and he tipped up the last lot of money he made from his painting sale. He's walking around in boots full of holes, his jeans are in tatters – and look at you, dolled up to the fucking nines. You clearly earn enough to keep both you and Paul without Sandy's contribution. You've ruined his life, why should he give up his career for you, too?'

Carol wiped her eyes and looked at her watch. She knew she was in the wrong.

'I didn't want to do this. It's Kevin's fault. I'm scared of him, but I don't know how to get out of it now.' She shot a look of desperation in Stevie's direction. She needed to get back. Kevin would be getting twitchy. 'And I didn't ruin Alex's life. *He* ruined mine, getting me pregnant and refusing to believe Paul was his. None of this is my fault.'

Stevie chewed his lip. Was she genuinely scared or playing for sympathy? Hard to tell with Caz.

'Well we all know how you getting pregnant happened, don't we? Fortunately, Sandy doesn't – yet. But if you value your marriage and your kid you'll stop selling drugs for O'Leary.'

Carol's face flushed red and she frowned. 'I don't know what you mean, and who's O'Leary?'

'You *do* know what I mean,' he growled. 'You stuck pinholes in something, remember?' he said as she gasped. 'You trapped Sandy in the worst possible way. And O'Leary is your boss.'

'My boss's name is Briggs, Kevin Briggs,' she said. 'So you got that wrong.'

'Nah,' Stevie said. 'That's just one of his aliases. Our regular guy Barry works for O'Leary. He lives in Woolton in a big fancy house with his missus and kid, just up the road from my parents' new bungalow. Only he keeps a low profile and rents flats in unassuming places around the city, so the scuffers can't keep track of him.'

Carol shook her head. 'His ex-wife and daughter live in Woolton, he's divorced, he told me. So you've got that all wrong.'

'And that's what he told you, is it? He's not divorced. He still lives there, most of the time anyway. He's using you, Caz. It's what he does. He gets young girls to trust him, then uses them and their kids to distribute his drugs around the city. I bet he's screwing you, too. It's his usual pattern.'

He half-smiled as her colour drained, and he almost felt sorry for her. Almost, but not quite. What she'd done to his best mate and Jackie was unforgiveable and he wanted to see her suffer for it. Patsy had told him how heartbroken Jackie was at giving up her baby daughter. He'd love to throw *that* at her, but he knew it would be a step too far.

'I have to go.' She snatched at the pram handle but he held on to it.

'You're going nowhere until you promise you'll tell Sandy the truth – about everything, including your affair with O'Leary. Sandy's got a night off and he's popping over to see you later, he told me earlier. He's not seen Paul for a couple of days.'

'I'll tell him when I'm ready,' she snapped. 'It's got nothing to do with you.'

'It's got *everything* to do with me. Sandy's my best mate. He's a great guy and you've screwed him up so much he doesn't know whether he's coming or going. You tell him tonight and let him have a divorce. If *you* don't, *I* will.'

❧

Carol settled Paul in his cot and switched off the bedroom light. He'd grizzled all the way back from town and she was glad of the peace. Kevin had nearly pulled her hair out by the roots when she'd told him no more sex, her baby needed her and she just wanted to drop the money in today. She'd also told him she was going to move away and she didn't want to work for him any more. He'd forced her to her knees, yanked her hips up and pulled her head back as he'd pushed into her from behind. She'd screamed for help but it seemed to excite him all the more, and no one came to her aid anyway. Afterwards he'd thrown her money at her and pushed her out of the door. She'd stumbled on the stairs and banged her head against the wall. He ran down and pulled her to her feet. She pushed him away and said that Alex was coming soon.

'Well in that case I'll pop down and pay him a neighbourly visit.' He'd grinned in her face and tried to kiss her, thrusting his tongue down her throat and making her gag. 'Tell him what a randy little whore his missus is and how she likes it rough.'

'You stay away from us,' she called as he sauntered back up the stairs.

'Not a chance, gel. You belong to me now. I'll tell him that too. And if you open your gob to him and land me in it, you'll never see him or the kid again, you hear me? See youse later, sweetheart.'

And with that he slammed his door shut.

❀

Trembling, Carol filled the bath, stripped off her clothes and scrubbed herself until her skin felt like it was on fire, removing the stench of sex and Kevin from her body. The bruises on her legs, thighs and buttocks were painful and she wept as she gently patted herself dry and rubbed Nivea cream into her skin to soothe it. She felt so depressed and down and hated her life. She took a long drink of vodka from the glass balanced on the sink, relaxing slightly as the liquid hit her empty stomach.

In the sitting room she pulled on the fresh clothes she'd laid out on the sofa so she wouldn't disturb Paul. She poured another glass of neat vodka; the Coke bottle on the kitchen worktop was empty, but she needed to drink to blot out her terrified thoughts.

She took a pad and pen out of a drawer in the kitchen and wrote a letter, which she folded and placed on the coffee table. She had written 'ALEX' on the back in bold letters. Taking a last quick peep at her sleeping son, Carol grabbed her coat and handbag and the remains of the bottle of vodka and let herself silently out of the front door, praying that Kevin wasn't looking out the window. Alex had his own key so would be able to get in when he arrived, which hopefully would be before Paul woke up.

She hurried up Golden Grove and onto Luxmore Road with her head down. There weren't many people around but there was a queue outside Nelson's chippy, so she rushed past as quickly as she could before anyone caught her eye and engaged her in conversation. A bus pulled up as she neared the stop and she jumped on board for the short journey, knowing her trembling legs wouldn't carry her there.

At Walton station she bought a one-way ticket to Lime Street. Once there she'd decide where to go, somewhere, anywhere, to escape her self-made nightmare. She'd just missed a train so was the only person in the waiting room, and she took the vodka out of her bag and finished it off, sliding the empty bottle under the bench seat. Kevin would find her, she just knew it. There was nowhere she could escape to that he wouldn't catch up with her. And he'd take out his anger at her vanishing act on Alex and Paul. She just hoped that Alex read her letter and got himself and Paul out of the flat safely before Kevin made his promised visit. She'd told Alex to take Paul to his parents, who she was certain would look after him well.

No matter what happened now, her marriage was well and truly over. She'd confessed all to Alex in the letter she'd left him. Nothing had been missed out. Whether he'd think it was drunken ramblings when he found her secret stash of vodka in the wardrobe was anyone's guess. If Stevie didn't tell Alex, she knew that Kevin would take great delight in doing so, as payback for her deserting him, so it was better that he read it from her first, along with her heartfelt apologies to both him and Jackie.

She'd lose Paul, as Alex would remove him from her care. She was an unfit drunken mother who sold drugs, left her baby outside pubs and had sex for money with the neighbour. No court would allow her near her child again. Her mam and dad wouldn't want to know, they'd be disgusted with her. She was disgusted with herself. She'd lose her friends for certain. Susan would be horrified. She got to her feet and strolled onto the platform, wobbling slightly. On the bridge above was a telephone box. She chewed her lip for a moment and then ran up the steps, rushed inside and dialled Stevie's number.

'Is Alex there?' she asked as Stevie answered.

'He's just this minute left to visit you, Caz.'

'Please, Stevie, go after him. Kevin will hurt him and Paul if you don't. I've left the baby at the flat, and a letter for Alex. I have to go now; I'm waiting for a train. But please go after Alex, he'll need your help.'

❀

Stevie stared at the receiver in his hand. He quickly called Patsy and gabbled out his tale; that baby Paul was alone and maybe Caz's parents could get to the flat quicker in the car than he could on his scooter. Patsy told him she'd dash to Dora's right away with the message. He grabbed his jacket and scooter keys and raced downstairs to follow Sandy.

He arrived at the flat just minutes after Sandy and ran inside. Sandy was holding Paul and staring at a piece of paper in his other hand. Of O'Leary there was no sign, nor was there a car outside on the street. Stevie breathed a sigh of relief. One less thing to worry about. Sandy's face had drained of colour and he handed his son over to Stevie as he spluttered out the contents of the letter Caz had written.

'How could she do this?' he yelled, waving the paper in the air. 'How?'

'Sit down, mate. Caz's folks are on the way over.'

'But look, read it.' Sandy collapsed onto a chair as Stevie took the letter and quickly scanned it to see Caz's scribbled confession about the damaged contraceptives and the fact she'd been working for Kevin upstairs and selling drugs as well as sleeping with him. She'd left no stone unturned. She'd finished by saying Paul would be better off without her and Sandy should get a divorce, find Jackie again and not bother coming looking for her as she was going away for good.

'We need to get you out of here,' Stevie said, 'before that neighbour comes back. He's a dangerous guy, Sandy. It's his little helper that supplies our dope. Come on. We'll have to leave our scooters and we'll walk to the main road and flag a taxi down. I'll get you to your parents' place. With a bit of luck we might see Caz's mam and dad in the car.'

☣

Outside the phone box Carol looked over the bridge at the railway lines below. She walked up and down waiting for the train to approach. There was no sign of it and then came a stuttering announcement over the tannoy that it was running ten minutes late. Typical; she wished she hadn't finished all the vodka now.

She leant her elbows on the parapet to stare up the track. Her head felt light and after what seemed like ages she heard a loud tooting noise as the train approached. She dropped her bag onto the floor, took off her coat, climbed up the parapet, sat astride the wall and kicked off her shoes. She could see people on the platform waving at her to get down and someone was pulling on the arm of the station master as he prepared to wave his flag. He looked up and his expression of horror was the last thing Carol saw before she was grabbed by the arms and forcibly dragged backwards onto the pavement.

☣

Dora screamed and her legs gave way as Joe dragged their daughter off the bridge seconds before a train pulled into the station. They'd been on their way to Carol's flat in answer to Patsy's frantic message after she'd practically hammered the front door down while they were eating tea in the kitchen. Joe had bundled Dora into the car and driven at speed to Walton Vale and their abandoned grandson. As they'd approached the bridge over the railway lines Dora had pointed to a girl who had flung her coat and bag onto the floor. Joe braked hard as they both realised at the same time that it was Carol, and as she climbed onto the bridge her intentions became apparent and they jumped out of the car and dashed across the road – just in time.

Dora cradled her sobbing daughter in her arms and cried into her hair. Joe stood by the phone box retching as a police car pulled up. The police, summoned by the station master, took charge. An ambulance was called and Carol, along with Dora for company, was dispatched to the hospital, with Joe and the policemen following in their cars.

Dora swept Carol's hair from her eyes and held her hand. There was a swelling on Carol's forehead where she'd banged it against the pavement, but that was the least of Dora's worries. Her state of mind was a greater concern. Carol was silent and staring into space. That vacant expression was familiar. Dora recognised it from her own spells of depression following the births of her babies. Why hadn't she recognised it in Carol?

Chapter Twenty-Eight

August 1968

Jackie wiped her sweaty brow and pulled her long hair back into a ponytail. She fanned her face with her hand and took several deep breaths before following the rest of the troupe out of the theatre to the nearest café on New Oxford Street. Rehearsals for the rock musical *Hair* were well under way and she was part of the cast – well, one of the dancers, at least. She couldn't believe her luck. The show had been a massive Broadway hit and was due to premiere in the West End at the Shaftsbury Theatre on September 27th.

She'd been so excited when she was chosen from the hundreds who'd auditioned for parts. Following the birth and adoption of her daughter, she'd allowed herself no time to grieve and had been accepted back into the dance troupe she'd taken leave of last year. It was the only way she knew how to cope and at least she'd been able to get out of Liverpool quickly after her spell in the mother and baby home. She'd built a protective shell around herself and allowed no one to get close, turning down the many offers of dates she attracted. Dancing came first; romance could stay on the back-burner for now. She would always love Sandy; there was no room in her life for another relationship at the moment. She was only eighteen anyway, so there'd be plenty of time for that once she'd established her career.

Last year had been the worst year of her life. And to top it all, her sister Carol, who she still despised for stealing the love of her life, and hadn't spoken to since, had left Sandy and their son and tried to commit suicide. She'd been diagnosed with severe depression just like their mam had suffered following both her pregnancies. The Reverend and Mrs Faraday had taken on Paul's upbringing and sent Sandy away to Paris for twelve months, to recover from the shock and to further his art career. The marriage had been annulled and when Sandy came home he would be a free man. Mam and Dad had struggled with Carol's illness and when she had been discharged she'd walked out of their home after just two weeks and gone away to join a hippy commune in South Wales. She sent the odd letter to Mam, but had distanced herself from everyone, including her son, telling Mam she wouldn't be coming back to Liverpool, ever.

Sandy would be back from his travels by the time the show opened. Jackie wondered if he would seek her out. He was free now, but he still had no idea that she'd had their baby and given her away. How could she tell him without causing him further distress? In the year that had passed since the adoption, there wasn't a day went by that she didn't look at her photos of Wendy and cry. The pain never lessened and she didn't think it ever would.

The café was crowded and noisy and she sat at a table near the window with some of the other girls from the dancing troupe, hugging a glass of Coke.

'You coming out with us later?' a girl with long dark hair directed at Jackie. 'We're going to the Marquee to see Jimi Hendrix.'

'Er, I'm not sure,' she replied. 'I've got a banging head and might just have an early night instead.'

She didn't want to go out and wasn't that keen on Hendrix anyway. She was bothered she might get chatted up and couldn't face it. It happened everywhere she went. She'd grown her blonde hair long again for the show and the number of times she was asked if she was Marianne Faithfull was laughable. Still, it was also flattering, especially when someone had asked the other day how Mick Jagger was doing. She loved it when they looked puzzled as she answered them in her Liverpool accent.

London wasn't a place that thrilled her as it did the others. But then *they* hadn't spent lonely nights sleeping in shop doorways in cardboard boxes, their young lives in ruins. She sipped her drink and tried to look enthusiastic as she joined in the general chit-chat about the show and how fanciable the leading man, Oliver Tobias, was.

It was the flower-power costumes that Jackie loved most. The wonderful hippy clothes in fabrics that hung in soft folds around her body. The rainbow colours and wide flares, floaty skirts and sexy gypsy blouses that were so easy to dance in as they moulded to every curve and contour. It was a style she'd adapted to her everyday wear now. The cast was to appear on *The Eamonn Andrews Show* soon and the thought filled her with trepidation, though not as much as the nude scene in *Hair*, where the whole cast emerged naked from beneath a tarpaulin sheet. Still, if the part led to bigger and better things for her, then it was a good first-rung-on-the-ladder experience.

❀

Sandy leant on the ferry rail as the white cliffs of Dover came closer. The wind whipped his long hair around his face, tangling with his beard. His mother wouldn't recognise him now and would probably think he was a tramp come knocking at the door when he arrived back in Liverpool. He was looking forward to getting home and reclaiming his life and his son. He'd missed Paul but had been in no fit state to look after him following Caz's startling revelations. He'd been on the verge of a breakdown and it had been a wise move on his parents' part to suggest he got completely away for a while. He'd managed to complete a number of works, which were on their way home in a packing crate and would hopefully sell well in the little gallery that had supported him in the past.

When he'd read Caz's confession he'd been horrified to learn of the destructive act that had led to Paul's birth. All he'd been able to think about was his and Jackie's last morning at Middleton Towers and how he could so easily and unknowingly have made her pregnant too. Thank God it hadn't happened. The chaos that would have ensued was unthinkable. He'd heard from Stevie and Patsy that she was part of a dancing troupe touring with shows, so at least she'd moved on and was enjoying the career she'd been desperate for. As soon as he'd got himself organised at home he would look for her. He needed her, still loved her with all his heart and hoped *she* still felt the same. If she did, they could pick up where they'd left off.

❀

'Who was it, love?' Joe asked as Dora put down the phone, a big smile lighting up her face.

'It was Sandy. He's back from Paris and he's bringing our Paul to see us later. We could take him down to play on the sands while the weather's nice.'

Joe nodded. 'Aye, why not. Be great to see the little fella again. He's into everything now and I bet Sandy's mother will be glad of a break.' He put his arm around Dora's shoulders and gave her a hug.

Following Carol's departure he'd moved them to a three-bed cottage in Hoylake. They'd paid for it between them using Sammy's money and Joe's from the sale of his house. Dora had taken ages to recover from almost losing Carol and she had blamed herself for not recognising the fact that she had been depressed and that was why she'd turned to alcohol. Getting Dora away from Fazakerley and the gossips had been a good move, although when Joe had told her where the new house was she'd seemed reluctant to move to the area, but wouldn't say why.

They were settled in now though and enjoyed the sea air when they got the chance. Joe had changed his job and drove a bus part-time, doing local runs out to the villages, and Dora did a bit of dressmaking and an alterations service, just as she had many years ago. She was slowly building up a nice little business, using the third bedroom as her workshop-cum-dressing-room. He'd bought her a new lightweight electric sewing machine to replace the old one she'd got from Jacobs' when Sammy had closed the business down. Neither of them needed to work really, but they liked to keep busy. Dora spent ages making beautiful clothes for herself, Jackie and her growing list of customers. He was proud of her. Life had been hard in the past, but making things up to her was all Joe lived for now.

His divorce from Ivy would soon be through and when it was he'd be down on one knee begging Dora to marry him again. There'd be no more mistakes in his life; he'd make sure of it. And thankfully Jackie seemed to be making a nice career for herself, but he worried about her while she was away from home and was always glad to see her when she came back for a break. The new show she was rehearsing for promised to be a big hit. She'd told them it had come from Broadway in New York. He felt immensely proud to think of his little girl on stage in the West End.

'I'll make us a picnic to take on the beach,' Dora announced. 'It'll be lunchtime when they arrive and they'll be hungry.'

Joe smiled. 'I'll go and dig Paul's bucket and spade out from the shed while you do that, chuck.'

❁

Sandy sat on the beach next to Dora's deckchair, watching Paul and Granddad Joe sailing a little red boat they'd bought from a shop on the walk to the promenade. His son was squealing with laughter as he ran in and out of the sea, the gentle waves lapping his fat little legs and soaking his shorts and T-shirt as he flopped down and splashed around.

'Good job my mum packed fresh clothes,' Sandy said. 'He's having a great time.'

'It's good to see him,' Dora said. 'He's the image of you, he really is. Your mum and dad have done a great job with him. It can't have been easy. But you needed that break after everything that came out about our Carol.'

Sandy nodded. 'As soon as I can afford it I'll get my own place and look after Paul as much as I'm able. But I need to work and the gallery has taken on the new stuff I did in Paris. That should fetch something in. Mum said she'd help as much as she can.'

'We can always have him down here for a few days, you know. But not when our Jackie's home. I don't want her upsetting again.' She looked up as Joe called out that he was going up onto the prom to get ice-creams and did they want one. 'Yes, a wafer for me, please.'

'Not for me, thanks,' Sandy called, wondering if he dared broach the subject now she'd mentioned Jackie.

'How is she?' He chewed his lip and focused on a single white cloud above his head.

'She's okay. She's in London rehearsing for that new *Hair* show in the West End.'

'And does she come home often? I-I'd like to get in touch with her.'

Dora stared at him, her face blanching and her eyes wide. 'No, Sandy, you mustn't. What's done is done. Best to leave it in the past where it belongs.'

'I still love her.'

'She's moved on. You must leave her alone.' Tears slid down her cheeks.

'But I have to put things right with her. Dora, please. There's nothing standing in our way now. I need to speak to her. I'm sure Jackie knows I still love her and I always will.' He got to his feet and turned to look at the sea as his own tears fell.

'You can't put it right, Sandy. Not now. It's too late. You ruined her life, leave her be.' She wiped her eyes with a tissue and looked across to where Joe was queuing at the ice-cream van with Paul in his arms. 'Just be grateful you've got that little lad to look after.'

'What do you mean, I *can't* put it right? The marriage was annulled. I'm free; Jackie's still free, according to Patsy. We can be together again, if it's what she wants. There's nothing to stop us now. And *how* exactly did I ruin her life? That was Carol's doing, as you well know.'

Dora looked at him. 'Yes, it was, to a point. But Jackie had a baby too. She was adopted last August from this very place, Hoylake mother and baby home. You have a daughter, Sandy. She was a year old on June the 1st.'

Sandy stared at her in astonishment, and then dropped to his knees and grabbed her hands. 'Is this true?' he demanded. 'Why did no one tell me? Why didn't Jackie tell me?'

'Because you were married to our Carol and you couldn't do anything about it. She had no choice but to make the decision by herself. Can you imagine how your parents would have reacted to the news if she hadn't been brave enough to do that? My daughter was crushed, Sandy, heartbroken. That's why she washed her hands of anything to do with Carol or Paul. Oh God, I shouldn't have told you like that. I'm so sorry.' She held his face in-between her hands and gently wiped away the tears that were rolling down his cheeks with her thumbs. 'Joe doesn't know. Only I, Agnes and Patsy know.'

'Patsy knows? I can't believe she didn't tell Stevie. Those two tell each other everything.'

'Well if she has, he's done the best thing he could and kept it to himself.'

Sandy nodded. Stevie had gone through a few bad months following Caz's near suicide. He'd confessed to Sandy that he'd made her promise to tell the truth, blaming himself for putting pressure on her. Kevin had been arrested for the part he'd played, and was serving a lengthy prison sentence for drug pushing, as well as rape and sexual assault on Carol and at least three more teenage girls, who had come forward once the case had been reported in the *Liverpool Echo*.

'Joe's on his way back. Don't say anything, please. Leave that to me for when I think the time's right.'

Sandy swallowed his tears and tried to come to terms with this latest bombshell. Christ, he wasn't yet twenty-one and stuff had happened to him that most people didn't get in a lifetime. But no matter what Dora said, he was off to London to look for Jackie as soon as he could get away. Maybe he'd wait until the show began in September, then he wouldn't be accused of getting her all upset beforehand. It would be hard to contain himself for the next few weeks, but he owed it to Jackie not to screw things up any more for her. He'd tell his parents he had an exhibition to attend or something.

❦

Sandy sat in the audience, his heart in his mouth. She was amazing, slim, lithe and supple, all the things she'd always been. As beautiful as ever, long blonde hair cascading down her back. Her face completely animated by what she was doing. He gasped as the nude scene evolved and the sheet went up and he caught a glimpse of her naked body. It was a blink-of-the-eye scene and he was glad when it ended.

As the audience left the theatre he followed them outside and made his way around to the stage door entrance. He sat down on a wall opposite to wait. No doubt they'd be ages with all the first-night celebrations to get through first, but if he had to sit here all night, he would.

She came out eventually with a gaggle of young women, all excited and talking at once. She was near the back of the crowd but he recognised her immediately. He hoped she'd recognise him. He'd shaved off his beard, as his mum said it made him look older, but his hair was still long. He got to his feet and moved forward. As she turned to walk away from the others he called her name. She spun around. Her eyes widened and she clapped both hands to her mouth.

'Sandy?'

He held out his arms.

She walked slowly towards him, her eyes never leaving his face.

He folded his arms around her and held her tight, his tears falling into her hair. It was over two years since he'd last held her and made love to her at the Scottie Road flat. It felt like a lifetime ago. She sobbed against him, clinging tight, ignoring curious stares from passersby.

'I've missed you so much,' he whispered. 'I love you.'

She pulled away slightly and looked up at him. 'I love you too, and I've missed you more than you'll ever know.'

'We need to go somewhere quiet where we can talk,' he said. 'I'm in the Jubilee Hotel around the corner; do you want to go there?'

She nodded. 'I'm sharing with three of the dancers so we can't go to my place.'

In the quiet lounge at the back of the hotel, Sandy bought them a drink each and they sat down at a small table.

Jackie took a sip of Coke and let out a long breath. 'I can't believe this. I knew you were home, Patsy told me. But when you didn't send me any messages via her I thought you didn't want to get in touch.'

Sandy sighed. 'You have no idea how hard it's been for me to stay away. I thought it best to wait until the show began and try and see you then. It was great, by the way. You stood out amongst the other dancers.'

'You saw the show?' she gasped. 'Oh, Sandy, the nude scene!' She blushed prettily.

He smiled. 'You're even more beautiful now than you were back then. Jackie, we've had a crap couple of years and I'm so sorry you had to go through it. There are things I need to tell you, things that Carol did that had a direct bearing on everything that happened.'

She looked away and tears filled her eyes. 'There's something I need to tell you, too.'

He nodded. 'I already know. Our daughter,' he said as her jaw dropped. 'Your mam told me. We'll find her, we'll get her back. I promise you with all my heart we'll find her.'

She put down her glass and shook her head. 'We can't get her back, Sandy. I had to sign to say that I wouldn't contact her. I have to wait until *she* contacts me, and that might be never.'

Tears ran down her cheeks and he knelt in front of her and held her tight.

'I don't think I can ever forgive Carol for this,' he said. 'I know I shouldn't speak ill of her when she's been not right, but even so…'

He told her what her sister had done and how it had led to both babies being accidentally conceived.

She let out a long breath and held on to him. 'In time, Sandy, it will all come right. At least now we have each other again, and we can really begin our lives. Let's try and look to the future and maybe one day our daughter will make the decision to look for us.'

'Did you give her a name, this girl of ours?'

'Wendy Angela.' She choked on a sob.

He hugged her tight. 'You once told me it was a name you would give your daughter if you ever had one.'

'You remember that?'

'Sefton Park, near the Peter Pan statue.'

She smiled and kissed him.

'Oh, Jackie, I'm never letting you go again,' he whispered into her hair. 'Stay with me tonight, please, darling. And I promise you that one day, when we're allowed to, we'll search for, and hopefully find, our Wendy Angela. If it takes forever, we'll never give up looking until we find her.'

Epilogue

Thirty-Five Years Later

Sandy put down the phone and called up the stairs to his wife.

'Jackie, that was your mam. She and your dad are coming over. She sounded really strange, as though she was crying.'

Jackie ran down the sweeping staircase, followed by a golden retriever, who leapt around excitedly, as though sensing a walk might be on the cards. Jackie grabbed his collar and ordered him to sit.

'What did she say, exactly?'

'Just that they're coming over, nothing else.'

'God, I hope one of them isn't ill. I can't stand to lose anyone else at the moment.'

Sandy shook his head. 'Life can't be that cruel to us.' Both his parents had passed away in the last twelve months and they were just coming to terms with their loss. 'We're due for something good happening, surely?'

'Paul's new baby might be all we're entitled to. All that God-bothering your dad did has done *us* no favours, has it?'

Sandy's son Paul had just become a father for the first time and next month they were planning a trip to Switzerland, where he now lived and worked, to see their new grandson.

He took her hand and led her into the lounge. As he opened the French doors, the dog shot out and ran like a mad thing around the large, well-kept lawn.

'He's batty.' Sandy laughed at Jasper's antics. 'Where *does* he get the energy from?'

Jackie smiled. 'No idea, but I wish I'd got half of it.'

They'd got Jasper as an eight-week-old puppy when they moved into their new house, in Hoylake, nearly twelve years ago. Following the annulment of Sandy's marriage to Carol, they'd married in 1970. Jackie had worked constantly in various musical shows up and down the country, but hated being away from Sandy and Paul, who she'd taken to as soon as she met him. Sandy had been given full custody of his son and Jackie had found him easy to love, as he didn't look anything like Carol. She felt happy to take on a mothering role to Paul, and she enjoyed it immensely.

Sandy knew that deep down the loss of their daughter weighed heavily on Jackie's mind. When the time of Wendy's eighteenth birthday came around they had begun to search, but reached dead-ends. They'd checked constantly to see if there was a trail that would show she'd been looking for *them*, but so far it seemed she didn't want to know. The Salvation Army had been unable to help them and the original adoption agency had no record that their daughter had tried to look for her mother.

As the years went by Sandy felt he'd failed Jackie in his quest to fulfil the promise he'd made that they would find her. Wendy would now be in her thirties, like Paul, and may well be married with a family of her own. She may not want to know. A very helpful lady at the adoption agency had told them there was a possibility that their daughter had no idea she was adopted. It often happened, apparently, when adoptive parents decided to say nothing to the child in their care. As there was no trail of Wendy looking for information, it was a definite possibility. And if that was the case, it would be impossible to trace her.

They'd more or less come to terms with the fact, although they'd never quite given up hope. They always celebrated her birthday and bought a little present at Christmas, just in case. The sadness in Jackie's eyes on those days broke Sandy's heart. They'd tried for another child, but it just didn't happen, so they'd thrown themselves into the careers they'd both worked hard for. His art work was displayed and sold world-wide, and he attended exhibitions in galleries, and gave lectures in art schools about his paintings, and where his inspiration came from. He told them each piece represented a passage in his life, and that his wife was always his inspiration. Jackie had semi-retired from her acting career, but still played a role as the matriarch of a large family in a long-serving television drama that was set in sixties Liverpool. She'd won awards for her earlier stage work, but preferred to spend most of her time at home now, or travel with Sandy when he was lecturing abroad.

Sandy called Jasper in before he churned up the lawn.

Jackie dropped to her knees and gave the dog a hug. 'You smell all damp and woolly, you big softie,' she said, laughing as he licked her face and rolled onto his back for a tummy tickle.

'I'll go and put the coffee on,' Sandy called, making his way into the hall. 'Put your feet up while we wait to see what your folks want.'

⸙

Jackie flopped onto the sofa with Jasper at her feet. She buried her toes into the silky curls on his back and he whimpered with pleasure. He was devoted to her, this furry baby who'd filled a huge hole in her heart.

On the wall above the marble fireplace was a large canvas that Sandy had painted, taken from the small postcard-sized photograph she'd been given on leaving Prospect House, following Wendy's adoption. He'd brought it to life, not in his usual surreal style, but in a way that filled Jackie's eyes with tears each time she looked at it. She knew his sadness that he'd never met their daughter at all overwhelmed him at times and she'd caught him crying while throwing paint at a huge canvas not long after their marriage. She wished with all her heart that she could have given him another child, but it wasn't to be. Although she wasn't particularly religious, she felt it was God's way of punishing her for giving away Wendy and for Sandy's disgracing his parents, who had never been informed of their granddaughter's existence. No point in causing further anguish until we find her, Jackie had told him.

He joined her on the sofa and checked his watch. 'They should be here any minute.'

Jackie's parents, who had remarried six months after their own wedding, lived a short drive away in the same village of Hoylake where they'd moved to from Fazakerley years ago. Jackie had picked the house she and Sandy now lived in when they decided it was time to put down permanent roots. She too had chosen Hoylake for the connection with their daughter. It made her feel closer to Wendy, even though it brought back sad memories. The Victorian detached house, set in several acres of gardens, was a bit too big for them, but it also housed Sandy's attic studio and a private suite of rooms that Paul and his wife Jill used when they visited.

Jackie blew out her cheeks. 'I feel really worried now, all churned up inside. It must be something serious or Mam would have told you on the phone.'

Sandy slipped his arm around her shoulders and hugged her close. 'Whatever it is, we'll deal with it together.' He kissed the top of her head as the doorbell rang. 'I'll go and let them in.'

Jackie moved over and patted the seat beside her as Mam came into the lounge.

'Your dad's just having a quick cigarette with Sandy in the back,' Mam said as she sat down, gave Jackie a hug and a kiss and took a deep breath. 'They'll bring coffee through.'

'Thought Dad had given up smoking.'

'He had, until yesterday.'

Jackie looked at her still attractive, slim mam, blonde hair streaked with silver now and pinned up neatly on top of her head.

Her blue eyes had a worried look in them and she fidgeted with the clasp on her handbag.

'Are you ill, Mam?' Jackie took one of her hands and squeezed it.

'No, chuck, nothing like that and neither is your dad, before you ask.' She stopped as Sandy and Joe came through, Sandy carrying a tray of mugs. They took their seats, Sandy sitting the other side of Jackie.

'Right, if you're not ill, tell us what's wrong then,' Jackie demanded. 'You both look worried to death.'

'I got a letter this morning off one of the women from St Paul's WI,' Mam began. 'Seems she's pally with the old lady we lived next door to on Fourth Avenue. Anyway, the old lady gave her a letter and asked her to forward it on to me. It was given to the old lady by a young blonde-haired woman who was knocking on doors, looking for her mother.'

She opened her handbag, took out a creased envelope and handed it to Jackie.

Jackie felt her head go light and beside her Sandy stiffened as she took the envelope from her mam. She opened it with shaking hands and pulled out a letter and a photograph of a slim blonde, the image of herself. She handed the photo to Sandy while she read the letter and then burst into tears. Sandy took the letter from her, his hands shaking. He read it and then grabbed hold of her and they cried together.

Mam picked up the letter, which had fallen to the floor. At last, the news they'd waited a lifetime for.

'Is it?' Joe asked, his voice barely more than a whisper.

'Yes.' She nodded as he pulled her close. 'Thank the lord.'

'There's a return address and the letter's dated three weeks ago,' Jackie cried. 'Oh, Sandy, to think that we may have walked past her in Liverpool while she was looking for us is unbearable. You were up on the docks a couple of days that week too, overseeing your exhibition.'

'I can't believe it.' Sandy looked stunned. 'After all this time. We'd better get writing, now, send it special delivery before the post office closes.'

'Oh, I'm so thrilled for the pair of you.' Mam wiped her eyes on a tissue. 'And so is your dad, aren't you, Joe?'

He nodded; his eyes were bright with tears. 'When your mam told me about Wendy I was upset at first that you'd kept it from me. But every night since then I've said a little prayer that you'd find her one day. All those years of searching and wondering and now it's finally going to happen.' He put his arms around his daughter and gave her a hug. 'Having your girl in your arms again will put all the wrongs of the last few years right.'

Mam got to her feet. 'I'll make some fresh coffee while you two get that letter written. Our Frank and Maureen are coming for tea tonight with their granddaughter Joanie; oh, I can't wait to tell them. They'll be over the moon for you. Come on, Joe, you can help me while they get their heads together. They need to be alone for a few minutes.'

Joe followed his wife into the kitchen while Jackie stared at Wendy Angela's handwriting, which was neat, like hers. She read and re-read the words over and over until she felt she could recite them by heart, while Sandy held her close. His eyes shone and his wonderful smile lit up his handsome face as Jackie smiled with him.

Wendy Angela explained that she had been searching for her mother from the day she'd discovered she was adopted, which hadn't been until she was in her thirties, and her search had begun immediately. She was hoping and praying that the letter would find its way safely into her hands and she was looking forward to hearing from her. A wonderful feeling of peace and contentment enveloped Jackie as she read the words again. Their daughter would soon be home. The wait was almost over.

A Letter from Pam

I want to say a huge thank you for choosing to read *The Liverpool Girls*. If you did enjoy it, and want to keep up to date with all my latest releases, just sign up at the following link. Your email address will never be shared and you can unsubscribe at any time.

www.bookouture.com/pam-howes/?title=the-liverpool-girls

To my loyal band of regular readers who bought and reviewed the first two books in the Mersey Trilogy, thank you for waiting patiently for the final instalment. Your support is most welcome and very much appreciated. Thank you also to Beverley Ann Hopper and the members of her FB group Book Lovers, and Deryl Easton and the members of her FB group The NotRights.

A big thank you also to the FB group Liverpool Memories, whose admin and members have kindly shared their lovely tales and memories with me during the writing of the Mersey Trilogy.

A huge thank you to team Bookouture, especially my lovely editor Abi for your support and guidance and always being there, and thanks also to the rest of the fabulous editorial team.

And last, but most definitely not least, thank you to our wonderful media girls, Kim Nash and Noelle Holten, for everything you do for us. And thanks also to the gang in the Bookouture Authors' Lounge for always being there. I'm so proud to be one of you.

I hope you loved *The Liverpool Girls* and if you did I would be very grateful if you could write a review. I'd love to hear what you think, and it makes such a difference helping new readers to discover one of my books for the first time.

I love hearing from my readers – you can get in touch on my Facebook page, through Twitter, Goodreads or my website.

Thanks,
Pam Howes

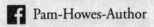 Pam-Howes-Author

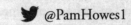 @PamHowes1

Acknowledgements

As always, my man, daughters, son-in-law and grandchildren. Thank you for your support. I love you all very much. xxx

Thanks again to my lovely 60's Chicks friends for their friendship and support when I'm feeling under pressure. Thanks once again to my friends and beta readers, Brenda Thomasson and Julie Simpson, whose feedback I welcome always.

Thank you to the band of awesome bloggers and reviewers who have given my Mersey Trilogy such fabulous support with your wonderful blog tours. It's truly appreciated.